D1159398

Resounding praise for the incomparable *USA Today* bestselling author

SAMANTHA JAMES

"A REMARKABLE WRITER."
Lisa Kleypas

"SAMANTHA JAMES WRITES EXACTLY THE SORT OF BOOK I LOVE TO READ."
Linda Lael Miller

"JAMES DELIVERS DELICIOUS AND EXCITING ROMANCE . . . WITH EXCELLENTLY DRAWN, COMPLEX CHARACTERS."
Publishers Weekly

"READERS WILL ADORE HER ENDEARING, THREE-DIMENSIONAL CHARACTERS."
Romantic Times

"SAMANTHA JAMES TUGS ON THE HEARTSTRINGS."
Catherine Anderson

By Samantha James

A Perfect Groom
A Perfect Bride
The Truest Heart
His Wicked Promise
His Wicked Ways
One Moonlit Night
A Promise Given
Every Wish Fulfilled
Just One Kiss
My Lord Conqueror
Gabriel's Bride

SAMANTHA JAMES

A Perfect Groom

AVON BOOKS
An Imprint of HarperCollins*Publishers*

This is a work of fiction. Names, characters, places, and incidents are products of the author's imagination or are used fictitiously and are not to be construed as real. Any resemblance to actual events, locales, organizations, or persons, living or dead, is entirely coincidental.

AVON BOOKS
An Imprint of Harper Collins*Publishers*
10 East 53rd Street
New York, New York 10022-5299

ISBN: 0-06-050279-7
www.avonromance.com

First Avon Books paperback printing: December 2004

Printed in the U.S.A.

10 9 8 7 6 5 4 3 2

Prologue

He always knew he was wicked.

Despite the fact that the Sterling children were of the very same parentage and grew up in the very same household, they were, in point of fact, all quite different.

His elder brother Sebastian was the responsible one, steadfast and dependable, studious and thoughtful and ever proper. His baby sister Julianna was possessed of a sweet, bubbly nature.

But Justin . . . he was every bit his mother's son.

Ah, yes, he was the most like his mother, not only in resemblance—he had inherited the crystal clarity of eyes that shimmered like the finest of emeralds, the exquisite artistry of features that were in perfect balance, her fine dark hair—but in . . . well, other ways as well. Indeed, he was convinced, in every way . . .

He still remembered those first few years after Mama ran off with her lover. Mama had many lovers, he suspected. Of course it was one of those things that no one talked about openly, but it *was* discussed in hushed, quiet whispers. And despite the fact that he wasn't bookish, Justin *was* a precocious little boy who absorbed every last word of the servants' gossip—the dark glances that signaled their pity over the way the marchioness had abandoned her three children, leaving them in the care of their father, a man who gave every impression he was at odds with the world at large. After all, it wasn't as if Papa liked anyone. Not Sebastian. Not even sweet, adorable Julianna, whom everyone loved. And especially not unruly Justin.

His tutors pronounced him hopeless. Undisciplined and disruptive. Inattentive and unruly. He didn't excel at his lessons like studious Sebastian.

From the time he was very young, he was well aware it was a good thing Sebastian had been born first; Justin knew he'd have made a horrible Marquess of Thurston once Papa was gone. Somehow, he was always doing things he shouldn't. Thinking things he shouldn't. Saying things that were perhaps better left unsaid . . . especially to Papa. Little wonder that he was ever at odds with his father. He couldn't sit still for hours at a time. He squirmed and fidgeted in his chair. He stared out the window and heartily wished himself elsewhere.

Justin disliked his studies from the very first day he'd joined his brother in the schoolroom. One day he simply decided he'd had enough. After the noonday meal, he slipped out of the schoolroom without telling anyone. Perhaps he should have expected that their tutor, Mr. Rutherford, would immediately tattle to Papa when he failed to return. Perhaps he had.

He was never quite sure he'd expected that Papa would deign to remove himself from his study.

Of course, to an eight-year-old boy, it was vastly amusing to see everyone searching for him. Perched high in the branches of a tree in the orchard, Justin peered down while the servants ran frantically to the stables and all about the grounds of Thurston Hall. He snickered when Papa paced to and fro before the tree. But all at once Papa paused . . . and looked up.

That the marquess was not pleased with his second son was evident in the sizzle of his gaze.

"Why aren't you in the schoolroom?" demanded the marquess.

"Because I'm here," retorted the little boy. "Is it not obvious?"

"Come down here now, you vile little wretch!"

The little boy stopped tittering. His jaw firmed. Green eyes flashed. "No," he said.

His father's hands balled into fists. "Come down this instant, I say!"

His father's rage did nothing but inspire the little lad's mutiny. Stretching out a thin arm, he caught the knobby branch above. Higher he climbed, too caught up in the moment to hear the creak beneath his foot. Exultant now, he glanced down through twirling leaves at his father's upturned countenance.

The branch gave way. Justin tried to break his fall and landed hard upon his wrist. He heard the snap as fire stabbed through him—a hot, sizzling streak like a dozen knives resounding in every part of him. For one paralyzing instant he couldn't move. He couldn't even breathe. The pain was so intense he thought he might lose consciousness.

At last he rolled to his back. His father stood over him, his features dark and livid. The marquess bent low. "On your feet!" he ordered. Curling his fingers roughly around the lad's other arm, he hauled his son upright.

At his side, Justin's wrist was cocked at an odd angle from his hand. It throbbed so abominably he wanted to retch. Bravely he swallowed the bile rising in his throat. He clenched his jaw against the pain and glared at his father.

"Don't!" came his father's familiar bark. "Don't!"

"Don't what?" The boy's calm did nothing but infuriate the marquess.

"Don't look at me like that!"

"Like what?"

"The way *she* did!"

Something was rising inside the little boy, a festering resentment, a twisted swirl of emotion he couldn't control—nor did he want to. In that moment, he hated his father. Hated him for the harsh control he exerted over his brother Sebastian. Hated him for the way he turned a blind eye to little Julianna. He didn't care if Papa took the birch to his backside.

He hated his father . . . as he sensed his father hated him.

"Who?" he inquired icily. "Do you mean Mama?"

Sheer rage flamed in his father's eyes. "Shut up, boy! Shut up!"

He struck the boy hard across the face.

The blow felled Justin to the ground once more. This time he shot upright of his own power. Through glittering green eyes, he regarded his father. "I won't!" he cried. "She didn't like you any better than I do, Papa, any better than Sebastian . . . or anyone, for that matter! Perhaps that's why she left!"

The marquess snapped. "How dare you speak to me so! Wicked, that's what you are, boy. Wicked!"

Vile curses spewed from his lips.

It wasn't the first time his father had called him names—it wasn't to be the last, either. Names that . . . well, names that he'd never confided to anyone, not even Sebastian.

All the while the lad proudly stood his ground. He never flinched—never even blinked—though every word pummeled his heart, his very soul. When at last a heavy silence descended, he merely tipped his chin.

"I trust, sir, that you are finished?"

Disdain dripped from his tone, a frigidity that should have been far beyond his years, far beyond his experience. A snarl twisting his lips, the marquess drew back his fist once more.

Suddenly Sebastian was there. He thrust his way between them. "Papa, stop!" cried the eldest. "Look at Justin's wrist . . . there's something dreadfully wrong!"

And indeed, there was.

A physician was summoned. Inside the house, Justin lay on his bed. The physician cocked a brow.

" 'Tis broken," he announced. "I believe I can set the bone back into place, lad, but I must be honest. It's going to hurt like the very devil. So if you feel the need to howl . . ."

The marquess hovered directly behind the physician.

Justin's gaze collided with his father's. There was a lump the size of an apple in his throat. His eyes burned . . . his father's image wavered, then righted into focus.

It was then he glimpsed his father's satisfied little sneer and he realized his father expected him to cower and wail and weep. His mouth compressed. Mother hadn't. Sebastian didn't. And he *wouldn't*.

Sebastian squeezed his shoulder. "Justin," came his whisper, "do you hear? It's all right if you—"

"It is not," the boy refuted fiercely. His gaze locked with his father's. "I won't cry. I will never cry!"

The physician gave a nod and stepped over him.

There was a sickly crack as the bone slipped back into place. Justin's thin body jerked. His back arched off the bed. The thin fingers of his free hand wound into the sheets. When it was done, he lay white-faced and panting.

But he did not cry. No hint of sound whatsoever passed his lips . . .

The marquess gave a snort of disgust. Without a word, he turned and stalked from the chamber.

* * *

Wicked.

As often as he could, *whenever* he could, the marquess taunted his second son. He shouted it. He screamed it. He whispered it, when no one else was about.

Not once, in all the years of his youth, did Justin Sterling chance to glimpse his father's chest swell at his accomplishments or his eyes shine with pride.

He was well aware there was little point in trying. The marquess held his son in disdain.

Time marched on, and the spindly-legged boy grew tall and straight and handsome. His attendance at Eton was marred by numerous incidents and letters to the marquess. His father's disapproval multiplied, in perfect parallel with Justin's defiance.

Ah, yes, his mother had put the blight on the family name, while he was the bane of it. His deeds were atrocious, his behavior appalling. If it displeased his father, it pleased *him*.

And he reveled in it.

He drank. He gambled. He whored. And if his father knew it, well, all the better.

One warm June night, the summer of his seventeenth year, he stumbled into the house just before dawn. He'd just spent a very pleasurable evening with a bottle of port and the miller's daughter, and the combination had left him deuced exhausted. Faith, but the girl was creative in ways he'd never expected. Ah, but she had a talent with her mouth that—

"Where the devil have you been?"

The marquess barred his path.

A slow smile curled Justin's lips. "What, my lord, you wish an account of the night's activities?" He didn't bother with a form of address. He'd stopped calling him Papa years ago. Now he wouldn't even deign to call him Father to his face.

He gestured grandly toward the door of his father's study, which stood ajar. "Perhaps we should be seated. This could take some time, for the evening's entertainment was interesting, shall we say. I give you fair warning, though, it's altogether possible you may be shocked—"

"Cease!" hissed the marquess. "I've no intention of listening to your filth!" His gaze raked Justin from head to toe. "Christ, you're drunk, aren't you?"

In the face of his father's sneer, Justin executed a courtly bow, as courtly as he could manage given his sotted state. "An astute observation."

His father's lip curled in disgust. "God, but I wish you'd leave. I wish you'd leave and never return!"

Justin's mocking smile remained. "All the reason to remain."

The marquess clenched his fists. "By God, I could make you. I have the power to make certain you never show your face here again!"

"Ah, but what would that say to the world? You drove Mother away, while you threw me *out*. At any rate, you needn't put up with me but a while longer. I'm off to Cambridge at the end of summer, remember?"

"And I shall be glad, for every day you are here is a living hell!"

Justin inclined his head. "A sentiment, I daresay, I return in full measure."

"Look at you, so drunk you can hardly stand!" the marquess burst out. "And you reek of cheap perfume! God, but you are so very much your mother's brat! She shamed me, the witch! She shamed my good name, as *you* shame me! And all these years I've had to look at you, staring back at me with *her* eyes, with *her* smile. Reminding me what she did, what she was—a whore who would spread her legs for any man who would have her. And you are no better. Your blood is tainted," he raged, "as she was tainted. No decent woman will ever have you, boy. No decent woman will ever want you!"

Justin's eyes glittered. In that instant, he wanted only to strike out, to strike *back,* to wound his father as his father had wounded him.

"If Mama was such a *whore,*" he stated cuttingly, "how then do you know your children are your own—"

All at once Justin broke off. He stared hard at his father.

"Sweet Christ," he whispered, the words but a breath. "You don't, do you?"

The marquess made no answer. The silence was suddenly stifling.

Justin's mouth twisted. "Oh, but that's rich! The Marquess of Thurston . . . abandoned by his wife, who was killed with her lover on her way to France . . . and forever saddled with her children. And he must ever wonder if any of them are his own! And of course you couldn't foist us off on anyone else, could you? You had to claim us, because you just didn't know."

The marquess was livid. "Shut up, boy."

Justin began to laugh. And once he'd started, he couldn't seem to stop . . .

"Shut up!" roared the marquess. Malice glittered in his eyes. He took a threatening step forward.

Suddenly everything changed. The marquess made a choking sound. His eyes bulged. He clawed at his cravat . . . and slumped to the floor.

Justin couldn't tear his gaze from his father's figure, lying prone on the polished marble floor. For one horrifying instant, he couldn't move.

Then sanity returned and he rushed to his father's side, falling to his knees. He stretched out a tentative hand. "Father?" he whispered.

The marquess stared toward the ceiling through sightless eyes.

Justin began to shake. A horrible, sickly sensation seized hold of him. He lurched upright. And then he was running, running toward his chamber, as if the devil himself were at his heels . . .

The marquess was dead. *Dead.*

Justin would never tell anyone about what transpired this night between the two of them. He would keep it a secret locked deep in his being. No one would ever know that he had been present . . . that he had killed his father.

One

London, 1817

The atmosphere at White's was not particularly different from any other evening. A number of well-dressed gentlemen circled the hazard table. The air was thick with the pungent smell of brandy and cigars. His long frame stretched out in a green velvet chair, Justin Sterling idly scanned the day's newspaper, as if he hadn't a care in the world—and indeed he did not. His long legs crossed at the ankle, his pose was one of redolent ease.

"Upon my soul!" intruded a mocking voice. "So you've at last deigned to grace us with your presence again!"

Justin glanced over the top of the paper, his green eyes meeting those of his friend Gideon.

Gideon eyed the empty chair beside him. "May I sit?"

"What, you're asking?" Justin laid aside the

newspaper. Gideon was a man known for doing what he pleased, when he pleased, and where he pleased—a man after Justin's own heart, to be sure.

"Well," Gideon said, "given the beastly frame of mind you were in when you departed the country, I thought I'd better."

It was true. Even his sister-in-law Devon had commented on his wretched mood before he'd left. Why it was so, Justin didn't know. He didn't lack for companionship, neither female nor familial. He had anything he could possibly want at his disposal. Indeed, what *more* could a man possibly want?

He didn't know. That was the crux of it.

To that end, he'd decided three months earlier that a change of scenery was in order, so he'd removed himself to the Continent. To Paris, Rome, Vienna . . . he'd traveled to his heart's content, *indulged* himself to his heart's content.

Now he was back.

And he was no more content than before.

Justin reached for his port. "And greetings to you, too," he murmured dryly.

"Oh, all right, then. I daresay, you are looking singularly well." Gideon eyed the perfect fit of snug wool across his shoulders. "Must be your tailor. Weston, I presume?"

Justin inclined his head. Weston was the premier—and most expensive—tailor in the city. "You presume correctly."

Nearby came a raucous burst of laughter.

"Two thousand pounds to the man who can take her!"

Justin glanced over just as Sir Ashton Bentley executed a wobbly bow. Justin was not surprised; Bentley's predilection for drink somehow always managed to surpass his tolerance.

"Raise the stakes and make it worthwhile," boomed another fellow.

The voices came from a group of men gathered just a few paces away from White's famous bay window where Beau Brummell and his cronies usually gathered, though they were absent this night. It appeared the discussion was growing quite animated.

There was a loud guffaw. "No one's seen her muff or likely to, lest it be on her wedding night!"

"She'll never consent to a bedding before marriage!" hooted another. "Ask Bentley!"

"Ha! It damn well won't take marriage, or even an offer, to make her mine. She'll be green-gowned by the end of the season or my name isn't Charles Brentwood!"

Another man chortled. "Her? Tumbled on the grass? Not bloody likely."

"Two thousand says I can mow her down!" boasted Patrick McElroy, second son of a Scottish earl. "And her husband, should she ever deign to choose one from the buffoons courting her, will never know he wasn't the first!"

"And just how will we know the deed has been done?" came the inevitable inquiry. "To lay claim to it is one thing, to succeed is quite another."

Indeed, Justin's mind had been pondering that very point.

"He's right," came the shout. "We'll need proof!"

"A trophy!" someone cheered. "We need a trophy!"

"A lock of hair ought to do the trick! There's not a soul in England with hair the color of flame!"

No doubt it was some young debutante who had captured their fancy. Trust the Scotsman McElroy to be vulgar. And Brentwood had no finesse when it came to the fairer sex. Justin almost felt sorry for the poor chit, whoever she was.

Justin's gaze hadn't left the group. "A randy lot, it would seem," he murmured to Gideon. "But I confess to an abounding curiosity. Who is this woman with whom they're so fascinated?"

Gideon offered a mocking smile. "Who else? The Unattainable."

"The what?"

"Not what, but *who*. You've been gone too long, my friend. Since she turned down three offers of marriage in a fortnight—Bentley among them—she's become known as The Unattainable. She's quite famously in vogue, you know. The toast of the Season thus far."

Justin's gaze lifted heavenward. "Just what London needs. Another drab, boring, insipid debutante."

"Not precisely a debutante. She's almost one-and-twenty, though I don't believe she's ever had a formal coming-out. And she's hardly insipid." Gideon erupted into laughter. "Ah, but that is the last word I should use to describe The Unattainable."

"And what word *would* you use to describe her?"

Justin lifted his glass to his lips, while Gideon pursed his lips. "Hmmm. Do you know, one simply will not do! She's truly quite delectable, but oh, how shall I say this? She is not a woman of convention, yet she's all the rage. She is most certainly never boring, and she's hardly drab. I don't believe I've yet to see her dressed in white. And her hair is indeed the color of flame." He nodded toward the group. "A fitting trophy indeed."

"She hardly sounds the usual diamond of the first water."

"She's not the usual debutante. But perhaps that's the lure. She is a woman of . . . how shall I put this? A woman of statuesque proportions." Gideon gave a dramatic sigh. "She has all the grace of a fish out of water. And she cannot dance to save her soul."

A perfectly arched black brow climbed high. Justin lowered his glass to stare at Gideon incredulously. He pretended a shudder of distaste. "The chit is a giant, a bumbler, nearly on the shelf, yet she's entertained three proposals?"

"Quite so," Gideon affirmed lightly, "and not even a fortune to commend her."

"My God, have all the men in Town gone mad?"

Gideon laughed softly. "Yes. Mad is what they are. Mad about *her*. Mad *for* her. I should estimate . . . oh, perhaps half are ensnared. Enamored. Entranced, falling at her feet and declaring themselves instantly in love with her. The other half are here at White's"—Gideon waved a hand—"seeking to slip beneath her skirts, as you can hear."

Ever the cynic, Justin quirked a brow. "You sound quite besotted yourself," he observed. "Have you fallen beneath her spell, too?"

A laugh was Gideon's only response. But almost before the sound emerged from his lips, Gideon's eyes slid away for a fraction of a second. Justin had known him too long and too well not to see what Gideon chose to hide. Justin gazed at him, in truth no less than shocked. Gideon was hardly the sort to embarrass easily.

"Never tell me," he drawled, "that you were among the buffoons paying court to her."

Judging from his glower, Gideon did not take kindly to his jibe.

Justin couldn't resist teasing. "Set you in your place, did she?"

"Don't be so damned smug," Gideon snapped.

Justin took a sip of port. "Why, I wouldn't dream of it." He contemplated the brew, his mind stirring. He was *not* fond of red-haired females, and for good reason. They put him in mind of—

"You're looking vastly annoyed, Justin. What is it?"

"If you must know, I was just thinking about a female who gave me a set-down some years ago."

"What, you?"

Oh, but the incident playing in his mind was not one he cared to remember. She'd dealt quite a blow to his pride; granted, it had been a bit inflated at the time. Why the girl had singled him out for her mischief, he had no idea. Of course, Sebastian persisted in reminding him of the minx's little scheme whenever he could. Child or no, he'd never quite forgotten—or forgiven!—that wild little hoyden's attempt to demean him.

He offered a tight smile. "Suffice it to say that perhaps we're not so dashing as we think, either of us." He didn't divulge that the female had been a mere child—though he had been a mere youth himself. God knew Gideon would have gloated to no end.

He steered the conversation back to the subject at hand. "She must be quite something, this chit known as The Unattainable, to send *you* sniffing about her skirts—and you the most notorious rake in Town."

"Oh, but I do believe that honor is solely yours." Gideon had regained his aplomb and proved himself fully up to par. "However, if you think you would fare better, perhaps you should put yourself into the running." He nodded toward the group where The Unattainable was still being discussed—and in ever more bawdy terms.

Before Justin could answer, Bentley's voice rang out again. "Three thousand pounds to the man who succeeds in deflowering The Unattainable!"

"Ah," said Gideon. "The stakes are rising."

Justin gave a shake of his head. "Good God, Bentley's drunk. Someone should get him out of here before he goes back to the hazard table and loses the very clothes on his back."

"Who is in?" There was a flash of hands, five in all—McElroy, Brentwood, Lester Drummond, William Hardaway—a lad barely out of the schoolroom!—and Gregory Fitzroy.

" 'Tis done," came the shout. "Three thousand pounds to any man among the five of us who claims The Unattainable!"

There was a raucous cheer, a flash of banknotes, and a footman was sent scurrying for the betting book. Justin was hardly shocked by the subject of the wager, for when it came to the matter of wagers, nothing was sacred here at White's—or any of the gentlemen's clubs, for that matter. They were rakes one and all, he decided with more than a hint of self-derision, and he and Gideon perhaps the worst of the lot.

Yet almost in spite of himself, Justin found himself pondering what it was about The Unattainable that everyone found so captivating.

His gaze returned to Gideon. It was disconcerting to discover Gideon's eyes already locked on his face. Justin wasn't certain he liked the flare of amusement in Gideon's gaze.

He knew it for certain when Gideon tipped his head to the side.

"Intrigued, are we, Justin?"

Justin shrugged.

Gideon's laughter rang out. "Admit it. We've known each other too long. You are, if not by the fact that the sum is a significant one, then because of the fact that *my* interest was once piqued by The Unattainable."

An elegant black brow arose. "She must be a veritable ice maiden to resist the likes of you."

Gideon neither confirmed nor denied it. Instead his eyes glinted. "If that is indeed the case, no doubt you think you can thaw her."

"I am not inclined to try," Justin said baldly.

"I confess, you disappoint me." Gideon affected shock. "You, the man with innumerable conquests. By God, you've gone and gotten almost . . . dare I say it? Almost respectable. You," came his drawling complaint, "are growing into a dullard."

Now, *that* was laughable.

He was a devil inside, and everyone knew it . . . everyone except, perhaps, his brother Sebastian, who liked to remind him of his occasional lapses into respectability. The way he'd ventured into several business dealings and profited quite fortuitously, for one. Too, he'd left the family townhouse two years earlier and leased his own just prior to Sebastian's marriage. Those were, he supposed, the trappings of respectability.

A pleasant haze had begun to surround him, for he was well into his third glass of port. Nonetheless, his smile was rather tight. "Don't bother baiting me, Gideon," he said amicably.

Gideon gestured toward the group still gathered

around the betting book. "Then why aren't you leading the way?"

Justin was abruptly irritated. "She sounds positively ghastly, for one. For another, no doubt she's a paragon of virtue—"

"Ah, without question! Did I not mention she's the daughter of a vicar?"

Justin's mind stirred. A vicar's daughter . . . hair the color of flame. Once again, it put him in mind of . . . But no. He dismissed the notion immediately. That could never be.

"I am many things, but I am not a ravisher of innocent females." He leveled on Gideon his most condescending stare, the one that had set many a man to quailing in his boots.

On Gideon, it had no such effect. Instead he erupted into laughter. "Forgive me, but I know in truth you are a ravisher of *all* things female."

"I detest redheads," Justin pronounced flatly. "And I have a distinct aversion to virgins."

"What, do you mean to say you've never had a virgin?"

"I don't believe I have," Justin countered smoothly. "You know my tastes run to sophisticates—in particular, pale, delicate blondes."

"Do you doubt your abilities? A woman such as The Unattainable shall require a gentle wooing. Just think, a virgin, to make and mold as you please." Gideon gave an exaggerated sigh. "Or perhaps, old man, you are afraid your much-touted charm is waning?"

Justin merely offered a faint smile. They both knew otherwise.

Gideon leaned forward. "I can see you require more persuasion. No doubt to you Bentley's three thousand is a paltry sum. So what say we make this more interesting?"

Justin's eyes narrowed. "What do you have in mind?"

Gideon's gaze never left his. "I propose we double the stakes, a wager between the two of us. A private wager between friends, if you will." He smiled. "I've often wondered . . . what woman can resist the man touted as the handsomest in all England? Does she exist? Six thousand pounds says she does. Six thousand pounds says that woman is The Unattainable."

Justin said nothing. To cold-bloodedly seduce a virgin, to callously make her fall in love with him so that he could . . .

God. That he could even consider it spoke to his character—or lack thereof. Indeed, it only proved what he'd always known . . .

He was beyond redemption.

He was wicked, and despite Sebastian's protestations otherwise, he knew he'd never change.

"Six thousand pounds," Gideon added very deliberately. "And worth every penny, I'll warrant. But there's one condition."

"And what is that?"

"She must be yours within the month."

A smile dallied about Justin's lips. "And what proof shall you require?"

Gideon chuckled. "Oh, I daresay I shall know when and if the chit falls for you."

He was drunk, Justin decided hazily, perhaps as drunk as that fool Bentley, or he wouldn't even give the idea a second thought.

But he was a man who could resist neither a dare nor a challenge—and Gideon knew it.

There had been many women in his life, Justin reflected blackly. He had reached the age of nine-and-twenty, and thus far no woman had ever captured his interest for more than a matter of weeks. He was like his mother in that regard. In all truth, what was one more?

And if everything that had been said about The Unattainable was true . . . if nothing else, it might prove an amusing dalliance.

He met Gideon's keen stare. "You're aware," he murmured, "that I rarely make a wager unless I stand to win."

"What a boast! And yet I think perhaps it will be *you* paying me. Remember, you've the rest of the horde to fend off." Gideon gestured toward Brentwood and McElroy.

Justin pushed back his chair and got to his feet. "Something tells me," he drawled with a lazy smile, "that you know where this beacon of beauty can be found."

Gideon's eyes gleamed. "I believe that would be the Farthingale ball."

Two

Miss Arabella Templeton strained to see around the marble column on the edge of the ballroom, doing her best to remain hidden.

The reflection of hundreds of candles glistened in the cut-glass chandelier that dominated the center of the Farthingale ballroom. While it was quite a breathtaking sight, Arabella wished she were elsewhere. *Anywhere* else would have done nicely. But thus far Aunt Grace and Uncle Joseph had displayed no indication that they were ready to leave.

"Is he gone yet?" she whispered.

"No." The lovely Georgiana was fervidly scanning the sea of faces. "The others have dispersed, but I spotted Walter a minute ago near the musicians. Now I fear I've lost him again."

Arabella stifled a groan. *He* was Walter Churchill, a pleasant enough fellow, she supposed. They all were, with the exception of Ashton Bentley. But Walter had proved most persistent tonight.

From the moment of their arrival, she'd been surrounded until she thought she would surely smother! Her feet ached abominably from being crammed into slippers that didn't fit—that was what came of having feet the size of a continent—and all she craved was her bed and a moment to herself. But her dance card was filled from now until Perdition. She'd managed to cry off the next several dances, but a number of gentlemen remained, hovering at her elbow, offering to fetch lemonade. In particular, Walter, who chattered in that nonstop way he had until she wanted to scream. Desperate, she'd announced the need to answer nature's call. There was silence—she knew they were shocked at such frankness, but Arabella no longer cared.

Luckily Georgiana had seen her plight. A year younger than Arabella, she had met Georgiana years earlier at the finishing school they'd both attended. In the room where the girls took their meals one evening, Arabella was on her way to the table in the corner where she usually ate her supper alone. She was walking past a group of girls when the inevitable comments about her hair and her height began, comments she was plainly meant to hear. Her face burning, Arabella lowered her gaze, set her shoulders straighter. There was nothing she could do to disguise her long limbs anyway, and besides, Mama had always taught her to be proud of what she was. And so she had marched on, determined to ignore them. Unfortunately, the only route to the corner took her directly by them.

There was a particularly unkind comment—from

her nemesis Henrietta Carlson—and the inevitable snickers. Arabella didn't stop to think—oh, but somehow that was always her downfall!—she simply did the first thing that came to mind.

The sight of slimy pea soup dripping from Henrietta's pink-beribboned curls had been most gratifying.

Aunt Grace and Uncle Joseph's afternoon-long session with the headmistress the next day was all that had saved Arabella's place in the school.

It also marked the last evening she ate alone in the corner. The very next night, Georgiana had shyly asked if she could join her. It seemed Georgiana liked Henrietta no better than she.

It didn't seem to matter that they were vastly different in many ways. The other girls' ridicule was no less virulent than before, but with Georgiana's friendship, it was easier to bear. Arabella was ever one to spout her feelings aloud, while Georgiana was quietly reserved, more thoughtful. Georgiana summed it up quite nicely one long-ago day: "The difference between us, Arabella, is that you have the courage to say what I should only like to."

Their friendship had not waned over the years.

Indeed, Arabella's upbringing was hardly the norm for a proper London miss. True, she was schooled primarily in England, but Papa's missionary duties often took the family off to such faraway places as India and Africa. Arabella had always enjoyed London, but at times it was difficult to conform to the many strictures required of a proper lady. To be sure, Arabella had never really quite fit in anywhere. When she was away with Mama and Papa, there was no need; thus, she'd grown rather used to going her own way.

Once again, she strained to see around the marble column toward Georgiana. "Georgiana?"

"I think it's safe to come out now," Georgiana ventured after a moment.

Cautiously Arabella stepped out from behind the column.

"Georgiana, I very much fear a fourth suit is imminent."

Georgiana laughed.

"Don't laugh," Arabella grumbled. "It should be you fending off unwanted admirers, not me." Petite, with silky flaxen hair and a heart-shaped face, Georgiana was the epitome of the very proper London miss—all that Arabella was *not*.

Indeed, Arabella's own mother, Catherine, along with Catherine's elder sister Grace, had both been beauties in their day. Arabella, on the other hand, was very much her father's daughter. Not only had she inherited his tall, rangy frame, but his abundance of thick red hair as well . . . all of which were *most* unfashionable in an age where petite, pale beauties like Georgiana reigned supreme.

"By the by, I adore your gown, Georgiana. You look like a princess." A slim gloved hand touched Georgiana's skirt of white bombazine. "I do wish I could wear white, but it makes my skin look like paste." She cast a wistful glance down at the blue silk of her gown.

"You sparkle like a jewel," Georgiana said

warmly. "That's why everyone is so taken with you."

Arabella reserved judgment. There was no way to hide her gaudy coloring; she'd learned by trial and error that there was little point in trying.

"I recognize that expression, Arabella. Don't argue. You're all the rage. Accept it, and enjoy it."

"You know as well as I that it's not *me*." She was as ungainly as the elephants she'd ridden in India. At affairs such as these, she felt gauche and awkward. She must constantly bite her tongue to keep from speaking her mind. She simply hadn't the patience to remember each and every one of Society's blathering rules, despite the tutelage of Aunt Grace and Georgiana.

Lord, but she hated all the attention she was getting this Season! She'd spent her entire life eliciting second glances. By now she should have grown used to jaw-dropping stares. She'd never quite been able to decide which was worse—having hair the color of fire, or being the tallest female in the kingdom (in the entire world, she was convinced). Oddly, Society had been most accepting of her *faux pas*, probably because Aunt Grace and Uncle Joseph were such well-respected members of the *ton*.

She sighed. "It's simply that I chanced to receive the first proposal of the Season."

"As well as the second and third." Georgiana struggled to keep a straight face. "Why, I could almost be jealous, but you're blissfully unaware of your own charm."

"Georgiana! It's all quite distressing, really. I

prayed I wouldn't cause a stir. I should have known better! Before I knew it, all of London was talking about me. And now it seems the whole of London is *looking* at me, and all these silly gentlemen are circling like vultures. I've seen them, you know, in Africa, and it's not a pretty sight."

Georgiana made no reply. At her silence, Arabella glanced at her.

"What is it? What's wrong?"

Georgiana was gazing across the ballroom, her lips parted. She gave a tiny shake of her head. "Arabella, he's here," she whispered. "He's here!"

"Walter!" Arabella gasped and would have darted behind the column once more if Georgiana hadn't reached out and caught her sleeve.

"No, Arabella! It's him, the handsomest man in all England! And he's coming this way!"

The handsomest man in all . . . Oh, for pity's sakes. At that precise moment there was a distinctly feminine squeal nearby, followed by a shrill of giggles.

Arabella locked her chin and deliberately looked the other way. Whoever he was, she was in no hurry to see him. It appeared as if every female around her was suddenly all a-twitter, their hearts all a-dither, but she was not a jiggle-brained idiot, to fawn over a mere man.

Georgiana poked her. "Arabella, look, he's with the Dowager Duchess of Carrington. She's giving him her hand to kiss."

"Georgiana, I'm in no need of a blow-by-blow account. If I wanted to look at him, I would."

"Oh, but he's quite splendid. I've never seen him so close before."

"Georgiana, really!" If she sounded cross, she couldn't help it. "I didn't think you were the sort to be taken in by such a man. No doubt he's the world's worst rogue."

Georgiana didn't argue. Instead she said in a strange voice, "Arabella, he's coming this way." She gasped. "I do believe . . . yes . . . *yes*! He's coming toward *you*."

Arabella pointedly turned her back. Just what she needed. Another vulture.

"Perhaps you're mistaken," she stated calmly. "Perhaps he's coming toward *you*."

There was no answer. Instead there was only silence, a silence that dragged on and on.

Arabella tapped her foot. "Where the devil is he now?"

Still no reply. An odd, heated feeling caught her in its midst. She could almost feel the hairs on the back of her neck sizzle in awareness.

"Georgiana?"

She turned impatiently . . . and it wasn't Georgiana she beheld, but the spotless knot of an intricately tied cravat. Her gaze strayed up—and up!—taking in a square masculine jaw, a long elegant nose and male lips that might have been sculpted by the hands of a master, all the way to clear, crystalline eyes the color of emeralds, set beneath a slash of dark, slanted brows.

And then the unthinkable happened. She, who usually managed a retort for everything, swallowed what she'd been about to say—and very nearly her tongue.

It was *him*.

Justin Sterling.

The Farthingale house was only a few blocks away from St. James's Street. After their arrival, Justin and Gideon stood on the fringes of the ballroom.

"Quite the crush, isn't it?" Beside him, Gideon raised his quizzing glass. "Lady Farthingale will be crowing tomorrow. I heard she invited half the city."

"And it appears few of them declined." Many of the guests stood elbow-to-elbow, shoulder-to-shoulder.

Hundreds of jewels glittered and winked in the candlelight. With a single, practiced stroke of the eye, Justin's gaze encompassed the room full of partygoers, the sea of shimmering ball gowns and elegant coiffures . . . until at last it settled across the room.

"I see you've found her."

Justin responded with a lift of his brow. "I daresay you were right. She's impossible to overlook."

"Yes, she is that, isn't she? And I see she's garnered her usual audience." Gideon snared two glasses of champagne from a white-gloved servant, handing one to him. "Silly young pups! Fools, all," intoned Gideon, "that they fancy themselves in love."

Love. For the swell of a heartbeat, an odd emotion churned in Justin's gut. It wasn't that he was incapable of that tender emotion. But he knew no woman could ever love *him*.

"So what was it if not love that sent you sniffing about the lady's skirts?" he inquired.

Gideon's half-smile left him in no doubt.

Justin's regard returned to the woman across the room. He'd noticed her right off, and it wasn't just the brightness of her hair that set her apart from every woman here tonight. Gideon was right, he surprised himself by admitting. The Unattainable was exceptionally tall for a woman, yet she didn't shirk from it or try to hide it. A twinge of reluctant admiration cut through him. She carried herself like one who was proud of it—and God knew, she carried it well.

She was gowned in ice-blue satin, a shade that should have clashed hideously with her hair, yet didn't. The empire waist fell in soft, delicate folds to the toes of her slippers. It made no secret of the fact that her breasts were delectably full and high on her chest. God knew he was a man who was an ardent admirer of bountiful, curvaceous breasts. Her shoulders were slim but broad for a woman, which somehow made the column of her neck, long and slender, appear all the more feminine, particularly when she tilted her head as she did just now. A froth of curls spilled over her shoulder, onto the generous expanse of her bosom.

Desire stirred, a dark stab in his middle. Her legs would be fashioned like the rest of her, he decided, long and slim and lithe, strong enough to wrap around his hips as he drove inside her. Granted, it was just as he'd told Gideon. He wasn't partial to redheads. And he'd always avoided virgins like the plague. But *this* one . . .

He had to stop himself from taking an involuntary step forward. He only caught himself just in time! For the first time tonight, he experienced the ripeness of anticipation. He'd yet to gain a glimpse of her face, just a hint of her profile, which held a great deal of promise, her figure a great deal of allure. No, he wasn't worried. His taste in women, as in everything, was fastidious. He wouldn't bed a toad and Gideon knew it. Ah, yes, he reflected in mute satisfaction, to win this wager would be no hardship at all.

Gideon had noted his appreciation. "Stunning, isn't she?"

There was no need to answer. "Well," Justin murmured almost lazily, "I suppose it's time I sent the pups scattering." Suddenly he laughed.

"Bedamned!" he said. "No need to bother after all. She's ducked behind the column near the dining room. And now another young woman has joined her—"

"Yes, that's Georgiana Larwood, I believe."

"No wonder she's known as The Unattainable. It appears she's determined to evade them. Or perhaps some*one* in particular."

"Probably you," injected Gideon with a smirk.

"Highly improbable," Justin said smoothly.

"Now, wish me luck, old man." He drained his champagne and placed it on the tray of a passing footman. "Oh, and don't bother calling for details early in the morn. I fear the night may be a long one."

Gideon hastened to help himself to another glass of champagne. "Ah, the master at work! Perhaps I should take notes."

"Oh, I'm certain you'll find another diversion."

Justin ambled across the ballroom, his path taking him ever closer to The Unattainable. He paused to chat with several acquaintances, among them the Dowager Duchess of Carrington.

The duchess peered up at him, her eyes a vivid hue despite her age.

"Justin!" she exclaimed, offering her hand. "How delightful to see you again."

Justin kissed her fingertips. "I assure you, Your Grace, the pleasure is wholly mine."

The elderly woman let out a resounding chuckle. "You know there was a time when I was convinced you were quite an irascible rake."

Justin feigned astonishment. "What! Do you mean to say I am not?"

Her shoulders shook with laughter. "Never mind your wretched reputation. I know better, boy. Indeed, I've become quite fond of you the last few years."

"A feeling I return in full sentiment, Your Grace." Justin spoke with genuine affection.

"Save your charms for the younger ladies, m'boy.

Which reminds me, I was just telling Sebastian and Devon very recently that I do believe it's time you set your mind to taking a wife. So if need be, keep in mind I shall be happy to lend my matchmaking efforts."

Justin laughed softly. "You do love to play matchmaker, don't you?"

The duchess settled both hands on her cane. "I do," she declared, her eyes sparkling like a girl's. "I once told your brother it was high time he married, and look at the outcome!"

Justin thought of Sebastian, blissfully enamored of his wife and family. While the hand of fate was squarely behind the fact that Devon landed in Sebastian's arms and life, the duchess had indeed played a part in steering the pair together when it appeared Sebastian might lose his ladylove.

"So," the duchess finished with a vigorous wave of her cane, "should my services become necessary, you have only to say the word."

Justin chuckled. The duchess spoke not with her hands, but with her cane. Many a word was punctuated with a stab of that infamous instrument, and God help anyone who chanced to get in the way when she wished to make a point. "I assure you, Your Grace, should it come to that, you shall be the first I shall call upon."

She beamed. "Excellent!"

He bade the duchess farewell, bowing low. When he straightened, he caught Gideon's eye.

Gideon raised his champagne in silent salute.

Justin smiled to himself. The chit's back was to

him now, but she was still there. He'd yet to see her face, and he was suddenly impatient.

Three steps closed the distance between them. He acknowledged her companion with a faint nod, but his attention was solely for her . . .

She turned then, this chit known as The Unattainable.

Even as a part of him acknowledged that she was a feast extraordinaire for the eyes and senses, he was pricked by a horrifying certainty.

A hundred thoughts, a hundred curses skittered through his mind in that instant. Oh, Christ, but he should have listened to his instincts . . . he should have known. Perhaps he *had*.

Justin did not thank Gideon in that moment. He did not thank Providence. For in his wildest dreams, he'd never imagined it could possibly be true.

But it was. Sweet Christ, it was.

The woman before him was none other than the bane of his youth. The wretched little brat who'd made such a nuisance of herself in her younger days . . .

Three

"Miss Arabella Templeton," he drawled as he recovered his powers of speech, a recovery he considered miraculously swift, thank God.

In truth, he was still reeling. But by God, he wouldn't show it. Not to her.

He glanced at her companion. "It's Miss Larwood," he murmured, "is it not?"

Georgiana blushed and swept a curtsy. "It is," she said breathlessly.

"Miss Larwood, it is indeed my very great pleasure to introduce myself. I am Justin Sterling. But you would indulge me greatly if you would allow me a word with my old friend Miss Templeton."

Georgiana's mouth opened and closed.

"What! Miss Templeton neglected to tell you of our acquaintance?" He shook his head. "Why, I've known her since she was a child!"

Georgiana seemed decidedly nervous. She glanced at Arabella, then back at him.

Justin slanted a half-smile. "I do not bite," he said lightly. "You have my undying promise to leave her in one piece."

"But of course, my lord." Georgiana curtsied again and swept away.

Justin transferred his gaze to Arabella. He bestowed on her the smile that invariably sent the ladies to swooning—all ladies but her, that is.

Her consideration of him was surely destined to put the fires of hell to shame, he noted. Blithely he ignored it. "It has been a long time, has it not?"

"Not long enough." The words emerged from between gritted teeth.

Still as charming as ever, he observed.

"What do you want?" she said tersely.

He feigned great affront. "Oh, come. Is that any way to greet an old friend?"

His gaze ran over her. Gideon had been right. A conventional beauty she was not, but she had a mouth like sin and eyes the color of heaven. Christ, had he really told Gideon she sounded positively ghastly? Lord, he was the world's biggest ass!

Up close, she was even more breathtaking than from across the ballroom. Gone was the thin, gawky child whose carrot-red curls seemed to eclipse the whole of her being. Instead there stood a vibrantly sensual woman who wreaked havoc on his senses.

The exposed skin of her shoulders glistened like porcelain. Affixed on a fine gold chain was a tiny sapphire that nestled in the velvet cleavage of her breasts. There were no feathers or pearls in her hair, no bracelets circling her wrists. He approved the costume for its very simplicity. In truth, she needed no other adornment to make her shine.

And shine she did.

His gaze, hot and avid, lingered on the tempting hollow between her breasts. A dark, swift heat seized hold of him as she took a breath. By God, he thought, every other woman in the room paled in her presence. She was ripe like a warm, sweet peach just waiting to be plucked.

He dragged his gaze reluctantly to her face, only to find her blue eyes dark with outrage, the fullness of her mouth pursed into a tight little knot.

He decided to remain at arm's length for now. If he got any closer, she might well fasten her fingers around his neck.

"Why are you looking at me like that?" she demanded.

"I'm simply marveling at how you've grown. Why, you must surely stand eye-to-eye with many a man."

Arabella stiffened. She'd always hated her body. For as long as she could remember, she'd been a full head taller than every other girl she knew.

But she didn't stand eye-to-eye with Justin Sterling. Indeed, if she gazed straight ahead, her focus came to the very center of his mouth, now curved into a lazily wicked grin. And yet, it was rather nice, actually, to feel for once that she wasn't a great behemoth.

If only it were any other man but him!

"Do not mock me," she said curtly.

He swept her his most courtly bow. "I do not mock you." He shook his head. Again his gaze slid over her, lingering on the swell of her breasts beneath her bodice, an unmistakably simmering appraisal. "Ah, yes," he murmured, "how you've changed!"

Silently, Arabella consigned him to a fate most reprehensible. Aloud she snapped, "And I see you have not." But in truth, he had. He was bigger, even taller than he'd been at eighteen. She'd noticed it right off. Beneath his jacket his chest was broad, his shoulders lean but wide. Broader than she recalled . . .

The realization was downright disturbing.

He stepped close. She resisted the urge to step back.

"Do you know," he went on, "when my friend Gideon made mention of The Unattainable, I was *pricked* by the oddest thought. Odd, that I should think of it that way, don't you agree?" He sighed. "Ah, but I have such memories of you, Miss Templeton. Not fond, but memories just the same."

"Indeed?" she inquired coolly.

"You don't remember? Well, then, let me refresh your memory. We were at the Dowager Duchess of Carrington's estate in Kent, as I recall. There was some sort of outdoor entertainment—"

"It was a play," she interrupted.

"Ah, yes. Well, then, since you've obviously recovered your memory, perhaps you'll remember crawling about on the ground, playing some game, or so I was convinced. Imagine my surprise when you crawled beneath my chair, took a pin, and stuck me through the shoe."

"Perhaps you should have worn boots," Arabella said sweetly.

"That's what Sebastian always said. Oh, but your little prank was always the source of much amusement for my brother."

Arabella winced. She wasn't proud of her behavior that day, but she wasn't about to let him have the upper hand, either. "I begin to recall. You were limping when you left, weren't you?"

"Indeed. I did my best to avoid you, but you saw my horse and came running. I thought you meant to apologize, so I stopped. You offered me your hand to kiss—so much the little lady!—and so I took it. I thought I was safe, for the duchess had her eye trained on us."

As he spoke, he edged nearer. This time Arabella *did* try to step away, but the column was at her back. There was nowhere she could go to escape him.

And indeed, escape was foremost in her mind. For the glint in his eye set her heart to leaping and her pulse to pounding. What the devil was he about?

She looked him straight in the eye. *The handsomest man in all England*. Yes, she'd heard tales of him. Some women, she knew, considered the man engaging. Disarming. Arabella considered him the worst sort of cad imaginable.

"Would you please leave?"

"Miss Templeton, how rude! I've not yet finished my story."

"I know the outcome."

He continued as if he hadn't heard. "But then the duchess turned away. You fisted your fingers and drew back your hand, and punched me with all your might. You left me bloodied and looking as if I'd been injured in a boxing match. Indeed, that's what I was forced to tell my friends."

"So you lied!" She made no secret of her disdain.

"Obviously you know little of a man's honor. Was I to tell them I'd been bested by a child?"

Arabella snorted, a distinctly unladylike sound. What did a man like him know about honor? He was a selfish scoundrel, who cared nothing about anyone but himself and his indulgences.

Her frame of mind was little improved when he laughed, the wretch! She disliked being the source of his amusement.

Her gaze slid beyond his shoulder. "I don't see your companion," she stated pointedly. "Hadn't you better find him?"

"Oh, but I cannot leave you here alone. Indeed, I count myself quite the gallant. I saw you hiding from your admirers, in particular dear Walter, and decided to rescue you."

Arabella fumed. Drat! He was too astutely observant for his own good . . . and for her comfort.

"I'm surprised you even remembered my name," she said stiffly. "It was only because I wounded your pride that you did."

Again that slow, simmering look. "Oh, but you do yourself an injustice. I've just spent three months on the Continent. And what do I find when

I return? All the *ton* raving about The Unattainable. And, I must say, with good reason."

Her back stiffened. "Pray do not make light of me."

"A mere statement of fact. My friend Gideon regaled me with countless tales of your suitors. And all true, it would seem, for it has come to my attention tonight that men do have a tendency to stare at you."

"Just as women have a tendency to stare at *you.*"

"And you, Miss Templeton? Are you among those women?"

His tone was cajoling, almost lazily caressing . . . accompanied by a smile in perfect harmony.

Arabella was amazed, and more than a little incensed. Did he truly think she would allow herself to be taken in by it . . . by him?

Apparently so.

"Let me say this, my lord. If I should ever chance to stare at you, 'tis only because of your arrogant impudence."

To her utter shock, that devastating smile only deepened.

It only made her all the more determined. "And if you should ever chance to make me shiver from head to toe, it will be in disgust. For I, sir, would never allow myself to be swayed by a handsome face and a winsome smile."

He was undaunted. "My, but you're prickly tonight. Perhaps I was wrong and you haven't changed at all."

"Nor have you, sir." Eleven years had passed since they'd last seen each other. Eleven years and he was still a prancing young buck. A profligate. A hellion. A heartbreaker, as she well knew.

"I'm flattered that you remember me so well."

"Don't be," she said flatly. "Even if your reputation did not precede you, I've an excellent memory for faces."

He regarded her, that wretched smile still lingering on his lips. "I confess, my dear Miss Templeton, that I am given to wonder what makes men flock to you like hounds to a fox. Certainly it is not your flirtatious mien."

Before she knew what he was about, he snared her hand. Arabella tried to snatch it away, but it was neatly trapped by the snugly unremitting pressure of strong male fingers.

"You doth not protest, my dear. We've an audience."

Oh, God, he was right. More than a few heads were turning their way. And Walter stood on the sidelines, looking for all the world as if he'd been whipped.

Justin stepped close. "Miss Templeton, our meeting has been"—he pretended to consider—"another memorable occasion."

Caution fled to the winds. On her lips was a parody of his mocking smile. "And I would say it has been a pleasure," she parried, "but indeed it has not."

The pressure of his fingers tightened even more.

He stepped close, so close he blotted out her view of the rest of the assemblage.

"A word of warning, my dear. Tread lightly, for my reputation is not unwarranted."

Her reply came swift as an arrow. "I am not afraid of you, my lord."

"Perhaps you should be."

"Ah, but you don't bite, remember?"

"And perhaps I lied. Indeed, I've been known to eat up tender little girls like you."

Arabella straightened to her full height. "I am neither a girl nor little. And I vow you'd find my hide quite tough."

He threw back his head and laughed. Arabella fumed. She was not pleased at being the brunt of his amusement.

"You denied me the chance to kiss your hand once before. I fear I must do so now."

There was no stopping him. Before she could form a protest, he was lifting her hand. Their eyes tangled in the instant before he slowly bent his dark head.

He released her, spun around, and walked away calmly.

Her eyes widened. Her lips parted. She stood, too stunned to move, to believe what he'd just done. She'd expected a light, airy kiss breathed upon her knuckles. But what she got was something else entirely . . .

Why, he'd nipped her, the rogue!

Four

Early the next afternoon Georgiana burst into the drawing room. Arabella sat alone as she prepared to take tea. Her aunt was upstairs napping.

"Arabella, you must tell me what happened! Oh, but I was so disappointed that Mama and Papa decided to leave early!" In a swirl of skirts, Georgiana settled on the sofa beside Arabella.

Arabella placed a hand on the silver teapot the maid had just deposited before her. "Tea, Georgiana?" she inquired.

"Tea would be lovely, thank you. Now, you must tell me everything."

"One lump or two?"

Georgiana very nearly shrieked. "Is that all you have to say?"

Arabella handed her a delicate silver and ivory cup. "What would you like me to say?"

"Well, I'd like you to tell me what happened with

Justin Sterling last night! Arabella, I'm amazed that you are so calm. He singled you out, you among all the other women there!"

Arabella suspected the only way to avoid Georgiana's questions was to answer them. "Only because he was on the Continent and newly returned to London. He was there only to meet The Unattainable." Her mouth turned down. Lord, but she despised that name. She hated it as much as she hated the attention she'd managed to garner this Season.

Of course, as Aunt Grace had demurely mentioned over breakfast this morning, it *would* end were she to accept an offer. And when Aunt Grace gently reminded her she was almost one-and-twenty . . .

It was all she could do not to flee the table in tears.

She hadn't, of course. She'd masked the hurt as she'd learned to do. There was no malice intended, of course. Aunt Grace and Uncle Joseph loved her like one of their own. Arabella also knew Aunt Grace and Uncle Joseph would like to see her make a good match—they'd done quite well with their own three daughters. Aunt Grace had subtly reminded her only a few days ago that her cousins had managed to snag an earl, a viscount, and the second son of a duke.

But Arabella didn't want to "snag" a husband. She was in no hurry to even *gain* a husband. And she certainly wasn't in London to acquire one. Indeed, the only reason she *was* here was because the last time she'd traveled to Africa, the heat had made her deathly ill; thus, Mama and Papa had insisted she stay with Aunt Grace and Uncle Joseph when Papa was sent back to Africa last month.

Perhaps it was because she hadn't grown up a proper London miss that marriage did not consume her every waking thought. Perhaps it was because she had never truly fit in anywhere. Her appearance had always made her the odd one out, so to speak. Not that a soul on this earth knew, even Georgiana, but Arabella wasn't quite sure where she belonged, or what her place should be.

Should she ever chance to wed, it would only be to a man who didn't mind that she was clumsy and didn't mind that she laughed when she shouldn't and said what she shouldn't . . . a man who loved her for herself, who loved her for what she was . . . wild, red hair, lanky limbs, freckles and all . . .

A man who loved her for all that she was not, and could never be.

The way Mama loved Papa.

It had caused quite a stir when her beautiful, elegant mother had wed a man who resembled a scarecrow, and a clergyman yet! Catherine's elder sister Grace had managed to land Viscount Burwell. But what Arabella's parents shared was a love that was deep and abiding.

And Arabella would settle for no less herself.

The Unattainable indeed, she reflected glumly. Aunt Grace was ecstatic when the first proposal had come—from an earl, no less! Aunt Grace had been shocked when Arabella refused Lord Thomas Wilbury's suit. She'd gazed at her as if Arabella were quite daft. Arabella was convinced that Aunt Grace thought it might be her one and only chance at marriage.

Incredulously, another followed almost immediately, this from Phillip Wadsworth. Faith, and it was probably terribly shallow, but it didn't help that he was half a head shorter than she. Perhaps it was vain, but that was the one thing about which she was incredibly sensitive.

When the last proposal came from Ashton Bentley—the wretch had actually tried to kiss her!—Aunt Grace had taken her aside. Of course, she'd been obliged to inform Aunt Grace his conduct had been quite ungentlemanly.

"Arabella, did you hear me?"

Georgiana's query brought her back to the present. "What were we discussing?" she asked, though she knew very well what it was.

"Justin Sterling," her friend supplied promptly.

"Oh, *him*." Arabella lifted her teacup.

Georgiana's mouth quirked. "Yes, *him*."

"He only came to see The Unattainable," she said again. "Trust me, Georgiana, he wouldn't have come near if he'd known it was me."

"Why do you say that?"

"He dislikes me as much as I dislike him."

"Arabella, I must confess, I was quite stunned when I realized you knew him. Why didn't you ever tell me?"

"What's to tell? Oh, of course I've known *of* him for many a year. But I hadn't seen him since I was a child. And indeed, I confess, there is but one occasion that truly marks the boundaries of our acquaintance."

"Do tell," pleaded Georgiana.

Arabella's mouth compressed. "I'd rather n—"

"Oh, please, Arabella," Georgiana begged.

"Very well, then. It happened at the Dowager Duchess of Carrington's country estate. I was on my way outside when I chanced to pass by a room where two people were talking. The door was ajar and—oh, I know it was quite untoward of me, but I slipped behind it and stopped to listen."

"Who was it? Justin Sterling?"

Arabella nodded. "He was with a girl named Emmaline Winslow. I'll never forget, for I thought her the most divinely beautiful creature ever to grace this earth. But she was crying, Georgiana, *crying*. And even as I stood there, Justin Sterling made no bones of his feelings. I will never forget his words. He told her there were other women just as fetching as she. Indeed, he stated, she was but one pearl among many and he intended to sample them all! And it wasn't just that, Georgiana. It was the way he said it, so cool, so carelessly indifferent!"

"Oh, the poor girl!" Georgiana's tone reflected her sympathy.

"She was nothing to him, Georgiana, nothing but his latest conquest. He walked out then. He walked out with his nose in the air, a prancing, preening peacock who clearly thought much of himself! He left Emmaline sobbing her heart out, alone in the house. But I determined that he should have his comeuppance." She relayed how she had followed him outside and slipped beneath his chair. "I settled for his shoe," she finished, "though I'd have dearly liked to aim for a higher vicinity."

Georgiana struggled not to laugh. "No wonder he remembers you."

Arabella refreshed her tea. "Well, he deserved it."

"That he did," agreed Georgiana, "but, Arabella, you say the most outrageous things sometimes!"

Arabella reached for her cup. Her blue eyes sparkled above the rim. "I know," she murmured demurely, "it's quite unseemly. But you won't tell, will you?"

"Not a word," Georgiana promised.

Her laughter faded. "At any rate, now you know why I consider Justin Sterling the most odious creature alive." What she *didn't* divulge was that his behavior last night had only affirmed her opinion. A part of her was still aghast, for clearly his audacity knew no bounds.

And yet she recalled, with vivid clarity, the bounding leap of her heart when he'd bent over her hand . . .

"I agree, he does have the most horrid reputation. Perhaps all he needs is the right woman to tame his wickedness . . ." Georgiana's voice trailed off.

Arabella glanced over at her. There was an odd expression on Georgiana's lovely features, somewhere between guilt and anxiety.

"What is it?" she asked briskly.

"It's nothing," Georgiana murmured.

"Obviously it's something or you wouldn't look like that." Sometimes Georgiana needed encouragement. She wasn't like Arabella, to blurt out whatever was in her mind. Indeed, Arabella decided wistfully, she wished she were more like Georgiana. It took strenuous effort to check her impetuous nature, and somehow she was never very successful.

"Georgiana?" she murmured.

Georgiana took a breath. "I was just thinking about the two of you last night—The Unattainable and the handsomest man in all England."

"Pray don't call me that. And don't call him that, either."

"I'm sorry. I know you're sensitive about that . . . But admit it, Arabella. Is he not the most wonderfully splendid man you've ever seen in your life?"

Arabella couldn't help it. Unbidden—most certainly unwanted—a vision implanted itself in her mind. Eyes of shimmering emerald and firm, masculine lips tipped up in a suave, masculine smile that made the bottom drop out of her stomach just thinking about it.

"I hadn't noticed," she replied primly.

She didn't fool Georgiana. Nor did she stop her.

"Oh, Arabella. You should have seen it, really. There was something almost spectacular about the way the two of you looked together . . . him so dark and dashing, the perfect foil for you and your vibrance. And the way he towers over you. Why, you barely reach his chin—"

Not so. Her eyes, Arabella was quite certain, were on the exact same level as his lips.

"I confess," Georgiana went on, "it was really quite romantic."

Arabella's cup hit her saucer so hard the liquid sloshed over the edge. She stood, intending to fetch a cloth to mop up the mess. But when she turned to dart for the door, her knee connected with the delicate table where the tea service sat.

The table tipped. China went flying in all directions. A dark stain began to spread on Aunt Grace's prized Aubusson carpet.

"Oh, bother," she muttered. Georgiana chuckled, already halfway out the door to fetch a maid. She returned with a cold cloth to press on Arabella's bruised knee, and resumed her seat.

"Thank you." Arabella slanted her a fond smile. "You are a dear." She paused, then said softly, "It's amazing that we ever became friends. We are such opposites, aren't we? You're graceful and tiny as a raindrop, while I'm grace*less* and thunder about like a great lout."

"Stop it, Arabella. You sell yourself short. Which reminds me: Are you going to the Bennington gala tonight?"

Arabella nodded.

"Hmmm," said Georgiana. An innocent pause, then, "Do you think he'll be there?"

There was no doubt who she meant. Arabella groaned. "Now, there's a dreadful thought."

Georgiana laughed, while Arabella wished she could.

Oh, but Georgiana could be such a tease. It was a well-known fact that when it came to women, Justin Sterling chose only the pink of the *ton*. Really, to even intimate that she and Justin looked spectacular . . . why, it bordered on the ridiculous.

Yet she couldn't deny, in some faraway place hidden deep inside her, a part of her was rather flattered.

There was, thank heaven, no sign of him. All in all, the evening passed rather pleasantly. At last, breathless from excitement, she started toward the side of the room where refreshments were being served.

"Arabella!"

Near the threshold, she turned. Walter Churchill was coming toward her.

"Walter, hello! I didn't know you were here." She almost hated herself for the way her heart sank. Truth be told, she'd been almost relieved that there had been no sign of him . . . or Justin Sterling, for that matter.

She liked Walter. She truly did. As for Justin, she told herself stoutly, he wasn't worth even a second thought.

"I've only just arrived," Walter said. "Arabella, please, I crave a word with you." He indicated a small room just off the ballroom. Arabella hesitated, then reluctantly followed him.

There was a small sofa just inside the doorway. It was there he led her, gesturing for her to sit. There was an expression of utmost earnestness in his brown eyes as he sat beside her, near but not touching her.

"Arabella, please, tell me you're not in love with him!"

Arabella blinked. His outburst wasn't what she'd expected.

"I beg your pardon?"

"I saw you together last night. I saw you with him!"

Arabella inhaled. "You mean Justin Sterling?"

"Yes. You know what he is, don't you? A rakehell. A black-hearted scoundrel. Why, he's kept half a dozen mistresses at once. Arabella—" Walter gazed at her pleadingly. "He'll break your heart, if you let him."

Arabella couldn't help it. She laughed. Dear God—Georgiana and now Walter, too!

"Set your mind at ease, Walter. Believe me, I am impervious. I should never be taken in by the likes of such a man."

"I cannot tell you how pleased I am to hear it." Lightly he touched her hand. "Arabella, I adore you. I worship you—"

"Walter, please." She knew what was coming. She just knew it . . .

"Marry me, Arabella. Marry me. For I swear, you'll break *my* heart if you don't."

Arabella sighed. She wasn't sure if she should laugh or cry. "Walter. Walter, please, say no more!"

His expression rent her in two. Oh, God, she thought half-hysterically, but she should have had the speech down pat by now.

She didn't. She was babbling, doing her best to ease his pain. "Walter, try to understand. I am very fond of you. Truly I am." She *was* fond of him, and they got along favorably, if not famously . . . but she knew she could never be amorously inclined toward him. And that was the crux of it. If and when she ever married, she wanted passion and excitement and . . . and she would never find those things with Walter. Yet how could she say that without hurting his feelings?

"You are a kind, sweet man," she continued, "and I am honored that you would think of me in such a way. Indeed, I foresee that someday you'll make some woman a fine husband." She paused, hoping it would be enough, praying it would!

Walter's mouth opened, then closed. "Arabella," he said quaveringly, "what are you trying to say? I have feelings for you. And I thought you had feelings for me—"

"But not those kinds of feelings. Walter, listen to me. I cannot be your wife."

God help her, he appeared ready to weep. Arabella's heart went out to him. She was the sort who wore her emotions for all to see, and it cut her to the quick to think that she was hurting him so.

"Walter, please understand how difficult this is for me. But I made a vow to myself a long time ago, a vow that when I marry it will only be for love."

He gulped. "You don't love me?"

"I'm afraid not," she said gently. "In time, I think you'll realize you don't love me, either."

The silence was horrid. He stared at her, his expression utterly hangdog.

"Walter, I'm so sorry," she said lamely, "but it's for the best. Truly it is." Slipping a hand beneath his elbow, she rose and started toward the door, which had been left ajar.

At the threshold, he stopped and looked at her.

Arabella winced. "I can summon your carriage if you like."

He shook his head. "There's no need." At last he turned and walked back into the ballroom, his shoulders slumped as if they held the weight of the world.

Rather anxiously, Arabella watched as he crossed the room and spoke to the footman near the stairs. Good. He wouldn't make a scene. She hadn't thought he would, but still, she was relieved. She rather doubted Walter would let it be known he'd asked for her hand, only to be rejected, which suited her perfectly. Why, if word of still another proposal got out, she was very much afraid the *ton* would *never* stop talking about her.

Smoothing the yellow muslin of her gown, she gathered herself in hand and prepared to rejoin the gala.

It was then she heard it . . . almost directly behind her.

Someone was clapping.

She froze. The skin on the back of her neck prickled in warning. She knew, even before she turned, who stood behind her.

* * *

"Yet another discarded suitor," Justin observed. "I should imagine they'll soon be able to form their own club."

Arabella made no reply. He'd startled her, he realized.

"It was good of you to let him down gently," he mused. "I wonder, were the others so fortunate?"

Her silence didn't last for long—not that he expected it would. "You were lurking behind the door, weren't you?" she accused. "Spying on me."

"I was not. I was with Lord Bennington in his study. He offered me a brandy he'd just acquired, which I confess quite hit the spot. But a word of advice, Arabella. If you wish to carry on a conversation in private, it's usually best to close the door."

"I've not granted you leave to use my given name." The primness of her tone was at complete odds with the fiery blue sizzle of her eyes. "You should have let your presence be known."

"Pray tell, what would have been a good time? In between 'I adore you' and 'I worship you'?"

If anything, the heat in her eyes flared hotter. Indeed, Justin decided, she was being remarkably restrained. Where was the explosion he'd expected?

He continued. "Obviously, though, he is not aware of our previous association or he wouldn't have thought you were in love with me."

Levelly she regarded him. "You wretch," she said evenly.

"Oh, but I do believe it's *I* who should be offended. You did not speak highly of me. However, I am compelled to inform you—that bit about half a dozen mistresses is greatly exaggerated." He shrugged. "Not that I wouldn't have liked to, I admit. But funds precluded it, I fear."

Her chin came up. "You have no decency whatsoever, do you? What kind of man would say such a thing to a lady?"

Justin knew full well she had a temper to match the fire of her hair. It occurred to him he was baiting her—and enjoying it immensely.

"Come, now, Arabella. You gave an admirable performance of a concerned, compassionate woman. I must commend you. Why, you should have been on the stage."

His efforts began to see fruition. She was growing agitated.

"Do you think I enjoyed that?" she flared.

"Didn't you?"

Her chin came up. "I am not like you," she stated coolly. "I am sensitive to his feelings."

"Then why don't you marry him?" He didn't give her the chance to answer. "Ah, yes. Because you intend to marry only for love."

She sent him an arch look. "Is that so hard to believe?"

Justin shrugged.

"I've heard it said that your brother married for love," she reminded him.

"But he didn't intend to. He set out in search of a bride who would fit his requisites for a wife. He was simply lucky enough to find love in the process." Again he gave her no chance to respond. "But we stray from the subject. What I find difficult to believe is that *you* are capable of that tender emotion."

Her lips clamped shut. She was practically spitting, just itching to launch into a tirade.

Admittedly, he found the prospect rather intriguing.

He tipped his head to the side. "What are you thinking, Arabella?"

Her eyes narrowed. "Believe me," she stated with forced politeness, "you do not wish to know."

"And if I said I did?"

"Grass before dawn," she said between her teeth. "Does that give you a hint?"

"A duel," he drawled. "How delicious. Oh, but I should have known you'd be contemplating ways to attack."

And indeed, he decided with wry amusement, her glare left him in no doubt she was contemplating the possibility. If she were a predator, he'd be gnawed to the bone.

"Forgive me, but did you not just claim to be a tenderhearted woman? My, but you certainly pulled the wool over Walter's eyes, didn't you?"

"My God," she gritted out, "if I had a pistol, I do believe I would shoot you on the spot!"

"Ah. Clearly my charm is utterly lost on you."

"You have no charm."

"Arabella!" He affected shock. "What a thing to say to a gentleman!"

"You, sir, are no gentleman!"

Ye gads, but she was a hoyden! As impetuous and strong-willed as ever, he suspected. And yet their encounter last night and tonight provided him the most entertainment he'd enjoyed in quite some time. He was enjoying her wit and their sparring—never mind that foolish, careless bet with Gideon. In the back of his mind, he made note to mention it the next time he saw him . . .

It was odd, but he felt suddenly buoyant. Alive as he hadn't in longer than he could remember.

"It's a good thing you declined poor Walter," he said smoothly. "It's clear he's simply not up to the rapier slice of your tongue. But I promise, you'll find me a worthy opponent."

Her eyes narrowed. "What the devil is that supposed to mean? And why are you smiling in that wolfish way, as if there's something you know that I don't?"

She was nothing if not forthright, he decided. "I don't know. Certainly it can't be the company."

"I shall ignore that," she announced. "Now, then. I should like to discuss the matter of your spying on me—"

"I was not spying. I thought we established that."

"We did not. But may I trust you will not disclose the nature of what you overheard?"

"Why?"

"Because I abhor gossip, that's why."

He arched his brows. "You mean you don't relish your reign as The Unattainable?"

"I do not," she muttered. "And if anyone else calls me by that horrid name again today, I swear I shall scream."

His mouth quirked. "That should help to discourage gossip."

Her eyes found his. "Do I have your assurance you will say nothing?" she demanded.

"Well," he murmured, "I might be persuaded."

"For what?"

A kiss, he almost said. Indeed, it was only at the last instant he quelled the unexpected impulse.

He was all at once vastly annoyed with himself. A kiss with Miss Arabella Templeton . . . how the blazes had his mind conjured up something so preposterous?

It was a startling admission, considering she was the most vexing female he'd ever had the misfortune to encounter. Yet on second thought, perhaps it was neither startling nor preposterous.

His gaze had drifted down to her lips. She had a mouth given to laughter, he decided. A mouth fashioned purely for a man's pleasure, full and lush and pink like the rest of her. He'd already mentally approved her choice of gown—the buttery yellow made her skin glow.

He found the prospect of kissing her—God, what was the matter with him?—provocative, at the least. In her zeal, she'd moved closer. That wasn't helping matters. Nor did the earnestness of her regard. She was staring up at him intently, awaiting his answer, her lips parted, offering a glimpse of small white teeth. Christ, he wondered crazily, what *would* she taste like?

"You haven't answered me. You won't tell, will you?"

Wicked. That's what he was. Wicked to even think what he was thinking . . .

The music had commenced. Hearing it, he cocked a brow. "Dance with me," was all he said, "and I shall consider it."

And he whisked her onto the dance floor.

Five

They wheeled so suddenly she clutched at his shoulder. "Justin!" His name was a sound of pure dismay. Belatedly it occurred to her she'd just called him by his given name. "What are you doing?"

"I should have thought it would be obvious."

They whirled past the Misses Wilmington, Abigail and Lucinda, who regarded him with open admiration. Justin inclined his head and directed a devastating smile at the pair. Abigail tittered behind her fan, while Lucinda openly batted her eyelashes at him.

Arabella's jaw snapped shut. "Did no one ever tell you it is the height of bad manners to dance with one woman while making eyes at another?"

"Jealous, are we?"

"In a pig's eye!"

He threw back his head and laughed. "Arabella, you are truly a delight."

He didn't mean it, of course. Indeed, she was well aware he meant the complete opposite.

"I've not forgiven you, you know," she told him stoutly.

"For what?"

She bared her teeth.

A heavy black brow climbed high. "My dear, is something wrong? Do you worry there is perhaps a bit of basil left from the cream sauce at dinner? Set your mind at ease, then. There is none."

Arabella longed to screech at the top of her lungs. She was forced to settle for a whisper. "This is revenge, isn't it? Your way of getting back at me for the prank I played on you as a child."

"My word, but you are suspicious! Why would you possibly think that?"

"Because I should have thought you would avoid me like the plague."

"Why would I avoid you? That would imply I am afraid of you."

"And you, of course, fear nothing, least of all a mere woman."

Their eyes caught. Within his, glimmered a spark of something . . . something she couldn't quite decipher. She knew only that whatever it was, she didn't trust it.

"Must you stare at me?"

"I'm sorry," he said smoothly. "I didn't mean to. It's just that I never before noticed your freckles."

No doubt he was comparing her to the elegant sophisticates with whom he usually associated. But Arabella had never hated her freckles more than she did at that moment. When she was a child, she'd scrubbed until her skin was raw. When she was older, she'd prodigiously applied Gowland's Lotion each and every night. Nothing had worked.

Her gaze was the first to slide away. She lapsed into silence. Lord, but this was awkward. She didn't like dancing. More aptly, she didn't like dancing with *him*. He was far too devilishly attractive, for one thing. It galled her to admit that she couldn't *not* be conscious of him. My God, that was a feat no sane woman could accomplish. And she was acutely aware of the weight of his hand on her waist. She felt as if she burned clear to the skin. And his other hand, wrapped around hers, large and brown and strong . . . Something wholly unfamiliar stabbed at her insides.

He whirled her again. Arabella stumbled, forced to grab at him for support.

"Justin, stop that!" she hissed. Her legs felt like stilts. Her face was flaming, she was certain.

"My dear, how else are we to dance?"

"You're holding me much too tightly!"

"Am I?"

It was a mild inquiry, but hardly a mild look. What was it he'd said last night? *I've been known to eat up tender little girls like you.*

Arabella was heartily annoyed with herself. She sounded as if she'd been running. In truth her shortness of breath wasn't due to the tightening of his arm around her waist. No, it had far more to do with the proximity of his lips, which hovered so near she could feel the warm rush of his breath across her temple. And his height . . . confound it, he managed to make her feel dainty and delicate, no small feat. And . . . oh, how she liked it! God above, but she did!

But this was Justin Sterling. Rake of all rakes. Cad among cads.

Confused by her reaction, disturbed by his nearness, she rallied her defenses, straightened her spine . . . and accidentally stepped on his foot in the process.

He grunted. "I'd heard that dancing was not one of your accomplishments. But you did that on purpose, didn't you?"

"I did not," she denied with a flare of resentment.

The clasp of his hand around hers tightened.

"Justin! For pity's sake—"

"Do you know, that is the third time you've uttered my name in as many minutes? I do believe my status is growing in your eyes."

"I wasn't counting," she said from between her teeth. "Now loosen your grip, if you please."

He was undaunted. "The waltz is not yet over."

"Justin—"

"Four," he intoned softly.

Arabella's head came up so suddenly she nearly clipped his chin. She shot him a look that would have withered many a man in his shoes. Alas, not him! He continued to regard her with the merest hint of a smile on his lips.

"Now, see here." She did her best to sound severe. “I do not want to cause a scandal. And surely you don’t, either—”

He laughed outright.

Her eyes were snapping. “Why do you find that so amusing?”

“Because it *is* amusing. Scandal? My dear, you’ve spent too much time away from the country with your parents. The Sterling family name is synonymous with scandal. Hadn’t you heard?”

“I thought it was only *your* name that was,” she stated daringly.

“If you seek to wound me, Arabella, you’ll have to do better than that.”

Faith, but he had an answer for everything! She decided her best defense was silence. He spun. Arabella stumbled, and only narrowly avoided crashing into a large vase at the side of the floor.

He sighed. “If you would only relax and follow my lead, this would not be an ordeal. I’m an exquisite dancer.”

Arabella set her lips. But of course he was. He was light on his feet, his steps deft. What else could one expect from a man as perfect as he?

Again she trod on his foot.

“My God,” he muttered, “what *is* this perverse compunction you have to see that I never walk again?”

Arabella flushed. She didn’t appreciate the reminder.

The music ended a moment later. Before she had a chance to draw a breath, a man appeared beside them. Fair-haired and ruddy-cheeked, he was nearly as tall and powerfully built as Justin. Arabella watched curiously, for there was a certain arrogance in the way he inclined his chin toward Justin.

"Sterling," he greeted. "Good to see you."

He spoke with a distinct Scots burr, Arabella noted. Justin acknowledged with a curt nod. "McElroy."

The man named McElroy transferred his gaze to Arabella. "I don't believe I've had the pleasure of meeting your dance partner. Perhaps you'll be so good as to introduce us."

"Certainly. Miss Templeton, Lord Patrick McElroy. McElroy, Miss Arabella Templeton."

Oddly, Justin sounded less than pleased.

McElroy gave a bow. "Charmed, I'm sure."

Arabella smiled and gave a small curtsy. "A pleasure to meet you, my lord."

Behind them, the musicians struck a chord.

McElroy turned to her. "Miss Templeton, may I have this next—"

He never got the chance to finish. "Sorry, old man," Justin cut in smoothly, "but Miss Templeton has already promised this next set to me."

Arabella had no choice but to follow when he practically dragged her into the middle of the dance floor.

Still rather stunned, she gaped up at him. "Why did you do that? Maybe I wanted to dance with him."

"Trust me"—his tone was clipped—"you didn't."

Arabella borrowed his phrase of but moments before. "Ah," she almost purred. "Jealous, are we?"

That he did not deny it with the utmost vehemence stunned her to her very soul. She was still contemplating his lack of dissent when his eyes snared hers.

"Let me put it this way, Arabella. You're better off with me than with him."

"I do believe I should be the judge of that."

He scowled. His lips were almost ominously thin, the set of his jaw stern. Why the devil was he suddenly so out of sorts?

"Where the welfare of innocent young maids is concerned," he said sharply, "he's dangerous."

"What! More so than you?" she asked tartly. The bent of their conversation was altogether shocking. Later she would ask herself how she dared. For now, she did not.

"That is not something you should know." He put his face close to hers. "You are an innocent young maid, are you not?"

Arabella gasped. "That, sir, is none of your affair!"

He smiled suddenly, his good humor restored. Ah, but at her expense, she feared!

They danced on in silence, until the tune ended.

He bent his head low. "That was much better," he murmured, his breath brushing her ear. "Why, not once did you trounce upon my foot."

He led her to the edge of the dance floor, but retained possession of her gloved hand. Reminded of his impertinence last night, Arabella didn't dare tug it back, as she wanted to. But there was a wicked slant to his smile. It held something she didn't trust in the least, especially when he raised her hand to his lips.

"Don't you dare bite me again!" she hissed. "Else I swear I shall bite back."

Laughing green eyes met hers. "Now, *that* I should like to see."

His dark head descended. And indeed, he did not bite. At the very last instant, he turned her hand palm up. A thumb grazed the inside of her wrist, where her glove ended and her skin was bared. And then she felt the warm, wet wash of his tongue trace the very same path . . .

Arabella was speechless. By Jove, he'd licked her instead!

Once Arabella was home, her lacy white gloves were consigned to the bottom of the drawer—they would not be worn again, she vowed. From there she marched across to the washbasin, where she scrubbed the offending hand as fiercely as she'd once scrubbed her freckles. If she never saw the man again, it would suit her just fine!

With luck, she decided blackly, he'd take himself back to the Continent, or wherever it was he'd been. Of course, that was hardy likely . . .

Twice in as many nights she had seen him. *Twice.* Would she be so unlucky as to encounter him a third? But what else could she do? She could hardly avoid him the rest of the Season.

But Arabella did not relish the prospect of seeing Justin again. Indeed, it was still on her mind the next day because Lady Melville's masquerade party was to be held that night at Vauxhall Gardens. Aunt Grace had been thrilled to pieces when the invitation arrived. According to her, rumor had it a thousand guests had been invited. Arabella had been excited at the prospect as well; she glimpsed a balloon ascent from Vauxhall one afternoon not long ago, but she had yet to experience the glorious wonder of Vauxhall after dark.

But that was before Justin had returned.

Now, she could have wailed aloud. Would he be in attendance?

She hoped not. She prayed not.

The prospect of seeing him again, wondering what he would do next, filled her with dread. Dancing with him last night . . . He hadn't lied. He was an exquisite dancer, and she had felt like such a clod! He'd held her altogether too closely. She remembered vividly the feel of his hand on her waist, his heat and warmth, a warmth that spread clear inside her. As for the warm slide of his tongue on her skin . . . God above, his *tongue*! And he was altogether too handsome, his behavior altogether too rakish. Furthermore, he was altogether too unpredictable.

She didn't trust him. She had the sneaking suspicion he had enjoyed tormenting her. He would delight in making a fool of her, she was convinced.

No, she most definitely did not look forward to seeing him again. Indeed, she almost dreaded it.

Nor could she put him from her mind—and that was most vexing of all!

Glancing into the drawing room later that day, Aunt Grace spied her sitting on the long cupboard near the window, staring into the garden.

"I must say, my dear, you're looking most disgruntled."

Arabella looked up. "Aunt! I didn't know you were back." Aunt Grace had been shopping with several of her friends. In invitation, Arabella patted the cushions beside her.

Aunt Grace joined her, arranging her skirts lightly over her legs. "My dear, I've watched you frowning and fretting and fidgeting from across the room for a full five minutes. What is on your mind?"

Arabella took a breath. "Nothing."

Aunt Grace studied her for a moment, then pursed her lips. "Any gentlemen callers this afternoon?"

Arabella shook her head.

Her gray eyes softened. "Ah, so that's why—"

"Oh, that's not the case at all! I actually had a moment to myself—and indeed I relished every second." Every second, that is, that was not given to thoughts of Justin Sterling.

Aunt Grace was startled at her vehemence. "I hadn't realized you were so unhappy, dear."

"Oh, but I'm not unhappy!" Arabella hastened

to reassure her. "I adore being here with you and Uncle Joseph. And I adore London, the gaiety and the parties. But this whole business of being considered The Unattainable . . . well, I didn't want it. I *don't* want it. I should be quite content with being on the sidelines."

Aunt Grace regarded her, her head tipped slightly to the side. "That may be hard to accomplish, my dear. Granted, the *ton* is fickle. But right now, you are the toast of the Season, and will likely remain so, unless you deign to choose a husband."

Arabella couldn't help it. "Aunt Grace, if I never have another gentleman caller this year, I do believe it would please me to no end."

"My dear, I think you're simply feeling rather overwhelmed."

Arabella slanted her a wan smile.

"Do you know, in our day, between your mother and I, I do believe we had callers queuing out the door. Why, your grandfather used to complain that his house was not his own!" Her aunt was almost giggling in fond remembrance. "And it was the same with your cousins, you know. Why, I do believe it runs in the family!"

Arabella couldn't help but smile. There was no question her aunt had been a beauty in her day. Indeed, her cheeks were still plump and pink, her eyes bright and vivacious. And when she smiled, the dimples in her cheeks lent her a youthful radiance that was almost infectious.

"The years have been kind to you, Aunt Grace, for you are still a very fetching woman."

Her aunt fairly beamed. "Thank you, child. That's most gracious of you. But come, will you not at least admit it *is* rather flattering to have all those gentlemen throwing themselves at your feet?"

Arabella bit her lip. "Well," she allowed, "perhaps."

"Yes, yes, I knew it. But back to the business of finding a husband."

Arabella sucked in a breath. "Aunt Grace," she began carefully, "I am not quite sure how to say this, but—"

"I think I know your point, child." Aunt Grace was once again brisk. "It occurs to me that I have been most persistent in urging you to choose among your suitors. Perhaps *too* persistent."

Arabella relaxed.

"I admit, I am overanxious. It's just that I do so enjoy planning a wedding. It has been two years since your cousin Edith wed, you know. But I suspect you will be like your mother and choose your own path. As for the matter of your future husband, I promise, my dear, I shall endeavor to say no more."

Arabella didn't speak. There was a restless questing inside her she didn't fully understand, and she felt as if she were suddenly flailing . . .

She didn't have the heart to inform Aunt Grace there was a very good likelihood she wouldn't be planning a wedding because Arabella might never wed. She wasn't beautiful or accomplished like her cousins. She was . . . different. She knew instinctively that she wouldn't be content with the missionary life, as her parents were. She wasn't a bluestocking or a crusader. And she didn't want to be an albatross around her parents' necks.

She didn't know what she wanted or even what she was suited for! She only seemed to know what she *didn't* want . . .

But she was lucky, she realized with a pang. Lucky to be loved the way she had been loved all her life, by everyone close to her. And she was all at once reminded why she had always cherished the time spent with her aunt. She'd never loved her more than she did right now.

Impulsively she reached out, clasping both of her aunt's hands in hers.

"Do you know, when I was young and in school, and Mama and Papa had to be away, sometimes I missed them terribly." An aching lump of emotion swelled in her chest, so vast she could hardly speak. But suddenly it was all spilling out, and she couldn't stop it.

"But then I'd think of you, and suddenly it didn't hurt so much. I didn't feel so alone, because I had you, Aunt Grace. Because you were there to hug me and hold me and mother me when Mama could not. I've never told you how much that meant to me."

Tears sprang to her aunt's eyes, and suddenly her own were swimming as well. With a tender hand, Grace smoothed a tendril of hair behind her ear.

"Arabella! Oh, Arabella, I cannot tell you how it pleases me to hear you say that. I shall always be here for you, whenever you need me. Why, you are as dear to my heart as if you were my own. You know that, don't you?"

"I do, Aunt Grace. Oh, but I do!" Fraught with emotion, the pair hugged.

Aunt Grace drew back, patting her cheek. "But you must promise me, Arabella. No more fretting. No more worrying. This is a time in your life for you to be happy and gay and . . . oh, I know this may not be the right time to say it, particularly when I vowed I would speak of husbands no more. But you know me, and I fear I must . . . You'll know when the right man comes into your life. You'll know it *here*"—she laid her hand on her heart and smiled—"as both your mother and I did."

Arabella blinked. "But you and Uncle Joseph . . . I always thought that your marriage was arranged."

"Oh, I should say not! A love match, my dear." Grace's eyes were twinkling once again. She let out a giggle. "I confess, I was quite the coquette, and I did lead him a merry chase. He had to vie for my affections, but once he . . ."

Arabella looked on in astonishment. Aunt Grace was blushing!

Grace cleared her throat. "Suffice it to say that it wasn't long before I knew he was the one." She rose and shook out the wrinkles in her gown. The dimple in her cheek deepened. "Oh, but he was quite the dashing rake, your Uncle Joseph."

Arabella was aghast. For all that Uncle Joseph commanded a purposeful, distinguished demeanor outside the family, when she envisioned his thinning pate, it was difficult to imagine him a rake!

Instead her mind veered straight to Justin Sterling.

From the corner of her eye, she saw that Aunt Grace had started toward the door. Arabella got to her feet as well. Halfway across the room, she stopped.

"You haven't forgotten the masquerade tonight, have you, dear?"

"Of course not."

"Excellent. I'll have Annie make up your bath. We wouldn't want to be late for such an event." Three more steps, and then she paused and glanced back over her shoulder.

"By the way, dear, I saw you waltzing with Justin Sterling last night."

Arabella sucked in a breath. "What?" she said weakly. Mercy, had she spoken Justin's name out loud? "Oh, yes, Aunt Grace, I know. We should probably have the dancing master back."

"Actually, I was going to say, dear, that the two of you looked quite striking together. I daresay, I wasn't the only one who noticed. The Dowager Duchess of Carrington quite agreed. His dark looks lend themselves perfectly to a woman with your vivacious coloring."

Arabella was speechless. Georgiana had said nearly the very same thing. And now Aunt Grace . . .

"I chatted with him briefly earlier last night. You'll recall we've known his brother the marquess for a number of years. Indeed, the marquess is hosting a house party next week. But Justin, well . . . I daresay he's a very charming young man."

"Aunt Grace, he's a reprobate! His reputation is—"

"Yes, yes, I know, it's quite scandalous. But you must admit, is he not the most divinely handsome man you've ever laid eyes on?"

"Aunt Grace!" she gasped.

Her aunt arched a brow in wicked amusement. "Come, child. I may be getting on in years, but my eyesight has yet to fail me." She winked at her. "I daresay, he puts me in mind of your Uncle Joseph some thirty years ago."

The woman continued to chuckle as she sailed breezily from the room. But Arabella had yet to recover. She was still gaping when the door closed. Stunned, she sank back onto the seat.

She didn't know whether to laugh insanely or bury her head in her hands and weep.

Georgiana . . . and Aunt Grace. Even the Dowager Duchess of Carrington, a most imposing woman who made Arabella quake in her slippers . . . Young and old, it didn't seem to matter. Did Justin Sterling command some brand of sorcery? Sweet heavens, was there a woman alive who could withstand his ability to charm and captivate?

It appeared that she alone was not susceptible. She alone would never succumb.

Six

On her way up the stairs, Arabella very nearly stopped at Aunt Grace's door, intending to cry off the masquerade. She could plead the headache. Or simply that she longed for an entire evening to herself.

But sitting in her bath a scant half-hour later, she resolved differently. If she should chance to see Justin, she wouldn't let him set her to quailing. Nor would she let him best her. She had more starch than to let him win.

And she wasn't about to let him turn her into a recluse. That would have given him too much satisfaction.

And indeed, once they arrived at Vauxhall, Arabella wouldn't have missed it for the world. Their arrival to the Grand Walk was perfectly timed. They had no sooner settled in than a crescendo from the orchestra sounded. The night exploded; hidden in the trees were lanterns of radiant color, in the shape of stars and half-moons. Arabella exclaimed in sheer delight, for it was a world like no other.

Despite her earlier resolve, she had been on edge as they awaited entry into the gardens. But from that moment on, the mood for the night was set. And there was no sign of Justin, which sealed her enchantment of the evening.

Most everyone in attendance wore masks and had chosen their costumes with care. It was vastly entertaining trying to guess who everyone was. There was a svelte young beauty draped in the garb of a Greek goddess, a couple who came as Romeo and Juliet. For her own costume, Arabella had chosen to wear a gown of gauzy layered silk in the Spanish style. A fine black lace mantilla shielded her curls.

Finishing a country dance, she laughed as a dashing pirate blew her a kiss from across the dance floor, set up near the central square. She knew it wasn't Justin—he lacked Justin's tall, lean physique. Her heart pounding from her exertions, she wandered into a miniature temple a short distance away from the guests.

Inside, a small bench beckoned invitingly. It was, she decided, the perfect place to rest and regain her breath. Tipping her head back, she listened to the sound of a waterfall tinkling nearby.

She was just about to rise when the trill of feminine voices reached her ears.

"You know he won't be long without a mistress," said one.

"He never is," agreed another. "But who will be the next lucky lady, I wonder?"

Arabella froze. They had stopped almost directly behind her.

"He does have a tendency to go through lovers. Why, I vow, it would not be beyond reason to say that he's bedded down with fully half the women here tonight, now, would it?"

More trilling laughter. Arabella's lips turned down, but she didn't dare move. She didn't want them to think she was spying on them.

"Ah, yes, and left a trail of broken hearts in the wake."

"And yours among them," said the first woman. "Ah, yes, well, hearts do mend, don't they? But perhaps you should cast your hat back into the ring."

"Oh, I would not be averse to it were he to look my way," the second woman said lightly. "But Agatha has her eye on him again, you know. They were lovers a few years ago, if you recall, just after she married Dunsbrook. But how many has she seen since? A dozen?"

"Ah, but what of him? Surely thrice that many!"

Arabella's entire body burned. How blithely they spoke of dalliances and indiscretions, of affairs and infidelity. How frivolously they spoke of love and lovers—dear God, they made but a mockery of the words!

Theirs was a world she would neither embrace nor understand, a world she deplored with all her being. And the gentleman in question—oh, but she used the term most generously!—why, he was the worst of all!

Love was faith and fidelity and all that went with it. Love was what her parents shared. And, particularly after her conversation with Aunt Grace, she was very, very certain that love was what Aunt Grace and Uncle Joseph shared.

"Yes, I remember the way Agatha carried on. Why, to this day I recall the jealous fit she threw when she discovered he was carrying on with Lady Anne—what a tizzy! You'd have sworn he was her first and only love. I won't deny Justin Sterling is a lover of superb finesse, but it's not as if he's the only man with such . . . skill."

The man they were discussing was Justin. Oh, but she should have known!

"Well," the first voice said cattily, "we certainly know who his next mistress *won't* be, don't we?"

"Ah, yes, The Unattainable."

"The very one."

"God, yes! Did you see her at the Bennington affair last night, lumbering about like a . . . a horse? I'm sure he only danced with her out of pity, though I can't imagine why."

The second exclaimed with snobbish delight, "I quite agree. God knows what the gentlemen see in her. Why, I do believe it's all a vast joke, that they're all secretly laughing at her!"

Oh, God. In but a heartbeat, Arabella's pleasure in the evening fled. Her happiness shattered, like a piece of fine china dashed to the floor. She cringed, sick to the dregs of her soul. She couldn't help but remember what Aunt Grace had said only this afternoon about the *ton* being fickle.

The toast of the Season indeed. Sweet Lord, she might well end up the laughingstock of the year.

She couldn't bear one more second. Only half-aware, she arose. Blindly she walked, her steps quickening. Then suddenly she was almost running, tearing along the path, twisting and turning.

When at last she stopped, her heart was pounding. The lights of the square were far behind her; her flight had taken her into a deeply wooded area. She glanced about in dismay, and no little amount of fear. She had strayed far from the rest of the party. She'd heard tales of thieves lying in wait for unwary females, and had no doubt they were true. Oh, why had she come so far!

Footsteps crunched on the gravel nearby. Her eyes darted into the shadows. She clutched her skirts and prepared to flee. All at once strong fingers whirled her about. A dark, featureless shadow loomed before her. Frightened almost beyond her wits, she opened her mouth.

"For pity's sake," a voice intoned irritably, "don't scream. It's only me."

The man restraining her stripped off his mask. Her breath caught on a gasp. Arabella looked up. Set between sharp green eyes was a long, elegant nose.

"Perhaps the very reason I should!"

His eyes flickered over her. "What are you doing out here? There are thieves and footpads—"

"And rakes and scoundrels?" she queried archly.

He made no response, but his lips thinned.

"You're following me, aren't you? How the devil did you recognize me?"

"My dear Arabella," he drawled, "masquerade or no, there is nothing about you that does not remain"—his gaze flickered over her, lingering on her hair—"distinctive."

Arabella was stung. She knew what he meant. Her height. Her hair. Justin Sterling, with his perfect, impeccable looks, had no idea what she had endured her entire life! He couldn't possibly know how it hurt to be jeered at, laughed at, sneered at.

She felt like a freak in a circus sideshow—and never more so than now.

Her mantilla had slipped to her shoulders. She dragged it up over the froth of curls pinned at her crown. Angry, bitter hurt crowded her throat. "Must you insult me?" she cried.

"God's blood, I meant no insult."

"Oh, but you did! I—I don't need to be reminded of my shortcomings. I know my hair is quite unattractive, but there's nothing I can—"

"Unattractive! Why, quite the contrary." Indeed, it was a startling admission . . . or was it? Justin wasn't quite sure. He knew only that he had come here tonight hoping to encounter her. She had grown into a woman of wit and intelligence—a woman fully capable of a wicked repartee that rivaled his own. Indeed, their first meeting, as well as the second, had inspired a rather reluctant admiration. Was it any wonder he looked forward to the next?

"It's . . . well, it's what makes you . . . *you.*" Lord, but he sounded lame. He, the master of seduction, the man who had wooed and won his way into the boudoirs of more ladies than he could even remember, found himself at a startling loss for words. Where was his usual glib flattery, the practiced ease which was second nature?

Not that it came as any surprise, but she appeared singularly unimpressed. Eyes flashing, she raised her chin. "Let me pass," she said calmly.

"Not yet. We have much to discuss."

"We have nothing to discuss."

"Don't we? If you recall, we have some unfinished business, you and I."

"What business?" she asked sharply.

"Do you forget so soon? We neglected to settle last night on the price of my silence about your *cher amour* Walter."

"He is not my love and you know it."

He merely gave her a mundane smile in return.

"You've decided to plague me, haven't you, Justin? It's revenge for the prank I played on you as a child."

"My, but you're in a mood, aren't you?"

Arabella said nothing. She lowered her head. He had moved close. Less than the span of her palm was all that lay between them.

"Arabella?" he queried.

His nearness was disarming. He was disturbingly, distractingly masculine. She felt helpless against him! All at once she couldn't think. Her heart was clamoring so that she could scarcely breathe.

"Not having the vapors, are you?"

The amusement in his tone brought her head up in a flash. "I never have the vapors," she stressed.

"No, I don't suppose you do." He eyed her. His tone had turned almost grim. "Why do you look at me as you do?" he asked curtly.

"How do I look at you?"

"As if you would do me harm. When you look at me, I see nothing but contempt." There was an edge in his tone that did not bode well.

"Our dislike is mutual," she stated bluntly. "There is no need to pretend otherwise."

His eyes narrowed. "You haven't answered my question."

"Nor will I."

"Why not? Are you a coward, Arabella?"

"I am not!"

"Then why do you refuse to answer?"

"And why can't you leave me be? If anyone saw you come after me—"

"And what if they did?"

Arabella pressed her lips together. As if there were any need to ask! He was baiting her, she knew. But if he wanted to hear her say it, then so be it.

"Because I've no wish for my name to be bandied about with yours."

His eyes grew frosty. "Indeed?"

"Indeed."

"Why, Arabella?"

"Simply because you are who you are! You are *what* you are!"

"You refer to my reputation."

Later she would wonder what possessed her, that she dared to challenge him so. "Yes. I despise men like you."

"Arabella, I do believe you cast aspersions on my character."

"Character?" She cast him a withering look. "You have none!"

"Oh, come. Am I not a man of eminent distinction?"

Now he mocked not only her, but himself. "Perchance a man of eminent delusion," she muttered.

He tipped his head to the side. "My, but this grows interesting. Truly, what do you think of me?"

"I think you would rather not know."

"Oh, come. Out with it."

Arabella glared. "You are a rake."

The merest lift of his brows. "What? That's all? That's why you dislike me?"

Another glare, more heated than the first.

"That's what I thought. Please, pray continue."

Her eyes narrowed. "I know what you are, Justin Sterling."

"You profess to know a very great deal about me. What, precisely, do you know?"

"All I need to know!"

"Such as?"

"You are a profligate," she said.

"And?"

"A cad. A Corinthian."

A slow smile edged across his lips. "Come, surely you can do better than that."

"Do you think I haven't heard tales of your escapades with your lady friends?"

"Clearly that distresses you."

Oh, but he was outrageous! Totally unrepentant. Arabella was reminded of poor Emmaline Winslow sobbing her heart out. How could he be so callous? "You are a rogue. A bounder."

He quirked a well-shaped brow. "I've never given my attention to any woman who did not want it."

"No doubt a masterly achievement in your eyes." Arabella hitched her chin high. His aplomb unraveled her temper. "You, my Lord Vice—"

"Lord Vice? Oh, that is rich, coming from you, Miss Vicar!" He directed his gaze heavenward. "Are you finished?"

Her eyes were snapping. "I am not!"

"Well, then, pray continue."

"You are despicable."

That brow remained cocked high. "Surely you can do better than that."

Arabella took a deep breath. "You are despicable—"

"You repeat yourself, my dear."

"Despicable *and* odious. I find you utterly detestable. Thoroughly unlikable—"

"Odd," he cut in. "It seems I only have this problem with you."

Arabella made a shrill sound. "You are vile. Uncouth—"

"Never in front of a lady."

"Clearly you find this a great source of amusement. But I'll have you know, unlike the rest of the willy-nilly females who giggle behind their fans whene'er they spy you, I see you through unclouded eyes. No decent woman will ever have you. Why, I doubt the woman exists who could penetrate your—" She gestured wildly at his chest.

"Heart?" he supplied.

"What! You have a heart?"

"Is that all?" he asked coolly. "You detest me because I've a fondness for beautiful women?"

"Your reputation is thoroughly reprehensible and you know it."

"I avail myself of what pleasures may come my way, though I admit my reputation is one I've probably cultivated."

"You are a womanizer and a wastrel, Justin Sterling. Furthermore, I don't like you very much! So let's just leave it at that, shall we?" She tried to step around him.

He didn't allow it. A long arm snaked out and stopped her cold.

"Unhand me," she said clearly.

"I think not."

Arabella turned her head. A chill went through her. Only then did she note his smile was wiped clean. His eyes had gone utterly cold.

Sharply she spoke. "What the devil are you doing?"

An unpleasant smile rimmed his lips. "I should think it would be obvious, my dear."

She had no chance to reply. Before she could move, before she could say a word, he snatched the mantilla from her hair.

Her hand went to her head. "Justin! Why did you do that?"

"Let us call it a token of your affection, shall we?"

He twisted so that they stood face-to-face. With his free arm, he crushed her against him. Arabella's breath left her lungs in a rush. She stared directly into his dark features. His intense regard was unnerving. Too late she recognized her rashness; too late she regretted it! She had challenged him, and a man like him wouldn't take such a thing lightly. Truthful or not, she had been unwise to taunt him so.

A blistering heat resided in his eyes, along with something she didn't fully understand. Anger? Most assuredly. Desire? No, she thought. Surely not desire. And yet . . .

"Give it back," she said levelly.

"You're in no position to make demands, Arabella."

Indeed, she thought frantically, she was in no position she'd ever thought to find herself in! His nearness was overwhelming. She could feel the rise and fall of his chest against her breasts. He was rock-hard and broad. Once again she was acutely conscious of the way he made her feel small and feminine.

"Let me be." She strived for disdain. Somehow she feared she only managed to sound desperate. "I know what you're trying to do, Justin."

"Tell me," came his silken invitation.

Nervously she wet her lips, summoning a bravado she was far from feeling. "You're trying to frighten me."

He smiled nastily. "Am I succeeding?"

"No!" she lied.

And he knew it. She knew it by the way his smile slowly ripened and his green eyes glittered emerald fire in the night!

"Perhaps you should be frightened," he said in a tone all the more lethal for its velvet softness. "Ah, yes, perhaps you should be."

His gaze slid over her, dwelling long and hard on the outline of her breasts. Arabella's heart lurched. Her stomach dropped to the ground.

"Don't," she said haltingly. "You use women, Justin. Discard them like old shoes, with nary a thought. But I won't let you do that with me."

"My dear, you couldn't stop me."

"Don't say that!"

"Must I remind you of your own words? I'm a scoundrel. A cad. So don't play with fire. Don't play with *me*! Whose reputation would suffer if our names were linked together, if it was known that you were here with me in the dark—here in Lovers' Walk—here in my arms? Certainly not mine! Yours, however . . ." He let the sentence dangle.

Oh, God. What had she done? She had unleashed something in him, something wild and primitive, something far beyond her experience . . . far beyond her ability to control. He was like an animal on the hunt, she thought frantically.

"You wouldn't," she whispered.

"Wouldn't I?" The slant of his smile was almost cruel. "Oh, yes, Arabella, I see you take my meaning. I could see to it that your prospects for marriage end this very night. You say no decent woman will ever have me. You're right. I do not deny it. But, by God, no decent man would ever have *you.* Not even poor, besotted Walter."

Their eyes collided. A simmering tension hung between them. His features were an ominous mask, his expression forbidding, each word a pelting blow.

For, God help her, it was true. She would be forever shamed. Forever shunned.

She had erred badly, she realized. Somehow she'd always known that Justin was dangerous. What she hadn't known was how much—or that he might prove dangerous to *her.*

A tremor went through her. She gave a tiny shake of her head. Her gaze grazed his, then skidded away. "Don't!" she said on a strangled breath. "Please, don't ruin me."

He wanted to, he realized. The ugliness inside him wanted to show her. He wanted to hurt her. To lash out and punish her for saying that no decent woman would have him.

His father had said that, too. The night he'd died. The night he, Justin, had *killed* him.

Damn her! he thought fiercely. Damn her feistiness. Damn her prim, prudish ways! For being such a spitfire, for being so defiantly strong-willed and impetuous. And damn her scornful, reckless tongue!

His arm around her back tightened. She was stiff in his embrace, but she didn't resist him. He wanted to give in to the wickedness inside him, the thunderous need that made his head roar and scalded both his blood and his temper. An elemental heat reared up in him. She had fired his lust, stirred his anger, and the wickedness inside him clamored for him to lower her to the ground, to taste and explore the hot, silken interior of her mouth as he would and say to hell with her innocence. To hell with his conscience. He wanted to drive between her thighs again and again until the world exploded in a crimson haze of pleasure.

Christ, but he was vile!

"Look at me," he demanded.

Slowly she raised her head. She didn't avert her face, though he sensed she wanted to. He saw her convulsive swallow, glimpsed the shimmer of wetness in her wide-set eyes, felt her struggle to control her emotions in the deep, tremulous breath she drew.

Something inside told him how much it cost her, to stand before him on the verge of tears. And somehow, that very sense told him he was the *last* person on earth she would want to bear witness to her tears . . . yet what had he done?

"Please," she whispered, so low he could barely hear. "Please, do not disgrace me. I . . . it would kill my Aunt Grace."

He cursed her in that instant, just as he cursed himself. He'd wanted her cowed. Beaten.

And she was.

Abruptly, he released her.

"Go," he said harshly. "Go before I change my mind."

She needed no further encouragement. Grabbing her skirts, she bolted past him toward the square.

Not once did she look back.

Seven

Back at his townhouse, Justin downed the contents of an entire bottle of brandy. Bleary-eyed and barely aware, he fumbled his way up the stairs to his chamber. Fully clothed, he passed out face-down on the bed.

In the morning he woke to a dozen hammers clanging in his brain . . . and the softness of Arabella's mantilla still clutched in his palm.

He rolled over with a groan, a sick feeling twisting his gut. God, but he was a bastard. He staggered from his bed and reached for the bottle yet again. Maybe someday, he thought bitterly, he would learn that drink wouldn't change what he was . . . and what he had done.

As for Arabella, well, The Unattainable had done the unthinkable.

She'd dealt a blow to his pride. Somehow, the chit had gotten under his skin! Never before had he regretted what he was, or what he'd done. He harbored no illusions about being the world's worst scoundrel. He'd made it a rule to never look back. But Arabella had succeeded in filling him with self-loathing, something even Sebastian had been able to manage but rarely.

And he didn't thank her for it. Over the course of the next few days, he strived to dismiss the incident—and *her*!—from his mind.

An impossible task.

Irritated with himself, tired of his own company, he called for his carriage and headed to White's one evening. There he went straight to the hazard table.

It wasn't long before Gideon sauntered over and stepped up beside him. Justin grunted in greeting.

"Well, well. Feeling out of sorts with the world, are we?"

His mood as black as his soul, Justin glared at him. "What does it matter to you?"

Gideon nodded at the dice. "I should hate to see you lose your fortune. I am after all, looking forward to seeing that a goodly portion comes my way."

Justin stared at him blankly. He'd been in a drunken stupor for two days—or was it three?—and it was an effort to slog through the muddle in his brain. "What the hell are you talking about?"

Gideon shrugged. "Indeed, it works to my advantage that you are here and not dancing attendance on a certain young lady whom I just chanced to see at the Barrington gala. I take it you're aware that, in your absence, your competitors are moving in on the lady in question? Rumor has it that she had a steady stream of callers both today and yesterday."

Scowling, Justin grabbed Gideon's elbow and steered him to the corner. He was not a pleasant drunk. He never had been and never would be. "Our wager is off," he advised tightly. "I should never have made it."

Gideon didn't back down. "It's too late for that now, my friend. You won't get off so easily."

Justin expelled a breath. "Dammit, Gideon—"

"Need I remind you a wager is a wager? I won't let you renege."

"And I have no intention of dishonoring it," Justin responded curtly. "I'll see that a draft is sent to you in the morning."

Gideon, it appeared, had other intentions. "Those were not our terms," Gideon reminded him bluntly. "Yours within the month, I believe it was. I'm a sporting man," he said with a shrug. "My only regret is that I'm off to Paris for the next month or so and so will be unable to watch your progress—or lack thereof, as it were."

Justin locked his jaw hard. He purposely maintained his silence, aware of Gideon's curious gaze.

"What! Losing ground already, eh? Is the lady so staunchly opposed to your suit, then? Ah, but I fear you are losing that golden touch . . ."

Gideon's smile did not set well. Arabella would hate him forever. He'd made certain of that last night. But he wasn't about to divulge such a thing to Gideon. "That's none of your affair," he said sharply.

At least the man knew when to back down. Gideon inclined his head. "Adieu, then. I shall look forward to seeing you upon my return."

Justin stalked back to the hazard table, where he lost a considerable sum. He told himself he didn't give a damn what nitwit Arabella chose to associate with, when she did it, or why. It was none of his business.

Yet a scant hour later, he was standing on the fringes of the Barrington ballroom, greeting Lord Barrington.

And there *she* was . . .

She sat not far from the refreshment table. She was dressed in green, a low, square-necked gown that revealed the rounded tops of her breasts. Her hair was caught up and away, coiled loosely at her crown. He approved the style, for it flattered to perfection the long, slim column of her neck. He pondered what it would be like to sweep aside the errant curls at her nape and plant his mouth *there*, in the vulnerable hollow that divided her nape. Her skin would be warm and soft, velvety smooth.

Christ! he thought disgustedly. What the hell had ever possessed him to come here? Why was he chasing after her like some foolish, lovesick schoolboy? He was a man about town, a man who confined his relationships to women of experience, women who knew the stakes and expected no more of him than he expected of them—an association uncluttered by nothing more complicated than a mutual lust. That was why he'd always avoided virgins like the plague!

Two men stood before her. Gideon had been right, he acknowledged grimly. He recognized both of them from that night at White's, Drummond and Gregory Fitzroy. The wolves had begun to circle indeed . . . Something savage welled in his breast. God rot it! It wasn't *her* they wanted, it was that damn bet! They would use her, discard her as carelessly as . . . as he would have, if it had been any woman but her.

He should warn her. Oh, but that should go over well, a voice inside chided snidely. She would see it as another insult.

A passing footman offered wine. He took it, draining it in one gulp.

When his gaze returned, yet another man had posted himself near her right shoulder—Charles Brentwood. Justin slammed his glass down on the table next to him. Brentwood was standing, and availing himself of the view from above. He was peering quite lasciviously into the generous swell of cleavage offered by a gown that Justin decided then and there was far too revealing. Granted, it was a tactic many a man employed, but it suddenly made him madder than blazes. Also granted, the gown was entirely the fashion, but what did that matter?

He wanted nothing more than to wipe that self-satisfied smirk off Brentwood's countenance.

It was then that Justin felt the bite of something utterly foreign. It brewed inside him like a fiery poison, seeping through him until he saw the world through a mist of crimson. A dull roar pounded in his ears. He wanted to stalk across the ballroom and tear apart every last man who surrounded her. At first he thought it was the wine; he'd had far too much to drink today. But this was a feeling so completely alien to him that it took a while before he realized what it was.

The stinging bite of jealousy.

Oh, but this was rich! he decided in some muddled, fog-laden corner of his mind. *He* was jealous. He, Justin Sterling, the most notorious rake in the city, who could have his pick of the most exquisite women in the land! Indeed, he felt almost *insanely* jealous.

How the hell had it happened? And why Arabella? How could she, a completely respectable innocent, have captivated him so? How was it possible that this flame-haired *hellion* had managed what no one else had managed to do? The most lush, beautiful women in Europe had tried to make him jealous. None had succeeded. None . . . save Arabella.

He wanted her. He wanted her almost violently. The way he'd wanted her that night at Vauxhall Gardens, a rampant, untamed hunger that burned like fire in his soul. He wanted her so badly that he had to clench his fists to contain it. And if he stood here much longer, the violent surge in his loins would be obvious to the entire ballroom.

If it had been any other woman, he would have taken what he wanted. He would have laid siege to her defenses with single-minded intent until he had her exactly where he wanted her, swooning and half-mad with yearning. Denying his desire for a woman wasn't something Justin was used to. It wasn't something he had done *ever*. It wasn't greed or arrogance that assured his success. It simply *was*.

But this was Arabella. *Arabella*.

And she couldn't stand the sight of him.

An acrid darkness stole through him. He'd been a fool to come here. If he left now, she would never even know he'd been here. But he knew he wouldn't leave. Not yet. Perhaps this was his own particular brand of punishment—God knew he deserved it!—to bear witness as she lavished her attentions on her devotees, scum though they were! But his temples were throbbing. That last glass of wine had done him in . . . The air in the ballroom was suddenly stifling.

Without a word, he spun around and directed his steps toward the terrace.

Arabella knew the exact moment Justin entered the ballroom. It was most peculiar, the way it happened. First her heart picked up its beat. Then a strange tickle prickled on her nape, almost as if someone had touched her there . . .

And she knew . . . *she knew* Justin was here.

And God above, there he was, talking with Lord Barrington. Tall, lean, clad in evening dress, a froth of snowy white lace at his wrists. No man had a right to look that virile, and she found the thought irksome.

She dragged her gaze away. One of the gentlemen asked a question. She heard herself respond, but for the life of her, she couldn't recall either her reply or the question! The faces before her were just a blur. There was George . . . or was it Gregory? asking to fetch her another glass of wine. Lord, she couldn't even remember their names!

When she dared to glance Justin's way again, his back was toward her. He was walking toward the terrace, with that fluid, unstudied grace so much a part of him.

She almost hurtled upright. "Please excuse me."

"Miss Templeton!"

"I say, wherever are you—"

She turned. "Gentlemen," she said pointedly, "I do not want wine, or lemonade, or a bite to eat. What I crave right now is a moment to myself."

She left them standing across the room. What they thought, she didn't know. Nor did she care. In truth, she couldn't quite say what came over her. All she could think of was Justin. Why hadn't he acknowledged her? A voice inside chided her. It wasn't wise to follow him, for he was surely the devil-at-large. Yet she could no more have stayed either her will or her steps than she could have stopped the earth from turning.

The terrace was deserted. Behind her, the musicians had struck up a waltz. Guided by the glittering lights of the ballroom, she followed a meandering path through the garden, enclosed on three sides by a high stone wall. There, in the far corner, at last she spied him. He stood before a gurgling fountain, staring at the sky as if spellbound.

Spellbound. That was exactly how she felt. What madness possessed her that she had followed him out here? The sight of him made her insides quiver and her knees quaver.

Yet somehow she managed to sound almost calm. "Hello, Justin."

"Well, if it isn't Miss Vicar."

Miss Vicar. Arabella flushed.

Deliberately he turned his back on her. Arabella remained where she was, tentative and uncertain. It seemed he was determined to ignore her. She couldn't blame him, but still, it hurt.

"What! Not gone yet?" He glanced over his shoulder.

Her mouth felt suddenly parched. She was suddenly floundering. "I . . . it's just that . . . I haven't seen you for several days. Have you been ill?"

"No."

He turned back to face her.

It took every ounce of courage she possessed to remain where she was. "I saw you inside," she finally blurted. "Were you going to leave without saying anything?"

"Yes."

Well, he was certainly direct.

"Look here, Justin. I suspect we are hardly going to be able to avoid seeing each other. So we are simply going to have to come to some sort of agreement. We must be civil to each other, at least."

"I quite agree. So if you've come to gloat—don't. And if you've come to deliver another diatribe, do not bother. Consider me duly chastised."

His manner was guarded, his tone cool. A gnawing guilt nagged at her. He couldn't know how she regretted her outburst the other night.

"Justin," she said, her voice low, "the other night . . . I spoke out of turn—"

"You spoke what was on your mind."

"But I didn't mean to—"

"Yes, you did," he cut in. "We both know it."

She peered at him. His shoulders were stiff and square. Why, she could almost believe . . .

"Never say that you've come to grief over my—" She broke off, staring at him. What was wrong with him? He sounded odd. There was something strange about his eyes, and he wasn't entirely steady . . . Merciful heavens, he was foxed!

And, it seemed, he wasn't finished.

"Does that surprise you, Arabella? Startle you? I see it does. Scoundrel that I am, I do have feelings. And contrary to your opinion, I *do* have a heart."

Arabella was too stunned to say a word.

"I believe I deserve an explanation. There must be some reason you dislike me so. From the beginning you've disliked me. Why, as a child you disliked me! But I've never done anything to you."

"No, not to me, but—"

She stopped short. This was not a discussion she cared to pursue, particularly in light of his sodden state.

"Justin," she said helplessly, "it's not that I dislike you—"

"Then why did you say such things?" His tone was almost accusing.

He stepped close. The heavy aroma of wine and spirits assaulted her. Dear Lord, it was a miracle *she* wasn't sotted as well!

"What if I told you I like you?" he went on. "What if I told you I'm fond of you?"

"You're fond of all women!"

"Not true. It's well known I have extremely fastidious tastes. Otherwise, I wouldn't have danced with you that first night. *Or* the second. God, I wouldn't be here right now."

Arabella stared at him dumbly. She couldn't help it. She was unaccountably flustered. What was she supposed to say to *that*? Dear Lord, how was she to interpret such a statement? She had come out here to apologize to him. She'd prepared herself for his mockery. His acid barbs. His arrogance. Anything but this . . .

A dozen different emotions rushed at her from all sides. Dismay. Alarm. She was charmed when she didn't want to be charmed. Flattered when she should *not* have been flattered. Was this how he managed to gain so many conquests? By catching them off guard and vulnerable? Oh, stupid question, that! A man with his looks had no need to coerce and cajole a woman into his bed.

"What if I said I want to kiss you?"

Things were progressing from bad to worse.

Her heart seemed to stumble, along with her breath. Perhaps he had no idea what he was saying. "Justin," she asked, "how much have you had to drink tonight?"

"Too much." He responded as if she'd asked the time of day. "But you haven't answered my question."

"I have no intention of answering it!"

"Why not? Don't you want to kiss me?"

"No. You're foxed." Why men relished spirits so, she couldn't imagine.

"But I'm the handsomest man in all England."

She feigned distaste. "Right now you're the most disgusting man in all England." As if that could ever be true.

"Oh, come. It's said that I—"

"Pray do not boast, Justin! I know very well what's said about you! You think you have only to enter a room and all eyes are upon you vying for your attention." Granted, they usually were, but he needed no encouragement!

"And what about you, Arabella?"

"What about me?"

"Are you drawn to me?"

Arabella blanched. He was inching closer. Her insides were fluttering. "Other women—" she began.

"I don't care about other women. I care about you. What you think. What you think of *me*."

She stepped back, only to discover she'd trapped herself in the corner. Justin stood before her. Tall. Strong. Powerful. Escape was impossible.

Their eyes caught. He smiled, then raised a hand. In shock she felt the tips of his fingers trace a slow path from her wrists to her elbow. In its wake a trail of fire smoldered.

Her nails dug into her palms. Even drunk, he was rakishly appealing. "Stop that," she said unsteadily.

He didn't. His gaze was roving over her face now. Foxed or not, it appeared he was well aware of her attraction to him! She knew it for certain when he asked silkily, "Have you ever wondered what it would be like to be kissed by me?"

I've wondered what it would be like to be kissed by any man, she nearly blurted.

"What makes you think I would let you kiss me?" she heard herself say. Was it a plea? A provocation? Heaven help her, she didn't know!

"What makes you think I wouldn't anyway?"

Dash it all, he had an answer for everything! "You're a man of . . . unseemly appetite."

"And you're a woman of untarnished reputation." A finger beneath her chin tipped her face to his. Arabella swallowed. She couldn't tear her gaze from the sculpted beauty of his mouth. He bent his head so that their lips almost touched. Almost, but not quite.

Every nerve in her body was screaming. Her heart hammered wildly. She couldn't have moved if she wanted to; the shocking truth was that she didn't!

His gaze had fallen to her lips. "The truth now, Arabella. You've never been kissed, have you?"

Mutely she shook her head.

His eyes darkened. "Then perhaps it's time you were," he whispered.

There was no time to think. No time to reason. For his mouth closed over hers, hot and slow, a kiss of leisurely exploration. Her muscles turned to wax, and she was quite certain that if his arms hadn't circled her waist, she would have melted on the spot.

For the kiss was like nothing she expected . . . yet everything she wanted. Everything she hadn't even *known* she wanted. She felt herself slipping. Falling into a realm where nothing existed save the exquisite pleasure of feeling her mouth trapped beneath his. His kiss was heady and potent, and she suddenly felt as if *she* were the one who had imbibed too freely.

He muttered something unintelligible. A tremor went through her when his tongue curled around hers. She didn't pull away, didn't want to. She felt . . . oh, heaven help her. Fascination, perhaps. Whatever it was, it was like nothing she'd ever felt before. It was as if a spark had been lit in her veins, even there at the tips of her breasts . . . *especially* there.

Beneath the insistent demand of his, her lips parted still more. For the span of a heartbeat, she sensed a curious impatience in him. She didn't understand it, any more than she understood the restless questing in her belly. She longed almost desperately to wind her arms around his neck, to lift herself on tiptoe and press herself against his length and revel in it. But coward that she was, she didn't quite dare. And just when she sensed they were on the verge of something . . . oh, she didn't know quite what it was, only that it was something . . . something *more,* he raised his head.

She made a faint, mewling sound of protest. Was it over so soon, then?

"Arabella?"

Still a little dazed, she opened her eyes.

He ran a fingertip down her nose. "A word of warning, my dear Miss Vicar. I saw you tonight with your beaux, flirting and laughing. Don't trust them, any of them. All they want is your virtue."

Arabella blinked.

"And the next time I try to kiss you . . ."

"Yes?" she said breathlessly.

"Run, sweetheart. Run as far and as fast as you can . . . lest I catch you."

Eight

"Arabella? Arabella, whatever is wrong with you this morning?"

Her aunt's voice seemed to come from a very great distance away.

Arabella pasted a bright smile on her features. "Yes, Aunt?"

Aunt Grace gestured grandly to her plate. "My dear, first you scooped oodles of orange marmalade on your toast. You then followed with berry jam—which Cook does quite wonderfully, I daresay—but you then smothered the whole of it with marmalade again."

Arabella looked down at her plate. The sight almost made her gag. Her toast was a mound of mush . . .

Which was exactly how she'd felt when Justin kissed her.

"Furthermore, I do believe you've put a dozen lumps of sugar in your chocolate."

"Oh, Aunt, surely not." Arabella took a sip and nearly choked. It was sickeningly sweet.

They were in the morning room for breakfast. Even Uncle Joseph, who usually resided behind his *Times* throughout the morning repast, had lowered it to regard her with one shaggy brow upraised.

"Arabella," he asked, "is something amiss?"

"Nay, Uncle," she denied quickly. "I didn't sleep terribly well last night, I'm afraid."

That, at least, was the truth.

She'd spent the entire night tossing and turning. Half a dozen times she'd bolted upright, unable to believe it had really happened.

Her first kiss, and it had not come from the man who would be her husband. That wondrous occasion that every girl dreamed of had come from the most notorious rake in London.

How on earth had it happened? She should have been mortified. She should have been horrified. Saints above, she should have had the presence of mind to stop it. She shouldn't have allowed it to happen in the first place! And indeed, it galled her to admit that it was not her willpower that prevailed in the end, but Justin's. Why, if it had been up to her, she'd have let him go on kissing her forever. Oh, and if he only knew the scandalous, wanton thoughts that even now ran through her brain . . . The exquisite warmth of his mouth sealed upon hers was almost sinfully delicious . . .

Miss Vicar indeed.

Her mind revived the memory with a clarity that was all too vivid. Her cheeks flooded with heat.

He'd bewitched her. Bedazzled her. After all, the moon was full last night. Why, if she believed in such nonsense, she would have seized on it as the perfect explanation for her scandalous behavior.

Instead, she thought glumly, she had only one. She had *liked* kissing Justin. The feel of his mouth on hers—the feel of *him*!—so hard and warm and purely male, was compellingly seductive. She hadn't known that a mere kiss could be so intoxicating. Almost addictive. She had liked it so much that she wished he would kiss her just once more . . .

Her fingers crushed her napkin in her lap. That would never happen, she told herself almost bitterly. He'd only kissed her because he'd been foxed.

Foxed or no, she did not relish the prospect of facing him again. No doubt he would see it as some sort of victory. Would he taunt her? Mock her weakness in that arrogant, infuriating manner that irritated her to no end?

She had succumbed. She, who had fancied herself above those giggling ninnies who batted their eyelashes and practically cast themselves in his path!

And he would delight in reminding her.

To him, it was nothing. Justin Sterling was a man who had doubtless kissed a hundred women in his lifetime. But to Arabella . . . she had felt his kiss in the very marrow of her bones. Indeed, now, the morning after, she remembered every subtle nuance. The startling width of his chest, the way his breath swirled in the back of her throat as her lips parted beneath his.

And indeed, that train of thought was proving treacherous. Uncle Joseph had resumed reading his paper, but Aunt Grace was still looking at her with eagle-eyed sharpness. "Arabella," she said sternly, "were you out in the garden again without your bonnet?"

No! But I've been out in the garden with Justin.

She had an almost hysterical desire to blurt out the truth. Instead she said primly, "No, Aunt Grace."

"You're looking quite flushed, dear. And you haven't eaten a thing." Aunt Grace fretted. "I do hope you're not coming down with a fever." Aunt Grace reached out and placed a plump hand on her cheeks. "No, no fever, thank goodness. That wouldn't do, you know. We must depart tomorrow morning, remember."

Arabella looked at her. "We're leaving?" she queried brightly. Oh, perhaps to Bath, she thought hopefully. She directed a swift prayer heavenward. She adored Bath. Aunt Grace and Uncle Joseph had a charming house there, and she loved nothing more than to take long walks in the surrounding hills, the perfect place to seek respite from the turmoil in her mind.

Best of all, they would be far, far away from Justin Sterling. There would be no further encounters—chance or otherwise—which pleased her to no end. She ignored the nagging little voice which reminded her she had been the one to seek him out last night.

"Yes, dear," Aunt Grace was saying. "We'll be leaving rather early."

Arabella smiled, the first genuine smile of the day. "Where are we going, Aunt?"

Aunt Grace finished the last of her tea. "The Marquess of Thurston and his wife are hosting a house party, remember? We're going to Thurston Hall, their country estate."

"What?" Her mind balked. She very nearly shrieked her dismay. She knew the Marquess of Thurston, of course. He was Justin's elder brother, Sebastian. Sweet Lord . . .

"Yes, dear." Aunt Grace pushed her chair back from the table. "The invitation arrived last week. I'm certain I mentioned it. It must have slipped your mind." She sounded almost gleeful. "A week at Thurston Hall . . . It's an enchanting place, dear. I confess, I'm quite looking forward to it."

Not so with Arabella. Long after Aunt Grace had left the table, Arabella remained where she was. Aunt Grace was right. The invitation *had* slipped her mind. Indeed, she'd completely forgotten it. Finally, she got to her feet, expelling a long-pent-up breath.

Was it too much to hope that Justin would not be in attendance?

She scoffed. She might as well resign herself to it right now. Justin would be there, no doubt, as dashing and as dangerous and daring as ever.

She didn't welcome the niggling little voice in her brain that suddenly reminded her of her speech last evening . . .

I suspect we are hardly going to be able to avoid seeing each other. So we are simply going to have to come to some sort of agreement. We must be civil to each other, at least.

What had she been thinking, to spout such nonsense? Why did she have the feeling those words would come back to haunt her?

She had no doubt he would find some other way to plague her.

Ah, well. But at least one thing was certain. At least she needn't worry that he might kiss her again. There was no possible way on this earth that would *ever* happen again.

Perhaps someday, if she ever wed, that is, she might tell her grandchildren that she'd been kissed by the handsomest man in all England . . .

They would never believe it. How could anyone, for she could hardly believe it herself.

The Burwell carriage was a well-sprung affair admirably suited for travel. Aunt Grace babbled on as they left the sprawl and bustle of London behind; both Arabella and Uncle Joseph listened with half an ear. They stopped briefly for luncheon at a roadside inn, then resumed their journey.

It wasn't long before her aunt and uncle drifted off. Arabella smiled at the picture they presented. Aunt Grace was snoring slightly, her mouth open, her head propped against Uncle Joseph's shoulder.

Her uncle had tipped the brim of his top hat forward to shield the glare from the sun. Aunt Grace shifted; he reached out and lightly squeezed her plump little fingers.

She marveled that she had been so blind. Oh, she'd always known that Aunt Grace and Uncle Joseph loved each other. She had just assumed it had come *after* they wed. But in these last few days, she saw what she had never really seen before. A touch here, a sigh there, a whisper, the slightest nod of the head, the tiniest exchange of smiles . . . all were signs of love, signs that they were comfortable in that love and didn't mind that others saw.

Her throat tightened oddly. Her parents were like that, despite the disparity in their appearance—her mother so dainty and fair, her father a great, hulking giant. Yet no two people could have been more in tune with each other. It was almost as if one were but an extension of the other. How many times did Mama begin a sentence, only to have Papa end it? Then they would both laugh, and gaze at each other in a way that occasionally made her think she'd almost been forgotten. For though her own heart swelled near to bursting with love, at times it was blunted by an elusive hurt. Oh, she knew they adored her. She had grown up knowing she was very, very loved. Not once did she doubt it. And yet, she couldn't deny that at such times, she felt . . . lonely. Lonely and wistful and envious of all they shared . . .

Oh, drat. *Drat!* What *was* this melancholy sadness that lurked in her breast? She didn't know, only that she wished with all her heart that it would cease.

Determined to banish it, she turned her attention to the window, to the open countryside north of London. Windmills dotted the landscape, and flowers seamed the meadows in riotous profusion.

The next thing she knew, she was being jostled awake by Aunt Grace. "Arabella," came her aunt's whisper, "we've arrived, dear."

Arabella glanced up. Her eyes widened. A massive structure of sprawling grandeur, the front of Thurston Hall was dominated by tall white columns. It was truly an awesome sight.

A liveried footman dressed in crimson and gold helped them alight and they were ushered into the house. They had no sooner stepped inside than the marquess met them in the entrance hall. A large man, Sebastian Sterling strode toward them with a grace that belied his great size. "Joseph. Grace. Welcome to Thurston Hall!"

"Good to see you again, Sebastian." The two men shook hands, and Sebastian turned to Grace. "Grace, you look enchanting as always." He turned to Arabella and took her hand. "And Arabella! It's been several years now, hasn't it?"

Arabella smiled up at him. She had always liked his calm, forthright manner, even as a child. "Hello, my lord."

"No need to stand on formality here. Call me Sebastian."

"Sebastian, then," she murmured.

"I hear tell you're the talk of the town. Do you

know, I predicted several years ago you'd take the *ton* by storm."

"She certainly has," injected Aunt Grace. "Did you know she's had three offers already?"

Her aunt was practically crowing. Arabella smothered a groan as she thought of Walter. What would she do if she knew the number was really four?

Sebastian chuckled. "A discerning woman, then. I can appreciate that."

Just then a woman emerged from one of the rooms off the entrance hall. She was petite, with bright, golden hair that shimmered in the sunlight. Her eyes, Arabella noted as she drew close, were almost the same color as her hair.

"Grace. Joseph!" she sang out. "How good to see you again." Extending her hands, she greeted them warmly, then slipped her arm through her husband's, slanting a smile toward Arabella. "Who is this lovely young lady?"

Sebastian made the introductions. "Arabella, my wife Devon. Devon, Miss Arabella Templeton. Her mother Catherine is Grace's younger sister."

Devon's eyes widened. "Arabella!" she exclaimed. She glanced at Sebastian. "Is this the same Arabella who gave Justin his comeuppance some years ago?"

Arabella bit her lip and glanced at her aunt. This was probably the only one of the escapades from her younger days that her aunt didn't know about.

"A female who got the best of Justin." Devon was almost squealing, her eyes sparkling. "Oh, what I wouldn't give to have been there. Oh, but I think you and I will get on famously."

Arabella couldn't help but smile in return. She liked Devon's warmth and openness immensely. But she had the distinct sensation Aunt Grace would have a few questions for her later . . .

For the time being, Grace transferred her attention to Devon. "We've hardly seen you in London since the little ones were born," Grace said.

"We've hardly been in London since they were born, which suits us just fine. We love it here in the country," Devon said simply. "It's here we want the twins to grow up."

Arabella gasped. She couldn't help it. "*You* carried twins?" she said in disbelief. Her gaze went up and down Devon's diminutive figure. "My word, how—" She colored and broke off. "Forgive me. I meant no offense."

"And none taken," Devon responded with a laugh. "Believe me, I was big as a cow."

"Not quite," her husband said with a chuckle. He covered her hand with his. "But no matter, you carried it off beautifully." He was staring down at her as he spoke, and in his eyes glimmered an unmistakable light. Devon flashed him a dazzling smile in return.

Arabella winced. Another obscenely happy couple. What was it these days?

She was just about to clear her throat when Devon dragged her gaze from her husband's.

"I'll have Jane show you to your rooms," said the

marchioness. "We'll dine at half-past eight. That should give all the guests a chance to rest. It's such a tiring journey from London, isn't it?"

Indeed, Aunt Grace was yawning. "A nap sounds just the thing, don't you think, Arabella?"

Arabella didn't, but she didn't say so. Nor was she the least bit tired. But she didn't mind shutting herself away in her room till the dinner hour. The longer the time till she encountered the beast in his lair, the better. Perhaps, she decided cautiously, luck was with her after all, and Justin would not be joining his brother's house party.

She was totally unaware of Devon's thoughtful gaze following her up the grand staircase.

"Love, you're up to something," Sebastian said sternly. "I know that look."

"Oh! I am not! I was only thinking that young Arabella seems a very spirited sort."

Sebastian cocked a brow. "*Young* Arabella," he stressed, "is probably not much younger than you, my love. But yes, she's definitely a woman of spirit."

Devon smiled a smile that sent warning bells clanging through her husband.

Sebastian expelled a breath. "Devon, what is on your mind?"

Her eyes opened wide. "Sebastian! Don't look at me like that. I was just thinking . . ."

"Yes?"

". . . that Justin may have met his match."

"Devon," he said dryly, "you don't understand.

While I have always regarded the prank Arabella pulled on our dear Justin as vastly entertaining—which is why I told you about it—Justin was never so amused. 'The vicar's child is the devil's child,' he always said. And if you saw his scowl when he—"

"But she is a child no longer, Sebastian. You made the observation yourself."

"Nonetheless, believe me when I say that Arabella Templeton is the last woman on earth that Justin would—"

"Precisely why she may well be the *right* one." Impish amber eyes twinkled up at him. "Look at the two of us."

Sebastian narrowed his gaze. "Has the duchess arrived yet?" he asked suddenly.

He referred to the Dowager Duchess of Carrington. "As a matter of fact, she has," Devon confirmed.

"And the two of you have had your heads together, haven't you?"

"Why, whatever do you mean?"

"Meaning that I'm well aware she loves nothing more than to play matchmaker, and I do believe you've decided to take on the very same role yourself."

"Oh, come!" Devon protested. "We've been wed for two years already and I've yet to do so for either your sister *or* your brother."

"Well, we both know how Julianna feels about marriage. As for Justin and Arabella—" He shook his head. "Devon, he's always regarded her as a veritable hellion."

She raised her brows. "Precisely the term I would use to describe your brother."

"True, but—"

He broke off when his wife picked up her skirts and stepped around him.

Now he was the one who was scowling. "Where the devil are you going?" he called after her.

She swiveled to face him, her expression one of the utmost innocence, which only made him all the more suspicious. "To see to the seating arrangements for dinner."

"But you did that days ago!"

She blew him a kiss. "I know," she said sweetly.

Arabella tried to nap after all, but she couldn't sleep. She was too restless. And it felt as if a hundred butterflies had taken up residence in her belly. An hour before dinner, her maid came in to help her dress. By then, Arabella was almost finished. All that remained was to pin up her hair, lace up her stays, and do up the myriad buttons on the back of her gown.

Standing before the mirror in the room she'd been given, Arabella gazed unsmilingly at her reflection. She looked well enough, she supposed. Her gown was made of airy peach gauze, a color that softened the brassiness of her hair. The cut was simple and flowing, trimmed by a row of iridescent beading around the neckline and high-waisted bodice. She chose it on purpose, for it was one of her favorites. She needed comfort. She needed courage. She needed whatever she could muster to rally her defenses against the enemy.

Exiting her room, she glanced to the right, then the left, an expression of consternation on her features.

Across the hall a door opened. "Oh! Hello, there," said a lilting, musical voice.

Arabella glanced up to see a stunning woman with rich chestnut hair standing across from her. "Hello," she said. "You're Julianna, aren't you?"

"I am. And you are . . . Arabella, yes?"

Arabella nodded. Like the marchioness, Julianna was tiny; Arabella noted wryly that she barely reached her chin. Her eyes were as vivid as Justin's, but they were blue—and without his icy penetration.

"I thought so. I recognized you by—"

"Yes, I know. My hair. No one ever forgets me. Ah, that's what comes of being a redhead, I suppose."

"Actually, I was going to say I recall you from some years ago." Julianna's eyes sparkled. "A particular incident involving my brother Justin—"

"Oh, dear." Arabella couldn't withhold a smile. "I fear I'm quite infamous in your household."

"Yes, well, Justin can be a swaggering oaf at times. He stomped around for days, while Sebastian and I laughed for weeks!" Julianna tipped her head to the side. "Shall we join the others?"

"Yes, thank you." Arabella gratefully accepted the offer. If left to her own devices, she should have been quite hopelessly lost. They had turned to the left and now traversed a hallway that seemed to go on forever.

"My word," she said. "How big is this house?"

Julianna let out a laugh that sounded like bells tinkling in the wind. "One hundred and two rooms. It's a monstrosity, isn't it? I quite prefer my own tidy little house in London."

Arabella eyed her curiously. "Do you live alone?" The question emerged before she thought better of it, but Julianna didn't seem to mind her forwardness.

"Yes. Sebastian, Justin, and I all resided together until Sebastian married Devon. Indeed, it was time for Justin and I to go our own ways. I am, according to the gossips, a spinster." Her beautiful eyes darkened. "It's beyond me why, when a woman passes the age of one-and-twenty, she is promptly put on the shelf. A man, on the other hand, is hailed as a gadabout and no one thinks the worse of him. That I have chosen not to marry is no one's business but my own. Why must I do what everyone expects? Why must *you*? Why must anyone?"

Arabella blinked. Julianna's vehemence was startling.

Julianna appeared to have noticed it as well. "Pray forgive me. I didn't mean to lecture."

"And I didn't think you were," Arabella assured her promptly. She smiled. "Frankly, it's refreshing to find a woman who isn't afraid to think for herself. I fear I've never been able to hold my tongue when I probably should, so I've acquired a reputation as the opinionated sort, and it's just so . . ." As usual, her hands began to flail about.

"So unfair," Julianna put in. "And so vexing!"

"Yes. Yes! As if our only goal in life is to marry and have babies . . . not that there's anything wrong with that—but I should like to make up my own mind without Society constantly looking over my shoulder and passing judgment."

"Oh!" Julianna declared. "Blessed be, a woman after my own heart. But you must find the whole business of being regarded as The Unatt—"

Arabella threw up a hand. "I beg of you, do not say it!"

By the time they reached the drawing room, they were chatting as if they'd been friends for ages. A little of her unease departed, and for the first time since yesterday, she was cautiously optimistic that this house party wouldn't be such an ordeal after all, particularly when she saw that Georgiana and her parents were present. She beckoned to Georgiana, who hurried across the floor.

Georgiana's face lit up when she saw her. "Arabella! I'm so glad you came! I confess, I feared you would cry off—" She broke off as Arabella sent her a warning look. "But it appears I've forgotten my manners. Who is your friend, Arabella?" Georgiana smiled at Julianna.

Arabella made the introductions. "Georgiana Larwood, Lady Julianna Sterling."

Georgiana bobbed a curtsy. "Lady Julianna, I'm so very pleased to make your acquaintance," she said hastily.

But the look that had passed between Georgiana

and Arabella had not gone unnoticed by the sharp-eyed Julianna.

"I do hope your reluctance to attend doesn't stop you from enjoying the house party."

"It wasn't that I was reluctant," Arabella said lamely, "I simply forgot about the invitation until Aunt Grace reminded me yesterday morning."

A dimple appeared beside Julianna's lovely mouth. "Good. For I should hate to think you *were* reluctant. Or that it had something to do with my brother Justin. His behavior can be atrocious, you know. I do hope he hasn't been rude to such lovely ladies as the two of you."

"Oh, he's been nothing but charming to me," Georgiana put in brightly.

Arabella could have cheerfully throttled her. She said nothing.

Julianna's gaze of mild inquiry had yet to leave Arabella. "Oh, dear," Julianna murmured ruefully. "Arabella, pray do not tell me he has been misbehaving again."

Oh, if she only knew . . . It was all Arabella could do to stop her hand from stealing to her lips, which tingled in remembrance of his kiss.

"Well," she stated without thinking, "he won't be doing it again, that much is for certain."

Julianna chuckled. "That's the spirit. Whatever it was he did, I do hope he wasn't too outrageous. You're not a hen-hearted miss, thank heaven. Indeed, I suspect, you're just the woman to set him in his place."

Just then Julianna was hailed by someone across the room. She raised a hand, then glanced back at Arabella and Georgiana. "The Dowager Duchess of Carrington is calling me. I'd best attend to her." Her smile encompassed them both. "Ladies, a pleasure meeting both of you. Welcome to Thurston Hall, and may your stay be an enjoyable one."

Julianna left, and Arabella and Georgiana looked at each other. "I like her," they announced in unison, then laughed.

"I wonder why she isn't married," Georgiana mused.

The very same thought had been running through Arabella's mind.

"We came downstairs together," Arabella murmured, "and she informed me quite openly that she's regarded as a spinster. She seems very much the independent sort, doesn't she? She told me she has her own house in London." She paused, then said, "I don't mean to sound unkind, but how old is she, do you think?"

"Twenty-five or -six, I should imagine. She's so lovely, it's a wonder that she's never married. I can't imagine she wouldn't have received a score of proposals her first Season."

Arabella bit her lip. "She stated quite distinctly that it was she who had chosen not to marry, and it was no one's business but her own."

There was an odd expression on Georgiana's features.

"What is it, Georgiana?"

"Actually, I heard Mama and Papa mention her

name on the way here, when they thought I was napping," Georgiana admitted, lowering her voice. "Papa said it was a shame what happened to her. Mama declared it had quite scarred her forever."

Something flashed in Arabella's mind. The night of the Bennington gala, Justin had laughed and said something about his family name being synonymous with scandal—yes, that was it! But what—

She was suddenly thoroughly disgusted with herself. "Would you look at us!" she exclaimed. "We both abhor gossip, yet here we are!"

"You're right, of course," Georgiana said immediately. " 'Tis *our* behavior that is atrocious."

The conversation turned to other things, and while they talked, Arabella scanned the room.

The gathering wasn't particularly large; she guessed there were perhaps thirty people milling about. She'd met most of them at some time or other in London. Across the room, a tall, powerfully built fair-haired man gave a brief salute. She frowned. She knew him, she thought vaguely. Ah, Patrick McElroy, the man who had asked her to dance at the Bennington gala. She inclined her head briefly in acknowledgment, then turned back to Georgiana.

And then she saw him. *Justin.*

And if there were a hundred butterflies residing in her belly before, there surely numbered a thousand now.

He stood near his brother. They were of equal height, the Sterling brothers. But Justin's build was leaner, his hair a shade lighter than Sebastian's, but still so very dark. Dastardly though he was, he was as elegantly handsome as always. He was clad in black evening clothes, the cut of his jacket so close and tight it outlined every taut, spare line of his back and shoulders. He laughed, a flash of white against his bronzed skin, and glanced idly away.

Their eyes caught . . . oh, but for the merest moment!

Arabella swallowed. His gaze was subtle. Yet the sense of awareness that swept over her was keen. Everything inside betrayed her. Her heart pounded, her pulse skittered, then began to clamor wildly. Oh, what foolishness was this? He would surely think she had been deliberately looking for him, the cad!

Silly girl, chided a voice inside. *You were.*

Justin said something to Sebastian, then began to saunter his way across the room.

And then he was standing next to her. "Miss Larwood, how nice to see you again. And Miss Templeton, you are ravishing as always."

Was that meant to be a slur? Knowing him, it surely was. Praying none of the turmoil she felt showed, she lifted her face. She was even smiling. Just what she would have said, she never knew, because the dinner bell sounded.

"Miss Templeton, please do me the honor of allowing me to escort you in to dinner."

Before she could say a word, her hand was whisked into the crook of his elbow, her fingers trapped beneath his.

Arabella was speechless. He did not ask. He simply assumed that she would accept. If she could have refused, she would have. But it wouldn't do to make a scene.

Fuming, she had no choice but to accompany him into the dining room.

Nine

In all honesty, Justin didn't know until the last minute that he would be seated next to Arabella during dinner. While the others were still streaming in from the drawing room, she let him know in no uncertain terms she thought otherwise.

She tipped her head and said under her breath, "You arranged this, didn't you? To spite me, I suspect. Well, you've evened the score, Lord Vice, several times over, I believe."

"My dear Miss Vicar, I suspect we have my sister-in-law Devon to thank for the seating arrangements. She has this insanely romantic notion that a wife will tame my wild, wicked ways."

"No respectable woman will have you!"

She detested him. Could it be any more obvious? He could almost hear her gnashing her teeth.

With an effort he leashed his temper. "Yes," he replied pleasantly, "I do believe you've made your opinion of that quite clear."

But inside he was smarting. Her disdain seared his soul. And now the gauntlet had been thrown, the die cast. She offered no quarter and he would give none.

He was at his most outrageous, roguish behavior. Within reason, of course, considering they were at the dinner table. While the conversation around them flitted from the theater, to the weather, to the appalling condition of the roads between here and London, he allowed the length of his thigh to ride against hers. Repeatedly. He reveled in the way she went rigid. When she requested wine, he poured for her, waiting for her to take it from his hand. When she did, he deliberately trailed a fingertip along her knuckles.

From the corner of his eye, he noted a flush had risen on her cheekbones. Most enchanting, he decided distractedly, and one which nearly matched the color of her gown. That, too, he had admittedly admired when he saw her come into the room with Julianna; it clung to her high, full breasts and swirled gently around her form.

He wasn't the only one who had noticed. A surge of possessiveness shot through him when he saw Patrick McElroy's eyes alight on her form as she'd entered the drawing room. Now McElroy sat some distance down the table from he and Arabella, on the same side; McElroy couldn't see them, and they couldn't see him, which was fine with Justin.

He began seething when he saw McElroy alight from his carriage earlier in the day. He'd wasted no time confronting Sebastian. It seemed Sebastian had originally issued the invitation to McElroy's father, the earl; they were in the midst of negotiating a business transaction and he'd hoped to finalize matters. The earl had written back stating that he had other plans for the week, requesting that his son Patrick attend in his stead. Sebastian had agreed, for his only experience with Patrick McElroy was the front McElroy put on in Polite Society.

Indeed, McElroy might fool others with his affable manners and pleasant countenance, but there was another side of him that Justin had never liked. His tongue could be coarse and vulgar. He had a mean streak a mile wide. Justin had witnessed it firsthand at a boxing match some months ago. McElroy had nearly taken his opponent's head off, and even with the other man battered and bleeding and down, he'd had to be restrained from battering the man even further.

But McElroy was far, far away at the other end of the table, and Justin would much rather concentrate on the beauty at his side.

In between the third course and the fourth, she dropped her napkin. He rescued it for her, allowing his hand to linger in her lap. Was she becoming flustered? He hoped so.

He knew for certain when he bent his head to hers, as if to confide some intimate secret in her ear. She nearly jumped out of her skin.

Her head swiveled. She leveled on him an icy stare. "If you are attempting to make advances toward me—"

He gave her a mundane smile. His lips hovered but a breath from the dainty shell of her ear.

"My dear," he whispered, "if I were making advances, you would know it."

He both saw and heard the breath she sucked in.

He lowered his head still further, so that his mouth brushed the skin of her temple. "Or do I misinterpret? Perhaps you are the one attempting to flirt with me."

"Certainly not!" Her chin jutted out. "Have you ever heard of scruples, sir?"

"Certainly not." He borrowed her phrase of the moment before.

"I thought not." Eyes sizzling, she turned back to her plate.

Their fiery exchange unexpectedly made his blood sing. His mood suddenly lightened. God, but he'd been dreading this house party. Thurston Hall was Sebastian's pride and joy, while it was Justin's bane. He hated it here. He presented himself here only when the requisite family affair demanded it and departed as soon as he could. The Hall reminded him of . . . far too many things he would rather not ponder. It roused anger and resentment and a host of other emotions that were better left buried. But with Arabella here, at least he wouldn't be bored. Hell, it might even be bearable.

He was a brute to torment her so. He'd frightened her the night of the masquerade, and then *he* was the one who had been afraid. But clearly Arabella was not one to wallow in defeat. She spoke what was on her mind, and there was usually plenty on her mind, he decided with wry amusement. Truth be told, he admired her resilience, her pluck.

And God above, the very sight of her stole his breath away. When she entered the drawing room, fire sparked within him. She was brightness and warmth, all color and light compared to the pale simpering misses of the *ton*. Behind her prim, proper exterior was an earthy, sensual creature, with a wildness to match his own. He'd tasted just a hint of it the other night.

The meal concluded, Sebastian rose and announced there would be entertainment in the music room. "Rest assured," he said with a warm gaze at his wife, "my wife will not be singing."

Devon wrinkled her nose prettily.

Beside him, Arabella rose. "I think I'll fetch my shawl," she stated coolly. "There is a decided chill in here."

She wasted no time heading toward the door. Justin remained where he was for a moment, surveying her as she crossed the room. She didn't glide, like a proper lady would have. No, he decided wryly, there wasn't a dainty bone in her body. She strode with her head held high and her shoulders back, her carriage straight and proud. He silently applauded. She couldn't hide her height and so she used it to advantage.

She paused to speak to her aunt. The lamplight burned on the fluted wall behind her. Oh, if she knew the picture she presented! The gauzy material of her gown was almost paper-thin, affording a view of long, well-shaped legs. He imagined those irresistibly long legs locked high and tight about his waist. Oh, but she would fit him perfectly . . .

Christ, what madness was this, that he was fantasizing about Arabella!

Yet the illicit vision remained high and bright in his mind's eye, starkly vivid, her curls spread out in wanton disarray on the pillow, those eyes like heaven half-closed in sultry promise, her arms reaching for him . . .

Arabella . . . reaching for him? Now, *there* was a fantasy. His lips twisting in self-derision, he rose and headed toward the music room.

Through some miracle, Arabella managed to find her room through the maze of hallways. There, she paused for a moment, pressing her hands against the flush of her cheeks. She wasn't cold. She hadn't wanted her shawl. She just needed a moment to gather her composure. Oh, but Justin was incorrigible, totally brazen! She'd glanced back at him as she left the drawing room. His gaze swept the length of her, and she had the most ridiculous notion he could see right through her gown. And how dare he insinuate that *she* was flirting with him? Why, the notion was totally preposterous!

As if she had a chance of capturing such a rogue . . .

As if she even *wanted* such a rogue!

Never mind the niggling little voice inside that reminded her he was the most devastatingly divine-looking man to ever walk the face of this earth.

For one perilous instant, when he had bent his head to hers, it tumbled through her mind that he was going to kiss her. She'd totally forgotten where they were, that they were surrounded by more than a score of guests. She totally forgot everything. That he was a scoundrel. A profligate. She forgot all but the moist heat of his mouth poised so near to hers. A part of her whispered that she had only to move her head ever so slightly . . . Thankfully, anger came to her rescue.

She paced the length of the chamber, trying to calm herself. When he was near, she knew not what to do, or say, or think. What was it about him that distracted her so? But she could never let him know it. Never. Somehow, she must learn to ignore him. He delighted in torturing her, she was certain of it. And she always managed to play right into his hand!

Picking up a lacy shawl, she set her lips firmly together. The next time, she vowed, would be different. She wouldn't allow him to faze her, no matter the provocation.

On that note, she left her room and retraced her steps.

The drawing room was empty. She'd tarried too long, she realized, and she'd neglected to ask where the music room was. Stepping out into the hall, she glanced first one way and then the other. The faint sound of laughter reached her ears, but with the vastness of the entrance hall, it seemed to echo all about her.

"Looking for something?" inquired a male voice from behind her.

Arabella whirled. "My lord. Heavens, you startled me."

He spread his hands. "My apologies, then."

She pasted a bright smile on her features. "Do you know where the music room is? Or are you as lost as I?"

He stepped forward, his hand on her elbow. "Allow me," he said smoothly. He ushered her down the hall and took the corridor to the right, where he opened a door.

"After you," he murmured politely.

Arabella stepped inside. Her gaze swept around a vast, dark, empty chamber. "I fear you're mistaken. This isn't the—"

Behind her, the door clicked shut.

Arabella turned. Patrick McElroy stood leaning against a wide mahogany door, arms crossed over his chest.

"What is the meaning of this?" she demanded.

An easy smile curled his lips. "It's deuced hard to be alone with you," he said mildly, "but I doubt we'll be missed."

He stepped forward.

Arabella stepped back. A prickle went down her spine. Too late she remembered what Justin had said that night at the Benningtons'.

Where the welfare of innocent young maids is concerned, he's dangerous.

He didn't look dangerous. But she disliked the glint in his eye. In fact, she disliked him, period.

"My dear Arabella, I only brought you here to declare myself—"

"Declare yourself what? Mad? Because that's what you are!"

"Come, aren't you the least bit attracted to me?"

"Attracted to you—" Why, the lout was even more conceited than Justin. Her pulse leaped. She should have been wary, for the cad had surely led her away from the others. Fool that she was, she'd fallen for his ploy.

She eyed the door. It wasn't locked. Moving quickly, she tried to shoulder her way past him.

He snared her arm in an iron grip. "No need to be hasty, love. A kiss is all I ask." He gave a grating laugh. "Well, a kiss and perhaps a bit more."

Arabella gasped and struggled to free herself. "Let me go, you oaf!"

"Is that any way to talk to one of your most ardent admirers?" With the heel of his hands, he slammed her up against the wall next to the door. Arabella struggled. Panic raced through her. She was strong for a woman, but no match for a man. She couldn't displace either him or herself. For the first time, she was truly alarmed.

"Let me go!" She tried to bring her hands up, but he caught them in his and jerked them behind her back. Pinned by the weight of his body, she couldn't move.

There was no way she could avoid his moist, wet lips. It spun through her mind that his kiss was nothing like Justin's. Justin's kiss was honey and magic. She felt nothing but revulsion when an insistent tongue rammed between the seam of her closed lips.

Arabella gagged and bit down, hard.

He cursed and jerked back. "You little witch!" He reached for her once more, but the movement allowed Arabella all the space she needed. She brought her knee up hard against his groin.

McElroy doubled over with a grunt. Arabella ducked beneath his arm and wrenched the door open.

She smacked straight into a broad chest.

Ten

Strong hands descended to her shoulders, steadying her even as she flung herself against him. It took Justin but an instant to assess the situation. His gaze swung from Arabella's stricken features to McElroy. The man was hunched over, one hand clamped over his bleeding lip, the other cradling his vitals.

"The chit is vicious!" McElroy gasped. "Look what she did to me!"

Justin's expression turned to stone. "Pack your things and get out," he said through his teeth. "Now."

McElroy attempted to straighten. "I will not," he snarled. "I was invited by your brother."

"And that invitation has just been retracted." Sebastian stepped inside, his gray eyes cold and wintry. Seizing his collar, he started to jerk McElroy from the room like the cur that he was.

Sebastian paused at the threshold. "I trust you'll see to the lady?"

"I will," he said grimly. "But after the entertainment, I suggest you inform her aunt she decided to retire."

Hearing the door close, Arabella moved her head slightly. "Is he gone?" Her voice was muffled against his chest. Her fingers were still wound around the edge of his waistcoat.

Justin nodded. He was so furious he could barely see straight. Arabella, however, glanced up and saw only the fierce clench of his jaw.

"Why do you look like that? It wasn't my fault. He—he tried to kiss me!"

Justin's eyes darkened. He didn't blame her. He'd underestimated McElroy. He'd never dreamed the man would have the nerve to approach Arabella here in the house. He'd seated himself in the last row of chairs to await Arabella's return. Julianna had just begun to sing when it came to his attention that McElroy was absent as well. Sebastian had seen him leap up and followed. Then there was the frantic fear when he'd first glimpsed her face. . . .

Arabella tried to wrench away. He didn't let her. His arms closed around her, a gentle imprisonment. "I don't blame you, Arabella. I don't," he stressed, holding her tight, stroking the curve of her spine until he felt some of the tension leave her.

Curling his fingers beneath her chin, he brought her eyes to his, slowly searching her face. With his thumb, he brushed the curve of her cheek. "Did he hurt you?" he asked, the timbre of his voice very low.

She drew a deep, quavering breath, then shook her head. "He didn't have a chance," she admitted. "I bit him, and then . . ." She colored.

Justin noted with relief that the cloudiness was fading from her beautiful blue eyes. At her words, one corner of his mouth turned up. He pictured McElroy's pose as they burst inside. Maybe the wretch would think twice before pressing his unwanted attentions on another female.

"I must say," he murmured dryly. "I begin to see why you're known as The Unattainable."

She flared. "Oh!" she cried. "You are insufferable. Is there nothing you take seriously?"

"Hush, Arabella. *Hush*. You were very brave." She tipped her head and stared at him rather oddly, and it was then he realized he was almost crooning.

After a moment he felt her push away. He loosened his grip and let his arms fall to his sides.

She glanced around. "What is this room?"

"My fa—" He caught himself just in time. "Sebastian's study," he finished. A band of tightness crept around his chest, until he thought he would choke. It was just outside this room, mere steps away that—

Abruptly he squeezed the thought shut. He would not go there. He *would* not. It was bad enough that he must endure being at the Hall without dredging up all the anger and hurt. God had delivered his punishment by relegating him to his own brand of hell. Twelve years of guilt was not enough, it seemed.

Only a lifetime would do.

Moonlight cascaded through tall mullioned windows. The draperies had not been closed. Arabella moved to stand near one. Justin lit several candles, then turned to her.

"Arabella," he said.

She pivoted, one hand idly caressing the heavy crimson fabric.

"There's something you should know," he said grimly. "There's a reason McElroy did what he did tonight."

Her eyes flashed. "Yes, I know. He's obviously a scoundrel."

"It's more than that."

"How could it possibly be more—" She halted when she saw him shaking his head.

"The night of the Farthingale ball. Five men made a wager at White's that night, a wager concerning you. McElroy was one of those men."

Her eyes didn't waver from his face, but her expression had gone wary. "What kind of wager?"

His gaze bored into hers. "Do you remember what I told you that night at the Barrington gala? About your beaux?"

"Fitzroy was there. And Brentwood and Drummond," she said slowly. Justin was aware of the precise moment comprehension set in. "You said . . . not to trust them, any of them." She flushed. "For they were only after my . . ." She flushed, unable to go on.

"Your virtue," he finished quietly. "The wager, Arabella, was three thousand pounds to the man who claimed The Unattainable's maidenhead."

Her eyes were huge, her skin pale. "Are you saying . . ."

"Yes," he cut in abruptly.

A mantle of silence hung in the air, and then her eyes found his. "That's only four," she said faintly. "What about the fifth man, Justin? Is that why you came to the Farthingale ball that night? To see the prize? To see The Unattainable?" She was standing behind a chair. She gripped the back so tightly her knuckles showed white. Her voice had gone utterly cold. "Was it *you*?"

A muscle tightened in his jaw. Something dark and bitterly ominous crept over him. *Yes . . . No.* Oh, Christ. He couldn't tell her about the other bet—that careless, foolish wager with Gideon. God, but he was a bastard. He couldn't! He was drawn to her in a way he'd never dreamed possible. How damned ironic, the sinner and the saint, he thought blackly. It was selfish, but so be it. She would hate him even more and he couldn't bear the thought.

She was right. He had no scruples. For even now it was himself he sought to protect.

"No," he heard himself say. "It was William Hardaway."

"Hardaway. Yes, of course. He called on me twice this week."

He saw her chin come up, and then she turned her back on him.

His eyes narrowed. "Arabella?"

"Yes?" She sounded perfectly normal. Admittedly, she was bucking up rather well, particularly in light of McElroy's assault.

"Aren't you going to say anything?"

"What do you expect me to say?"

She pivoted to face him. The way her hands locked before her gave her away. Yet when she spoke, she sounded utterly calm. "It seems I must thank you for guarding my virtue. After all, it is worth a good deal of money, isn't it? Granted, you're the last man in the world I'd have expected to do so, considering our feelings for each other. Though perhaps it's some grand joke to you."

Justin sucked in an impatient breath. Did she truly think so little of him? "I only told you so you would be careful. It was certainly *not* my intention to wound you."

"Of course not." Her tone was one of the utmost formality. She crossed to a side table where a decanter and two glasses sat on a silver tray, paused, then glanced at him.

"May I?" she inquired.

A dark brow climbed high. "By all means."

Her hand hovered over the glasses. "Will you join me?"

He declined. "Whisky is not my drink, I fear. It's a little too potent. My tastes run to brandy instead."

He thought she might heed his warning. She did not. Instead, she tipped the neck of the decanter into the glass. A considerable amount splashed inside. As daintily as if she were about to indulge in a spot of tea, she raised it to her lips.

The glass tipped. The liquid went down in one gulp. She pressed the back of her hand against her mouth. Her eyes watered, but to her credit, she neither coughed nor sputtered nor choked. To be sure, it was expensive stuff. Sebastian favored only the best.

She proceeded to pour another. His brows climbed higher still. "Well, well," he murmured. "Miss Vicar has a vice."

Her eyes blazed. She whirled on him. "Don't you dare make light of me, Justin Sterling!"

He held up both hands in a gesture of defeat. "I wouldn't dream of depriving you of your pleasure."

She moved to the seat beneath the window, staring out into the night. Justin watched her, silently standing vigil. Her mood was odd. He felt just as odd, out of step somehow. He sensed her hurt, yet he also sensed he was not the one to ease it. His insides twisted. God, he thought blackly, who was he to offer advice? Besides, she wouldn't welcome it. Not from him. But he wasn't about to leave her alone, either.

"Justin?"

"Yes?"

She held out the crystal glass. "Will you fetch me another?"

Justin glanced at the decanter. Ye gods, it was half-empty! And Sebastian would blame him . . .

"I think you've had enough, Arabella."

"Fine," she said testily. "I'll do it myself."

Hands on his hips, he surveyed her. Her gait, he noted, was none too steady.

He positioned himself before the table. When she attempted to step around him, he reached for her glass, only to find she was determined not to give it up. He ended up having to wrest it from her grip.

"I want another." Her lip thrust out in petulance.

"No."

She glared her defiance. "Why not?"

"Ladies don't drink," he said sternly.

"*You* drink," she accused. "You went to the Barrington gala when you were foxed."

"I'm a man."

She snorted. "So?"

"It's different for men."

"Why is it men can do what women cannot?" she demanded. "It's patently unfair that the rules are so different for men and women! Julianna and I came to that very conclusion on our way downstairs."

Julianna. He almost groaned. For all her fragile looks, his sister was sometimes rather stubbornly outspoken and opinionated.

She blinked up at him, attempting to focus, he suspected. Suddenly she lifted a hand. "Your mouth is crooked," she announced with a cackling laugh. "You're not the handsomest man in England after all, are you, Justin?"

At her touch, Justin froze. The temptation was strong to remove her hand immediately. He didn't allow anyone to touch his face. Ever. He never had . . . He willed away the impulse.

"Sweetheart, that's not my mouth. That's my nose."

Her fingertips fell away. She scowled fiercely. "Sweetheart? Why do you call me that? You called me that before, you know. Do you call all your women sweetheart? Well, I'm not one of your doxies, Justin Sterling."

No, he thought. Dear God, never that.

She was swaying unsteadily. He caught her by the waist.

"Let me be," she protested loudly. "I am not a helpless female. I've never swooned in my life. Indeed, I have only the utmost disdain for women who swoon."

She wasn't swooning. She was staggering. Arabella, the vicar's daughter, was a drunk! And, it seemed, a rather belligerent one, at that. A dry smile touched his mouth. For the first time, he began to appreciate what Sebastian had put up with many times over the years taking care of him.

Her gaze had fixed on the door behind him. "Where's the rest of the party?"

"They're in the music room." The party was still in full swing. Someone was playing the pianoforte. He guessed it would go on for at least several hours. "I'm afraid, Arabella, you're in no condition for a party."

She surprised him by agreeing. "No. I suppose

not." Her eyes climbed to his face. "Is this what it feels like to be foxed?"

"Yes, sweetheart," he said softly. "And I think it's time you went to your room. Are you on the third floor?"

She nodded. "Across the hall from your sister." Her voice had begun to grow fuzzy.

"We have to pass the music room. We must be quiet, all right?"

A shadow passed over her features. He sensed her sudden change of mood, her uncertainty.

An arm about her slender waist, he led her outside into the corridor. She stumbled along, close to his side. The stairs might prove problematic; he was half-afraid she'd stumble and turn an ankle. Swiftly, he slipped an arm beneath her knees and swung her high into his arms.

She gasped and clutched at him for all she was worth. "Put me down. You can't possibly carry me all the way."

"Rubbish." She had a stranglehold on his neck. "I do believe I'm in danger of being strangled, though."

"Oh," she said weakly. Her grip on his neck loosened slightly.

He carried her up the stairs with ease. At the door of her room, he paused, feeling for the door handle.

"Justin, wait."

"What is it?"

She turned her face into his neck. "My maid," she said in a small voice. "Annie. She'll be waiting for me. I—I don't want her to see me like this."

"I'll take care of it."

Indeed, her maid rose from the chair in the corner when the door opened. "Your mistress is indisposed," Justin said smoothly, "but you may go. Someone will be up shortly to tend her."

The maid bobbed a curtsy and left.

Candlelight flickered from the wall sconces. Justin made his way across the room and set her on her feet near the bedside. She sat, one hand feeling for the bed behind her.

On her features was an expression of utter consternation. Justin sat down beside her. "What is it?" he asked quickly. "What's wrong?"

She raised her face to his. Her skin was pasty white. "Don't tell anyone, Justin. Please don't tell what McElroy did. That horrible wager . . ." She shuddered. "Everyone will laugh."

"Arabella," he said helplessly, "I know how you must feel."

"You don't!" she burst out. "How could you? No one has ever laughed at you. You—you're too perfect!"

She covered her face with her hands. Her shoulders heaved. She began to weep.

Justin was shocked. His arms closed around her. "Arabella, what nonsense is this? You're the pink of the *ton*. No one laughs at you—"

"They do!" she cried. "They always have. They always will! I've heard people talking. Whispering. All my life. It's not enough to have this—this horrid red hair that I cannot hide. It's not enough I'm as tall as most men! It's always been like that, always.

Oh, I've pretended not to notice, not to care that people stare as if—as if I'm a freak! And now everyone gossips and calls me by that horrible name—The Unattainable." She gave a dry, broken sob that stabbed his chest like the point of a sword.

"All my life I just wanted to be like everybody else—*look* like everyone else. Do you know what it's like to gaze into the mirror and cringe? To hate what you see and know there's nothing you can ever, ever do to change it?"

The muscles in his throat locked tight. God help him, he did. But not in the same way as Arabella . . .

His arms tightened. Her sobs scalded his heart.

It was the whisky, he knew, that opened the flood tide of emotion inside her, combined with the shock of McElroy's assault, and his revelation about the wager. Hell, it was all of it!

He held her as she rocked against him, feeling her pain, her bitterness. He knew her stubborn pride would never have allowed her to expose herself to him otherwise. He'd just been given a glimpse into a part of her he'd never dreamed existed, a vulnerable part she hid deep within herself.

He ached inside. He ached in a way that had never happened before. "Listen to me, Arabella. You're beautiful. Yes, you're different. But don't you see, that's the attraction. That's why when you walk into a room, there's scarcely a man who can take his eyes off you. You're like a brilliant, exotic flower."

Her head was nestled into the notch between his

neck and his shoulder. "Don't say things you don't mean."

Her contrariness made him want to smile. Even now, she argued with him. But that was a part of what drew him to her. But at least she'd stopped crying.

One corner of his mouth turned up. He dropped a brief kiss on her brow. "Sweetheart, rest assured, I am not a man to say things to a lady that I don't mean."

"For pity's sake," she grumbled, "stop calling me sweet—" All at once she pressed her fingertips to her lips. "I don't feel very well." She lurched from his arms to her knees beside the bed.

Justin was beside her in a heartbeat.

By now she lay sprawled on the floor. "I think I'm going to be sick!" She raised stricken eyes to his.

"No, you're not," he said firmly. "Just take a long, deep breath and don't even think about it, much less say it . . . That's the way, sweetheart. A few more, just like that . . ." After a few moments, he ran a finger down her cheek. "How are you feeling now?" he murmured. "Can you rise?"

Her eyes widened in alarm. Vehemently she shook her head, still a little green. Justin shifted, propped his back against the bed, and eased her head into his lap.

Arabella winced. "My head hurts," she moaned.

"It's all these damned pins." One by one, he removed the pins from her coiffure, dropping them in a pile by his side. When the last one slid from its berth, he threaded his fingers through the heavy mass, gently sifting the silken strands away from her scalp, the movement soothing and monotonous.

"Better?" he murmured.

"Yes. Thank you." She lay against him listlessly. Her lips barely moved.

His belly tightened as he looked down. Her hair was incredibly long and soft, spilling over his legs and onto the floor, a glorious waterfall of gleaming red strands. Against his will, against all his better judgment, he felt his rod stiffen and swell. Desire struck, swift and merciless, an arrow in the loins. It seemed his body had a mind of its own. He held his breath when she shifted her head. Her brow furrowed, and she settled her cheek at the very top of one hard thigh. Sweet Jesus, now her mouth was perilously near the head of his . . . She sighed. Even through his trousers, he fancied he could feel her breath, warm and . . . He drew a shaky breath. With every second, he could feel himself pulsing . . . pulsing in time to his heart. Oh, Christ. *Christ*. This was altogether more temptation than he could handle.

"Arabella. Arabella, I need to get you into bed." It slipped out unwittingly. He suppressed a groan.

"No. I don't want to, Justin. I can't move."

"We must, Arabella. It would hardly do for me to be caught in your room come morning, now, would it? Here, I'll help you."

"Everything's spinning."

"I know, sweet. I've much experience in these things, remember?"

"Yes, I suppose you do, don't you? Will it go away soon?"

"Yes," he lied. She'd never remember, he was certain.

She was limp as a wet rag, but he managed to get her on her feet. He made brisk work of the buttons on the back of her gown and unlaced her corset, dropping both in a heap at her feet. She stood before him, clad only in her shift.

"I need my nightgown," she fretted.

"No, sweet, you don't. You can sleep as you are just this one night." He'd tested his willpower as far as he could . . . or so he was convinced.

He turned her in his arms. The shift she wore was no real barrier at all; she might just as well have been naked. Behind her, the candlelight glowed, revealing the lushly erotic outline of her body in stark relief. Her breasts were round as melons, deliciously full. The disks of her nipples thrust against the sheer silk, plump and dark. He wanted to rip away that damned shift and bare her completely. He wanted to curl his tongue around and around her nipples, knowing she would taste like warm honey. Unable to resist, his gaze swept the length of her. He wondered vaguely if the dusky triangle between the juncture of her thighs was as red and curly as her hair.

"Come," he said brusquely. "Into bed with you." He lifted her onto the mattress, whisked away her slippers and stockings, and drew the sheet up over her.

She immediately thrust it down to her waist.

"I'm hot," she complained. "And it feels strange without my nightgown."

"You'll get used to it, Arabella. It's just for this one night."

"I won't," she pouted. "Wouldn't you feel strange going to bed without your nightshirt?"

"I don't sleep in a nightshirt."

"What do you sleep in, then?"

"Nothing."

Her eyes rounded. She gaped. "What?" she said faintly. "You mean you sleep . . . naked?" She said it as if it were a curse.

"Yes, dear," he said blandly. "I sleep naked."

"Oh! That's wicked, Justin."

He wanted to laugh at her censure. Somehow he couldn't.

Instead he sucked in a painful breath. He'd never put a woman to bed chastely in his life, yet he just had. Oh, but wouldn't the bucks of the *ton* hoot if they knew!

It took every ounce of willpower he possessed to battle the heated rush that sizzled in his loins. Never before had he been so achingly aware of one woman. Never had he wanted a woman the way he wanted this one—the one woman he couldn't have! Was that the allure? Was it simply that she was the one woman who resisted him?

"Justin?"

"What, sweetheart?"

"You said you wouldn't tell anyone about McElroy. You won't, will you?"

"Of course not."

"You didn't promise."

He sighed. She was babbling, yet completely adorable. "I promise," he said gravely.

"And Walter. You never promised you wouldn't tell anyone he proposed."

"I promise now. I won't tell anyone about Walter."

Slender brows met in a frown. "How can I be sure I can trust you?" she asked suspiciously. "I probably shouldn't, you know. One should never trust a rogue."

"You're right, Arabella. You probably shouldn't. But I swear, I'll keep your secrets."

That appeared to satisfy her. She leaned back on the pillows. He took her hand, idly toying with her fingertips. Soon her eyes began to close, but suddenly they popped open.

"You asked me why," she said suddenly.

"Why . . . what?"

"The night of the masquerade. You asked me why I disliked you."

Justin went very still inside. "Why do you dislike me?" God, it almost hurt to say it aloud.

"It was Emmaline Winslow."

"Emmaline Winslow?" He was stymied. Who the devil was Emmaline Winslow?

Her head bobbed up and down. "That day at the Dowager Duchess of Carrington's country estate . . . when I crawled under your chair and stabbed you with my pin. I—I heard the two of you in the house. You told her there were other women just as fetching as she. Indeed, you said, she was but one pearl among many and you intended to sample them all! You made her cry, Justin. You were so callous! You walked away and—and left her crying."

Comprehension dawned in a flash. For one paralyzing instant, Justin couldn't move. His mind hurtled back. He suddenly understood so very much.

"But I don't dislike you anymore," she confided earnestly. Her gaze scoured his face. "You don't mind, do you?"

"No," he said hoarsely. For the life of him, it was all he could say.

"Good. Will you stay until I sleep?"

He nodded, watching as she weaved her fingers through his, closed her eyes, and brought their joined hands to rest on her belly.

He stared until his eyes grew dry and the moon was high in the sky. And all the while, a hundred different feelings crashed around in his chest.

Something was changing between them. *Everything* was changing. He didn't know what it was. And he didn't like not knowing, not one damn bit.

But he couldn't stop it.

And that terrified him. It terrified him, as nothing or no one else had ever frightened him before.

Eleven

It was late when Arabella woke the next morning. Sunlight poured through the draperies. With a groan she heaved to her side, seeking to evade the light. Even through her closed eyelids, it seemed to burn. Her mouth felt as if it had been stuffed with muslin. Her throat was dry as the sands of the Sahara. Her head was pounding as if a blacksmith had taken up permanent residence in her brain. She wanted to drag her pillow over her head and go back to sleep. But something naggingly insistent wouldn't allow it.

Snatches of memory sifted back. McElroy. Justin's appearance in the study. The rest was vague. She recalled sitting at the window, a finely cut crystal glass in her hand . . .

Oh, Lord, *that's* why she felt so horrid. Never again, Arabella vowed, would she indulge in spirits so strong. Indeed, never again would she indulge in *any* kind of spirits.

Just then there was a knock on the door.

"Come in." The words came out a hoarse croak.

It was Aunt Grace, bright-eyed and chirpy. "Good morning, Arabella," she sang out. "I brought a pot of chocolate and some pastries for breakfast." Grace deposited a tray on the bedside table, then sat on the bed. "How are you this morning?"

Arabella rolled over and pushed herself up, dredging up a wan smile. "Fine," she murmured.

"You don't look fine. You look quite dreadful." Grace handed her a delicate china cup. "I'm sorry you're feeling so poorly, love. Perhaps it was something you ate."

Oh, if she only knew . . .

"Unfortunately, you weren't the only one to take sick. Patrick McElroy had to depart quite suddenly, too. Perhaps it was the same malady."

McElroy! Just the thought of him made her sizzle again. Aloud she said, "I'm sorry to have missed the festivities."

Aunt Grace patted her hand. "Well, the important thing is for you to get better. Just rest, dear, and perhaps by this evening you'll be well enough to join us for dinner."

Arabella smiled gratefully. "Thank you, Aunt. Will you make my apologies to the marquess and his wife? I do hope I haven't spoiled any of their plans."

"Not at all, dear. Why, I spoke to Devon just now, and she asked me to pass on her concern."

"That's very kind of her," Arabella murmured.

"Would you mind closing the draperies just a bit on your way out? I confess, the light is quite glaring."

"Consider it done, my dear." At the window, Grace tugged at the drapes, glancing back. "It rained dreadfully last night. Did you hear it?"

"No, I'm afraid I didn't hear much of anything." Mercy, but wasn't that the truth?

"You'd never know, looking outside now." Her aunt was practically chirping. "It's gloriously warm and sunny." Grace stopped at the bedside and dropped a kiss on her brow. "I hope you feel better soon, dear." Suddenly Aunt Grace frowned. "Did Annie forget to pack your nightdress?"

Arabella glanced down, then froze. Not until then did she realize she was clad in her shift. Memories assailed her anew. Memories of lean, male hands skidding down the bare skin of her back . . . *Justin's* hands. She recalled the brisk efficiency with which he'd dispatched her gown. Which made perfect sense, of course—obviously he'd undressed many a woman in his lifetime.

But Aunt Grace was still waiting for a reply. "Oh, no, Aunt. It's just that . . . I fear I didn't feel up to bothering with it." She winced. What a lame excuse!

But Aunt Grace merely nodded and left. Alone, Arabella sank back into the covers, mortified beyond measure. This time she *did* drag the pillow over her head. She didn't know if she should laugh or cry. Justin had put her to bed. *Justin*. Would there ever come a day she didn't dread seeing him again?

She was patently convinced there would not.

She had no intention of lying in bed all day, though. Despite Aunt Grace's reassurance otherwise, she considered it dreadfully rude, particularly in light of the fact that she was a guest in someone else's home. Yet, miraculously, before she knew it, she was dozing.

When she woke, it was early afternoon. Cautiously she lifted her head from the pillow. The throbbing in her head was gone, thank heaven. After eating the pastries Aunt Grace had left, she felt much better than she had earlier. Washing quickly, she brushed her hair and dressed in a blue-sprigged muslin gown.

The house seemed empty. Quizzing a passing maid, she discovered most of the others were out riding. Tea, she was informed, was to be served outdoors near the rose gardens.

A bit of exploring was in order, Arabella decided quickly. The thought of negotiating all those steps again was tiresome, but if Aunt Grace saw her without a bonnet and gloves, she'd never hear the end of it. Retracing her steps, she retrieved a bonnet from her trunk, disdained the gloves, and ventured outside.

Aunt Grace was right. It was a lovely day, far warmer than it had been for quite some time. The grounds around Thurston Hall were lovelier still. She wandered at will, letting her steps take her where they would, up the side of a hill and down the other. The sun beat down. She hadn't expected it to be quite so hot. Trudging down the hillside, she came to a place where a small brook dashed madly through the trees before disappearing around the bend.

Hazy spears of sunlight twirled through the treetops, spinning a golden web all around. Arabella paused. Tiny beads of sweat collected on her forehead, and she wiped them away with the back of her hand.

Biting her lip, she cast a hasty glance around. She was quite some distance away from the house. There was no one about. Temptation beckoned—the lure was irresistible. With nary a second thought, she dragged her bonnet from her head and dropped it on the grass. Her slippers, stockings, and garters came next. Reaching down, she grabbed the hem of her skirt and tucked it into her bodice, baring her legs to just above her knees.

Without hesitation she waded into the stream. The water was cold, but deliciously so. She stopped, watching in almost riveted fascination as the water rushed around the middle of her calves. Ah, but she was supposed to be a proper young Society miss. No doubt it was decidedly improper to be traipsing through a stream in such a fashion . . .

The thought kindled another. A mischievous smile rimmed her lips. She recalled one of the summers she'd spent in Africa with Mama and Papa. She'd been perhaps fifteen or so at the time, and the heat had been unbearable. One night she'd crept from their hut to the shores of the river. And with no one to see, no one to care, she had shed her clothing . . .

And swam naked.

What would Society think if they knew that she, Arabella Templeton, the vicar's daughter, had splashed and swam *naked* to her heart's content . . . and that but the first of many times? Poor Aunt Grace, she was certain, would have been most scandalized. Why, Aunt Grace would be scandalized if she saw her now, baring her legs! Throwing back her head, she laughed aloud, a ringing, robust sound she couldn't withhold.

And it was then, at that precise moment, that she knew . . .

She wasn't alone.

It was Justin, of course. *Of course,* her mind echoed. Why, who else would it be? Oh, if she could only pretend she did not see him! Alas, he stood at the bank where she'd left her bonnet, shoes, and stockings. Her heart leaped. He was dressed informally—a loose white flowing shirt, tight buff breeches, and boots. She had to consciously slow the beat of her heart.

Damnation! He was smiling as his gaze traveled from her face to the slim curve of her exposed legs. Several things ran through her brain in that instant. Modesty commanded that she drop her skirts immediately and bolt. Yet if she did, they'd be instantly soaked. And once she returned to the house, which was inevitable unless she stayed out till after dark, how the devil was she to explain it?

And he knew it. Oh, yes, he was keenly aware of her predicament, for a maddening smile lurked about his mouth. He shook his head. "Ah, Arabella, I can almost reach out and catch hold of your thoughts, you know."

"Indeed," she retorted pertly. "And what am I thinking?"

"You're wondering if you should run. Or if you should drop your skirts and hide yourself from me."

"I fear, sir, that I can do neither."

His maddening smile widened further. "This is true."

Arabella's cheeks burned with the heat of a blush. "It occurs to me, sir, that you have a most decided predilection of coming upon me at the most inconvenient of times."

Her prim tone made Justin want to laugh aloud. Lord, she was sweet!

"Odd that you should see it that way," he mused lightly. "I'd begun to fancy myself your rescuer. Do I not always appear in your hour of need?"

"You?" She was clearly aghast.

He cocked a brow. "A misconception, then?"

"Indeed! I do believe you've decided your sole purpose in life is to torment me."

"Now, why would you say that?" He allowed his gaze to slide slowly over her form.

Her mouth turned down. "Stop staring at me like that!"

"Like what?" She regarded him with eyes both pleading and distressed. She was right, he decided vaguely. He *was* tormenting her. But . . . sweet Christ, he couldn't resist teasing her just a little.

"My dear Arabella, you cannot stay there forever. However, if you so choose, then I am compelled to inform you that I am ever so willing to continue to avail myself of a view that is most pleasing to the eye."

"Oh!" Her cheeks were flaming, almost the color of her hair.

He took pity on her. "Here, now. Come out before you catch your death."

He was right. She couldn't stay there forever. Her feet were beginning to go numb.

"Turn your back," she pleaded.

To her utter surprise, no argument was forthcoming. He turned to the side.

Biting her lip, Arabella began to wade toward him. But the rocks beneath her feet were slippery. Concentrating on her feet, she carefully made her way toward him, unaware that Justin had glanced back over his shoulder. Avid green eyes tracked her progress. She was almost there when she slipped precariously.

"Ohhh!" A cry escaped.

A long arm shot out, closing about her waist and swinging her high. The next thing she knew, there was dry ground beneath her feet.

A husky laugh rushed past her ear. "There, now—safe, sound, and nary a drop of water on your pretty gown. Aren't you glad I wasn't a gentleman after all?"

For the span of a heartbeat, her fingertips rested

on the plane of his shirt. Her mind registered warmth. Hardness. A taut masculine strength that sent a tremor of reaction all through her.

She recovered herself quickly, drawing her hands away. "You are a rogue," she accused without heat. "But thank you anyway."

He swept her a gallant bow. "I remain, as ever, your most humble servant."

"Justin Sterling, humble?" She smiled. "Now, that I should like to see."

The rogue had clearly reappeared. "And that is the most enchanting smile I've yet to see this Season," he declared. "More enchanting yet since I believe it's the first you've ever directed at me."

Arabella wrinkled her nose at him. She moved to sit on the grass near her slippers and stockings. Her legs were still wet, she noticed absently. She'd have let the breeze dry them before donning her hose again. It struck her then . . . a lady never exposed her hands to a man unless she was eating. Yet here she was, without gloves, sitting here in her bare feet before Justin . . . and it was like she'd done so every day of her life.

She watched as he dropped down on the grass beside her. "How long were you watching me?" she murmured.

"Long enough to know I'd give a fortune if I knew what the devil you were thinking about prior to the moment you noticed me. I found your expressions most intriguing, Arabella. You reminded me of a sly little imp up to mischief."

Arabella couldn't help it. A betraying flush crept

beneath her skin. She could feel it moving from her neck to her face.

"Ah, you're blushing," he said knowingly. "I daresay it was something shockingly untoward you were thinking of."

"I doubt there's anything that could shock you," she retorted promptly.

"Probably true." He leaned back on an arm. "We're much alike, you and I."

Arabella gasped. "We are not!"

He plucked a blade of grass and fingered it. A gleam in his eyes, he glanced at her. "Aren't we?" he said almost lazily.

Arabella set her chin firmly. "I suppose you mean last night." She looked away. "Now, see here. I'm not usually given to—to drink."

"If it's any consolation, you were no less argumentative than usual."

"Well, that's reassuring," she snapped. "And pray do not laugh at me."

"I wouldn't dream of it. But you have a wild side, Arabella. I've seen it. I sense it. We are . . . kindred spirits, if you will."

She gritted her teeth. "We are not."

"You bristle. But I know you, dear girl. You were wading in the stream because no one was about, because you figured no one would catch you." His eyes were alight. "I suppose it's lucky you stopped with your shoes and stockings. Indeed, if I had happened upon you swimming . . . naked . . . say, whatever would Society think of dear Arabella, the vicar's daughter . . ."

Her mouth opened and closed. It was as if he'd reached in and plucked her thoughts from inside her mind! Was he right? Was she as wild as he was convinced? She winced, reminded of all the scrapes she'd been in as a child.

"Oh, my, I do believe I've done the impossible. You're speechless, Arabella. But tell me. Is it because I'm right? Or because I'm wrong?"

"I refuse to dignify that with a response," she said sternly.

"Be that as it may, I, at least, am honest. I am what I am. Every one of those things you once called me. A womanizer. A wastrel. A rogue."

"Be serious, Justin."

"I am being serious."

She regarded him levelly. "But if you know what you are, surely you can *change* what you are."

"Can I? Can you? Ah, Arabella, I think not." Unbidden, Justin thought of his mother's faithlessness. Her infidelities. A bittersweet band of tightness crept around his heart, and darkness threatened. Deliberately he kept it at bay.

Arabella was shaking her head. "I think you're wrong, Justin."

"Mercy!" he mocked. "Careful, now, Arabella. Or are you trying to reform me?"

"I don't know," she said earnestly. "Perhaps I am."

He leaned close. An unholy light glimmered in his eyes. He gave her a slow, simmering appraisal. "I might be persuaded, you know."

His tone was low. Lazily seductive. Arabella's

stomach knotted. She couldn't take her eyes from his. A breeze ruffled his dark hair. His handsomeness struck her in a way that had never happened before—she, who had thought herself immune to it! Her gaze traced over the perfect contours of his features, the slightly aquiline nose, the way his lower lip was fuller than the upper, his jaw dark with his beard.

He was so close their shoulders brushed. What was it about this man that made her heart race? That made forbidden longings spill through every part of her, despite everything she knew of him. Despite knowing what he was, all the rakish things he'd done.

"Justin," she blurted, "you've been with many women, haven't you?"

She'd startled him, she realized. He gave her a long, slow look. "Where the devil did that come from?"

Her tongue came out to moisten her lips. "The night of the masquerade at Vauxhall Gardens, I overheard some women talking about you. One said you were a lover of—" oh, surely her entire body was on fire, "of superb finesse."

For the space of a heartbeat, he stared directly into her eyes. She had the unsettling sensation he was wondering if he'd heard her correctly. Indeed, Arabella could scarcely believe her daring. Perhaps he was right. Perhaps there was a wild, wanton streak in her.

"I see," he said after a moment. "And are you wondering if it's true?"

"Well . . . if you're so wicked and depraved and immoral, then why do women want you?" It all came out in a rush, and then she couldn't seem to stop. "I've seen them, you know. Their lips say one thing, but when they look at you, why, it's almost as if they wish to be debauched."

It was all Justin could do not to burst into laughter. The very idea that prim, proper Arabella dared to broach such a subject was mind-boggling. When he'd followed her here, never in his life did he imagine the turn of their conversation.

Nor was she finished, it seemed.

"Have you done licentious things?" she queried tentatively.

"And if I said yes?

"Then I would ask if . . . if licentious things . . . are pleasurable."

He raised a rakish brow. "Why are you asking me this? Last night you claimed you were not flirting with me."

"And I'm not. I'm simply . . ." She floundered.

"Curious?"

"Yes," she said breathlessly. "And I know of no one else to ask."

"Thank you," he said dryly. "That was flattering."

Slender brows drew together over her brows. "Aren't you going to answer?"

"I am not." He got to his feet and extended a hand.

She took it, allowing him to pull her to her feet. "Why not?"

She stood with her back against the trunk of the

tree they'd been sitting under. Very deliberately, Justin placed first one hand, then the other, on the rough bark beside her.

Her gaze slid from one arm to the other, then jerked back to his eyes. He knew the exact moment she realized she was trapped.

He adopted his most roguish tone. "My dear Arabella," he said softly, "I am alone with a beautiful woman. There is no one here to see. You want to talk about licentious things, while I would rather *do* licentious things." As he spoke, he leaned in even farther.

She nearly jumped out of her skin. She wasted no time ducking under his arm. He turned as she grabbed up her shoes and stockings, holding them to her breast like a shield. Her expression, a mixture of uncertainty and righteous indignation, nearly set him off.

He raised his brows. "What! Did you think I was going to kiss you?"

She sniffed. "As if I would let you!" Yet despite her bravado, she scuttled to the other side of the tree and began to tug on her shoes and stockings.

"Are you properly shocked?" he said mildly.

"Hardly," she snorted.

He smiled. "Rest assured, Arabella, whatever licentious activities I may have engaged in, it was not with innocent young maidens." He glanced toward the house. "We should be getting back. It's almost teatime."

Arabella took the arm he offered, her bonnet dangling from her fingertips. They began to amble toward the house. "For a man of such vast experience," she remarked, "you are remarkably closemouthed. I thought men had a decided proclivity to boast about such things."

He assisted her over an exposed tree root. "Mostly to other men. Not to—"

"Yes, I know." She rolled her eyes. "Innocent young maidens. But I'm not young, you know. I'm nearly one-and-twenty. So perhaps *you* should rest assured that I wouldn't be shocked at anything you decided to tell me."

He laughed softly. "Trust me, Arabella. Your tender ears would be singed. The smoke would be spied all the way to London."

"I was always a precocious child." She had no trouble keeping up with his long-legged stride. Suddenly she pointed. "Oh, look! What is that?"

Justin followed the direction of her finger. "It's the gazebo."

"Oh!" she exclaimed. "May we stop?" She didn't wait for an answer, but picked up her skirts and began running toward the small white structure on the hilltop.

Justin quickened his pace. "Oh, but this is lovely!" she sang out. Slanting him a smile, she leaned forward to sniff the dainty pink roses that climbed the twin columns of the entrance. "I do so adore roses."

Justin stopped at the bottom of the stairs. No, he thought raggedly, she was the one who was lovely. He found her disregard for convention quite enchanting. The strings of her bonnet still trailed from her fingertips. Exertion or perhaps the sun had tinted her cheeks the fairest rose. He had to wrench his gaze from lips that were practically begging to be kissed. God, but what was behind this cursed attraction to her? She was all wrong for him. Yet being with her this afternoon . . . Christ, it felt so right . . .

She turned to him. From where she stood on the first step, they were eye-to-eye. "Now," she said briskly, "where were we? Oh, you were about to tell me all your secrets."

"Are we trading secrets, then?"

"Indeed, you are the keeper of all my secrets," she grumbled. "Or the ones that matter anyway."

He chuckled. "That grates, doesn't it?"

Her lips pursed. "Yes," she muttered. "I think it's only fair that I should have just one of yours."

"A secret of the licentious nature, eh?"

"Well, yes . . . it makes sense, doesn't it? Licentious. Lascivious. Libertine. What do all those things have in common?"

"Me, I suppose."

Her eyes crinkled. "Very clever," she praised. Smiling brightly, anticipating victory, she stationed herself on the top step, where she gazed down at him. Oh, he was so smug and superior! Just once she longed to have the upper hand, so to speak.

It proved a victory short-lived. He quirked a brow. "I know what you're doing, Arabella, and it won't work." Setting his hands firmly on her waist, he swung her from her perch above him.

"Cad," she charged.

"Vixen," he shot back. "But I will admit, you win points for being persistent. However, I am compelled to inform you, no matter how hard you try, I won't tell you what you wish to know."

"Why not? I suppose it is a matter of principle now."

"Principle be damned. I've no intention of sinking even lower in your eyes, so my lips are sealed. Besides which, I begin to wonder if perhaps *you* are so insistent because it is indeed a trifle more than a matter of curiosity."

She frowned. "I don't know what you mean."

Justin began to walk on. "Simply this." He cast a sidelong glance at her. "Are you even aware how the act of procreation is done?"

"Of course I am. My mother told me, as well as my Aunt Grace. And—" She stopped short.

Justin placed his hands on his hips. Her expression was decidedly guilty. "And?" he coaxed.

She was blushing fiercely. "The night before my cousin Harriet married, I heard Aunt Grace telling her what to . . ." She ran the tip of her tongue around her lips. "What to anticipate in the marriage bed."

Justin dissolved into laughter. "I should have known! You were spying behind closed doors again!"

Arabella scowled. "I wasn't spying."

He only laughed the harder. "The devil you say!"

"Forgive me for interrupting your amusement, sir." She gestured grandly to the path before them, where the night's rain had collected in a wide pool.

"What?"

"There is a puddle before us," she pointed out.

He smiled. "So there is," he agreed.

Her gaze ripened to a glare. "A gentleman, on seeing that it is too wide for me to traverse on my own, and seeing that he is wearing boots and I have but thin slippers, would offer to carry me across."

"My dear, you have called me many things, but never a gentleman." His smile widened. "However, since you insist . . ."

Bending low, he pitched her over his shoulder and strode through the puddle. She was still sputtering as he set her on her feet on the other side.

Her chin climbed high. "And now I see why," she informed him icily. "You, sir, are no gentleman, nor will you ever be."

Justin threw back his head and laughed as she stalked away. Now, this, he thought, was the Arabella he knew . . .

Twelve

Tea was just being served when they arrived. Arabella chatted with Georgiana and Julianna for a time, then moved to sit with her aunt and uncle. Finally, she wandered off a short distance away from the others. A pair of chaise lounges beckoned beneath the shade of a tree, and it was there she directed her steps. Uncle Joseph had been discussing his prized hunting retriever with Sebastian, and Aunt Grace was busy flitting from guest to guest.

All the while, there wasn't a single moment she wasn't aware of Justin—where he was, who he was with, everything about him.

It was distracting. Disturbing. And most disconcerting.

For something had changed last night . . . and she had the oddest sensation that she was falling for him . . .

Which would be most unwise.

Indeed, downright foolish.

Yet she found herself battling the helpless sensation there wasn't a thing she could do to fight it. And deep down, she wondered what it would be like to be wanted—to be pursued—by Justin Sterling.

Exciting, to be sure.

Dangerous, without question.

He's broken half the hearts in London, warned a voice. *If you let him, he'll break yours, too.*

He was the kind of man she had always despised, the very antithesis of all she believed in, of all she held dear.

Yet she had only to catch the merest glimpse of him, and she was curiously short of breath. There was a strange flutter in her chest. When he wanted, he could be completely engaging and wholly charming. By heaven, she herself had been charmed!

She winced as she thought of all that happened last night. McElroy's advances—the wretch! And then there was the matter of that disgusting bet at White's. Just thinking of it made her shudder all over again.

But Justin hadn't disclosed it to be nasty or mean. Somehow she knew, in some strange, unfathomable way she didn't fully comprehend, that he'd been trying to protect her—which was totally at odds with the type of man she thought he was!

It made no sense that she should confide in him as she had. The details were fuzzy, but she remembered pouring her heart out, revealing all her deepest fears and flaws, sobbing against his shoulder.

And what had he done? He hadn't been appalled. He hadn't been disgusted. He'd simply held her, and it had felt remarkably good and right. And . . . oh, but she'd wanted him to hold her again this afternoon, back at the stream. She wanted him to kiss her as if there was no tomorrow . . .

Oh, but she was a fool! He'd kissed her once—*once!*—and surely it wouldn't happen again. It was well known the woman didn't exist who could put his heart under lock and key.

So why had he called her beautiful? Had he meant it? Of course not. Her heart contracted. From his own lips, he was a womanizer, a niggling little voice reminded her. No doubt it was naught but habit, a slip of the tongue, in much the same way he called her sweetheart.

Still, a curious sadness dwelled in her breast. Ah, if only . . .

On and on her emotions squalled and blustered in her chest. But he was right about one thing. She was wild. Wanton, and a little shameless. Lord, but she was a hypocrite! To think she had lectured him as she once had . . . Her conscience was proving most troublesome indeed. She was shocked at her own audacity as they had sat at the stream. Why had she queried him as she had?

Oh, indeed, she had no doubt that many of the tales she'd heard of his scandalous behavior were true. He'd admitted as much this afternoon. Never had he pretended to be anything but what he was. A rogue and a rascal. A rake and a libertine.

And yet . . . a part of her whispered that he

wasn't the cold-hearted man he pretended to be, though everyone was convinced he was.

From the corner of her eye, she saw him drop a fond kiss on Julianna's cheek. Her throat tightened oddly. When he was with his family, he was . . . different somehow. With them, he was care*free*, not care*less*. He wasn't what she'd first been so convinced he was, uncaring or insensitive. Last night, she realized shakily, had proved it.

She didn't know what to make of it. She didn't know what to make of *him*.

A high-pitched squeal pierced the air, followed by another. Sebastian and Devon's little ones were tottering across the lawn as fast as their chubby little legs would carry them. Every so often they glanced behind at their pursuer, Justin. A woman Arabella suspected was their nurse trailed behind. Arabella shook her head as if to clear it.

Even as she watched, he caught up with them, laughing, scooping them up, one in each arm. It was a sight so unexpected, so startlingly unlike the man she thought she knew, that her jaw nearly dropped open. At that precise instant he raised his head.

Their eyes tangled. Arabella couldn't have looked away if the earth had crumbled beneath her feet. Indeed, she decided hazily, that was how he made her feel.

Long legs closed the distance between them. The little ones were still giggling in delight as he came to a halt directly before her. The merest hint of a smile lurked on his lips, a smile that somehow managed to both dismay and disarm her.

"I don't believe you've had the privilege of meeting my niece and nephew."

"Indeed I have not." There was a breathless catch in her voice. Was he aware of it?

"Then may I present Geoffrey Alan Sterling, and his sister Sophia Amelia—or Sophie, as we call her." He glanced at the chaise next to her. "May we join you?"

"You certainly may."

Arabella smiled at the children. They were darling, with plump round cheeks and wee little noses.

"Oh, my. What little angels." She tipped her head to the side and regarded them. "Geoffrey has his father's hair, but his mother's eyes. And Sophie has her mother's hair, with her father's eyes." She shook her head. "Their coloring is so different, it's amazing they're twins."

"That's what everyone says." Justin moved to sit in the chair, only to find it a bit narrow with the two little ones in his arms.

"Here, let me take one of them," she said immediately. She patted her lap. The little boy promptly scampered from Justin's lap onto hers. Sophie, however, clung harder to Justin's neck, clearly reluctant to leave the safety of her uncle's arms.

"They're just over a year old," Justin commented, "so of course they don't speak much yet, except for Mama and Papa—and Uncle Justin, of course."

"Of course," Arabella echoed, biting back a smile. She nodded at Sophie, who had popped a finger into her mouth and regarded her with wide gray eyes. "She's adorable."

Justin's smile widened. He glanced at his niece. "I predict, Sophie, that you'll someday be a beauty and take the *ton* by storm, just like Miss Vicar here."

Arabella bit her lip and looked away. There. He'd said that she was beautiful again. She wished he wouldn't say things he didn't mean, that weren't true. Unsure how to respond, she said nothing. She didn't notice that Geoffrey was busy playing with the ribbon ties that closed the front of her bodice. All at once Justin cleared his throat. His gaze slipped down, then quickly away. It was then Arabella noticed the little boy had undone the ribbon. The opening in her bodice had begun to gape.

She gasped. "Oh," she cried, flustered. "Oh!"

"Only a year old," Justin teased, "and drawn to the ladies already."

Swiftly Arabella did up the ties again. She didn't want to laugh, but she couldn't stop herself, either. "Perhaps he's been too much influenced by the company of his uncle!"

Justin chuckled. "Perhaps. But let's see if we can find something else to amuse this young man." He fished his pocket watch from his trousers and dangled it before Geoffrey, who immediately grabbed for it.

In the meantime, little Sophie's eyelids had begun to droop. A companionable silence settled over them. Geoffrey played with his watch, while Sophie drifted off to sleep.

There was an almost imperceptible tightening of Justin's arms around the little girl. Or was it a trick of her eyes? Even as the thought spun through her mind, he pressed a fleeting kiss against her curls. There was a strange tugging on her heart at the sight of Justin, so dark and striking, with Sophie's golden head tucked beneath his chin, one booted leg stretched out before him. Something stark and strong stirred within her.

A week ago she'd have soundly denounced a rake such as he as being utterly incapable of loyalty and devotion. But seeing him with a child in his arms . . . His love for his niece and nephew was so very much apparent. That they adored him in turn was unquestionable. It was a side of him she had never dreamed existed. A side of him she had never thought to encounter.

Her head was suddenly whirling. Was she wrong about him? Was there more to the man than the cavalier façade he presented to the world? Was it possible his arrogance was just a mask, his cynicism a shield?

Alas, there was no time to consider. The Dowager Duchess of Carrington had stopped before them. Her snowy white head tipped first one direction, then the other as she beheld them. A slow smile crept across her lips. Before either Arabella or Justin could say a word, the duchess spoke.

"I knew it." Beneath her shawl, her bony shoulders shook with laughter. "I knew it the first night I saw the two of you dancing together at the Farthingale ball."

Justin arched a brow. "Your Grace?" he murmured.

The duchess was gazing at Arabella. "Walter was never the man for you, dear. I daresay you'd have been bored silly with him within a month."

Arabella gaped.

The duchess continued, leaning on her cane. "But you and Justin . . . well, 'tis just as I told your aunt. The two of you look remarkably fine together. La, but I can almost hear the wedding bells now!" She was almost giggling as she transferred her gaze to Justin. Raising her cane, she shook it at him almost playfully. "Now," she stated briskly, "all that remains is to find the right man for Julianna. Ah, but she has proved remarkably stubborn thus far, hasn't she?"

Arabella was speechless as the duchess sauntered away. To her utter shock, when she turned her gaze to Justin, she discovered an utterly wicked amusement dancing in his eyes. Oh, how dare he laugh! Moreover, how *could* he, particularly in light of what the duchess had said about wedding bells?

It appeared Justin did not share her loss for words. "As you can see," he said mildly, "the duchess is a woman who does not hesitate to speak her mind. And she does fancy herself a matchmaker extraordinaire."

Arabella eyed him over Geoffrey's head. "How did she know about Walter? You promised you wouldn't tell anyone he proposed!"

"And I did not."

"Then how could she possibly . . ."

"My dear Arabella, it was obvious dear Walter was smitten with you."

But Justin was hardly smitten with her. Why, then, had the duchess said what she had? And why hadn't Justin set the duchess to rights regarding the two of them? Merciful heavens, why hadn't *she*?

Arabella's gaze slid away. She swallowed, no longer able to meet his amused regard.

Her heart constricted. A sense of helplessness assailed her. Oh, Lord. She couldn't . . . wouldn't . . . *shouldn't* fall for a man like him.

Yet the oddest thought kept running through her mind. What if it was already too late?

The seating arrangements at dinner were the same as the previous evening, with the exception of McElroy's absence. Afterward, the gentlemen gathered for port and cigars, and the women retired to the drawing room. Arabella, however, was restless. She and Georgiana walked outside for a time, and when they returned to the house, they stopped to inspect the heavy, gilt-framed paintings in the portrait gallery. One by one they paused before the generations of Sterlings. In truth, Arabella paid scant attention to Georgiana's idle chatter. Her mind was elsewhere. But suddenly Georgiana exclaimed, "Why, look, it's Sebastian, Justin and Julianna!"

Her attention piqued, Arabella leaned closer. The three Sterling siblings were easily recognizable, as they had changed but little since childhood.

"My word, but look at Justin! The likeness to his mother is amazing."

Arabella caught her breath. Georgiana was right. Their mother was truly a vision. It was clear Justin had inherited his looks from her. Each possessed the same fine-boned elegance, the same dramatically gleaming dark hair, the same exquisite plane of perfect, symmetrical features. But it was the mother's eyes that captured Arabella's notice the longest. Bright, startlingly vivid green, long-lashed, and spectacular, particularly in contrast with her hair . . . it was like peering into Justin's eyes.

But their father, the previous marquess . . . A chill swept over her. He was thin-lipped and austere, and she took an instant dislike to him.

"Good evening, ladies."

So engrossed were they in the portrait that they both jumped.

It was Justin, garbed in black evening clothes, so dashingly handsome he nearly stole her breath. His gaze rested for a disturbingly long moment on Arabella, then slid to Georgiana. He inclined his head. "Miss Larwood, your presence has been requested in the drawing room. Something about a game of charades."

Georgiana clapped her hands together. "Oh, but I do love charades!" She started off, only to stop an instant later. "Arabella, what about you?"

Arabella gave a slight shake of her head. "Perhaps later." Her gaze returned to Justin. She frowned, rather puzzled. He had been charming and light and teasing during dinner. But the warmth he'd displayed throughout the day was gone. He seemed suddenly distant. Almost cold.

She struggled for something to say, feeling suddenly awkward. "Georgiana and I were just commenting how much you resemble your mother."

"Yes, I'm quite aware of that. But we all have our curses, don't we?"

His tone was no less than icy, his expression drawn in cold, frigid lines. He regarded the portrait unsmilingly.

Arabella floundered. "I'm sorry. Georgiana and I, we didn't mean to intrude where we should not—"

"Don't be silly. The gallery is hardly off-limits to guests." He drew his shoulders up tensely, then released a breath.

"I'm sorry, Arabella. I have a particular aversion to this portrait. Sebastian thinks it belongs here. Family and duty and all that." He grimaced. "My father had it removed when we were young. It was painted just before the scandal and he couldn't stand the sight of it."

Arabella frowned. "The scandal?"

"Oh, come. You don't have to be polite and pretend you don't know how my mother ran off with her lover."

Arabella blinked. "Her lover?"

Justin gave a mocking laugh. "Innocent Arabella. Yes, my mother had lovers—quite a number of them, I suspect. She was killed crossing the Channel with her lover of the moment."

"Oh," she said in a small voice. "I'm afraid I didn't know."

He eyed her. "Truly?"

"Truly." But she suddenly recalled how, the night of the Bennington ball, he'd mentioned his family and scandal.

"I'm surprised you didn't. These things have a way of resurfacing."

"Well, I didn't. I wasn't even born," she reminded him. "And I was often out of the country with my parents when I was young."

"I'd forgotten," he admitted. "Suffice it to say that Sebastian did a far better job of being both mother and father to Julianna and I when we were young than either of our parents."

"I'm sorry," Arabella murmured.

"Don't be." His tone was still rather curt. He stared at the image of his mother.

On unfamiliar ground, Arabella struggled for something to say. "I suppose that explains your closeness, then," she said softly. "When I was a child, I remember wanting a brother or sister so badly I would plead with Mama and Papa. But Mama had fallen ill with infection after I was born, and was never able to conceive again. Of course, it was some time before I understood why."

Still he said nothing. He hadn't taken his eyes from the portrait. He stared as if transfixed, his expression half-hurt, half-angry. Arabella had the oddest feeling he wasn't even aware of her presence.

His silence was beginning to scrape on her nerves.

She glanced wistfully up and down the gallery. "You're very lucky to have grown up in a place like this, though. Papa was always being called abroad for his missionary work, and it was exciting to travel to India and Africa, but we never really had a place to call home. We stayed with Aunt Grace when we were in England, and when I was in school. That was nice, but my cousins were older than I, and so I was the one always having to entertain myself. I should have loved to have had a home in the country like this. Not so grand, of course, but something cozy and—"

All at once she stopped. She'd succeeded in diverting his attention, at least. "I'm babbling, aren't I?"

"You are," was all he said.

A guarded tension defined his stance. Words seemed to dry up in her throat. She felt acutely lame. "And saying all the wrong things in the bargain, too, aren't I?"

She heard him inhale then release his breath as if he were striving mightily to relax. He gave a shake of his head; his gaze avoided hers. "It's not you. It's me, Arabella. Not you. I can be a beast sometimes."

"Yes, my Lord Vice," she agreed mildly. "You certainly can."

He startled her by taking both her hands within his, turning to face her directly. "Will you come onto the terrace with me? If I stay inside much longer, I—I feel like I might choke."

Arabella's lips parted. She gazed up at him. He

was taut and tight-lipped, his voice oddly strained. She didn't pretend to understand what he meant, yet there was a terrible, terrible tension within him. She could see it. She could *feel* it. What was behind it, she didn't know. She didn't care. All she knew was that if her mere presence could help ease it, then by God, she would help him.

She squeezed his fingers. "If that's what you want."

"It is." Arabella clung blindly to his hand as he led her quickly to the end of the portrait gallery, down a passageway, and through a door that took them to the rear of the house. In order to keep up with him, she was almost running. Only when they were outside did his pace slow.

They walked at a more leisurely pace now. The terrace ran the entire length of the house. Her hand was still anchored within his. Just thinking about it made her pulse skitter madly. Was Justin even aware of it? she wondered. She ignored the prick of disappointment. No doubt he'd forgotten, too preoccupied to even notice. But she liked the feel of his hand wrapped around hers, his grip warm and strong.

It was a clear, wonderful night, the temperature so mild she had no need of a wrap. Though the moon was no longer full, the lights from inside the house blazed a path for them to follow.

"Oh, look!" She pointed to the outline of a cherry tree on the edge of the orchard. "Now, that," she announced, "is the perfect tree for climbing. See the way the branches spread wide and hang low? Easy to simply leap up, grab hold, and swing a leg up."

Justin came to a halt. "My dear Miss Vicar, never say you used to climb trees when you were young." He arched a brow. "You?"

Arabella wrinkled her nose. "Oh, stop pretending to be shocked."

There was a small silence. "Actually, I was going to say I fell out of that tree once and broke my wrist."

Arabella didn't see the shadow that flickered across his face. "Well, I was never so clumsy," she went on breezily. "There was a tree much like that one at Uncle Joseph's estate near Yorkshire. I'll never forget the day my mother walked outside to find me hanging upside down, my skirts swirling about my head."

"I daresay that's probably not a feat every mother wishes to see her daughter engage in."

Arabella stole a glance at him. She was relieved to note some of the harshness had left his face. "Yes. My mother was quite horrified. And my father . . . I vow he's the gentlest soul on this earth. As I recall, that's the only time I ever heard him raise his voice to me. Though I certainly gave them both enough provocation," she added thoughtfully.

"Do they know you're the darling of the *ton*?"

Arabella lifted her gaze heavenward. "Well, I haven't mentioned it in my letters," she said dryly, "though I'm sure Aunt Grace has."

They walked on a bit farther, past a high stone

wall. The air was filled with the scent of roses. Justin paused, a wide stone bench behind him. The drawing room was nearby, casting out hazy fingerlings of light that etched his profile in silver.

When he released her hand, she felt curiously bereft. But they stood close, so near his scent eclipsed that of the roses. Man. Musk. Heat. All combined to send a tremor through her. Oh, Lord, he was so handsome he made her ache inside.

The merest hint of a smile curled his lips.

"What is it?" she murmured.

"I was thinking about the night I came here from London once. Sebastian and Devon were here. And I think—no, I am almost *certain* they were out here kissing when I arrived."

"Why is that so unusual? They do, after all, have two children."

His smile widened ever so slightly. "They weren't married then."

"Oh." Arabella felt her cheeks pinken.

Justin gave a husky laugh. "Don't look so shocked, Miss Vicar. Remind me sometime to tell you the tale of how those two ended up together. It's quite a story."

"Really? They're such a perfect couple. It's obvious they're very much in love."

"That they are," he agreed.

Her eyes widened. "I'm surprised to hear you say that."

"Why?"

"Well, I—I just assumed you didn't believe in love."

Justin made no comment.

"My parents are like that," she confided, her voice very low. "They look at each other and—and it's like no one else in the world exists, save the two of them. And yet, the truth is . . . my parents are so much in love that I—sometimes I almost feel like an outsider."

"I'm sure they love you very much, Arabella."

"Oh, they do. I know they do! But . . . I suppose I'm not making much sense." She gave an embarrassed laugh. "I don't know what I'm trying to say."

"You told Walter you would only marry for love," Justin said suddenly. "Is that why?"

She lifted her hands, then let them fall to her sides. "Yes. I can't imagine marrying someone I don't love. Can you?"

He merely raised his brows.

Arabella bit her lip. "Yes, yes, I know. You're hardly the person to ask. Men like you spend much of your adult life seeking to avoid marriage."

Justin crossed his arms across his chest. "Ah, Miss Vicar is getting testy now. Let us consider the requisites of a wife, then."

"Obviously she would be a diamond of the first water."

"Without question."

"Ah, then. So you would require a *beautiful*, docile, biddable maid."

"Beautiful, docile, and biddable, perhaps. But a maid?"

"Oh, so you prefer used goods?" She shot back an arch retort.

He gave her a wry smile. "Not used. That sounds so sordid. Let us say . . . experienced."

Well, at least she had succeeded in raising a smile. "Ah, yes, so you could engage in your licentious activities. But I would venture to say you would make a horrible groom."

"My brother said much the same thing once."

Arabella went on as if he hadn't spoken. "However, I do believe you would make an excellent father."

"What! Can it be true?" He feigned astonishment. "Why, Miss Vicar has just flattered me!"

"Oh, stop," she commanded. "You're very protective. You're good with children. It was very clear today with Geoffrey and Sophie."

"On to you, then." His tone was grave, but his eyes were alight. "What sort of man would you prefer to husband?"

"Well, a woman wants a man with more than good looks." It was her turn to needle him. "A man of fervent and not idle ambition."

"What, is that where poor Walter fell short?"

"No," Arabella muttered, "that was Phillip Wadsworth."

"I beg your pardon?"

She clenched her teeth. "Short. He was shorter than me, Justin. Must you make me say it? He only came to *here*." She gestured in the vicinity of her chin.

Justin laughed.

Her eyes flashed. "Must you make light of it?" She flounced away, so she didn't have to witness his mocking smile.

Silence drifted between them, as thick and heavy as the night.

"I'm sorry," he said quietly. "I didn't mean to be cruel." When she said nothing, he edged closer. "You're not crying again, are you?"

Mutely she shook her head.

"Then look at me. Please, sweetheart, look at me."

Sweetheart again, and spoken in a husky, tender note that made her tremble. Her eyes climbed slowly to his. His smile had evaporated.

His hands were on her waist, devastatingly large and warm, drawing her near.

Arabella's heart lurched. Her eyes widened. His were dark and heated.

"Justin," she gulped. "What are you doing?

"You're shivering. Don't be afraid, Arabella."

The trembling was spreading through her, to her limbs, to her very toes. In sweet confusion, she looked up at him. She remembered telling him that if he ever chanced to make her shiver from head to toe, it would be in disgust. But that was the furthest thing from her mind right now.

His head was lowering. As if . . . as if . . .

"I must be mad," he muttered.

"Why?" she asked wildly.

"Because I think I'm going to kiss you again."

His eyes seemed to burn clear through her.

"Oh, my," she said faintly.

"Why do you say that?" he demanded fiercely. "Why do you look like that?"

There was havoc on her skin, there where his hands rested. But most of all, there was havoc in her heart . . .

"Because I—I think I want you to."

Thirteen

His searing gaze trapped hers. "You shouldn't. I'm a rake. A scoundrel. Every one of those things you said I was."

Her fingertips crept to the front of his jacket. "I don't care, Justin. *I don't care.*"

God, he never should have brought her out here. She was such a contradiction—all prim, proper innocence combined with lush, earthy sensuality. And vulnerable . . . so very vulnerable. He'd forgotten how sensitive she was about her hair and her height. Indeed, she had cried about it last night. The memory stabbed at his heart. Proud, stubborn Arabella . . . didn't she know how lovely she was?

Her eyes were like sapphires, shining with moon dust. A red, silken curl tumbled over her shoulder. He longed to drag it around his fist and pull her close. And her mouth . . . the color of crushed roses, moist and dewy.

He burned inside. These past few days had been

nigh unbearable. It was harder and harder to be near her and not touch. Not yearn for her. And now, here in the dark, in the moonlight, he knew he hadn't a prayer of stopping himself. The devil might take his soul, but nothing would stop him.

With a groan he dragged her close. His mouth came down on hers.

With a breathy little sigh, she yielded, parting her lips beneath the fiery urgency of his. He felt himself swept back to that magical moment when he'd kissed her before. But this was so much better than what he remembered. He wasn't foxed and she wasn't shocked. Instead, she was sweet, almost unbearably sweet.

He braved a glance at her face. Her eyes were closed, her lashes, long and thick, dark crescents lying on her cheeks. But he knew if they were open, they'd be shining blue and heavenly and . . . God, she tasted like heaven and felt like the most tempting, delicious of sins. He could feel himself hurtling into a realm of pleasure—mind, body, soul.

He couldn't be slow and easy. His blood had begun to boil, hot and primitive, and he hadn't a prayer of stopping it. But Arabella didn't seem to care.

If it had been any other woman, he would have taken her right there on the bench. Ripped open his breeches to bare his hardness, and brought her down astride his thick, rigid erection, again and again until they both cried out in ecstasy. The erotic image shook him to the core.

But some brief remnant of sanity remained. This

was Arabella, young and sweetly naive. His conscience was screaming at him, but he didn't care.

A strong hand curled around the nape of her neck, tilting her face up to his more fully. He kissed her again, with hungry ferocity. With the other hand, a brazen fingertip traced the cream-laced edge of her low-cut bodice. Sweet Jesus, he could feel the tantalizing curve of her breasts.

A whimper escaped her lips, echoing in the back of his throat. His tongue circled hers, then traced the ridge of her teeth. She arched and the movement thrust her breasts against his chest more fully. Round and full. Soft yet firm. The contradiction was thrilling. Desire exploded in his veins. He ached with the need to taste her, touch her . . . *feel* her.

He whispered her name, the sound low and pleading and hoarse. "Let me touch you, Arabella. Let me see you."

His hand plunged into her bodice, cupping her breast. He squeezed that delicious fullness, aware of the way her nipple thrust against his palm, hard and peaked. He made a choked sound deep in his chest. She was trembling all over, he thought vaguely.

His mouth was on the side of her throat. "Arabella," he muttered raggedly, "you make me forget myself. Make me stop."

She moaned. "Why?"

He nipped the lobe of her ear. "You're an innocent."

"Yes . . ."

"And if we continue much longer, you won't be."

"Then perhaps we should stop," she said weakly.

But he didn't. *She* didn't.

His mouth returned to hers. She swayed against him. No longer content to merely feel, he slid her bodice down over her shoulder to bare her naked flesh. He wanted to touch her. Suckle her until she cried out her pleasure.

Near the terrace a door creaked open. Footsteps tapped on the flagstone. "Arabella?" sang out a gay, feminine voice. "Are you out here? We're being soundly trounced and we are in dire need of you—"

Arabella froze in his arms. Her eyes flicked open. They stared directly into his. "Georgiana!" she gasped. She jerked away, dragging her bodice up over her shoulder.

It was too late. Georgiana stood not three feet behind them, staring at them in wide-eyed horror, her dainty little mouth opened in shock.

But alas, that wasn't the worst of it.

Right beside her was Grace.

Throughout the many scrapes in which she had found herself embroiled over the years, there was none to compare with the way Arabella felt in that moment.

Aunt Grace spun around without a word. Round-eyed and speechless, clearly in a quandary, Georgiana ducked her head and hastened after her, back into the drawing room.

"Aunt Grace!" She started to charge forward. Justin caught her elbow and held her back.

"Wait," he warned. "Wait here."

Within seconds Aunt Grace reappeared. Uncle Joseph was at her side, his expression black as a thundercloud.

"Arabella! Christ, girl, have you no sense? Must you always make a spectacle of yourself?"

It wasn't his way to bluster and rage—his rare outburst made her shatter inside.

She was vaguely aware of Justin stiffening beside her. "If anyone is making a spectacle, my lord, I daresay it is you. May I suggest you lower your voice?"

Joseph's face turned purple. "And may I suggest you remove your hand from my niece?"

"Certainly." Justin's hand fell away from her arm.

"Now. Have the two of you anything to say for yourselves?"

Justin's mouth twisted. "What, are explanations truly necessary?"

"Spare me your sarcasm, boy!" Joseph snapped.

Justin's eyes flickered. "Nothing happened," he said curtly.

"Really? It is my understanding you had your hand on my niece's—"

"Uncle Joseph!" Arabella cried.

She was mortified. She wanted to die. She wanted to sink through the ground, never to be seen or heard from again, lost in the middle of the earth. Lost anywhere, anywhere but here. A feeling of utter shame consumed her. And Aunt Grace looked ready to faint.

By then Sebastian had appeared as well. "Is there a problem?" he asked, glancing from Joseph to Justin.

"A regrettable incident," Justin stated smoothly.

Joseph growled in his throat. His hands fisted. He looked ready to explode.

Sebastian stepped between them. "I suspect no one here wishes to cause a scene," he stated calmly, "so perhaps the four of you would like to adjourn to my study for further discussion."

"Not now." This came from Grace, her voice low and thick with tears. "Joseph, I cannot do this now. Perhaps in the morning."

"Grace, that's an excellent idea." Sebastian was every bit the gracious arbiter. "A good night's sleep may improve everyone's disposition. Say . . . seven o'clock sharp? The other guests won't be breakfasting until half-past eight. That should assure your privacy."

"I suppose that will do," Joseph said coldly.

Grace clutched at her husband's arm. "Joseph, please, take me to our room."

Joseph covered his wife's hand. "Of course, love." Raising his head, he gazed straight at Justin. "I trust you'll be present to settle this, young man."

"Oh, you need not worry, my lord." Justin's tone was pure frost. "I shall be there."

Arabella bit her lip. Aunt Grace had yet to meet her gaze, and it appeared she had no intention of doing so. Hesitating, Arabella glanced back at Justin. His features were set in implacable lines. He remained where he was.

"Arabella!" Her uncle rapped out her name.

Feeling crushed inside, Arabella had no choice but to follow.

Inside the drawing room, the game of charades was in full swing. At their entrance, however, the game came to a halt. Every eye in the room rested on them. Joseph cleared his throat.

"I fear the day has been a tiring one for my wife and my niece. We shall be retiring early."

Did anyone believe it? Arabella was afraid to look. As they left, she was aware of more than a few speculative gazes following them. Someone whispered; she couldn't tell who. As for Georgiana, there was no sign of her friend.

Her stomach was churning as they mounted the stairs. Her reputation was ruined. *She* was ruined. Her aunt returning inside to fetch Uncle Joseph, and their subsequent exit to the terrace would not have gone unnoticed . . . their abrupt departure from the party. There were bound to be questions. Rumors . . . An almost hysterical laugh bubbled up in her throat as Arabella collapsed in her room.

Oh, my, she thought, but I should be glad. The Unattainable has just been dethroned . . .

She was barely inside when someone tapped on the door. Gingerly Arabella opened it.

It was Georgiana.

"Arabella! Are you all right? What happened?" Georgiana grabbed her hand and pulled her across to the bed. "I saw your aunt whisper to your uncle and the two of them go out to the terrace. I was so rattled I didn't wait to see more."

Arabella's throat clogged tight. "Uncle Joseph was furious," she admitted. "Then Sebastian must have realized something was wrong, because he came out as well . . . We're to meet before breakfast." She shook her head, anguished. "I'm such a fool! I didn't even think . . . I should never have gone out to the terrace with Justin. Aunt Grace was utterly distraught. She wouldn't even look at me. Neither of them said a word to me after we left the terrace. I'm so ashamed," she admitted. "And so embarrassed. Everyone knows something is amiss . . . Oh, Georgiana, I fear I've disgraced the family."

Georgiana squeezed her hand. "It's all my fault. I should never have charged out the way I did. If I'd known that . . . that . . ."

Arabella smiled slightly. "That I was kissing Justin?"

Georgiana's cheeks pinkened. "Well, yes . . . if I'd known, Arabella, I'd have left well enough alone. I'm so sorry! It's all my fault."

"Of course it isn't." Arabella made the reply automatically. Dear God, what *had* she been thinking? To allow Justin to kiss her in that hot, consuming way that made her feel as if she were melting? Not only that, but to allow him to bare her breast. Her flesh had seemed to swell and burn; she'd wanted to feel his fingers, there on the very tip . . .

"Arabella?"

It was clear from Georgiana's expression it wasn't her first attempt to snare her attention.

Georgiana searched her face. "I asked what it was like."

"What?" Arabella said faintly.

"You know," Georgiana blurted. "Being kissed!"

Being kissed? Or being kissed by Justin Sterling? For Arabella had the very distinct sensation that being kissed by any other man would not have been at all the same as being kissed by Justin. For Justin's kiss had been wonder and magic. Bliss and . . .

Georgiana clapped her hands to her cheeks in horror. "Oh. Oh!" she cried. "I cannot believe I asked you that! Oh, do forgive me, Arabella!"

Surprisingly, Arabella laughed. Georgiana did as well, and Arabella walked her to the door a few minutes later. There Georgiana gave her a quick, fierce hug.

"Do not fret, Arabella. Whatever happens tomorrow morning, it will be for the best. I just know it."

Arabella's eyes softened. She bade her friend good night, closed the door and leaned against it with a sigh. If only she could be as certain as Georgiana . . .

What was it Justin had said to Sebastian? A regrettable incident, he'd called it. An odd little ache pierced her heart. What was it he regretted? That he'd kissed her? Or that they had been caught?

She had no answer. And suddenly she wasn't sure she *wanted* an answer.

What was done was done. It was too late to change it. As for tomorrow, all she could do was hope that Georgiana was right . . . that all would turn out for the best.

Not so very much later, in another part of the house, Justin had just closed the draperies in his room when a knock sounded on the door. He opened it to find Sebastian on the threshold. In his hands was a tray topped with a bottle and two finely etched crystal glasses.

Justin opened the door wider and gestured Sebastian inside. "Let me guess," he drawled. "You've come to dispense advice."

Sebastian slid the tray onto the table nested between two chairs that flanked the fireplace. "Not advice per se. But I thought you might like to talk."

Rolling his eyes, Justin settled himself in one of the chairs. "I can do without either, but I won't say no to the brandy."

Sebastian chuckled. "I thought not. It's your favorite—and my finest."

Tugging off his cravat, Justin tossed it aside, watching as Sebastian tipped the neck of the bottle into each of the glasses, pouring a generous portion into each. Sebastian handed one to Justin, then settled back in his chair.

Justin drained it in one swallow, balanced the empty glass on his knee, and glanced at his brother. "I suppose now is when you intend to inquire as to my intentions tomorrow."

"I would not presume to tell you what to do," Sebastian responded politely, "though I must say"—he cocked his head toward the window—"there *is* something about that terrace, a moonlit night . . . and the right woman, isn't there?"

Justin groaned. "Christ, now you're beginning to sound like the duchess."

Sebastian's mouth quirked. "And my wife," he added.

"I suppose you find this vastly amusing, don't you?" Scowling, Justin held out his empty glass.

Sebastian obliged him by refilling it. "Not at all."

Justin stared into the liquid. "I lost my head," he muttered. "I have no one to blame but myself."

"Unfortunately, this is not a matter that can be tossed aside. For I suspect that Arabella is not a woman of the world, shall we say."

"She is not," Justin admitted.

"Add to that the fact that the Burwells are a well-respected family."

Justin grimaced. "Must you always be so logical?"

Sebastian shrugged. "The way I see it, you either marry her or you do not. It's as simple as that, really."

It's not simple at all! Justin nearly argued.

"But if you aren't of a mind to marry her," Sebastian added cheerfully, "I suppose it won't be long before someone does. I hear she's had three offers already."

It wasn't three, it was four! Justin bit back the

words and instead sent Sebastian a withering stare.

He clenched his teeth. Goddammit, he didn't like having his hand forced. What man would? But it was just as he'd told Sebastian. He'd lost his head. And he could be no less than honest with himself! In that moment, in the moonlight, with the darkness swirling all around, no power on earth could have stopped him from taking Arabella in his arms. From bending his head to hers and kissing lips so temptingly sweet and soft. From tasting . . . and touching . . . And if Grace and Georgiana hadn't come upon them, he would have gone on kissing her. He would have gone on touching her, not wanting to stop, unable to stop . . .

He took a burning swallow of brandy. "Sebastian." He spoke without meeting his brother's eyes, his tone very low. "What if I hurt her?"

"You can't think like that," Sebastian said sternly.

Justin gave a shake of his head. "I can't help it. Sebastian, I . . ." He fell silent, his mind whirling. He hesitated, battling an unfamiliar uncertainty inside.

Something flickered in Sebastian's eyes. "You're thinking about Father, aren't you?" he said quietly.

"Yes." The word almost choked him. He should tell Sebastian, he realized. Dear God, wasn't it time Sebastian knew that he—Justin—had killed their father? Something dark and bleak began to seep through him. An acrid bitterness seared his being, and the words refused to come.

"Whatever it is you're thinking," Sebastian observed with soft deliberation, "don't. Father and Mother created their own hell. It had nothing to do with us. Surely you know that."

It had nothing to do with us. Something twisted inside him. What if Sebastian was wrong? What if it did?

"Sebastian," he said tonelessly. "Didn't you ever wonder . . . if Mother . . . if Father . . . if we, the three of us—you, Julianna, and I—" His jaw tensed. "Oh, hell. *Hell*. Forget it. Forget I said anything."

Sebastian gave him a long, slow look. "Whatever it is that's bothering you, Justin, we can't undo it, any of it. When we were young, there were days I prefer to forget, days I'll *never* forget. But when I think of our childhood, the one thing that stands out in my mind is this. We were lucky, the three of us, to have each other." He smiled slightly. "The past is over and done. It's time to look to the future. *Your* future. You deserve to be happy, Justin. Don't you know that yet?"

Justin's throat felt scratchy. "And what of Julianna? She deserves happiness, too. And for all that she claims she is, I wonder if it's really true."

A shadow slipped over Sebastian's features. "I know," he murmured.

Justin's face went hard. "When I think of what that bastard Thomas did to her . . . I wish I'd called him out—"

"That wouldn't have solved a thing," Sebastian

reminded him. "But I'm quite aware of what you mean. Still, I have to believe that happiness will come to her, too, Justin. There are times we must trust in a power greater than our own."

Justin raised a brow. "Your patience never ceases to amaze me."

Sebastian chuckled. "If my wife were here, I think she'd dispute such a notion completely." He got to his feet and reached for the tray.

Justin immediately raised his now-empty glass. "Leave the bottle!" he advised.

Sebastian laughed. "Careful, brother. If you're not in my study at seven sharp, I'm quite certain Joseph won't be inclined to generosity. And I don't particularly relish the thought of standing in as your second."

It wouldn't come to that, Justin decided, watching the door close. Whatever he was, whatever he had been, he couldn't . . . *wouldn't* . . . embarrass Arabella further.

Not only that, but Sebastian was right. If he didn't marry her, someone else would. And the prospect of Arabella with another man was . . . well, unthinkable, really.

Marriage, he thought, turning the word over in his mind. *Marriage.*

He was petrified, he realized. And yet, she sparked a fire inside him, in his blood, in his very soul. His awareness of her was ever-present. Her scent. Her heat. He could not be near her without longing to touch her the way he had tonight. He wanted more.

From the night he'd first seen her at the Farthingale ball, not one day had gone by that he hadn't thought of her. Wanted to be with her, the way he had tonight. He wanted to make her his, make her belong to him, feel her softness yield beneath him. The very thought of being with her like that—the way he wanted—brought the blood rising beneath his skin. But how long would it last?

Faithfulness and fidelity . . . was it any wonder he was terrified? He had little experience with such virtues—with *any* virtue! There had been no reason. And—he wasn't Sebastian. He was like his mother. *His mother . . .*

But he couldn't bear the thought of hurting Arabella. By God, he could not.

His desire was real, he reminded himself. He craved Arabella with every fiber of his soul. Her love was beyond his reach. He must be practical, he reiterated. Arabella would never love a rogue like him. But if he could not have love, he could have desire and passion, and by God, it would have to do.

And with that realization came the answer he sought, and some semblance of peace.

Justin knew, without question, precisely what he must do.

Fourteen

At five minutes before the hour of seven the next morning, Arabella, Aunt Grace, and Uncle Joseph were ensconced in Sebastian's study. A black pall hung in the air. Arabella sat on the edge of a chair, her hands clasped in her lap. Aunt Grace and Uncle Joseph sat on the sofa opposite her. Uncle Joseph was stiff-lipped and stoic. It wasn't his way to bluster and rage—she almost wished he would! And Aunt Grace . . . her eyes were red-rimmed and swollen. She'd been weeping.

And all because of her.

The door opened. Justin strode inside. He seated himself in the wing chair next to Arabella's.

Uncle Joseph wasted no time in niceties. He addressed himself to Justin. "In the absence of Arabella's parents, her aunt and I stand in their place. And it seems we have a dilemma on our hands."

Arabella leaned forward. "Uncle, Georgiana won't say anything. She's my friend—"

"Whether she will or will not is of no consequence!" Uncle Joseph's tone was blistering. "*I* know, Arabella. Your aunt knows! This is not one of your petty childhood pranks, to be dismissed and swept under the rug."

Beside her, Justin spoke. "This wasn't her fault, my lord. The blame is entirely mine," he stated bluntly. "I seduced her."

Arabella's eyes flew wide. "What!" she cried. "But you—"

"Hush!" Both Justin and Uncle Joseph thundered at the same time.

Chastened, subdued, Arabella sank back in her chair. Her gaze slid to Justin. He appeared totally calm and unruffled.

Uncle Joseph transferred his burning regard to Justin. "My niece has been compromised by you, sir." Uncle Joseph's fingers rapped on the arm of the sofa. "I demand satisfaction."

Justin inclined his head. "And you shall have it, my lord."

Arabella made a faint, choked sound in her throat. No, she thought wildly. Surely not a duel . . .

"I have dishonored your niece and damaged her reputation irreparably. Clearly, there is only one thing to be done. Therefore, I will marry her."

Uncle Joseph's tone was hard. "It had best be soon, for I warn you, I'll brook no delays."

Arabella's mouth opened and closed. The two of them were talking as if she weren't even present. Either she was going mad, or *they* were. Her heart was hammering so that she could scarcely think. So many emotions were roiling through her breast, she couldn't breathe. She couldn't even speak.

And did her ears play her false? Surely it was so. Surely Justin hadn't just said . . .

"I'll see that a special license is obtained, my lord. Your niece and I will be wed as soon as it can be arranged."

Stunned, she watched helplessly as the two men rose and shook hands.

By afternoon, everyone at the house party knew of the betrothal. When presented with the news, Devon promptly threw her arms around Arabella. "Oh, I knew it! I just knew you were the one."

Sebastian was less effusive, bowing over her hand, but there was a warm twinkle in his gray eyes. "I'm glad it's you," he said simply.

Throughout the congratulations, Justin merely smiled, but said very little. Arabella's heart sank like a stone. She promptly berated herself. It wasn't as if he were in love with her. Dear God, at times she wondered if he even liked her! What foolishness was this, that she expected him to act as if he were smitten?

With profuse apologies, the Burwells headed back to London at once—to see to the wedding preparations, as Aunt Grace declared. To Arabella, it all seemed like a dream. As if she saw everything from a place outside herself.

Two days later, Uncle Joseph informed her the license had been procured. The ceremony was set for three days hence.

Even then it didn't seem real.

The day before the wedding, Arabella sat in the salon, her mind whirling. Her aunt was out seeing to the flowers she'd ordered. Indeed, she thought numbly, Aunt Grace was the only one excited about the upcoming nuptials. The tea she'd poured sat on the tray, cold and untouched. It was difficult to believe that only a week earlier, they had arrived at Thurston Hall . . .

There was a light rap on the door. It was Ames, the butler. "Miss, you have a caller."

"I'd rather not see anyone, Ames."

He was unusually insistent. "You may wish to reconsider, miss."

Arabella sighed. "Ames, please—"

"It's your fiancé, miss."

Fiancé. Her mouth went dry. Never in the world had she dreamed Justin would be called *that*. Her heart was suddenly crashing wildly about her chest, while her mind had gone completely still.

"Miss?" inquired Ames. "If you wish, I can tell him you're indisposed."

It spun through her mind that that probably wouldn't work with Justin. He'd probably barge his way inside anyway.

She took a deep, cleansing breath. "Please show him in, Ames."

"Very good, miss."

A moment later, Justin strolled in. He was clad in

riding clothes, black boots that hugged his calves, buff leather breeches that clung to his powerful physique like a second skin.

"I hope you don't mind my calling on you unannounced."

"Not at all," she murmured. She indicated the striped silk damask chair across from her. "Please sit."

"I thought we should see each other at least once before tomorrow." He stripped off his riding gloves as he spoke, laying them on the rosewood table.

Nervous awareness collected inside her. His hands, she noticed vaguely, were like the rest of him: long, lean, elegant, yet devastatingly masculine. Her face began to heat. Her mind veered in a direction and she had no hope of restraining it. What, she wondered crazily, would the rest of him be like, beneath the civilized veneer of clothing? He was surprisingly strong. That night at Thurston Hall when he'd carried her to her room, she'd been amazed at how easily he lifted her . . . The memory displayed a surprising tendency to linger. She'd found herself thinking of it at the most unexpected times.

"Arabella?"

Her gaze jerked back to his face. "Yes?" Her voice was thin and thready.

He was watching her steadily. "I asked if you were ready for the wedding tomorrow."

Arabella didn't answer. She couldn't. It seemed her tongue was suddenly an unwieldy instrument she hadn't learned to master. Her mind was still all awhirl. By this time tomorrow, she and Justin would be husband and wife. She would be his wife. *His wife*. Oh, God, it would be heaven . . . No, it would be hell. Wife or no, every woman would still want him. Worse, he would want every woman . . .

"Yes . . . No. I—I don't know what I mean." Lord, she was an idiot. "It's all so unreal. So unexpected." Her tone was unsteady. She gathered every ounce of her courage and met his gaze. "Why?" she asked baldly. "Why are you doing this? Why did you agree to marry me?"

A brow arched. "Agree?" he said mildly. "Arabella, it may have escaped your notice, but it was my idea, not your uncle's, that we wed."

How could he be so calm, so matter-of-fact, when she felt as if she were flying apart inside?

"I should have thought you would bolt at the thought of marriage!" she blurted.

He gave her a long, slow look. Carefully he said, "I am many things, Arabella, but I am not a coward."

She drew a deep, almost painful breath. "How did it come to this?" she asked, the pitch of her voice almost a whisper. "We—we don't suit. You know it as well as I. And I know you had no intentions of marrying anyone, let alone me."

Justin tensed. His tone was almost dangerously low. "Why do you say that?"

"You're the most notorious rake in London. Everyone knows that rakes do everything they can to avoid being caught in the parson's mousetrap."

Justin leaned back. It took supreme effort of will

to prevent his jaw from tightening. My God, could she make it any more plain that she had no desire to wed him? Perhaps this was justice, he decided blackly, for his many sins.

"You are a lady, Arabella. The fact that in the past I've chosen to involve myself with women who were not always so proper has no bearing on our circumstances. I dishonored you and—"

"But you didn't dishonor me, not really! We—we simply kissed."

"We did more than that. I touched your—"

Her face flamed. "Must you remind me?"

"My conduct was hardly that of a gentleman toward a lady. We were caught in a compromising situation, and I will not allow it to ruin you. I have more respect for you than that."

His tone was curt. Arabella blinked. She hadn't thought he had any respect for anything or anyone. Well, that wasn't quite right. He respected his brother, and his sister-in-law, or at least she thought he did . . . For the first time, she realized there was much she had always assumed about this man.

And much she didn't know. Whether that was bad or good remained to be seen.

"I'm sorry," she murmured. "I didn't mean to insult you."

His expression told her he wasn't so sure.

She floundered. "I just . . . I don't want you to hate me, Justin. I don't want you to resent me."

His expression underwent a lightning transformation. Before she knew what he was about, he was beside her on the settee and had seized both her hands in his. "How odd that you should say that. Because that's the very thing I was going to say to *you.*" He gave a lopsided smile. "Indeed, that's the real reason I stopped by."

The feel of his hands around hers was oddly reassuring. Their gazes met, and something else, too. She didn't know precisely what it was, but it made her heart stumble and her pulse hasten.

But the next instant she sighed wistfully. "I just wish my mother and father could be here. I doubt the letter has even reached them by now."

He squeezed her fingers. "I know. And for that *I'm* sorry. But your uncle will brook no delays. He'll have my head if we wait. Besides . . . I think I prefer it this way."

Arabella frowned. "Why?" Oh, no doubt he feared that if they waited, he would reconsider. And then where would she be?

A smile began to dally about his lips. "It's certainly easier to simply marry you than court you. Now, at least, I won't have to fend off the horde of admirers surrounding you at every event."

She wrinkled her nose. "This is the first time you've even called on me," she said wryly.

"And after tomorrow, there'll be no need. You'll be right in my own house whenever I want you."

Whenever I want you. Precisely what he meant by that, Arabella wasn't certain. Nor, she decided shakily, was she prepared to speculate.

"I don't even know where you live," she murmured.

"I have a townhouse on Berkeley Square. I think

you'll find it quite charming." Out in the foyer, the longcase clock chimed the hour. "As much as I'd love to stay and chat, I must go. I've a business appointment soon."

Arabella's brows shot high. "You? A business appointment?"

He chuckled at her doubtful expression. "Actually, I've been quite successful. My most recent acquisition is a bank in Scotland. So you see, you're marrying a stodgily respectable gentleman after all."

Stodgy? That was the last word on earth she would use to describe Justin Sterling. Her lips quirked. "A pity," she replied mildly, "for here I was, looking forward to taming a scoundrel!"

"Oh, there's plenty of that left in me," came his brash rejoinder. The wholly wicked light that appeared in his eyes should have served as warning. She should have known better than to challenge a man like him! Before she knew it, strong arms swept around her and dragged her onto his lap. One hand anchored firmly around her waist, and with the other he captured her chin. Her lips parted in sweet surprise as his mouth closed over hers. He proceeded to kiss her mouth with a thoroughness that made the world spin and drove the very air from her lungs.

Her head was still whirling when he rose and set her on her feet, so much so that she had to clutch at his forearms for support.

He righted her, his hands large and warm on her waist. "All right now?"

Arabella nodded and reluctantly opened her eyes.

To her shock, his easygoing smile had vanished. In its stead was an expression so intense, so fierce, she caught her breath. "What is it?"

"I was just thinking."

"*What?*"

His gaze scoured her features, one by one, until at last it came to rest on her lips. "The next time I kiss you, you'll be my wife."

Fifteen

The ceremony began at precisely three o'clock the next afternoon at her aunt and uncle's townhouse. Other than Georgiana, who was her maid of honor, and Georgiana's parents, those present were limited to family—Sebastian, Devon, Julianna, the twins, Arabella's aunt, her cousins and their respective families. The only exception was the Dowager Duchess of Carrington. Sebastian stood as Justin's best man. Reverend Lynch, who had been a friend of her father's for many years and whom Arabella had known since childhood, presided.

She entered the drawing room on Uncle Joseph's arm. Her knees were quaking so badly she marveled that she could even walk. Her eyes widened when they paused at the threshold. Aunt Grace had decorated the room with dozens and dozens of fragrant red and white roses.

Yet in the very next heartbeat, her eyes strayed inevitably to Justin, looking very tall, very dark, splendidly attired in dark chocolate that made his light eyes blaze like emeralds. His carriage was proudly erect, but his expression was unreadable. He neither smiled nor frowned. His demeanor was solemnly intent, and she felt herself suddenly plunged into turmoil. They weren't even wed . . . did he regret it already?

To spend a lifetime joined to someone who would never love her . . . oh, God, how could she do it? she thought desperately. How could she bear it? This was her wedding day. *Her wedding day.* From the time she'd been old enough to entertain the notion of her own marriage, she had always been so certain that should this day come to pass, she would be hopelessly, helplessly in love with her husband . . . and he with her. But this wasn't the love match she'd wanted. Nothing had happened as it should have, and here she stood, mere inches away from the man who would be her husband for the rest of her days, teetering on the brink of the rest of her life . . .

A week ago she'd have sworn she most certainly did *not* love Justin Sterling, that she could never love a man such as he. But all at once she wasn't so certain . . . Did she love him? *Did she?* A hand seemed to close about her heart and squeeze. Within her churned a mass of such quivering, jumbling emotions that in all truth, she wasn't certain she knew up from down, right from left, the moon from the stars.

Yet one thing stood out above all. The thought that Justin might never love her caused a crushing pain in her chest. It hurt as nothing in the world ever had . . . as nothing ever would.

She had the most hysterical desire to turn and run screaming from the house.

Instead, three steps closed the distance between her and Justin. Three small steps and her life would be forever changed. They were at once the hardest—and the easiest—she'd ever taken.

Reverend Lynch cleared his throat. "Dearly beloved," he intoned, "we are gathered here together in the sight of God . . ."

The rest of the ceremony passed in a blur. The next thing she knew, Reverend Lynch had turned to Justin.

"Wilt thou have this woman as thy wedded wife, to live together after God's ordinance, in the holy estate of matrimony? Wilt thou love her, comfort her, honor and keep her, in sickness and in health, and forsaking all others keep thee only unto her as long as ye both shall live?"

"I will."

Quiet as his tone was, beneath was a note of such gravity, such clear, unfaltering conviction that Arabella was momentarily stunned. Reverend Lynch was speaking again, but she scarcely heard. Why, if one were not familiar with both the man and his reputation, it would be only too easy to believe he meant every word!

Reverend Lynch had paused.

Almost belatedly it occurred to her it was her turn. Her hands began to shake. The small bouquet of roses she held was quaking so that they were slipping and sliding against the silk of her gown . . .

The only sound in the room.

Arabella couldn't help it. Her gaze sped straight to Justin. He regarded her, one dark brow cocked arrogantly aslant, a glint in his emerald eyes, as if in a silent dare.

Her chin came up. "I will," she heard herself say all in a rush, then wondered madly if she sounded as tremulous and terrified and elated as she felt inside.

The next thing she knew, the reverend announced, "You may kiss the bride."

It was done.

Justin turned to her. Her mind recorded a fleeting impression of burning green eyes, and then hard arms encircled her. His mouth captured hers in a kiss that stole her breath and her heart and made a thousand shivers play over her skin. Would it always be like this? she wondered achingly. She hoped so. She prayed so.

The world was still spinning when at last he lifted his mouth. She blinked up at him. "Oh, my," she whispered unthinkingly.

He threw back his head and laughed, the rogue, for all to see and hear! Arabella promptly fixed him with what she hoped was a suitably admonishing frown.

He was undaunted. To her shock, he proceeded to kiss her again—and just as rousingly.

This time when she opened her eyes, it was to the sound of applause!

Arabella felt a fiery blush start at her neck and seep upward. "You are a scoundrel," she accused without heat.

He slipped her hand into the crook of his elbow. "Well, I did warn you, didn't I?"

A celebratory dinner followed. Uncle Joseph's stiff, formal manner toward Justin had thawed considerably by the time the main course was served, and for that, Arabella was glad. But almost before she knew it, dinner was over and it was time to go.

Near the door, the family gathered around to wish them well. It was a wild scene. The twins were squealing and darting everywhere, along with her cousins' little ones. There was much laughing and jesting. Aunt Grace was the last to step forward. She was smiling, but her eyes were glistening. In her hand was a dainty handkerchief.

At the sight of her aunt's tears, a hot ache filled her chest. Blindly Arabella reached out. She buried her face against Aunt Grace's cap. "Aunt Grace," she whispered on a watery half-sob, "I'm so sorry you didn't get to plan a proper wedding."

Grace hugged her fiercely. "It's all right, dear," she whispered back, the words meant for Arabella's ears alone. "You can make up for it by allowing me to plan the christening of your firstborn."

Justin had fallen back several steps to speak with Sebastian. He chose that exact moment to glance over at her. Over her aunt's shoulder, their eyes met. His were bland, but Arabella was quite certain hers were huge. She swallowed and averted her gaze, her mouth dry as bone. She had hardly dared to think beyond the wedding, let alone to children. Would Justin even *want* children? Her mind skidded forward to the night ahead. For that matter, would he claim his husbandly rights?

Her breath wavered. The kiss they'd shared earlier blazed high in her mind. Her entire body went hot. Justin was an extremely healthy, virile man who was known for his sexual appetites. Unless she was mistaken, she decided cautiously, she was fairly certain he would . . .

The subject was still very much on her mind when the carriage rolled up before a brick-fronted home on Berkeley Square a short time later.

Justin turned to her. "I thought we'd spend the night here," he said in a casual, offhand manner. "Given the speedy nature of our wedding, I'm afraid there simply wasn't time to plan a lengthy wedding trip. But if you like, I thought we might leave in the morning for a week or so in Bath. I hope that meets with your agreement."

"Oh, I adore Bath," Arabella said brightly. "It's particularly lovely this time of year."

No, Justin thought vaguely. What was particularly lovely was her . . .

A footman opened the carriage door.

He tore his gaze from her lips. "Come. Let me show you my—" He stopped short. "Your new home."

An odd little thrill went through Arabella. Some of her apprehension fled.

Her fingers on his elbow, Justin introduced her to the staff, then led her through the house. It was utterly charming, roomier than she expected without being ostentatious, the furnishings comfortably elegant without being pretentious. She exclaimed her pleasure, and though Justin said nothing, she could tell he was pleased.

They ended in what he explained was his bedchamber, a large, masculine room done up in maroon and browns, dominated by an immense four-poster bed.

She tried not to stare at it, but she couldn't stop herself, either.

"Are you hungry?"

She actually jumped. "Oh, no." Her voice was high-pitched and strained. "I couldn't eat a bite after that huge dinner." Somehow she dragged her eyes from the bed.

She was nervous, Justin knew. He sensed it. He could hear it in her voice, see it in the way her gaze grazed his, only to flit immediately away. He wanted to laugh, but wasn't quite sure he dared. Wedding night jitters were to be expected. He'd married a gently bred maid, after all, despite her claim that she knew very well how the act of procreation was done. Indeed, he wondered if that had been sheer bravado.

"Well, then, I expect you'd like some privacy. I'll send Annie in."

Arabella blinked. "Annie? Annie is here?"

He nodded. "I managed to persuade your aunt to allow her to enter my employment instead."

"Thank you, Justin." She paused, oddly touched by the gesture. "That was very kind of you."

He inclined his head. "It was my pleasure."

He left, and Annie came in to help her from her wedding gown. A small trunk containing some of her things had apparently been transferred earlier in the day. It was from there that Annie removed the nightgown and wrapper she would wear tonight. Her presence was comforting, but after brushing her hair, Annie promptly withdrew.

Alone, Arabella rose from the dressing table and began to pace, only to catch sight of herself in the cheval mirror sitting in the corner. Her jaw literally dropped open. She regarded herself in dismay. A stranger stared back at her, a stranger with burnished red waves tumbling about her shoulders and down her back. The nightgown she wore was but a wisp of sheer lace—and hardly worth the exorbitant price she knew Aunt Grace had paid. There were tiny little ties at the shoulders and at the waist. Her entire body was clearly visible, from the ivory sheen of her skin, the rouge of her nipples, to the downy triangle of reddish gold curls between her thighs.

It was a gown meant to entice. To tempt. To. . . . Lord, but her mind almost refused to form the word . . . to titillate. She felt quite . . . oh, sweet mercy, quite scandalous! Fast on the heels of that thought came another.

Would Justin like it? She wanted him to, she realized with a pang. She wanted him to be entranced. Enthralled. She longed for it with an intensity that made her ache inside.

It was in the midst of that very thought that the door opened and closed.

Arabella turned. The urge to clamp her arms over herself was almost more than she could stand. Yet she didn't shirk from Justin's gaze. It slid over her from head to toe, leaving no part of her untouched. Holding her breath, she stood her ground, the hopes of a hundred prayers and dreams lifting her heart and the corners of her lips.

Sixteen

Justin didn't move. He couldn't. He couldn't even breathe. She looked like an angel in white, her eyes brilliant and blue and shining like heaven itself. The air of utter purity that surrounded her stabbed at him like the prick of a knife.

Oh, Christ. What had he done? She was his wife. His *wife*. And she didn't deserve this. She didn't deserve a blackguard like him. Pain ripped through him like the slash of a blade. He was weak-kneed . . . weak-hearted. It was all he could do not to spin around and run, for he despised himself in that instant. He was black inside, as black as she was sweet and innocent. And though she might not see it tonight, she would someday. She would hate him if she knew what he was, what he'd done. Hate him, and he couldn't stand the thought.

Through sheer dint of will, he dragged his gaze from the vision before him.

Arabella didn't know what was wrong, only that something *was*. But she saw the way his eyes darkened, like a cloud across the sun, the way the muscles of his face seemed to freeze. Her smile wilted . . . along with her heart.

What folly had seized hold of her? Her new husband was the handsomest man in all England. And what was she but a graceless, awkward clod of a woman whom he would never have wed if Aunt Grace and Georgiana hadn't caught them kissing? How could she have possibly deluded herself into believing he wanted *her*?

She felt as if a sick coil of dread were slowly strangling her. Clasping her hands in a white-knuckled grip before her, she spoke. "I'm sorry," she said wildly. "I just assumed that since it was our wedding night . . . But no one need know if you prefer that we are not . . . not . . . intimate."

"Arabella—"

"I know a marriage is supposed to be consummated in order for it to be valid, but really, it's no one else's business but ours—"

Justin had gone very still. "Arabella, what the hell are you babbling about?"

There was a stark, empty hole where her heart should have been. Her throat ached with the effort it took to hold back tears. She wouldn't cry, she told herself. She absolutely would not.

She plunged on. "I understand. Truly I do. I know that I'm not beautiful like your other women. I'm quite aware I cannot hope to compare with—"

His expression underwent a lightning transformation. "Damnation!" he swore. "What nonsense is this?"

"I saw you, Justin. I saw! You looked at me as if you could not stand the sight of me!"

He made a sound low in his throat. "Come here," he demanded.

"I will not." Through some miracle, she managed to hold on to a shred of dignity. "Just . . . just tell me what to do. Where I should sleep . . ."

He crossed to her. Her hands were clenched like fists; he had to nearly pry them apart. Her skin was ice-cold, but he took her fingers firmly within his. Her expression was still painfully half-defiant, half-wounded.

This was all his fault, he realized tautly. How could he explain? He wasn't sure he could find the right words. It wasn't the thought of being with one woman that frightened him—it was fear of failing *her*. Arabella. He didn't know how or when it had happened, but somehow she had become very precious to him. He was terrified that he would do something to drive her away.

If he was wise, he would let her go this instant. But he was who he was. A greedy, selfish bastard. And he knew, beyond anything, that there was no way he would allow her to leave this room.

He took a deep, unsteady breath, caught in the grip of some vast, powerful emotion he could not deny. He knew then. He knew why he had married her: This was what he wanted. What he'd wanted all along. This night. This moment. This *woman*.

"It wasn't you," he said quietly. "It *isn't* you. It's *me*. I walked in, and there you were, looking so much like an angel that . . . well, you know my past. You know my reputation. I'm a devil. Everyone knows it. *You* know it. And I know it wasn't the wedding you dreamed of. I know I'm not the husband you dreamed of. But I would not—I *will* not—dishonor you."

The pitch of his voice had gone very low. "We can't undo it, any of it. Not now. It's too late. We're married. You're my wife, Arabella. And strange as it sounds, in a way, I think we've been heading toward this night almost from the moment I walked into the Farthingale ball and saw you again."

As he spoke, his palm slid against hers, square and strong and warm. Arabella glanced down, her every sense keenly attuned to the way his fingers caught at hers, lean and strong and dark. She swallowed, aware of everything inside going painfully weak.

"Look at me, sweetheart."

Sweetheart. Arabella's heart squeezed. She lifted tremulous eyes to his.

Her throat closed. The unexpected tenderness she glimpsed on his face caught her squarely in the chest. Oh, God, he was going to make her cry after all . . .

"Justin," she said unevenly. "Oh, Justin—"

"Listen, sweet. Please listen. You are . . . I know of no other word to describe you except . . . exquisite. Don't you know that?" His fingers weaved through hers.

"Oh, but I'm not—"

"Oh, yes, you are. You *are*. And when I lay with you tonight it will not be out of duty, or because our marriage must be consummated, or any other such silly reason. It will be because I want you. *You,* my darling Arabella. Because I desire you with every fiber of my soul. Is that understood?"

Her eyes clung to his. "Yes." It was but a breath of sound.

Her uncertainty was like an arrow to the heart. He decided then and there that perhaps he could show her much better.

He rested his forehead against hers. "Ah," he said huskily, "but you don't sound terribly certain that your husband has every intention of being *intimate* with his wife." A pause. "Perhaps we are doing far too much talking and not enough . . . *doing*."

Bemused, Arabella stared straight into green eyes alight with the merest glimmer of amusement. "What?"

His hands were already on the ties of her wrapper. Before she could stop him, the garment puddled around her feet. In the span of a heartbeat, his frank, unhurried appraisal made her flush self-consciously. It was most disconcerting standing here almost naked when he was still fully clothed.

"A most delightful gown," he remarked almost conversationally, "that I suspect is not your usual nighttime attire. Is it new?"

She felt herself nod. "Aunt Grace picked it out," she said faintly.

He smiled slowly. "Remind me to thank Aunt Grace for her impeccable taste." Strong hands descending to her shoulders, he continued in the same lazy vein. "For now, I think we can do without this . . . extraneous apparel."

Before the statement was finished, she was naked. Her gasp of shock at finding herself so was swallowed by hard male lips warm upon hers, a long, devouring kiss that made her tremble inside. She was scarcely aware when he lifted her and carried her to the bed. The world and everything in it slipped away whenever he kissed her. Twining her arms around his neck, she pressed herself against him, but a sharp button digging into the soft flesh of her breast made her draw back.

Justin lifted his mouth reluctantly, only to be confronted by a disgruntled frown. "What?" he said.

"It's most disconcerting to be lying here naked," she pointed out almost grudgingly, "when you are not."

Justin chuckled. God, but she said the most outrageous things! It had been in his mind to go slow and easy, to take his time and not rush her, though God knew, the sight of her in that gown tested his control sorely. The taste of her mouth was intoxicating, the scent of her dizzying. And holding her lithe, naked form against him, it was all he could do to stop his hands and mouth from running wild, to keep himself from ripping his trousers apart, baring his shaft, and bringing her down upon him hard and fast standing right in the middle of his chamber.

Hardly the way to take an innocent, much less his wife.

"A discontented bride," he teased. "How remiss of me."

Sitting up, he quickly shed his jacket, shirt, and boots. Standing with his back to the bed, he stripped off his trousers, straightened, and turned . . .

Which put his member at the exact level of his wife's unabashedly curious regard.

Or at least it had been until that moment. Her eyes widened. Her gaze on his rigid erection made him swell even more. Her mouth parted in a shocked little O. Her tongue came out to dampen her lips. Oh, sweet Christ, now, *there* was a tortuous sight.

Stretching out beside her, he forced a light tone. "My eager bride is suddenly not so eager. You've never seen a naked man before, have you, sweetheart? Let alone one who is clearly anxious to acquaint himself with the intimacy of bedding his wife for the first time?"

Arabella buried her head in the springy dark hair on his chest, muttering something unintelligible. He hadn't known a blush could encompass the whole of someone's body, but he did now.

Justin took a breath. He was chafing inside, for holding back his desires was an entirely new experience for him. Fiery curls spilled over her shoulders and breasts. Peeping between the silken strands, pale, pink-tipped flesh rose and fell with every tremulous breath, a sight that tempted him almost past bearing.

"I saw you with your hair down at Thurston Hall, the night McElroy accosted you. I thought I'd never seen anything quite so lovely then," he said softly. Lifting a ribbon of reddish hair around his fist, he brought it to his lips, inhaling deeply of the scent of roses and lavender, then carefully arranged it over one silken shoulder. "It's glorious," he murmured.

"Thank you." Her voice was very small. She had to will herself not to jump when he anchored a hand on her hip, but he did nothing but trace an idle pattern over her skin. It was true the sight of Justin naked made the bottom drop out of her belly. But his body was . . . extraordinary. As extraordinarily perfect as his features. The contours of his shoulders were sculpted and hard, his skin gleaming and smooth, the muscles of his arms lean and taut. A wiry thicket of dense, dark hair covered his chest and belly.

Her gaze moved slowly up the corded column of his neck to his face. Her breath slowed to a trickle. Unbidden, her eyes traced the chiseled beauty of his features, one by one. "You're very handsome, too," she whispered. A tremulous smile touched her lips. "Aunt Grace even thinks so."

His brows shot high. "Aunt Grace?" he echoed.

"Oh, yes," she assured him. "She said she might

be getting on in years, but her eyesight had yet to fail her."

He laughed huskily, a sound that made her heart turn over. Emboldened, Arabella stretched out a hand to touch his face.

Strong fingers closed about her wrist, thwarting her in mid-reach. Arabella had the oddest sensation she'd done something wrong, but he pressed a kiss to her palm, then settled it in the center of his chest. Her hand looked very small and white and dainty amid the dense, dark fur. The sight sent a thrill all through her. Justin's hand, meanwhile, settled on the curve of her waist, drawing her close. The other slipped beneath the fall of her hair and brought her mouth to his.

He fed on her mouth endlessly, long, languorous kisses that made her spine turn to water. Her fingers clutched at his shoulders. Beneath her fingertips, his flesh was firm and hard, warm like the sun. She sighed when he ran his tongue behind the shell of her ear. "I love it when you kiss me," she confided breathlessly. "You kiss very well. But then, I expect you know that."

His mouth returned to hers. "Thank you," he said against her lips. "I don't believe anyone has ever told me that." She could feel him smiling. "But there's a great deal more to kissing than just here"—he kissed each corner of her mouth—"and here . . . and here." He sucked in the center of her lip.

Arabella felt suddenly reckless. "Perhaps you should show me."

"An excellent idea." His head ducked low. He

pressed his open mouth against the slender grace of her throat, allowing his tongue to gauge the dancing rhythm of her pulse.

"Mmmm. That's very nice, Justin."

Nice? Justin thought in amazement. He wanted much more than . . . *nice*.

Leaning back, he allowed his gaze to wander the entire sweet length of her, lingering on the fleece between her thighs, the pale, unblemished flesh of her breasts, round and delectably full, hidden beneath a screen of reddish curls. With a wicked smile, he brushed aside her hair. Those pink, peeping nipples were an enticement he could no longer ignore. Arabella blushed furiously but she didn't retreat from either his touch or his scrutiny.

Still smiling, he bowed his head low. He loved the way her eyes widened when his mouth traced the pouting thrust of one breast. Her breathing hastened when he paused at the jutting peak.

He grazed it with his mouth, the merest caress.

Her breath sucked in.

Somehow he'd always known that beneath her prim, proper exterior was the body of a temptress. She was perfect. Absolutely perfect. Greedy now, he closed his hands around her luscious breasts. His palms filled with her jutting flesh so that her nipples were offered up to him in wanton invitation.

He kissed first one, then the other. With the last, he curled his tongue around and around the rouged center in a slow, lazy circle, leaving it wet and shiny and quiveringly erect.

She gasped aloud.

"More?" he asked silkily.

Her lips parted. Her mouth formed the word *yes*, but not the sound.

He obliged.

It excited Justin beyond bearing, knowing that she watched in dazed fascination as his mouth closed around the dark, straining peak, licking. Tugging. Her hand slid up to cup his nape; he felt her fingers tighten, as if to trap him and hold him in place.

Arabella couldn't speak. She couldn't even breathe. It was bliss. Sheer bliss. She was drowning in sheer sensation. It was as if lightning flashed, there at the peaks of her breasts. Heat showered through her. And now there was an unfamiliar questing deep in her belly. Her legs shifted restlessly. There was something missing, something more . . . She didn't quite know what it was . . .

But Justin did. His blood thundering, his rod pulsing, he caught her against him. His mouth captured hers again, a scalding, demanding kiss that sent blistering flames through every part of him. But when lean fingers traced a shattering path across the hollow of her belly, she tore her mouth away. Her hand clamped down on his.

"Wait," she said wildly. "Wait!"

His head came up. Her stricken little cry very nearly failed to penetrate the crimson haze of desire surrounding him.

He closed his eyes, willing away the pulse of desire clamoring in his veins. "This is going too fast for you, isn't it?"

"A little," she admitted. She was flustered, embarrassed, suddenly uncertain. She had liked what he was doing, but . . . "I'm afraid, Justin. I'm afraid."

The clamor in his head began to ease. He brushed a stray curl from her flushed cheek. Suddenly he was the one who hesitated. "I cannot promise there will be no pain. But it's my understanding that—"

"No. It's not that." She was adamant.

"What, then?" Puzzled, he searched her features.

You make women fall in love with you, she nearly blurted. *You're making* me *fall in love with you.* "I know you've been with many women. I—I know that and I accept it." An elusive hurt speared her heart, but she ruthlessly swept it aside. "From your own lips, you said that you prefer a woman of experience. And I have none. I've never even kissed anyone but you. I feel inadequate. Inept, to be perfectly honest. What if I'm not the passionate sort? I don't want you to be disappointed. I don't want you to be displeased."

There. It was out. She held her breath and waited.

Justin was suddenly furious with himself. Christ, was there anything he hadn't said or done that wouldn't come back to haunt him?

He looked at her, at her quivering lips, the way her beautiful blue eyes were half-pleading, half-hurt. A swell of some powerful, possessive emotion rose like a tide inside him, even as a sizzle of outrage shot through him at the thought of Arabella kissing another man. He'd never felt possessive of a woman before—had never imagined he would—and it came as something of a shock, just as his jealousy had. Did all new husbands feel like this? And yet . . . he discovered he liked feeling possessive of her. He liked knowing she belonged to him.

He ran the pad of his thumb over her lips. "You worry for nothing, Arabella."

"Do I? I—I liked what you were doing, Justin. Truly I did. But I want to please you, too."

His finger against the center of her mouth stemmed her speech.

"You will. You do."

"But how can you be certain?"

For a moment, a smile quirked at the corner of his lips. "Because I can feel you here, sweetheart." Catching her hand, deliberately he guided cool fingers around his rigid arousal, keeping them there with the pressure of his for the span of a heartbeat. Her eyes widened, along with his smile.

All at once, his smile faded. His glance sheared into hers. "But most of all," he said in a voice that made her tremble all over again, "I can feel you here." Kissing her fingertips, he guided her other hand directly over his heart. "And I must be honest, sweetheart. That's never happened with any woman but you."

Tears misted her vision. "Justin," she said, her voice catching breathlessly. "Oh, Justin." Slender arms wound around his neck. She kissed him with all the tremulous feelings held deep in her soul.

When at last she drew back, he smoothed her hair. An odd, half-smile curled his lips.

"I have a confession to make, as well."

"What?"

"I'm afraid, too."

"You?" She gave a lopsided grin. "I don't believe that."

"Oh, but I am," he assured her gravely. "You see, I've never lain with a virgin before. I want this night to be unforgettable. For both of us."

Arabella gazed at him, mesmerized by his expression, stunned by the tenderness in his tone. She felt as if he'd reached clear into her heart and laid it bare.

"Justin," she said shakily, some painfully sweet emotion catching in her breast. "You make me feel so special."

"You *are* special. Unique, and—and I've never known a woman quite like you, my darling Arabella."

My darling Arabella. She loved the low, melting way he said her name.

"I like knowing you've never kissed another man," he went on, a low rough timbre in his tone that thrilled her to the tip of her toes. "I like knowing you've never seen another man naked. I like knowing I'm the first man to lay with you." There was a shattering pause. "And now, I do believe it's time we took up where we left off before. Does that meet with your approval, my dear wife?"

Her eyes were shining. "Yes, my lord. Oh, yes."

The words acted like a floodgate flung wide. Twining his fingers in her hair, he turned her mouth up to his, bringing fiery red curls tangling about the both of them. He took her lips in a soul-blistering kiss that tasted of unmistakable male hunger and unleashed her own hunger. His breath filled her mouth . . . as he would fill her body.

He toyed with the tips of her breasts, wringing a cry from deep in her chest. A lean hand coursed over the hollow of her belly, tangling in the soft fleece above her thighs, initiating a daring rhythm that left her utterly weak. She gasped but did not fight it. It felt too good. *He* felt too good. Instead, her thighs parted helplessly.

There was more. So much more. Daring fingers traced the cleft of her womanhood, again and again. Flames shot through her as his thumb joined the evocative play, circling a tiny nub of flesh that seemed to swell and grow and weep. It was acutely, achingly sensitive. She shivered both inside and out, her mind a tangle of pure sensation. Showering currents raced through her, centered *there,* in the place he now claimed with blatant possessiveness, taunting, circling, pressing. She gasped as a finger slid deep inside her, a tauntingly wicked parody of the act to follow. She began to pant, writhing and twisting, searching for something . . . what it was she didn't know, only that she was close. When it came, that burst of pleasure, tiny, whimpering cries tore from her throat.

Her eyes opened, smoky and dazed. Justin's face filled her vision, her world. Imprisoned in the searing web of his gaze, riveted by the blistering hunger on his face, her heart knocked wildly as he spread her thighs with his knees and knelt before her. One hand on his rod, he leaned forward, rubbing himself against her fiery red curls. Arabella couldn't tear her gaze from his organ. He was rigidly, stiffly erect. Even as the thought vaulted through her mind, he was inside her. Within her.

She gasped.

At the sound, Justin froze. He could feel her maidenhead now, the fragile membrane that sealed her virginity, butted up against the most sensitive part of his body, the part that needed her most. He nearly groaned, for it was tearing him apart, the need to thrust deep and hard, to lose himself in her clinging wet heat. But this was the test, the moment he dreaded. He didn't know how to be slow and easy, he didn't know if he could.

Though it nearly killed him, he gritted his teeth and withdrew. A shaky laugh emerged at the sight of his innocent little wife. She looked half-terrified, half-mesmerized. Justin glanced down as well and nearly groaned. The rounded spear of his sex was sleek and damp, slick with her liquid heat. Passion soared.

Bracing himself on his elbows, he kissed her lips. "Tell me if I hurt you," he muttered, a touch of ragged harshness to his voice. He eased forward again, little by little, until he was resting again against her maidenhead. God, it felt good . . . too good, the walls of her cavern clinging tight to his swollen erection.

"I will," she promised, a wisp of a smile on her lips. "Please, Justin, just take me now. Make me your wife . . . make me yours."

He moaned. There was no help for it now. There was such trust in her gaze, such naked desire in her heated, shattering plea that he could hold back no longer. Blinded by passion, he thrust forward until at last he lay embedded full and tight within her.

"Oh, God," she whispered.

Justin's breath scraped harsh and ragged. "Do not swear."

Yet in those words lay a world of frustration . . . a world of passion . . . a world of feeling. Burying his head against her shoulder, he calmed his racing heart and allowed her body to adjust to the feel of him embedded deep inside her heat. So acutely sensitized was he that he was just a hair away from spilling his seed.

"I cannot help it." She gave a tiny shake of her head. "Justin, this feels so—so . . ."

He kissed the arch of her throat, then raised his head. His eyes found hers. "I do not hurt you?" That he could speak was a miracle.

Her smile was blindingly sweet. "No," she breathed. "God, no . . ."

Her smile faded. She guided his mouth down to hers, twining her tongue around his and driving him half-wild.

Slowly he began to move. His hands slid beneath her buttocks, bringing her closer still. Unable to stop himself, he drove in to the hilt, loving the way she clutched at him, the way her nails dug into the skin of his shoulders. Her hips were churning, seeking his again and again. Faster and faster he plunged, torrid and intense, loving the way she wrapped her arms and legs around him and clung.

He cast back his head, the cords in his neck taut. She scorched him, both inside and out. "Arabella," he said thickly. And then again, "*Arabella!*"

In some faraway corner, he remembered that night at Vauxhall Gardens when he'd first kissed her . . . He'd told himself that what he felt was lust. Passion. That she was the one woman who denied him, thus, she was the one woman he wanted, the one woman he must have.

But nothing had prepared him for this moment. For this night. Nothing had prepared him for *her*. For it was impossibly sweet . . . *she* was impossibly sweet. The world was blazing, and stars were shattering, falling down all around.

The night exploded . . . and so did he.

Seventeen

One week later they returned to London from Bath.

From the achingly tender moment Justin made her his, Arabella harbored no regrets, no doubts. Marrying Justin had been the right choice—not that there had been much choice in the matter. But in truth, that was of little consequence. There would never be another man for her, never in this world. She'd promised herself she would marry only for love . . .

And she had.

She knew, deep within the depths of her soul, that Justin Sterling was the only man she would *ever* love.

But it was a secret tucked close within her breast, a secret that would remain undisclosed for now. There existed between them an easy camaraderie that she suspected had come as a pleasant surprise to both of them. Arabella was loath to do anything to upset the balance. She didn't know if Justin wanted her love; she didn't know if he could ever return her love.

But he desired her—she had learned that much in nearly two weeks of marriage. Not a single night had passed that he did not make love to her. Beneath his tutelage Arabella discovered there were many sides of lovemaking—playful, hot, tender. She experienced them all at the hands of her new husband, and Justin appeared quite delighted at her response. Some nights he claimed her with a burning intensity, an almost wild, possessive frenzy that thrilled her beyond reason. At others he was almost painfully slow, so meltingly sweet and tender she wanted to cry. But always . . . always he made her feel as if she were the only woman on earth. Arabella could hold nothing back, nor did she wish to.

From that very first night came the yearning hope that from such a beginning, the seeds of love might grow. And she would continue to nurse the hope that her love could tame the wildness in him.

Indeed, there was every reason to believe it already had. Upon their return from Bath, Arabella was rather startled to find her things had been moved into Justin's bedchamber. There was an adjoining one, and she had somehow convinced herself that was the one she would occupy. Arabella knew it was the norm for Society husbands and wives to occupy different chambers, though her own parents slept in the same bed and always had, as did Aunt Grace and Uncle Joseph. Perhaps it was her way of staving off disappointment, for she didn't want to hope for too much . . . too soon.

She turned to find him watching her, his arms crossed over his chest.

"I hope you don't mind," he said with a supremely arrogant arch of his brow, "but I find I dislike the idea of separate bedchambers for husband and wife." Despite his formal tone, there was a faint light simmering in his eyes.

Hers were suddenly sparkling mischievously. She bowed her head, her tone in perfect accord. "Sir, I am in complete agreement."

They returned downstairs, where a brief repast had been prepared for the noonday meal. They had just finished when Arthur, Justin's butler, appeared with a silver tray. He set it before his master with a flourish.

"You were missed, my lord."

Justin began to sift through the stack of invitations. "Apparently word of our wedding has spread quickly," he commented. "Our presence is much in demand." He studied the gilt-edged invitation in his hand. "The Farthingales are having a fete tonight. I daresay it shall be quite the crush. Shall we make our debut as husband and wife there?"

The Farthingales' was where they had met again. Did he recall? Arabella wasn't certain, for he sounded rather blasé. Disappointment shot through her, quickly masked. "Must we?" she murmured.

Justin glanced at her inquiringly.

Arabella pulled a face. "You just said it will be quite the crush."

"Ah, yes. Lady Farthingale spares no half-measures when it comes to her parties. Everyone who is anyone will be there."

"Wonderful. And everyone who is anyone will be talking about *us*. Lord, but I detest gossip!"

"And I submit there is only one way to squelch gossip. Besides, why delay the inevitable? The sooner everyone sees us together and discovers we are happily wed, the sooner we can quiet those wagging tongues."

Did he mock her? Arabella looked at him sharply, but his demeanor was one of utter calm.

"What if there are questions?"

He chuckled. "I'm sure there will be, given the precipitous nature of our wedding. But who says we must answer them?"

Arabella released a breath. "I suppose you're right. And there is one thing that shall give me a great deal of pleasure." She smiled with sudden brilliance.

"And what is that?"

"I shall never be called The Unattainable again!"

"True enough." He leaned over and gave her a perfunctory kiss on the cheek. "I regret that I've some business at the bank I must attend to this afternoon. I fear it won't wait. Will you be all right if I leave you alone for a while?"

She smiled. "I hardly need a keeper, my lord."

"Good. If you need anything, just ring for Arthur."

Arabella nodded. Once he was gone, she rose and wandered about the house rather aimlessly. She considered a nap but quickly discarded the idea; in truth, the notion came to her out of boredom, certainly not because she was tired. It occurred to her then that she and Justin had been in each other's company almost constantly since their wedding day. And now that he was gone, she was—oh, but she couldn't deny it!—rather lonely. She missed him, she realized, then immediately wondered if he missed her . . .

Oh, but what foolishness was this? She chided herself sternly and retraced her path down the stairs. At the door to Justin's study, she paused. Would he mind if she used his desk? She owed Mama and Papa a letter, she realized guiltily. She'd never been the type of correspondent to write daily when her parents were away, but there had never been a lapse of more than a week, either. Feeling a bit of an interloper, she made her way into the room and sat in the leather chair. Opening the drawer, she found a few sheets of vellum. Dipping a quill into a small pot of ink, she began to write.

Dear Mama and Papa,

I hope this letter finds you well. Justin and I have just returned from Bath. The weather was surely delightful.

She stopped. What the devil was she doing? Mama and Papa would not want to hear about the weather in Bath.

Taking a breath, she tore the sheet in half and began anew. It proved more difficult than she imagined, for somehow the right words simply would not come. The process was repeated three more times until she was satisfied with what she'd written. Putting aside the quill, she read her efforts.

Dear Mama and Papa,

I trust the two of you are well. I know the news of my marriage must have come as quite a shock, being so sudden, as it were. You may have heard tales of my husband, but I know what others do not. Justin is a good man—the best of men, the perfect husband for me. And so I pray you, do not worry. I assure you, I am the happiest of brides. I look forward to the day when we are all together again and you may see for yourself.

Your loving daughter,
Arabella

Twice more she reread the letter.

She halted. All at once the words began to waver. She struggled to bring them into focus, but it was no use. She saw them through a watery mist. A terrible ache filled her chest, even as her eyes filled and overflowed. She bent her head, trying to will the tears away. But alas, she blinked. A single teardrop skidded down her cheek and splashed onto the vellum, smearing the ink. She gave a stricken sound, for now the letter was hopelessly ruined . . .

That was how Justin found her.

He stared, for an instant unable to believe what he was seeing. Her head was bowed low, her shoulders were shaking, and the tiny little sound she made wrenched at his heart.

He approached. She had yet to be aware of his presence, and so he spoke. "Arabella?" he said tentatively.

Her head jerked up. "Justin!" she cried. "I didn't hear you come in!"

He'd startled her, he realized. It took an effort to steady his voice. He'd hurried home, anxious to see her, impatient with even this brief absence. All he wanted was to take her in his arms and kiss her lips. The last thing he'd expected was *this*.

"What's wrong, Arabella?"

She began to babble. "Why, nothing. Nothing at all. You'll have to forgive me, I fear. I didn't mean to intrude. I was just dashing off a note to . . . to Mama and Papa."

Justin eyed the pile of torn stationery, then the single sheet that still sat in the center of the desk. Whatever possessed him, he couldn't say. Reaching out, he picked it up.

"Justin!" she cried. "That letter is private!"

Justin made no answer. Quickly he scanned it. A

teardrop stained the ink, a teardrop in the shape of a heart. Seeing it, he felt his own heart grow cold.

Slowly he shifted his eyes back to Arabella's face. With his thumb he blotted the dampness from her cheek and held it up.

His gaze never left hers. "Blind I am not," he said, his tone very low. "And while the business of being a husband is new to me, I am quite sure this is not a sign of the happiest of brides."

She snatched the letter from his grasp and clamped it to her breast. When she would have stepped around him, he caught her arm.

Coolly she faced him, her lips pressed together.

Bemused, confused, and frustrated, he stared at her. "What, have you nothing to say?"

"What would you like me to say?"

"I would like for you to tell me what the bloody hell is wrong!"

"There is no need for such language, Justin."

"The hell there isn't!" he exploded. "Why can't you tell me what's wrong?"

Her gaze flitted away. Her lips trembled. For one awful moment, he was certain she would burst into tears. She bowed her head low, and an empty silence yawned between them.

"It's nothing," she said in a rush, her tone very low.

"Nothing," he repeated. "I return home to find my wife in tears, and you say it's nothing? God's blood, I thought something terrible had happened! I thought . . . Christ, I don't know what I thought!"

Still she looked away, everywhere but at him. "Please release me, Justin. I should like a bit of privacy to recover myself, if you don't mind."

Her dismissal cut him to the quick. But Justin knew what was wrong. Clearly she was unhappy. Clearly she regretted their marriage. The letter to her parents proclaimed her happiness . . . yet her behavior told the tale only too well.

His mouth tight, he released her. "Very well, then."

She whirled, clearly anxious to be quit of him.

His voice stopped her just before she reached the door. "We'll leave for the Farthingales' at half-past seven."

He saw the way her back stiffened before she turned back to him. "I prefer to stay at home tonight," she stated with implicit politeness.

Justin was already shaking his head. "I'm afraid that's not an option, my love. You see, I chanced to see Lord Farthingale and several of his friends while I was out. I mentioned we would be in attendance tonight. If we are not, that will surely set tongues to wagging. And I understood you to say that's the very thing you wish to avoid, is it not?"

Clearly she did not appreciate his reminder. She glared her displeasure. "As you wish, then."

Shortly before eight o'clock, their carriage rolled to a halt before the Farthingale mansion. Arabella was staring dully out the window in the opposite direction.

"We've arrived," Justin stated flatly.

A footman opened the door and assisted her out.

Not a word had passed between them in the carriage. The tension was stifling. Justin was cool and distant; he'd said barely a word since the incident in the study.

In all her days, she didn't know when she'd been so miserable. Pride alone stayed her tears, sheer willpower her trepidation.

They had no sooner set foot inside the ballroom than they were immediately surrounded. There were congratulations and well-wishes—but off to the right, someone smirked.

"Aren't you the lucky gent, to succeed with The Unattainable where the others failed, eh, Sterling?"

Oh, and to think she'd been convinced she would never be called The Unattainable again!

Beside her, Justin gave an easy laugh. He made a great show of curling her hand possessively into his elbow and covering it with his. "Ah, but my wife is no ordinary woman. I knew I must get her to the altar as fast as I could—and so I did."

"Why, whatever do you mean, McElroy?" cried a female voice. "There are many of us who wonder how *she* managed to capture the handsomest man in all England!"

There was an answering snicker from a beauteous blonde dressed in green. "Perhaps the better question is how she will manage to keep him!"

An elegant turbaned head turned in the direction of both women. There came the distinct thump of a cane. "A pity that has escaped your own marriage," proclaimed a familiar voice. "Why, I've heard it said 'tis a marvel you and your beloved still manage to recall each other's names. Furthermore, had you been given the privilege of witnessing their first kiss as husband and wife—as I was—I daresay not a soul here would presume to question their devotion to each other."

Arabella blinked. A part of her wanted to applaud the Dowager Duchess of Carrington. Another part of her wanted to march over to the beauteous little blonde and bloody her pretty little nose—hardly a ladylike reaction.

Her gaze slid to Justin's features, only to discover one dark brow hiked in wicked amusement. He gave a little salute to the duchess, then lowered his mouth to her ear. His lips brushed the curve of her cheek as he spoke for her benefit alone. "I would suggest another demonstration is in order, but that was well said, was it not? Besides, who better to have as our staunchest defender than the Dowager Duchess of Carrington, eh, my love? Now, what say we greet our host and hostess?"

Arabella bit her lip as they walked away. "She's outrageous."

"And revels in it, too," he agreed. "If ever there's a woman to have as your champion, it's the duchess." He laughed softly. "She wields her cane like a weapon. It's a sight unlike any other. I give you fair warning, Arabella, should you see it come up, leap back and stand clear."

"Her cane?" Arabella queried. "I rather thought it was her tongue she wielded like a weapon."

"That, too, and between them, you understand why few dare challenge such a formidable opponent."

"Well, I like her," Arabella announced.

"Yes, I do believe you two are rather alike," Justin observed.

Justin remained at her side throughout most of the evening. To all appearances, he no doubt presented a thoroughly attentive husband, for he retained a possessive hand at her elbow, bending his head close whenever she spoke, as if he hung upon her every word.

But neither had forgotten the argument that preceded their arrival. She sensed it with everything she possessed, and it made her ache inside. She longed for the closeness that had marked their week in Bath. To make matters worse, for the life of her, she couldn't explain her behavior, not even to herself! She had no idea what had made her cry, only that something had.

She managed to maintain her composure, however. The muscles of her face began to ache from smiling, but above all, she had no intention of causing further gossip.

Lord Farthingale approached. "May I steal your husband away for a moment? I'm sharing a bottle of my best brandy with several of the gentlemen and I should like to offer a toast to the happy groom."

Ah, if he only knew, Arabella thought half-hysterically. Lightly she said, "Who am I to keep you gentlemen from such an occasion?"

Farthingale grinned. "I shan't keep him away long, I promise."

Arabella chatted with several acquaintances, then moved to stand near a marble column at the far side of the ballroom. It was then she spotted Georgiana, who gave a wave and joined her.

"Arabella! How are you?" Georgiana laughed. "Oh, I confess it seems so odd to think of you as a married lady now!"

Arabella wanted to scream, certain she could not endure one more comment about her new marital state. But she gave herself a mental kick. Georgiana was the one person who would know something was amiss if she was not careful.

"I may be married," she said lightly, "but I hardly consider myself a matron."

Georgiana frowned. "I say, are you feeling quite the thing?"

"Splendid," Arabella lied cheerfully, "though it has been a very full day. We only arrived back from Bath at noonday, you know."

They chatted for some time, and made plans to go shopping next week. It had been quite a while and Justin still hadn't returned. Arabella scanned the ballroom.

Georgiana saw and laughed. "Such an anxious bride," Georgiana teased. "There he is."

Arabella frowned. "Where?"

"Coming this way . . . Oh, but now I see Lady Dunsbrook has stopped him."

Arabella's heart seemed to trip. "Agatha Dunsbrook?"

"Yes. I didn't know the two of you were acquainted."

"We're not," Arabella said quickly. "I believe I've heard the name, though."

Indeed, Arabella thought vaguely, it was true. For she suddenly remembered vividly the night of the masquerade at Vauxhall Gardens, the conversation she'd overheard about Justin . . . and his many mistresses. What was it they had said?

It would not be beyond reason to say that he's bedded down with fully half the women here tonight, now, would it?

And this woman among them.

She couldn't stop the sheer, stark pain that wrenched at her insides. Nor could she tear her gaze away from Agatha Dunsbrook.

She could scarcely imagine anyone more beautiful. Soft, blond ringlets were caught up on her crown. Petite, Agatha did not even reach Justin's shoulder. She was, Arabella decided, a study in grace and loveliness, all the things that she could never be.

Tipping her glass to her lips, she drained the champagne.

"I met her last week," Georgiana went on. "I do not intend to be mean-spirited, but I confess, I really did not care for her. Do you remember Henrietta Carlson?"

"Implicitly," came Arabella's response.

"Well, she put me in mind of Henrietta."

Which was not a good thing. It was one thing to be pretty. After all, Georgiana was pretty *and* sweet. But to be pretty and unkind . . .

"Oh, I hear my name," Georgiana said. "I shall see you next week, if not before, love."

Arabella bade her good-bye. Her attention returned to Justin, who was still with Agatha. Even as she watched, Agatha tiptoed her fingertips so they snuggled into Justin's elbow. She stepped closer, then reached up to touch Justin's cheek.

Agatha has her eye on him again, one of the women had said.

Ah, but Arabella could well believe it, for the gesture was shamelessly bold.

She felt dizzy. Weak. It was the champagne, she thought hazily. Hauling in a breath, she forced herself to look away, gathering herself in hand.

In that instant, Arabella made a vow to herself.

She would not be rash. She would not be hasty. But she would not allow Agatha Dunsbrook to make a fool of her, either.

In three seconds, if Agatha Dunsbrook was still with her husband—by God, *her* husband—she would march over and pry Agatha's pink little fingers from her husband's arm, then wrap her own around Agatha's pretty little neck. At the thought, one hand began to flex.

One.

Two.

Three.

She looked up. Neither Justin nor Agatha was in sight.

"Not getting tipsy again, are we?"

Her husband stood before her. Taking her empty champagne glass, he gave it to a passing footman.

Arabella regarded him unsmilingly. His gaze sharpened. "Are you unwell?"

Slowly she let out her breath. "I'm fine," she said with a shake of her head. "Truly, I am."

He studied her, as if to assess the truth of her statement. "Do you realize," he said softly, "we are standing in the very place where we renewed our acquaintance last month?"

Arabella bit her lip. "I didn't think you'd remember."

He cocked a brow. "How could I forget?"

"I was hiding from Walter that night," she confided. "I was afraid he was going to propose."

"And instead I found you. Instead *I* proposed."

Their eyes locked.

Agatha was forgotten. *Everything* was forgotten. She wanted to throw herself against him and start the day all over again. Forget that stupid, silly argument . . .

He caught her hand within his and raised it. He did not kiss it, but held it suspended so close to his she could feel the moist warmth of his breath upon her skin.

She smiled slightly. "What, sir, are you going to lick me again like you did the last time?"

"Your memory errs," he said immediately. "I bit you the first time. I licked you the last time." The corners of his lips flirted at a smile. He retained possession of her hand. "Ah, I see more than a few heads turning in our direction. Should I do so again, it might cause more talk."

"Ah, but we are wed now."

He kissed her knuckles, then weaved his fingers through hers. "You tempt me, sweet. But I warn you, I would not be content with tasting merely the inside of your wrist. Why, I vow I would lick you all the way up to your lips, and there I would feast." With his free hand he traced a flaming line up and down the length of her bare arm, exposed above elbow-length lace gloves.

The prospect sent the blood rushing to her cheeks. "Justin," she said faintly, "as you just noted, we have an audience."

"I anticipate the moment when we *don't*."

"You shouldn't say things like that," she stated weakly.

"Why not? As *you* just pointed out, we are wed. I can say such things knowing you won't slap me."

"Yes, but still . . . Stop looking at me like that!"

"Like what?"

"As if . . ." Hot color rose from her throat to her cheeks; she could feel its betraying heat.

"As if I should like to devour you inch by inch?"

"Yes!"

"And I shall. But that, I fear, must come later."

She could feel everything inside going weak. "Are you making advances toward me, my lord?"

"I once promised that when I did, you should know it."

"Yes, and you shall give husbands a bad name, should you appear quite taken with your wife."

"Perhaps because it's true."

Arabella's throat constricted. When he gazed at her the way he did just now, it made her stomach plummet clear to her feet and her pulse race as if she'd run a very great distance. He made her feel as if she were the only woman on this earth. Was that his secret? Was this how he captivated so many women?

"Indeed," he murmured, "I do believe it's time to take our leave."

Arabella did not argue. The night was almost over, and she was suddenly anxious to be home—in Justin's arms.

In the foyer, they waited for the carriage to be brought around. Behind them, someone coughed. Both she and Justin turned at the same time.

"Walter!" gasped Arabella.

"Hello, Arabella." Walter's gaze encompassed Justin as well. "My congratulations to the two of you. Do you mind if I give your bride a congratulatory kiss?"

Justin inclined his head. "Not at all."

Arabella was allowed no chance to either agree or object. Reaching out, Walter grasped her elbows and kissed her lightly on the lips. Drawing back, he studied her, and she sensed there was something more he wanted to say. Yet all she could think was that she would die of mortification if he made a scene . . .

Walter glanced at Justin, then held out his hand. "You're a lucky man, old chap. You'll take care of her the way she deserves, won't you?"

For the span of a heartbeat, Justin simply stared at Walter's extended hand. Arabella held her breath uncertainly, for his expression was rather strange.

But then he shook Walter's hand. Briefly he inclined his head. "I shall," he said smoothly.

"Excellent. Now, if you'll excuse me, I've engaged Miss Larwood for this next waltz."

Justin said nothing as he escorted Arabella into the carriage. He was polite but distant on the ride home; Arabella's heart plummeted. The closeness that had sprung up between them had shattered, as surely as if it had never been. But one thought thundered through her, and try though she did with all her might, it refused to be vanquished.

Their first day back in London as husband and wife . . . and it was a disaster.

Eighteen

In bed that night they lay near to each other, but without touching. For the first time since they had wed, Justin did not take her in his arms, and Arabella felt the loss in every corner of her soul.

The minutes slipped by. The room lay smothered in darkness. Half an hour surely passed, perhaps another. But while her body was still, her mind was not. Wide awake, not wanting to move for fear of waking Justin but feeling she would surely scream if she laid still an instant longer, she eased to one side, then the other.

Still sleep eluded her. She half-rose, peering over at Justin. He lay unmoving, one sinewed arm propped beneath his head, his face turned away from her toward the window. Licking her lips, she rolled over.

"Is it your intention to squirm the night through?"

Arabella froze. She experienced the prick of his tone as surely as she felt the prick of his gaze digging into her back.

Biting her lip, she said nothing.

"Is something wrong?" he queried flatly.

Her fingers curled and uncurled around the blanket she clutched to her chin. "No," she stated wildly, then clearly thought better of it. "I mean yes. Or rather . . . I—I don't know."

"I do so love a woman who knows her own mind."

Sarcasm or wit? she wondered. She was never sure. In either case, it only made her more miserable.

"I'm sorry," she said in a small voice. "I didn't mean to wake you."

He sighed. "You didn't. I can't sleep, either."

She heard him fumbling in the dark, then candlelight melted the darkness. Arabella eased to her back, staring up at the plasterwork on the ceiling. Beside her, Justin pushed himself to a sitting position, leaning back against the headboard.

"Why can't you sleep, Arabella?"

"My mind will not be still," she confided. "I cannot stop thinking!"

"About what?"

"Everything," she blurted.

"Ah," he said dryly, "that clarifies things quite nicely. Now, I shall ask again. What is on your mind? And pray do not tell me it's nothing."

She turned her head, trying to glean his mood

from his expression. Encountering only the naked expanse of his chest, she balked but managed to cover her discomfiture.

She compressed her lips. "Why can't *you* sleep?" she countered. "And pray do not tell me it's nothing."

There was a small silence. "Point taken," he said at last. "Since you insist, I shall—"

But Arabella was shaking her head. His words were just the impetus she needed to summon her pride.

"Wait. I—I shall go first." Bravely she sidled up to her elbows, then swallowed. "Is it true you and Lady Agatha were lovers?"

There was a long, drawn-out silence. Arabella braved a look at him, then wondered no longer as to his mood. His features were grim.

"Where did you hear that?"

"The night of the masquerade at Vauxhall," she admitted. "I heard two women talking—"

"Oh, yes. The women who claimed I was a lover of superb finesse. That is correct, is it not?"

He sounded most annoyed.

"Yes." Arabella's tongue stabbed the inside of her cheek. "But is it true?"

"That I'm a lover of superb finesse?" He shot her a look. "Obviously not, or you wouldn't be asking."

The fierceness of a blush heated her cheeks. "Not that," she said quickly. "I mean about Lady Ag—"

"Yes." His voice cut across hers. Abruptly, he

seemed to hesitate. Strong hands closing around her shoulders, he pulled her around to face him. "Why do you ask, Arabella?"

"Because I saw you with Lady Agatha tonight and . . . well, dare I say it? You looked quite spectacular together." All at once she was babbling, her insides a mass of fury and confusion. "And I hated it, Justin. I hated being in the same room with her, knowing the two of you were lovers. I hate the idea of coming face to face with such a woman! I realize it can hardly be avoided, given your experience. But I wanted to slap her when she dared to touch you. I wanted to march across the ballroom and strangle her pretty little neck—"

His lips quirked. "Oh, dear. It appears I have acquired a jealous wife."

His amusement was the last straw.

"I am glad you find this so entertaining!" Alas, what was meant to be defiant was anything but. Her lips quivered along with her voice. She tried to wrench away before he glimpsed her weakness.

Too late. With his thumb and forefinger he caught her chin and brought her eyes to his.

"Arabella! I'm sorry, sweet, I'm sorry. I did not mean to hurt you. I *do* not mean to hurt you. Arabella—" This time he was the one who floundered. "I am not a saint. But neither have I been with the legions of women that you seem to think. What happened with Lady Agatha was years ago. It meant nothing to me then. She means nothing to me now. Yet should you chance to come face-to-face with her, or any other woman with whom I've been intimate—"

"It almost happened tonight," Arabella said wildly.

"And I repeat, should it ever happen, I want you to remember one thing."

"What?" she said miserably.

"That no matter how many others are in the room, the only one who matters to me is you. The only woman I see is you. There is only one woman in my life now. That woman is you. To me there is no one more beautiful than you, Arabella."

Her lips parted. "Truly?"

"Truly." His gaze captured hers, dark and searing. "The vows we took on our wedding day . . . I do not forget them, Arabella. I *will* not forget them. I do not know if I can be the husband you want, the husband you need, the husband you've dreamed of. But God help me, I will try."

Arabella searched his features, stunned at his intensity, the fierceness of his declaration. It washed through her like warm spiced wine. Everything inside her was churning. She was afraid to read too much into all he revealed, and just as afraid not to.

"Now. Do we understand each other?"

She nodded, all at once absurdly happy. But then her eyes darkened.

Justin frowned. "What is it?"

She laid her fingertips on his forearms. "This afternoon in your study . . . Are you still angry?"

Something that might have been pain crossed his features. "I was never angry, Arabella."

But she could feel his sudden tension in the way his muscles bunched beneath her fingertips. "I should like to explain. I—I don't know quite what I was feeling, Justin. I don't know quite why I was crying . . . but suddenly I was, and . . . and then you walked in." Her words came out in a rush. "It's not you. Everything has happened so fast. There's scarcely been a moment to think. Perhaps it's just the strangeness of it all. But suddenly I found myself missing Mama and Papa . . . and realizing how I wish they had been here." Her voice began to quaver all over again.

Justin caught her against him with a groan. "You're right. It has been a whirlwind, hasn't it? Perhaps I shouldn't have left you alone this afternoon. Perhaps we shouldn't have gone out tonight."

Arabella clung to him as he pulled her against him. Sliding down into the covers, he simply held her. At length, he drew back. With his palm he cradled her cheek.

"All right now?"

She smiled through her tears. "Yes. It's been an odd day, hasn't it?"

"That it has," he agreed. The merest hint of a smile crossed his lips. "But I fear I must tell you something."

"And what is that?"

"I, too, was jealous when Walter kissed you. *Insanely* jealous."

"Oh, my," she breathed. She snuggled back into his arms, then suddenly a peal of laughter rang out.

Justin cocked his head to the side. "What was that for?"

"I fear I must tell *you* something, my lord," she teased.

Her smile faded. She took a deep breath. "The dowager duchess was right, you know. Walter could never make me feel the way you do, Justin." She laid a hand on the center of his chest, her fingertips splayed wide.

He arched a lazy brow. "Are you making advances toward me, wife?"

"I am," came her shy, swift reply. "Will you oblige me, sir?"

A low, deep laugh erupted. "Lady, need you ask?"

He started to reach for her. She stopped him with a tiny shake of her head, the pressure of her hand pushing him back to the pillow. Leaning over, she kissed him, at first gently, and then with an ever-mounting passion, parting her mouth, angling her head first one way and then the other. Justin allowed her the freedom to explore as she would, fighting to keep his hands at his sides, loving the way she kissed him with wild abandon.

His breath sucked in as she ran her tongue along the plane of his jaw. Closing his eyes, he reveled in the feel of her palm on his skin, tracing the span of his shoulders, the curve of his bicep. A sense of awe swept over him. This was Arabella, his mind chanted. Arabella touching him. Arabella wanting him . . .

Each gliding caress resonated through him, penetrating his skin, through muscle and bone . . . as if she touched his very heart. Her hand coursed over his chest, twining in the thick fur. He could feel her trembling, as if she thought he would stop her.

He could not. He *would* not.

"Sweet Lord." The words were nearly lost in a ragged rush of air, for now her fingertips plied across the grid of his belly, across the jutting ridge of his hip, grazing the tip of his rod. Sweat broke out on his brow. Her innocent touch made his blood roar. A tempest of sensation roiled through him, settling in his groin. His shaft swelled and leaped, and he felt her sudden inhalation. A dark, piercing ache shot through his loins. Christ, he thought vaguely, if she kept this up, he would surely burst his skin.

Her mouth returned to his, and he caught her head in both hands, kissing her with greedy hunger, their tongues tangling in wanton intimacy. She shifted, bringing one slim leg to bear around his; her mound rocked against his thigh, a taunting, evocative rhythm that matched the curl of her tongue around his. He could feel her shadow-cleft, sleek and hot and damp . . .

It was beyond bearing. Beyond reason. Desire burned inside him, out of control. He could bear it no longer. With strong hands, he caught at her, bringing her above him, settling slim thighs down beside his own.

Impatient fingers dragged her nightgown down,

baring her breasts. Propping himself up, he caught a nipple in his mouth and sucked, first one and then the other. With one hand she braced herself on his chest, her neck arching as a long cry of pleasure broke from her throat. Panting, writhing, driving them both half-mad. The light from the fire glistened on the dampened pout of her nipples, wet from his tongue. With her gown hiked up to her waist, her breasts free and full, it was a sight more erotic than if she'd been naked.

He touched her then, there where her feminine nest cradled the head of his shaft. He touched her heated core. Touched velvet, pink flesh weeping with desire. And when she jerked against his fingers, pressing, seeking, Justin knew he could stand no more.

His hands slid around to cup her buttocks. "Take me," he directed, his voice strained. His hands on her hips, he guided himself into her silken sheath. And he filled her, thick and hard and strong. Arabella looked down at herself, impaled on his swollen hardness. Justin wanted to laugh at her expression, but instead it turned into a ragged groan.

And then he was surging, driving. Her hair fell around them, a shining mantle of fiery red. She melted into each thrust, arched into each plunge. He made love to her with a desperation he didn't understand, knowing only that he needed her.

Yet still it wasn't enough. Not nearly enough. He rolled, bringing her beneath him. He needed her, needed her as he'd never needed anyone or anything before, and for an instant he almost faltered. He felt . . . frightened somehow. Almost panicked.

Beneath him, Arabella moaned. She clutched at his shoulders. Her eyes opened, her pupils dilated with passion. "Justin. I want . . ."

"I know, sweet." He kissed her lips. Her throat.

His thrusts quickened. He redoubled his efforts to please her. Her hands slipped to ride the frantic plunge of his hips.

"Yes," she whispered. "Oh, yes."

A primitive tempo pounded through his body. A purely male satisfaction rolled over him. *Yes*, his mind echoed. *Oh, yes*. What he needed was now. What he needed was this. What he needed was *her* . . .

And that was his very last thought before wave after wave of dark, sweet ecstasy broke over him.

Nineteen

Beyond that first day back in London, the next few weeks passed with no further incidents. They were settling into marital life quite nicely, Arabella decided cautiously. Some nights they spent at home alone, just the two of them. On those occasions when they went out as husband and wife, to Arabella's utter delight, Justin scarcely strayed from her side. He was attentive and caring, considerate and thoughtful, both in public and in private.

He was, Arabella decided rather dreamily, a perfect groom.

"I must say, dear," Aunt Grace had commented when Arabella stopped by for tea one afternoon, "that you look positively radiant."

Arabella poured cream into her cup. "Thank you," she murmured.

"I daresay this has something to do with your new husband?"

Arabella blushed. Grace beamed. "He's treating you well, then."

Arabella laid down her spoon. "Aunt Grace, may I tell you something?"

"Of course, dear."

"I'm happier than I've ever been in my whole life," Arabella confided. It was just as she'd written Mama. "Happier than I ever dreamed I could be."

Grace laughed delightedly. "Can you believe it? Six weeks ago you were trying to convince me you were not suited for marriage!"

"It isn't being married that's made the difference, but marriage to the right man." The observation emerged unthinkingly.

"It pleases me to no end to hear you say that, too. I don't think I could bear it if you were unhappy." Grace lightly squeezed her fingers. She took a sip of tea, then lowered her cup to the saucer. Arabella took note of her aunt's expression. She was looking very much like the cat who'd swallowed the cream.

"Aunt," she said dryly, "I can see you're dying to say something. What, pray, is it?"

"Oh, nothing much," her aunt stated breezily. "I was simply thinking perhaps I'd best begin plans for that christening now."

Arabella gasped. "Aunt Grace!"

Grace laughed delightedly. Her eyes were still twinkling when they made their way to the door a short time later. Arabella started to bid her goodbye, then stopped.

"I nearly forgot," she exclaimed. "Have there been any letters from Mama and Papa?"

Grace shook her head. "I'm afraid not, dear."

Arabella frowned. She was anxious to discover her parents' reaction to the news that she had wed, and her mother usually wrote at least weekly. Odd that there had been no word . . .

It was Aunt Grace who pointed out what should have been clear in the first place. "Do not fret, dear. The post is not always reliable, particularly when coming all the way from Africa."

Arabella relaxed. "You're right," she murmured. She put aside her disappointment and smiled.

"But that reminds me, dear. I should like for you and Justin to join us for dinner the Wednesday after next—a family dinner, just the four of us."

Wednesday was nearly a week off. "I shall have to check with Justin," Arabella said automatically. "But I'll send a note around if we cannot make it."

As it happened, the drive home took her past the Larwood townhouse. Georgiana was just alighting from her own carriage, and waved madly when she saw her. She stopped, Georgiana invited her inside, and before she knew it, it was nearing eight o'clock . . .

Justin was just coming down the stairs when she arrived home. He stopped on the last step, the merest hint of censure in his expression. Perfectly arched black brows rose high as he glanced from her to the clock, which had just begun to chime the hour, and back again.

"Oh, no!" she exclaimed, handing her umbrella and reticule to one of the downstairs maids. He looked particularly dashing tonight, dressed in splendid evening clothes, his cravat very white against the bronze of his neck. As always, the sight of him made her pulse beat faster.

"Are we expected somewhere this evening?" She hurried toward him. "Just give me a minute to change. I won't be long, I promise."

One side of his mouth quirked up. "I began to fear you'd forgotten the way home," he said mildly. "Tell me, my love, have I cause to be jealous?"

"Hardly." Arabella laughed, hurrying toward him. "I'm sorry I'm late, but Aunt Grace invited me to take tea with her, and then I chanced to see Georgiana on the way home."

"Ah," he said gravely. "Now, if you said you were with Walter, it would be quite another matter."

She blinked. "Never say you are still jealous of Walter."

"And if I said that I was?"

His possessiveness thrilled her to the bone. "Then I shall simply have to see what I can do to remedy the situation."

There was a decided gleam in his eye. "Excellent idea," he approved. "Shall we begin now?" He extended a hand.

Breathlessly Arabella laid her fingers in his. She smiled up at him as he escorted her up the stairs to their room. He opened the door wide.

"After you, my dear."

Arabella stepped inside, only to stop short, catching her breath in amazement. Masses and masses of brilliant red roses were everywhere. The room was lit only by dozens and dozens of candles. They were everywhere, upon the bureau, the mantel, the bedside tables. The effect was stunning. A small table before the fireplace had been spread with delicate crystal and china.

"Justin." Wonderingly she spoke his name. "How incredibly lovely!"

He closed the door and leaned against it, watching the play of expression across her features. "I quite agree," he said, but his eyes were on her lips, still parted in astonishment. He gestured to the table. "Shall we dine while the food is still warm?"

"Certainly." Arabella allowed him to take her hand and seat her. He served her himself, though precisely what it was they ate, she was never quite sure. She really didn't know or care. All she could think was how Justin had arranged this incredibly romantic setting, and it thrilled her to the bottom of her soul.

When they'd finished, she took a sip of wine. Their eyes met over the gold-filigreed rim. "That was delicious." Her gaze encompassed the room once again. "But you've yet to tell me the reason for all this."

He shrugged. "I thought it would be nice to spend an enjoyable night alone with my wife in our room."

The heat in his eyes made her quiver inside. "Odd," she heard herself say, "but I thought we were alone practically every night."

"What! Are you complaining already?"

"I have no cause to complain," she responded. "As of yet anyway." There was an impish slant to her smile.

His eyes never leaving hers, he removed her wine glass from her hand and set it aside. Rising, he rounded the table and drew her up before him. "That sounds like a challenge."

"Does it?" Arabella was secretly startled at her daring. "I rather thought of it as an invitation."

His low, husky laugh turned her heart upside down. She liked making him laugh, for it wasn't often that he did so. When he did, she treasured it like nothing in this world. It struck her then, she'd never seen him quite so at ease as he was tonight.

All at once she remembered what he'd said their wedding night as she stood before him in her nightgown. Deliberately she slid two fingers under the lapel of his jacket. "I do believe I think we can do without this . . . extraneous apparel."

For one delicious instant, his eyes seemed to blaze. Arabella went hot all over.

He shrugged from his jacket and waistcoat. "Anything to oblige." His shirt met the same swift end.

When at last he stepped from his trousers, Arabella's mouth had gone dry. He possessed not only the face of a god, but the form of one. The candlelight threw his body into stark, golden relief. He was all muscle and shadow, all heat and sinew and man.

As if to lend credence to that very fact, his staff quickened before her eyes, boldly erect between the corded strength of his thighs.

Her breath caught high in her throat. That she could do this to him—that he wanted her so—was still a source of utter amazement.

Seeing where her eyes resided, Justin smiled lazily. "My dear Arabella, it's most disconcerting to be standing here naked"—his smile widened—"when you are not."

Arabella felt her cheeks heat. So he, too, was thinking of their wedding night . . .

She pursed her mouth prettily. "Then perhaps you will lend your assistance." She turned, giving him access to the myriad buttons at the back of her gown.

"But of course." He stepped near her. Before she knew it, her clothing was puddled around her feet. His fingers were in her hair, pulling the pins from the knot at her crown and sending it spilling around his hands.

A steely arm caught her close, dragging her back against him. The rigid stiffness of his staff prodded between the soft flesh of her buttocks. Sweeping aside her hair, he pressed his mouth against her nape.

"God, you taste so good," he muttered. "So damn good."

With a cry Arabella turned in his arms, lifting her mouth to his. Their lips met again and again; they were both ravenous, as if starved for each other.

"Touch me, sweet," he said against her lips. "Touch me here." His voice went low and guttural. "Touch me now."

Strong fingers clamped around her wrist, dragging her hand down . . . down. Her knuckles skimmed that taut plane of his belly. The tip of his rod, like a brand of fire, seemed to jump into her palm.

His sudden movement wrung a gasp from her, but there was no more hesitation. To pleasure him was her only desire, her only care. Without thought, her fingertips tripped along the length of his shaft, circling the root of his swollen flesh, scaling the shape of him, clear to the arching tip and back again. His size made her heart clamor madly. He was hotter than fire. And hard, so very hard, like marble, yet beneath the ridges of his skin she could feel him pulsing, a throb that echoed the rhythm of her heart.

"Like this?" she whispered.

She could hear the jagged intake of his breath. Emboldened by the fiery hold of his eyes, filled with a heady sense of power, her cool fingers daintily stretched to encircle him. Guided by instinct, by the flex of approval in his jaw, she stroked with first one hand, then the other.

His gaze seared hotly into hers, his eyelids half-lowered. He smoldered, both inside and out. "Like that . . ." The words were hoarse, thready with need. "Just like that . . ."

He shifted his position, catlike, sliding even more

of himself inside her grasp. With her thumb, she explored the very helm of his member, sheathed as if in silk, so utterly smooth.

His sharp inhalation was her reward. "Arabella." Her name was half-laugh, half-groan. "Do you have any idea what you do to me?"

Her pulse thundered wildly in her ears. She did, she thought hazily. She could feel a glistening, satiny pearl drop rise from the center of his shaft; molten passion, she decided vaguely. For indeed, he looked as if he were steaming. Unbidden, she glanced down at all her hands encompassed. Mesmerized by the sight, she couldn't look away. The tip of her tongue came out to moisten her lips.

"Sweet Jesus, don't do that!"

He jerked away. The next thing she knew, strong arms clamped around her waist. She felt herself crushed against him, borne high aloft, and then the softness of the mattress beneath her back.

His body followed her down. But he did not kiss her lips, nor toy with the bounty of her breasts, as she expected. Instead, his mouth brushed the span of her belly. "I think you deserve a little torment of your own, don't you, sweet witch?"

With the sleek width of his shoulders, he spread wide her thighs. With his tongue he traced a taunting, scorching pattern from the inside of her knee. Up . . . ever upward.

Arabella's mind teetered. As she gleaned his intention, her hands fell back alongside her head where it rested on the pillow. Every time he made love to her, it brought new wonders. She'd been convinced he'd taught her much about passion in the past two weeks. Clearly, she decided hazily, she had much more to learn.

"Justin." She could scarcely breathe, let alone talk. Anticipation raked along every nerve in her body, but especially there, where his breath warmed her skin. "The night we wed . . . when you said there was a great deal more to kissing, is this what you meant?"

She took his low growl to be a reply in the affirmative.

The sight of his dark head poised *there*, in stark contrast with her white pale flesh, sent a hundred shivers racing along her spine.

"Oh, my," she said faintly. "And does what you're doing . . . come under the nature of lascivious?"

With his thumbs he parted red-gold fleece, baring damp, pink flesh. His head began to lower. "What do you think?" he muttered.

But he allowed no time for either thought or speech, no time for anything at all. His mouth was shockingly, brazenly intimate, his tongue a divinely erotic torment, a torrid, evocative rhythm that lashed and swirled and licked, until she thought she could bear no more.

Slowly he raised his head to look at her, his eyes fever-bright and burning. "Tell me, sweetheart. Do you like this?"

Her fists were clutched in his hair, but not to push him away. "Yes," she gasped. "Oh, yes."

And when he touched her again, blistering flames licked through her. She was writhing. Hurtling toward the edge of bliss. When it came, dimly she heard herself cry out, again and again.

His breath left his lungs in a rush, for Justin could bear no more. He levered himself above her, his features tense and strained, rigid with need. He locked his fingers with hers. His mouth took hers with almost frantic urgency.

"Arabella." Her name was a hoarse, rasping sound. "Oh, Christ." His belly skimmed hers. He lunged deep and hard, pumping and churning, unable to stop himself, perilously close to the edge. Her body clamped tight around hot, engorged flesh, seeking his in a frenzy that matched his own. He gritted his teeth against his climax, determined to hold back, to pleasure her again. But, God help him, it had never been so good. So right. She was melting him, from the inside out, melting his heart, his soul.

He caught her hips in his hands. Each driving thrust brought him closer to bliss. Her whimper of pleasure obliterated all hope of control. Casting his head back, he groaned aloud. His release erupted, scalding and hot and honeyed.

They collapsed together, a wanton tangle of limbs. Long moments passed before either of them was able to move. Satiated, utterly drained, Justin rolled to his side and cradled her against him.

She was smiling, he saw. He traced her lips with his fingertips.

"What is this for?" he murmured.

"I was just thinking of Aunt Grace," she murmured.

"Aunt Grace again. How flattering."

"We've been invited to dinner the Wednesday after next, by the way. Is that all right?"

He nuzzled the wispy hairs on her temple. "My love, my only wish is to please you."

Arabella rested her head against the hollow in his shoulder, gazing up at him.

A dark brow climbed high. "Aunt Grace again?" he guessed.

Arabella nodded. "Yes," she confided a trifle breathlessly. "Justin, my aunt loves nothing more than planning parties and such. So I must warn you, so you aren't surprised at anything she might chance to say . . ."

"What, another outspoken woman? I begin to see you've gained your tendencies from your mother's side."

His warm teasing forestalled her anxiety. "Yes, well, I fear I must tell you that with our hasty wedding, well, she's anxious to begin planning the christening of our—our firstborn."

"Is she, now?" His smile was almost lazy.

Arabella held her breath. He hardly looked displeased at the prospect. She regarded him cautiously. "How do you feel about children, Justin?"

He shrugged. "I must be honest," he said dryly. "Prior to the last few weeks, I've given little thought to the idea of marriage, let alone children."

Arabella took a breath. "If we ever have children," she said solemnly, "I hope they resemble you."

Justin froze. Did she know what she was saying? A child who looked like him . . . He blanched inside. For an instant, he couldn't breathe. He thought he might choke.

"I saw the portrait of your mother at Thurston Hall." Arabella sighed dreamily. "You are the very picture of her, you know. I confess, I like the idea of a daughter with your striking coloring. Or a son with your exquisite features." Still smiling, she touched his cheek.

Justin couldn't help it. He recoiled.

"Good God. Do not say that. Do not even think it."

His sudden harshness stilled her smile.

She sat up, drawing the sheet over her breasts. "Is the idea of children so abhorrent to you?" she asked carefully. "Or is it that you fear they will look like me?"

He made a sound in his throat. "For pity's sake, Arabella, I refuse to dignify such a ridiculous statement. If I were afraid of how our children would turn out, I wouldn't have married you, now, would I?"

Timidly she asked, "So you wouldn't mind a daughter with flaming red curls?"

"No," he stated flatly.

It was hardly the reassurance she craved. Seeking some measure of encouragement, she stretched out a hand toward his face.

He stopped her cold, winding his fingers around her wrist and thrusting her hand back in her lap.

He might as well have slapped her in the face. A treacherous little pain knotted her heart, yet somehow she found the courage to lift her chin. "You did that on our wedding night. You did it again now. Twice," she pointed out quietly. "Justin, why won't you let me touch your face?"

He flung the sheets aside and rose, patently ignoring her as if she hadn't spoken.

Arabella had gone very still inside. Numbly she stared at the rigid lines of his back as he reached for his dressing gown. "Justin?" she whispered.

Almost savagely he jerked the ties of his robe closed. "This whole discussion of children is premature." He didn't look at her as he spoke. In fact, he was already striding toward the door.

Arabella slid from the bed. She grabbed her own dressing gown from the hook on the wall. She was still trying to shove her arms in the sleeves when the door slammed shut.

She was undeterred—and not three steps behind him when he entered his study.

He went straight to the table near the window and reached for a crystal decanter. Her lips compressed when he poured a generous splash, for she knew he was well aware of her presence. But he chose not to face her. Instead he raised the glass to his lips, staring out the window, his back to her.

Behind him, Arabella crossed her arms over her chest. "You're right," she said evenly. "The subject of children can wait, though we certainly haven't done anything to prevent the prospect, have we? But I want an answer to my question, Justin. Why won't you let me touch your face?"

At first she'd been puzzled, then hurt. Now she was determined.

He drained the glass and reached for another.

"Please look at me when I talk to you."

He turned, his green eyes distant. "Must we discuss this now?"

Her tone was as arch as his. "And when would be a good time? Never?"

His eyes flickered. "If it pleases you, Arabella, I should like to enjoy my brandy in private."

"Well, it doesn't please me," she shot back hotly. "What did I do? What did I say that was so wrong? Answer me, damn you!"

His lips pulled into something that scarcely resembled a smile. "Not very pretty language for a vicar's daughter, my love."

Arabella stared. He was thin-lipped and stony. It was as if she could see him withdrawing, pulling away inside himself . . . away from *her*. But why? *Why?*

A pulse was ticking inside her. Ticking like a clock in an empty room, until she wanted to scream. She stood motionless, aware in some strange, unfathomable way she didn't fully comprehend that something was deeply wrong. Beneath his handsome façade was something hidden, something he refused to share.

Her anger drained away as suddenly as it erupted. But her composure was shaken badly. She felt bewildered, hurt, anxious, and it took every ounce of courage she possessed to remain where she was.

"Why do you look like that? Justin, what happened to you?"

He gave a curt laugh. "My God, three weeks wed and you'd think she'd known me forever."

Arabella caught her breath. God, but he could be cruel!

"It was you who said we were alike." She shook her head. Her gaze turned pleading. "Why are you doing this? Why are you so cold?"

"What, Arabella!" He raised his hands high at his sides. "You don't like what you see? What I am? Perhaps you should have married Walter."

His voice pricked her deeply. "I know what you're doing, Justin. You're trying to push me away, aren't you?"

"For pity's sake! Can't a man have a moment to himself?"

More than anything, Arabella longed to go to him. To wrap her arms around him and cling. But somehow she knew he would shut her out, shut her away. How could a night that began so perfectly have turned so ugly?

The breath she drew was deep and racking. "Something's wrong, Justin. I know it. I can feel it. Something is very—"

"There is nothing wrong!"

The tension spun out endlessly. Seized by a bone-deep despair, she hugged her arms around herself, as if to ward off a chill. Indeed, she acknowledged vaguely, she felt as if she'd been plunged into a vat of ice.

"Is this how it will always be?" Her voice was very low, thick with the threat of tears that lay just beneath the surface. "Will we share nothing but passion? Nothing but a bed? Can you *tell* me nothing—"

"Arabella," he intoned politely, "I invite you to leave." With that he turned, staring out the window, his chiseled profile etched in silver. His posture inflexible, his face a mask of stone.

The silence was unending. It was as if she hadn't spoken, as if she weren't even there . . . as if he'd forgotten her.

As if she didn't even exist.

"Justin—"

With a curse, he whirled. "Must you keep hounding me?" he demanded tautly. "Have I wed a harridan? Go back to bed and just leave me the hell alone!"

His regard was fierce. His tone was fierce. Both scalded her. A sharp, tearing pain speared through her heart.

Arabella waited no longer. With a stricken little cry she bolted.

Twenty

The instant she was gone, Justin spun around. A wrenching pain ripped through him. He wanted to howl and rage like the monster he was.

His eyes squeezed shut. But even then her image danced against his eyelids. Arabella, staring up at him, chalk-white and pale, her wounded hurt shooting like an arrow straight into his heart.

"Sweet Christ," he whispered. "What have I done?"

In the aftermath hung an eerie silence.

You bastard, jabbed a scathing voice in his skull. *You filthy bastard.*

Self-disgust churned in his belly. Never had he hated himself as he did in that moment. He'd always known he was a demon inside. But he'd never known how completely vile he was until now.

Feeling as old as the heavens, he made his way into a chair. Numbly he realized his glass was still in hand. He downed the fiery liquid in a single gulp.

A bitter, ominous darkness slipped over him.

How strange that fate had brought her into his life, into his bed . . . into his heart. Little by little, she had pulled down the barriers around his heart as no other woman ever had . . . as no other woman ever would.

It struck him then, that in the days since his marriage, the restlessness that had plagued him for years was no more. With Arabella, each day was unique and fresh . . . like morning dew upon a newly formed leaf bursting into the world, cherished by nature, glistening bright in the sunshine. It was like seeing the world all over again, after a long, long journey into darkness, returning to find a world full of vibrance and color. For Justin, it was a feeling utterly foreign to him.

And the nights . . . sweet Lord, the nights! She turned to him eagerly, denying him nothing. Giving all that he asked and more.

And what had he done?

Exactly what she had said. He had pushed her away.

His lips twisted. Was this God's way of punishing him? he wondered blackly. Of making him pay for what he was? For the life of him, he could not explain what drove him.

It was just as he'd told Arabella. He was . . . who he was.

He would never change, he thought bleakly. He couldn't.

He didn't know how.

The night eroded. The moon sank low in the sky.

Hours later his heavy footsteps trudged up the stairs.

In his room—*their* room—Arabella lay sleeping. Sliding off his robe, he slipped into bed beside her, taking care not to wake her. In her sleep, she turned toward him, as if to seek him out, though God knew it was the last thing in the world she should have done. Knowing he couldn't stop himself, Justin pulled her into his embrace.

Her hand came to rest in the middle of his chest. For a timeless instant, her fingertips lay poised directly above his heart. Then she relaxed, nestling against him as if he were all that she desired.

Overcome by the need to touch her, he slid the back of his knuckles over her cheeks. They came away wet with tears.

He froze.

Wrenching shame spilled through his gut. His arms tightened. He felt charred inside.

"Arabella," he said raggedly. "Oh, God." He'd been so afraid he would hurt her . . . and he had. He'd made her cry. *Cry*.

The blackness within him yawned deeper. She was sweet and pure and he was a fiend. He'd always known it. His father had known it.

Perhaps it was better this way, he thought bleakly. Better that she see him for the wicked, heartless bastard that he was.

She might have walked into his life, into his arms, but she would never stay. Never in a million years. Best to take what he could, while he could, for as long as it lasted.

Because God knew, it wouldn't last forever.

In his heart, there was never any doubt.

It was inevitable, perhaps: He dreamed that night. He dreamed he was back at Thurston Hall. It was June. The night was warm. Through the fog in his brain, he realized he was drunk again. Stumbling just outside his father's study . . .

The memory sharpened, spreading like a bloodstain.

His father barred his way.

"Where the devil have you been?"

"What, my lord, you wish an account of the night's activities? Perhaps we should be seated. This could take some time, for the evening's entertainment was interesting, shall we say. I give you fair warning, though, it's altogether possible you may be shocked—"

Again he heard his father's voice, stabbing at him, the prick of a knife.

"Cease! I've no intention of listening to your filth . . . Look at you, so drunk you can hardly stand! And you reek of cheap perfume! God, but you are so very much your mother's brat! She shamed me, the witch! She shamed my good name, as you *shame me!"*

In his sleep, Justin flinched. Yet still he could hear his father, thundering through the walls of his mind, hurtling through the dark, ripping through the barriers of time and death—until it was just the two of them, standing outside the study.

"All these years I've had to look at you, staring

back at me with her *eyes, with* her *smile. Reminding me what she did, what she was—a whore who would spread her legs for any man who would have her."*

"No," Justin muttered. "No."

"And you are no better. Your blood is tainted, as she was tainted."

There were hands on him. Hands shaking his shoulder. "Justin," said a voice. "Justin, wake up."

He was still caught up in the past, snared in the tangled web of the dream.

"No decent woman will ever have you, boy. No decent woman will ever want you!"

His arm thrust wide. "No," he shouted. "No!"

A sharp, feminine cry shattered the night.

He bolted upright. His head came around wildly. Arabella was scrambling up from the floor beside the bed.

Sanity return in a rush. "Arabella! Christ, did I hurt you?" He dragged her up beside him.

"No," she said jerkily. "I'm fine. Really."

She was on her knees beside him, her eyes scouring his face.

"You were dreaming, Justin. Shouting."

"Yes." Releasing her, he sank back against the wall. He stabbed his fingers into his forehead, as if to drive out the memory.

Tentatively she touched his shoulder. "Are you all right?"

He didn't answer. He couldn't. He was still shaking.

"It seemed . . . so real. What were you dreaming of?"

"My father," he whispered.

He raised his head. In his eyes was something naked, something stark and lonely and beseeching. He looked so like a hurt little boy she nearly cried out. She had the strangest sense that he was floundering, uncertain of himself. But why? *Why?*

Blindly she spoke. Blindly she pleaded. "Please, Justin. Please, just . . . talk to me. I can't live like this. With this festering between us." She gave a tiny little shake of her head. "I don't want to."

He touched her then. With the pad of his thumb, he whisked away the dampness on her cheek. "I hurt you before," he said with a touch of ragged harshness. "I'm sorry. I don't want to hurt you again. But—" his shoulders hunched up, then down. "I'm not sure I can tell you. I'm not sure I can tell . . . anyone."

The tension that constricted his body was immense. She sensed he was fighting some fierce inner demon.

"Try, Justin. Please try."

The silence of the world seemed to drift between them.

Finally he spoke. "If I tell you, you'll hate me." It was a flat, hollow prediction.

"No. *No*. I could never hate you, Justin. Never."

Something bitterly dark and ominous crept into his features. "Even if I told you I killed my father?"

"You didn't. You couldn't. You wouldn't." Conviction gathered full and ripe within her.

"Believe it, Arabella. Believe it, for it's true." He shook his head when he saw the puzzled frown settle upon her brow. "Oh, not in the way you might think."

"How, then?" she challenged. "How?"

He spread his hands wide and looked at them. "With my wickedness," he said in an odd, strained whisper.

"Tell me what happened," she said softly.

The story emerged bit by bit. His voice, his features, were void of all emotion. He didn't look at her as he spoke.

Listening to him, Arabella's chest began to ache. She began to gain a very clear picture of his childhood. A little boy who struggled to please his father, to no avail. No wonder he said that Sebastian had been both mother and father to him and Julianna, more than his own . . . and little wonder that he and his father were ever at odds. Little wonder that he had grown rebellious and bitter.

"When I was seventeen, he caught me stealing into the house at dawn. I was foxed. He was furious." A harsh laugh emerged. "Nothing new there, of course. We quarreled. He called my mother a whore. Of course, I knew it was true. All of England knew it was true. My mother was a vain creature who knew of her beauty and used it to entice men. To seduce them. Sometimes I do believe my mother, with her own *joie de vivre,* would have spread her legs for any man simply to spite my father. And my blood was tainted, you see. My blood was *hers*. That's why he hated me. Because I looked like my mother. He held me in the same contempt, the same disdain. He told me so . . . oh, so many times! Never in front of Sebastian, of course. But that night . . . he shouted that I was a wastrel. That I was just like my mother."

Arabella was shocked. "Justin, it was he who was wicked, not you . . . never you!"

"No. You're wrong. I wanted to hurt him. I *wanted* to spite him."

"But who can blame you?" she protested. "My God," she burst out, "what kind of man would say such awful things to his own son?"

"Ah, but there's the thing, you see. It's entirely possible I'm not his son. That none of us are. Not me. Not Julianna. Perhaps not even Sebastian."

Arabella's mind whirled giddily. Her lips parted. "Are you saying that he is not your father?"

For the longest time Justin said nothing. "I don't know. Don't you see? Given my mother's reputation, it's entirely possible . . . I've often wondered if my mother was the only one who knew for certain . . . but if she did, it was a secret she took to her grave."

His eyes darkened. "It was that night that I realized . . . and I taunted him with it. I taunted him with my mother's infidelities and asked if he knew if his children were even his own.

"He was livid. And I was so very pleased! And I laughed, Arabella. I *laughed*. He started to shout at me . . . It was then he fell to the floor. He clutched his chest. And I left him there. *I left him there*."

His mouth twisted. "My conduct, as usual, was abhorrent. I rode off to London that night, so no one would know I was there. The servants found him in the morning. I never told a soul I'd been there, that I was the one who killed him. No one, not even Sebastian."

Her heart went out to him for the guilt he'd lived with all these years, the mistaken belief that he'd killed his father.

"Justin—"

"There's more," he said in a tone that sent prickles all down her spine.

He rose and walked to the mirror next to the armoire.

His voice stole softly through the silence. "Remember that night at Thurston Hall, with McElroy? I'll never forget what you said. That all your life you wanted to be like everybody else, *look* like everyone else. You asked me if I knew what it was like to gaze into the mirror and cringe. To hate what you see and know there's nothing you can ever, ever do to change it."

His voice plunged further. "I know what that's like, Arabella. I *know*. I'll never forget, not long before that night with my father . . . I stood before the mirror in my room, staring at my reflection. Before I knew it, the glass was shattered. I'll never forget bending over. Lifting a shard of glass and holding it to my face . . ." In the dark, he made slashing movements with his hand.

A suffocating tightness in her chest, Arabella

stared at him in horror, at his exquisite, perfectly sculpted features. "Justin," she said on a strangled breath. "Justin, no—"

His hand fell to his side. "Obviously, I couldn't do it. But now you know, Arabella. Now you see the ugliness inside the handsomest man in all England. Now you see me for the coward I was. But then, you always did see me for what I am."

"Oh, God, Justin. It wasn't you. It was never you. He poisoned you—"

"Poison. Yes, that's what I am."

His scathing self-disgust brought her to her feet. A single, scalding tear slid down her cheek but she paid no heed. Sliding her arms around his waist, she clung to him, laying her cheek against the sleek gold skin of his shoulder.

"Stop that. If—if you had cut your beautiful face, I don't think I could bear it."

He twisted around. "Why don't you blame me? Why don't you hate me?"

"Don't," she said with utter fierceness. "Don't say that. Don't even think it!"

"Didn't you hear what I said? Didn't you hear any of it?"

"I heard everything. *Everything*."

"Then why are you still here? How can you stand to be near me? To touch me?"

She heard the way he tried to stifle the emotion from his voice and couldn't. Something painful caught at the corner of her being. She'd been given a glimpse inside his soul, and she couldn't turn from him now. He needed her. He might not know it yet, but he did. She couldn't desert him. She *wouldn't*.

Her throat aching, she drew a deep, quavering breath. Her vision misted by tears, she gazed up at him, uncaring that her heart lay in her eyes. "I'm your wife, Justin. And what kind of wife would I be if I were not here to share your life and your pain? A wife belongs at her husband's side . . . and I belong with you."

"Oh, Christ." His voice caught roughly. "I've made you cry again."

"It's all right," she said bravely. Brokenly. "Just hold me, Justin. Just hold me and—and don't let go."

Powerful arms swept her against him, close and tight, exactly where she wanted to be. He fiercely kissed the tremulous lips she offered, wrapping his arms about her back and lifting her clear from her feet.

This time when he carried her to the bed, there were no more words, no tears . . . nothing but the breathless splendor of being his.

Twenty-one

Wednesday of the following week, Justin was whistling as he vaulted onto the seat of his curricle. He'd just made a visit to his solicitor, and while it was a visit that cost him a goodly sum, it was, he decided with supreme satisfaction, well worth it.

His mouth curled upward. Lord, how things had changed in the past year. His stylish townhouse in London had been the first of his acquisitions. Then a wife. And now a country house in Kent. He laughed to himself. Ye gods, he was now unquestionably a man of respectability!

It was odd, he reflected, how with the addition of a wife his life had become . . . simpler somehow. It should have been the opposite, he suspected. For most men, that probably would have been the case.

But he could be no less than honest. If his wife had chanced to be any woman other than Arabella, it wouldn't have happened. He'd probably be trying to figure out how to extricate himself from the marriage trap, he decided dryly, instead of burrowing deeper. Hell, if it had been any woman other than Arabella, he wouldn't even be married! Justin harbored no illusions. Compromised female or no, he would have found some way to elude impending matrimony.

But he didn't feel tied down. He didn't feel chained. He didn't feel trapped.

He felt curiously . . . free.

And, perhaps for the first time in his life, he looked forward to what the future would bring. Indeed, he welcomed it. In all truth, he'd never really cared before, for every day had always held the same monotony.

But now every day was different.

Up from Thurston Hall last week for a day of business, it was Sebastian who had chanced to mention the father of one of his friends had passed on. His friend had decided to sell his father's small country estate, furnishings and all. That had given Justin the idea: With precise clarity, he recalled Arabella's wistfulness at Thurston Hall the evening he'd kissed her; how she'd confided that as a child she'd never really had a home, not really. Because for all the starkness of his youth—of his entire life—the security of a home was the one thing he'd always had. Indeed, perhaps it was something he'd taken for granted, never really considering the absence of one.

But he did then. Or perhaps it was their talk of children, a prospect which was still rather daunting. He knew why, of course. Rake that he had been for so many years, he'd never considered his future would include marriage, let alone children. But, he realized dryly, it was also no doubt inevitable, considering the way his desire for his lovely wife burned stronger every day . . .

Children, he thought again. When the time came, he would be ready. More than ready. He was changing, he decided in amazement. Being with Arabella made everything different. With her at his side, he felt invincible.

His mind returned to the house. As soon as Sebastian had left, he'd made inquiries at once.

He'd taken a day to see the estate for himself. The first thing that struck him was the small cherry tree that stood just outside the drawing room window. He'd chuckled, remembering Arabella's confession about the way she'd shocked her mother by climbing trees when she was young.

From there, it all just seemed to fall into place. And difficult as it was to pinpoint, *everything* about it just seemed right. It was all so perfect . . .

Ah, but he couldn't wait to see the expression on Arabella's face when he told her. Anticipation warmed his veins. She would look at him in that wide-eyed way she had, launch herself into his arms, and kiss him in wild, sweet abandon—which was exactly the way he would take her that night, he decided with relish.

He grinned outright.

Upon his return to Berkeley Square, it happened that Arabella was outside and was just about to climb the steps to the door when he leaped from the curricle. Spying him, she waited at the bottom step.

He bent and kissed her lightly on the lips, feeling as if he might burst inside. "Just the person I wanted to see," he said lightly.

"And you, sir, are just the person I wanted to see. I've just come from Georgiana's—"

"Well, at least you weren't out shopping," he teased.

She frowned good-naturedly. "Oh, come. I believe I have yet to spend any of your money."

"Nor have I been besieged by requests to redecorate. How fortuitous that I chose such a thrifty bride and need not worry that I'm on my way to the poor farm."

"Why would I want to redecorate? This house is perfect just the way it is."

It pleased Justin to hear her say that. "However," she continued, "at any rate, I have some news you might be interested in hearing."

"And I have some news for you, too. But ladies first."

"Thank you. Now, as I was saying, my visit to Georgiana proved to be rather enlightening."

Justin offered a hand to escort her up the stairs. "In what way?"

"While I was there, Georgiana had a most unexpected visitor. And you'll never guess who it was."

Justin glanced down at her. She was practically beaming. "You're right," he said dryly. "I shan't."

She wrinkled her nose prettily. "You're no fun," she protested.

"Sweetheart, I can see you're just dying to tell me, so why don't you?"

"Very well, then. It was Walter. And when I left, they appeared to be getting on quite cozily. Her mother also confided this is the third time this week Walter has come to call on her."

Justin stopped short. "Georgiana and Walter?"

"It would appear so."

Justin didn't mean to smile so broadly—it just happened.

Arabella laughed at his expression.

"Perhaps theirs will be the next London wedding."

"I shouldn't be at all surprised," she agreed, tucking her fingers into the curve of his elbow.

Their eyes caught and held for an immeasurable moment. Justin took a deep breath, all at once rocked to the depths of his soul. Her eyes were a soft clear blue, shining like the sky above. She looked so happy, so unutterably content, even radiant. He was half-afraid to give voice to the thought that spun through his mind for fear it would evaporate. Was it possible? he marveled. Did *he* make her happy? That he might was a thought that nearly sent him crashing to his knees.

God, but she was lovely. A warm breeze teased a few errant curls at her temple. A tinge of rose bloomed on her cheeks. Her lips carried the faintest hint of a smile. And knowing she was his kindled potent, primitive urges. Desire flamed in his veins. He experienced a sudden urge to carry her upstairs, close the door, and make love to her until they were both exhausted.

His hand came out to smother hers, there where it rested on his sleeve. He was about to put forth that very proposition when Arthur opened the door and they stepped inside. Then Arthur was hovering at his elbow with the day's post and invitations. When he turned around, he saw that she'd disappeared up the stairs.

Which was all well and good, Justin decided, since she was exactly where he wanted her . . .

The brass knocker sounded at the front door. Arthur opened it and Gideon stepped inside.

Justin raised his brows. "Back from Paris already, I see."

"My good man, it's been over a month. And pray forgive my dropping in so unexpectedly, but I'd thought to see you at White's."

"I'm afraid I haven't been there in several weeks."

"Ah," Gideon said smoothly. "Busy with other things, such as your new bride, I expect."

An amused curiosity glimmered in Gideon's eyes, but Justin wasn't about to indulge it.

"I don't mean to be rude, but this is not a good time."

Gideon raised both hands. "Oh, no need to worry," he stated breezily. "I'll be brief. Indeed, I only came to settle up our affairs."

Justin's gaze flickered. "There is no need," he said stiffly. Christ, until this moment he'd forgotten his damned wager with Gideon.

"Indeed there is," Gideon insisted. "We had an agreement, that the lady in question would be yours within the month, and so she was. Granted, I certainly never expected that you would be forced to wed the chit—"

"I wasn't forced," Justin said tightly.

Gideon shrugged. "The fact remains, I trust the terms of our agreement have been . . . gratifying nonetheless. However," he went on, "I am a man who always pays his debts."

With a wink Gideon dropped a pouch into Justin's hand.

Before he could say a word, there was a whisk of skirts behind him—Arabella!

"Oh, hello!" she said upon seeing Gideon.

Justin half-turned. He knew the pouch contained the money from their wager. He mouthed a silent curse. Goddammit, he couldn't give it back, not without making a scene!

Pointedly he said, "Gideon was just on his way out."

"Yes." Gideon executed a low bow. "Again, my heartiest congratulations to the both of you."

The door was no sooner closed than Arabella nodded at the pouch.

"Ah," she teased. "I saw his sly wink. What did he bring you?"

Justin's heart sank. "Nothing of any consequence," he said quickly. "Really."

"Nothing of any consequence, is it? Hmmm, that sounds mysterious. Perhaps it's a treasure. Let's give a look, shall we?" Laughing, she snatched the pouch from his hand and peered inside.

Her eyes widened. "My word, there must surely be half a fortune here." She glanced up, her expression curious. "Are the two of you in business together?"

Justin hesitated. "No," he said.

"I thought not. Frankly, I should be astonished, for Gideon has never struck me as a particularly industrious sort." She pursed her lips. "Indeed, I know he is your friend, but he asked me to dance once—a tiresome experience, as I recall. All he could speak of was his excellent luck at the hazard table earlier in the evening. I've heard tales of men foolish enough to wager an entire fortune on a single roll of the dice. Let us hope he is not one of—"

All at once she broke off. Her gaze slid to the pouch in her hand.

Her smile slipped. Slowly she raised her head. "Justin," she said haltingly, and then, "It cannot be. Surely this is not—"

She stopped. Something pleading flashed across her expression. "*Justin*?" The sound of his name verged on desperate.

For the longest time, Justin couldn't say a word. His eyes bored into hers. It was as if he'd been turned to stone . . .

Quietly he spoke. "Do you remember the wager I told you about?"

Her breath caught. Every drop of blood surely

drained from her face. Anguish filled her eyes, those beautiful blue eyes, the only hint of color in her face. And Justin was aware, with stark, chilling certainty, of the precise moment he shattered her trust and she splintered apart.

"Oh, God," she whispered, the sound half-strangled.

Arabella knew what it was. Payment for the wager to the *man* who claimed her virtue.

The knowledge slipped into her heart like a dull, rusty knife.

She floundered helplessly, still reacting when he guided her into his study. He wrestled the pouch from her grip and dropped it onto the corner of his desk.

Arabella remained where she was. It was as if an icy chill swept across her soul. Cold to the tips of her fingers, for a heartbeat she felt herself waver, like a flame in the wind.

He caught her under the elbow.

Quickly she righted herself. "I'm all right."

"Yes." He smiled slightly. "I forgot. You never have the vapors, do you?"

His hands displayed a tendency to linger. "And I won't now," she informed him. Wrenching herself away, she marched toward the far corner of his desk. She had to put some distance between them. She absolutely couldn't bear it if he touched her.

Her voice scraped the silence. "I believe you said there were five men who entertained the wager. Five men who bet on who would claim my virtue. I recall quite distinctly, Justin, that you told me you were not among them. I remember it clearly."

He shook his head. "And I was not."

Arabella made a sound of impatience. "You make no sense!" she accused sharply. "You just said—"

"I know what I said. But I was not among those who entertained that particular wager."

Arabella lost her temper. "Do not lie to me!"

"I am not lying. I *will* not lie." He paused. "Gideon and I entered into a wager of our own. A private wager. We doubled the terms of the other men's wager."

"The wager for my virtue. Say it, Justin."

He seemed curiously reluctant. The seconds ticked by, one by one, and with each Arabella was suddenly fiercely, bitingly angry. "Say it!"

"Yes. *Yes*. We agreed to double the terms of the wager for your virtue."

"Was it a competition then between the two of you?"

He shook his head. "Gideon told me you'd already spurned his advances. The wager was that *I* could take your virtue." A pause. "Within the month," he added softly.

And he had. *He had*. Oh, God. *God*. In the span between one heartbeat and the next, she relived the achingly tender way he'd taken her on their wedding night, every fleeting, burning caress . . . She was cringing inside, the memory suddenly tarnished. And now he stood motionless, leaning against the side of his desk, arms crossed over his chest, watching her.

How could he be so calm? Arabella wanted to

scream and rage, to pummel him with her fists. Though she was blistering inside, she forced herself to match his aplomb.

"How much?" she asked.

He said nothing.

Her gaze skidded to the pouch. "I can always look," she reminded him.

"Six thousand pounds."

She was right. Half a fortune. "Well," she said coldly, "you certainly must have been very confident of your . . . persuasive abilities."

There was a taut, rippling silence. It flashed through her mind that he didn't know what to say, and so he said nothing.

"Ah, of course," she mused aloud, "the game was never to wed me . . . but to bed me." She was torn between the urge to laugh hysterically and cry in sheer, utter shame. In truth, she might have well surrendered her virginity to him without benefit of marriage. Oh, perhaps not that fateful night Georgiana and Aunt Grace had come upon them, but in time . . .

After all, he was the handsomest man in all England, and she was but a plaything. And she, fool that she was, had played right into his hands! For when she was in his arms, his expert mouth draining her of strength and will, nothing else seemed to matter.

Oh, but she'd forgotten what a rogue he really was. God knew, he'd made no secret of it. Being caught by Georgiana and Aunt Grace had simply forced his hand, forced him into marrying her.

The sense of betrayal was incredible. Wave after wave of burning shame washed through her, shame that bled to her very core.

But she wouldn't let him know it. No matter how much it hurt, she wouldn't.

Instead, she tipped her head to the side. "Is that why you agreed to wed me so quickly—that you might win?" She allowed no time to answer. "And here I was convinced you were to be commended for offering to marry me to save my reputation. Ah, poor Justin, forced to give up his name simply because he had the misfortune of being caught in the act of a mere kiss! I wonder, are you to be pitied or lauded? At least I needn't worry that we will have pockets to let, now, will we? At least I am aware of your priorities. Money over honor and all that—"

His jaw tensed. "Stop it, Arabella."

"I will not!" she flared.

A dull flush crept beneath his cheekbones. "For what it's worth, when I made that wager, I didn't know The Unattainable was *you*."

She snorted. "Why, thank you for that assurance! It makes it all the more palatable, doesn't it? Of course, a man with your looks would never have deigned to lower yourself to being seen with a graceless clod like me."

"That is not what I meant and you know it."

"There is no reason you could give that would make you less of a cad in my eyes."

His mouth twisted. "I'm quite aware of that. Nonetheless—"

Ignoring him, Arabella started for the door.

His hands descended to her shoulders when she would have skirted him.

She flung her head up. "Release me," she said evenly. "I must dress for dinner."

His mouth was as tight as hers. "That can wait."

"It cannot! Aunt Grace and Uncle Joseph are expecting us for dinner tonight."

He swore. "Goddammit, Arabella, we are not going anywhere until this is settled."

"Oh, yes, we are," she snapped. "I refuse to disappoint or disrespect my aunt and uncle by failing to appear. And if you will not accompany me, then I shall simply go alone. In any case, this discussion will have to wait."

His hands fell away. What he thought of her speech, she didn't know, nor did she care. Aware that her expression was mutinous, she sailed past him, her chin angled high.

In the carriage, the atmosphere was stifling. Arabella sat stiffly on one side of the cushioned velvet interior, Justin on the opposite. Not once did their gazes collide. She offered no small talk, nor did he.

As the carriage rolled to a halt in front of Uncle Joseph's townhouse, she realized Justin hadn't had the chance to tell her his news. Her lips compressed. She was not inclined to ask, not now. Clearly it hadn't been important.

Through some miracle, both of them managed to maintain a modicum of civility as they greeted her aunt and uncle.

Aunt Grace took her hands. A dimple appeared

in her aunt's cheek. "I have a surprise for you, dear," she said gaily.

Arabella smiled slightly. "Yes, Aunt?"

Beaming, without a word, Grace led her into the drawing room. There, two forms rose in unison from the sofa—one diminutive and blond, flanked by a tall red-haired man.

Arabella blinked, then shook her head, as if to clear it. Her lips parted. "Mama," she heard herself say faintly. "Papa . . ."

And then she burst into tears.

Twenty-two

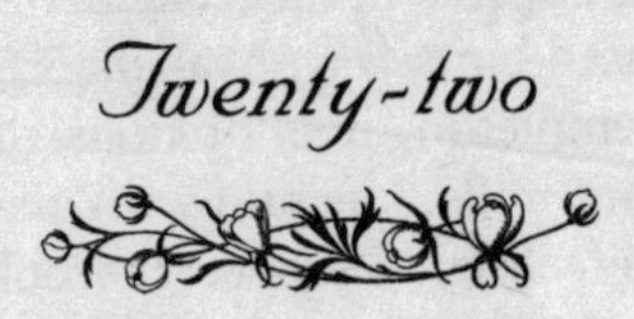

Her tears were not, Justin was convinced, tears of happiness. Tears of entreaty, perhaps. Tears of helplessness . . .

Dinner was a strained affair. Arabella's parents were polite but restrained. Justin didn't miss the way their eyes strayed to Arabella over and over. Arabella sat beside him, her face pale, still streaked with tears. Every so often, her teeth dug into her lower lip, as if she were fighting hard not to break down. For a time, Grace tried to rescue all of them with her usual bright, vivacious chatter, until at last she, too, lapsed into silence.

It was obvious to all present that Arabella was miserable. Justin was convinced it couldn't get any worse.

He was wrong.

After dinner they filed into the drawing room. Arabella took a seat near the fireplace, to the left of where her parents sat on the settee.

Justin cleared his throat. The direct approach was the right approach, he decided.

He addressed himself to Arabella's parents. "Mr. and Mrs. Templeton, it is obvious there is something on your minds," he said with an easy smile he was far from feeling. "I suspect it would serve us all if we simply got things out into the open."

Daniel Templeton wasted no time. "Very well, then," he said with a lift of shaggy red brows. "I shall begin by saying that the news of Arabella's marriage came as a total surprise. Had we been here, I doubt her mother and I would have allowed it."

Now even Grace appeared ready to cry. God above, but the evening was showing every sign of turning into a catastrophe.

Joseph reached out and covered his wife's hand. "Now, see here, Daniel. Considering the circumstances, Grace and I did what we thought was right," Joseph declared defensively. "You've left Arabella in our care many times and never before questioned our judgment."

"And there's never been any reason to. But my word, Joseph, can you imagine our distress when Catherine and I learned Arabella had wed such a . . ." He paused. His gaze flitted back to Justin, who gritted his teeth.

"Go ahead and say it," Justin invited baldly. "You certainly won't hurt my feelings."

"Very well, then. We were appalled upon discovering our daughter had wed a man of his ilk." Daniel's mouth was thin with disapproval. "Needless to say, we were already well aware of your reputation."

"That is why we set out for home at once," Catherine put in.

"And what do we find?" Daniel continued. "I know my daughter, sir. And despite what she wrote to us, that is not the face of a happily married woman."

Every eye in the room slid to Arabella.

Justin's heart sank. Her expression was pinched, her lips tremulous. He saw her convulsive swallow, the way her fingers plucked at each other in her lap.

A fist knotted in his chest, so that for a moment he almost couldn't breathe. It wrenched at his insides, seeing her like this. God knew, he didn't expect her to defend him. But if only she would say *something . . .*

"I submit, sir, that you took advantage of an impressionable young female. Her mother and I have already discussed this. Arabella has not yet reached the age of majority. We did not give our consent to this marriage. Therefore I am confident it can be nullified."

Justin surged upright with a curse.

Grace gasped. Catherine was clearly horrified. Joseph shot him a silent warning.

"Please." Arabella's voice was very low. "Will you all stop talking about me as if I weren't present? I am not a child anymore." She gazed at her father. "Papa, do not blame Justin, or Uncle Joseph or Aunt Grace. The truth is that if anyone had found out we were . . . kissing . . . I would have been quite done for."

Daniel's face softened as he looked at his daughter. "We all make mistakes, Arabella. But this is one that can be rectified. I'm certain an annulment can be obtained."

Justin was incensed. It was only by the most stringent effort that he clamped the lid on his temper. "Sir, I must remind you that this is a matter between husband and wife, and I do not welcome your interference. And now, if you would all be so kind, I should like a word with my wife in private."

His gaze locked with the reverend's.

Daniel's brows drew together over his nose. "Now, see here, boy, I am still her father—"

"And however much you regret it, I am still her husband." Justin's tone was clipped and abrupt. "And I wish to see her alone."

Daniel showed no sign of relenting; Justin *would* not. Catherine, Joseph, and Grace had already moved to the door and stood waiting. Justin and Daniel remained deadlocked, oblivious to everything but each other.

Finally, with a sound of impatience, Justin swung his gaze to Arabella. "Arabella?" he said softly. Within that quiet sound lurked both a demand and a question.

The tension spun out endlessly. Her gaze remained focused on her lap. She was silent for so long he almost wondered if she'd heard him. Just when he thought he might explode, she raised her head.

"I . . . please, Papa. It's all right."

Daniel's lips compressed, but he got to his feet. Walking over to where she sat, he pressed a kiss upon the fiery curls so like his. "Call if you need us," was all he said.

The door clicked shut behind him. Justin and Arabella were left alone.

Justin hadn't moved. Arabella's regard had returned to her hands, still clasped tightly in her lap. She was white and subdued as he'd never seen her.

"Well," he said with a sardonic smile, "that went well. I knew I was a cad, but I never guessed I'd have to seek permission to be alone with my wife."

That brought her head up. Her eyes flashed blue fire. "Don't you dare say anything against Papa!" she lashed out. "My father is the kindest, most gentle man on this earth."

Justin took a deep breath, feeling his way carefully. "Yes. Your parents are decent, respectable people. It's obvious they are wholly devoted to you, so I understand perfectly their loyalty to you. And certainly the situation is . . . out of the ordinary."

Arabella neither agreed nor disagreed. Her gaze skittered from his. Once again, she ducked her head. Her pose was one of utter despair.

Striding across the room, Justin got down on his haunches before her.

"Arabella," he said quietly, "won't you look at me?"

Her soft mouth trembled. Her lashes swept low, her head lower still.

A dull pain unfurled in his chest. On impulse, he stretched out a hand to cover hers.

It was a mistake. She drew back with a hiss. "Don't," she whispered. "Please don't touch me."

His jaw clenched. He willed away the angry demand that swelled in him. Instead he said, very low, "Please, Arabella. Let us go home and discuss this."

"No."

"What?"

She shook her head. "No. I—I don't think I want to go home. Not with you."

His eyes narrowed. "What are you going to do? Stay here?"

Her nod was jerky.

Justin inhaled. "Sweetheart—"

"Don't! Don't call me that. And don't look at me like that!" Her voice was thin and high. "Perhaps Papa is right and our marriage should be annulled."

"I don't want that." His statement was quietly emphatic.

Her eyes climbed slowly to his. If Justin hadn't already been on his knees, the torment he glimpsed on her face would have surely put him there.

"And what about what I want?"

He tipped his head, as if to peer clear into her heart. "What do you want?" he asked gently.

Her breath grew ragged and belabored. "I don't know," she said with a shake of her head. "But I can't think with you here. I can't think with you *near*. I need to be alone, Justin. I need to be alone!"

"No. What you need is me. Your husband."

"My husband. My husband!" she burst out. "My husband, who married me to win a wager!"

"That's not true—"

"Then why didn't you tell the truth? You told me about the wager at White's," she charged. "Why didn't you tell me about your wager with Gideon?"

He despised the betraying flush that seeped beneath his skin. "Perhaps I should have. I told Gideon before he left for Paris that the wager was off. He refused to listen. Arabella, for what it's worth, the wager was of no consequence to me."

It was the wrong thing to say. He knew it the instant the words were out. He gestured vaguely. "Arabella, I'm sorry—"

"Oh, I'm sure you are—sorry that you were caught!"

"I am sorry that I was so stupid, so foolish, so callous for making the wager at all! And yes, perhaps I'm being selfish, but I wish you hadn't found out." He gestured impatiently. "My God, how could I tell you? I didn't want to hurt you."

Arabella said nothing, merely stared at him in silent accusation.

"Arabella, the man who made that wager . . . he no longer exists. Being with you . . . everything's different. *I'm* different. For the first time in my life, I've felt . . . happy. Content. I—" He cast about for the right words, praying he could find them. "I've never felt like this, love. *Never*. And it's because of you, Arabella. I know it. I can *feel* it. When I think of our wedding night . . . what we shared . . . it's very precious to me, sweet. What we had . . . no, what we *have* . . . I don't want to lose it. I don't want to lose *you*."

But she was shaking her head, over and over and over. Denying it. Denying *him*.

"Please leave," she said tonelessly.

"Arabella! Don't do this. It can't end like this."

"It should never have begun!" she cried.

Justin stared at her. They were mated. By God, they were married. They belonged together in spirit and in soul. Didn't she know it?

"Don't say that." Against her will, against all reason, he caught her hands in his. He was burning inside—his lungs, his throat, but most of all, burning at the center of his heart.

"You said a wife belongs at her husband's side, Arabella. The night I told you about my father, you said—"

"I know what I said. But . . . everything's changed."

He heard the words, despairing and thick.

He wanted to shake her, to demand that she listen. He wanted to close his arms around her and never let go. Christ, he thought helplessly, it was almost as if he could see her slipping away, drifting beyond his reach.

"You're wrong," he whispered. "Nothing's changed. Only me. *Only me.*" His eyes were stinging. He saw the world through a watery blur. Saw *her* through a blur. He didn't care, nor did he care that *she* saw. All he could think was that he had to bring her back. He had to at least try.

"Please, sweetheart. We'll work this out, I promise. Just . . ." There was a deep, rough catch in his voice. "Come home with me. I—I'm begging you. *Come home with me.*"

A stricken sound tore from her throat, a cry that ripped his heart to shreds. "Don't say any more. And don't look at me like that!" She wrenched away and bolted for the door.

Justin knew then. It was no use. There would be no arguing. There would be no pleading.

And when he left . . . he left alone.

The next afternoon, Sebastian whistled a merry tune as he mounted the steps to his brother's house on Brooke Street. He and Justin shared the same solicitor, and having just come from that good man's offices, he was eager to congratulate his brother on his recent purchase.

Arthur let him in. "My lord," he murmured, taking Sebastian's hat and umbrella, "your arrival is most welcome."

The butler directed him to Justin's study. He didn't think twice of Arthur's statement until he saw Justin.

He lounged in a chair by the fire, booted legs sprawled wide. His usually impeccable appearance was anything but. His cravat was undone, his shirt wrinkled and untidy, his jaw dark with stubble.

"Good God, man!" Sebastian exclaimed. "You look bloody awful!"

Justin saluted with a half-empty bottle of wine. "Thank you. May I return the compliment?"

Sebastian looked into bleary, bloodshot eyes and swore. "Are you foxed?"

Justin's mouth twisted. "Not yet. But I *am* trying." He started to lift the bottle. "Ah, but where are my manners? Please, join me. It's a fine year, I promise you."

Sebastian wrested the bottle away and set it aside. "Where the devil is Arabella?"

Justin's eyes glinted. "My lovely wife spent last night at her aunt and uncle's. This morning, a footman came to collect some of her things. I trust that she is, at this very instant, contemplating whether or not our marriage should be annulled—per her parents' counsel, I might add."

Sebastian's mouth thinned. "Spare me your sarcasm. What the hell are you doing here, then? This is the last place you should be."

"She doesn't want to see me."

"Oh, that's absurd."

"She told me, Sebastian. She *told* me. She . . . she's left me," he ground out. "No, that's not right. I drove her away. I drove her away with my—my vileness. My God, Sebastian, you should have seen her."

Sebastian sighed. "Perhaps I will have that glass of wine." He retrieved the wine, poured himself a healthy portion, then sat back in the chair opposite Justin. "Tell me what happened," he invited.

Quickly, without a surfeit of words, Justin began to talk. He began with the evening of the Farthingale ball, and summed it up with Gideon's visit and the remainder of the evening last night.

Sebastian listened quietly throughout. One corner of his mouth crooked upward when Justin had finished. "Well," he murmured, "I certainly don't envy you."

Justin eyed his brother. "Your sympathy overwhelms me."

Sebastian leaned forward. "This isn't doing either of you any good. But I doubt an annulment would be so easy to obtain as Daniel thinks. For one, Arabella did have consent—her aunt and uncle. For another, the marriage has been consummated, has it not?"

Justin simply gave him a thoroughly disgusted look.

Sebastian's lips quirked in turn. "I agree, a stupid question."

"Perhaps it's better this way." Justin stared dully off into the corner.

"She's the best thing to ever come into your life," Sebastian said bluntly.

"And I'm the worst thing to come into hers."

"That's precisely the kind of thinking that will gain you nothing. Justin, sometimes things happen that we don't expect, that we can't control. Perhaps it's just as she says. Perhaps all Arabella needs is a little time. She'll come around."

Justin was quiet for a very long time. "And what if she doesn't?"

"Then make her."

Justin's mind veered to Arabella. He saw her as he'd left her, her eyes huge and wounded, shaken and but a shadow of the woman he knew.

Darkness slipped over him. "I can't. I won't." He faltered. "Sebastian, I've hurt her enough."

"And you're content to leave it at that?"

"What the hell am I supposed to do?" Justin grew bitter. "Snatch her away from her parents? That should go over well. Her father would probably have me hunted down for kidnapping!"

"I hardly think so. Daniel is a reasonable man. When he sees how unhappy Arabella is, he'll change his mind. So will Catherine."

"Sebastian, you haven't been listening. She doesn't *want* me. I think it would suit her just fine if she never laid eyes on me again. Christ, she could barely stand to be in the same room with me."

"She's angry and hurt," Sebastian reminded him gently. "And you forget, I *have* seen her with you. She can barely take her eyes from you—and you from her."

Justin dropped his head into his hands. Somehow he'd known his newfound happiness wouldn't last—that it was too good to be true. After all, *she* was too good for him. His whole life, he'd been floundering; in Arabella, he'd found something worthwhile. He'd felt *whole*. But now he'd lost her, and he had no one else to blame.

"That was before," he stated heavily. "And this is now, and . . . and it's just as she said. Everything's changed."

"No, Justin. Nothing's changed. Not really."

Justin raised his head. "I swear I do not mean to be rude, but what the hell would you know about it?"

Sebastian smiled slightly. "Quite a lot, actually."

"What the devil does that mean? And why the devil are you smiling?"

"If it's any consolation, I remember having a similar conversation with *you* several years ago, only then the tables were turned. As you may recall, there was a time when Devon refused to see me as well."

Justin's mouth flattened into a grim line. "Yes, and whose fault was that? Mine. I was the one who almost ruined your chance at marriage."

"Oh, no, it wasn't you, Justin. I mucked things up quite tidily." Sebastian paused. "It seems we both have a way of making fools of ourselves with the women we love."

Justin went utterly still, both inside and out. He stared at Sebastian until his eyes grew dry and he could no longer see. Scarcely able to breathe, he broke out in a cold sweat inside. Oh, God, was that what this was? This rending, tearing feeling deep in his soul? Was it love? It was like a red-hot knife tearing deep inside, over and over. A brand on his soul . . . on his very heart.

Love couldn't hurt like this. It *shouldn't* hurt like this. Love was supposed to be good and sweet and pure . . .

Like Arabella.

And in loving Arabella . . . well, it was not an admission that Justin made either easily or gracefully. He had fought it for much of his life.

But he could fight it no longer.

Yet the knowledge did not make his heartache easier to bear.

Indeed, it only made it all the harder.

Twenty-three

"Madame," Ames announced, "a caller for you."

From her seat on the settee, Arabella glanced up. "For me?"

Her pulse was suddenly wild and erratic. Was it Justin? A dozen feelings rushed at her from all sides. Hope . . . fear . . . everything in between. Her heart lurched as a tall figure strode into the drawing room.

It wasn't Justin, but Sebastian.

She could have wept. Two days had gone by since the awful scene here in this very room. As soon as Justin departed that night, Arabella had excused herself and gone upstairs. She had been too numb to feel anything but her own pain. Certainly not his.

But upstairs, in the bed where she'd spent so many nights before, sleep eluded her. It felt . . .

wrong somehow. The bed felt . . . empty. In the morning, she wavered between indignation and misery, hurt and yearning.

But now . . . Her gaze flitted to the tea service on the tray at her knees. "Would you like tea?"

Sebastian declined.

Arabella bit her lip. "You've seen Justin, haven't you?" The question spilled out before she could stop it.

"Yesterday," he affirmed.

Her hands fluttered back to her lap. "Did he ask you to come here?" Before he could say a word, she came to her own conclusion. "No, of course not. He's too stubborn. Too proud."

Sebastian smiled slightly. "I see you know him well."

"How is he?" The question almost burned her tongue. She didn't want to know, she told herself wildly. But she had to.

Sebastian hiked a black brow. "Must you ask?"

"Oh," she said weakly. "Foxed, I take it."

"If it's any comfort, I don't think it's helping." He watched her for a moment. "He doesn't know I'm here, Arabella. And I haven't come to plead his case, if that's what you're thinking. I'm not here to try to convince you to return to him."

"Then why are you?"

"I don't really know," he answered honestly. "But now that I am, I should like to tell you something. So please, Arabella, hear me out, if you will." He paused. "It's strange," he said musingly, "but all morning, my mind has been consumed with an incident that occurred long, long ago. I can't get it out of my mind and . . . well, frankly, that's why I'm here, I suppose."

Arabella regarded him curiously. "What is it?"

"We were at Thurston Hall," he went on. "Justin was perhaps eight or nine, no more, if memory serves me correctly. One afternoon, Justin failed to return to the schoolroom. Soon everyone was searching for him, frantic as the hours passed. But no one could find him, until at last my father spied him sitting in the branches of a tree in the orchard, watching as everyone dashed madly about for hours. He shouted for him to come down. And I'm not sure that Justin would have, but then he fell. His wrist was cocked at an odd angle—I knew it was broken. I ran over, for my father was in a rage such as I'd never seen before."

Arabella had gone very quiet inside. She suddenly recalled how Justin had pointed out that very tree . . .

"My father . . . he was not a gentle man, Arabella. He had no compassion for Justin's pain. The physician was summoned. I could tell it hurt like the very blazes—and Justin but a boy! But he didn't make a sound when the physician set the break. I recall telling him it was all right to cry. But Justin merely gazed at my father and vowed most insistently that he would *not* cry, that he would *never* cry. Oh, and my father *wanted* him to, I could see it in his eyes! But Justin never did," Sebastian finished. "Not then. Not ever."

He looked at her then. "That's odd, don't you think? For a child to never, ever cry?"

Arabella's throat constricted. Etched in her mind was a vision of Justin as a child, lying helpless and hurt while his father raged . . . And to think she had laughingly chided him about his clumsiness that day!

Her mind whirling, she went very still inside. For she was remembering something else, too, a memory that suddenly battered her. She cringed inside, recalling how Justin had stood in this very room a scant two days earlier, a telltale rustiness in his voice, an unfamiliar sheen in his eyes . . . She cringed inside. What was it she'd told him?

Don't say any more. And don't look at me like that!

She gave a tiny shake of her head and looked at Sebastian. "How do you know he didn't?"

"Because I know my brother," Sebastian replied. He seemed to hesitate. "Arabella, our childhood was not particularly pleasant—"

"I know," she said quickly. "Justin told me." She didn't tell him about the night their father had died, how Justin blamed himself. Justin had revealed it in confidence, and she would not betray that confidence.

But Sebastian was speaking again. "Julianna has no memory of our mother. She was too young when she left. That's a blessing, I believe. But Justin . . ." He shook his head. "I've always thought it was hardest on Justin. He needed a mother, and she wasn't there. It changed him, I think. And he's spent his life believing what he thought everyone else believed, that he was wild and rebellious and defiant. And the world believes it, too, that he is a man without scruples, without morals. But Julianna and I have always been aware that's not what he is, not really. I think you know, too, that he's not what he pretends to be."

Arabella did. God, how she did!

"He's been walking in shadow his whole life, wandering, searching for something he didn't even know he wanted. But I think he found it in you, Arabella. He's *different* with you. It's like he's stepped into a ray of sunlight." He gave a tiny shake of his head.

"Don't send him back into the shadows, Arabella. Please don't. I know I said I wouldn't interfere. But you and Justin belong together. Devon knew it even before I did. But this rift between you and Justin . . . it's beyond my power to repair, or I would."

He paused. "Please," he said softly, "just go see him. Before you decide anything, just—just go see him. I believe you'll find him in Kent. He told me he had some unfinished business at the house there."

She peered at him blankly. "What house?"

"The country house in Kent. He bought it just a few days ago."

Stunned, Arabella merely gazed at him.

"You didn't know, did you?"

Arabella took a breath. "He never said a word—" She broke off. Was *that* the news he'd wanted to tell her? Guilt washed through her. Oh, merciful Lord. Gideon had arrived, and then—then she hadn't even given him the chance.

Through a haze she saw Sebastian rise to his feet. "I must be off. Devon is expecting me."

Arabella saw him to the door, then returned to the drawing room. Her tea sat before her, cold and untouched.

There was a painful catch in the region of her heart. Sebastian's visit was a stark reminder of all Justin had endured as a child—his mother's abandonment, his father's censure. Arabella had the awful sensation it was surely far worse than Justin had let on, than Sebastian even knew. The night Justin had told her of his nightmare, she had guessed that Justin loved his father, loved him despite all the hurt his father had inflicted upon him. She had no trouble envisioning Justin as the proud, stubborn little boy Sebastian spoke of, for he was just such a man. If he was hurt, he wouldn't show it.

Yet he had begged her to return home with him. He'd *begged* her, with tears in his eyes . . .

Tears from the boy who never cried.

And she had turned her back on him.

Suddenly she was crying, too, silent tears that slid unheeded down her cheeks.

It was then she realized . . . the walls he'd built around himself were not meant to keep others out—to keep *her* out!—but to defend his heart, to shield himself against further pain.

She had failed him, failed him most cruelly!

Why had he wed her? she wondered achingly. If he'd wanted to coldly seduce her, he could have. If he'd persisted, she wouldn't have resisted.

Instead he had married her, this man who defied duty. And she wanted desperately to believe that what they had shared in those few precious weeks of marriage was more than passion. More than desire . . .

In was in the midst of that thought that she glanced up to find her parents, aunt, and uncle had filed into the room. Hurriedly she wiped the moisture from her cheeks with the back of her hand.

Mama wasted no time expressing her concern. "We saw the Marquess of Thurston leave. I hope his visit didn't distress you, Arabella. Are you—all right?"

"I'm fine, Mama," she said, and smiled.

"Oh, Arabella, it's grand to see you smile again! Why, we were anxious to cheer you, so Grace and I asked Cook to prepare your favorite—"

"I won't be staying for dinner, Mama." She stood, only to find the change in position made her head spin. Her father stepped to her side and steadied her.

She blinked. "Oh, my," she said. "How strange. That's the second time that's happened the last few days."

An odd look passed between her mother and Aunt Grace. Arabella looked from one to the other. "What is it?" she started to ask.

Her jaw sagged as the significance sank in. "Oh. *Oh!*" This last was almost a squeal.

"It's strain, surely," her mother said quickly.

Arabella put a hand on her belly. A faint wonder crept inside her. "Perhaps not," she said softly.

Her mother inhaled. "Arabella, no. No! Never say you're breeding by that man—"

"Mama!" Arabella's voice rapped out sharply. "Watch what you say! That man is my husband. Do you hear? My *husband*. And his name is Justin. It would please me if you would begin using it."

Mama appeared utterly stricken. "Arabella," she whispered, "what are you saying?"

Arabella stepped forward, taking her mother's hand. "Mama, I'm not a child anymore. I haven't been for a long time. You and Papa have been gone so much that I think you still see me as a child. But I'm a woman now, a woman who knows what she wants." She smiled faintly. "When you and Papa left for Africa, I didn't. Why, even when the Season began, I didn't. I felt out of step somehow. But now I know what's wrong—or rather, I know what's *right*."

"I agree you're not a child. But Arabella—"

"Mama," came Arabella's reminder, "you flaunted convention when you married Papa."

"Yes, but—"

A finger on her lips, she stemmed her mother's protest. "You and Papa followed your hearts. So did Aunt Grace and Uncle Joseph. And that's what I'm doing." Her gaze slid to her father. "Papa, there will be no annulment."

The lines had begun to ease from her mother's face. Her father was watching her as well. "Arabella, are you certain this is what you want?"

"It is, Papa." Her eyes were clear and shining. "I'm going home to my husband. I should never have let him leave without me. And it would please me if you welcome him into the family with open arms."

Daniel gave a tiny smile. He put an arm around his wife. "It's difficult to watch your child hurt, Arabella. We simply wanted you to be happy."

Mama gave a rather watery smile. "Of course, dear. That's all that really matters."

Arabella could have burst inside with all she felt in that moment. She'd never loved them more than she did right now. She kissed each of them.

Uncle Joseph had already left the room to call for the carriage, and Aunt Grace was at the door, calling for a maid to pack Arabella's belongings.

"Well, Aunt Grace, I can see you're eager to be rid of me again."

Grace started to titter, then clapped a hand over her mouth so Catherine wouldn't see. "My dear," she whispered, "I simply marvel that it took you so long to see what I saw long ago."

"And when was that?" Arabella teased.

"Why, that very first night at the Farthingale ball when you waltzed with your husband-to-be. You were quite dazzled. He was quite smitten. Oh, but I had such high hopes that night!"

"Aunt Grace!" Arabella gasped in amazement. "Even then?"

"Even then."

Arabella hugged her fiercely. "You know you always were my favorite aunt."

"Child, I am your only aunt!" Grace's eyes were sparkling with mirth. She clapped her hands together. "Oh, happy day!" she sang out. "I shall begin planning that christening this very night!"

Arabella chuckled shakily. "It may be a trifle soon," she cautioned, "but I should imagine it won't be long."

Twenty-four hours later, Arabella was inside a carriage that hurtled through the countryside of Kent. The hour had been late when she'd finally departed London, and the carriage had no sooner left when the road had been blocked by a carriage that overturned. Reluctantly she'd spent the night at a roadside inn.

Though it wasn't so very far from London, the city seemed a world apart. On each side of the road, lush green grass ascended the rolling fields on either side. She sat on the edge of the seat, peering out the window, chafing inside.

Sebastian had told her of several landmarks, such as the village with an ancient Celtic cross in the town square. She searched for them eagerly. It wouldn't be long now. Only a few more miles.

As the carriage rounded a curve, a small manor house came into view. Arabella leaned forward as the building grew larger and larger. She caught her breath, entranced by the stone towers that rose on the front corners. It was lovely beyond words. Beyond wishes. Exactly the kind of house she'd always dreamed she might live in . . .

When the carriage rolled to a halt, the driver leaped down, then scurried to help her alight.

Arabella stepped outside. The scent of some sweet, unknown flower lingered on the breeze. Her gaze swept around, then stopped on the low-hanging branches of a cherry tree that stood in the front of the house. A wistful yearning bloomed in her breast. Oh, but she could imagine waking here, every day for the rest of her life.

Mounting the wide stone steps, she reached for the brass knocker. The door was wrenched open before she laid a finger on it.

She squinted upward. A spare masculine form filled the doorway. He was dressed in boots, tight fawn breeches, and a white shirt that revealed a slice of dark, hair-roughened chest.

Her heart lurched. "Hello, Justin," she said breathlessly. A streak of longing shot through her. Had it only been a few days since he'd touched her? Kissed her?

God, but it seemed a lifetime! She longed to cast herself against him and forget the tumult that raged in both their hearts, forget everything but the warm strength of his arms tight around her back.

But he would not welcome it. For while her heart gladdened at the sight of him, she couldn't say the same for Justin. He regarded her, the cast of his jaw was locked tight, his features stony. His lips were set in a thin, straight line.

"I suspect I have my brother to thank for you being here, don't I?"

His acid greeting was not what she'd hoped for. It took every ounce of hope and courage she possessed to meet his eyes. "Sebastian told me where you were," she said quietly, "but I came on my own. And he has only your best interests at heart, you know."

Justin's eyes were a stormy green. She thought he might argue, but he said nothing.

"Do you think I might come in?" She ventured the question tentatively, and for one treacherous moment she had the terrifying sensation he might refuse.

Finally he stepped aside. Arabella set her reticule on a table in the entrance hall and followed him into a large drawing room to the left.

She turned in a slow circle. "Why didn't you tell me you bought this house?" A faint smile curved her lips. "Justin, I adore it! I've never seen anything quite so beautiful—"

"I'm selling it," he interrupted curtly.

She looked at him sharply. Her heart began to pound so hard her chest actually hurt. "Why?"

"Because I should never have bought it, that's why. I only came to clarify a few matters with the estate manager."

Arabella shook her head. "Please don't be so hasty. Buying this estate . . . that's what you were going to tell me the other afternoon, wasn't it?"

His eyes flickered. "It doesn't matter."

Arabella felt like she was bleeding inside. He was

so distant, so remote. "It does matter. Please, Justin," she blurted, "can we talk?"

"What more is there to say?"

"I should think a great deal."

"I should think *not*."

He turned his back on her and strode to the window. "You'll forgive me if I don't see you out."

His manner was coolly defensive. Arabella stared at him, stung. He was so stubborn. So arrogant and prideful. My God, he wanted her gone! A wave of despair washed over her, but she battled it back.

"If you're trying to drive me away, you're going to have to do better than that," she said, her tone very low. "For I won't leave. Not until you tell me outright that . . . that you don't want me as your wife."

In the heartbeat before her voice wobbled traitorously, her gaze cleaved to his.

Time hung never-ending. Something splintered across his features. He raised his eyes to the ceiling, the cords of his neck standing out in stark relief.

Without a word, he turned his back on her. He strode across the floor to the window and stood staring out, his arms crossed over his chest.

But in the heartbeat before he swung away, she glimpsed something in his eyes, something that made her bite back a cry.

She knew it for certain when she heard his voice, low and half-strangled.

"Go, Arabella. Just go and leave me be!"

Her heart constricted. She stood rooted to the spot. Sebastian's story came back full force. She remembered the little boy who wouldn't cry, no matter how much he hurt. And for that mind-splitting instant, she saw clear inside. She saw him as he was now—stripped of his pride, raw and naked and still so vulnerable.

And she knew then why Sebastian had come to her. *Don't send him back into the shadows,* Sebastian had pleaded.

And she couldn't. She wouldn't. Something came over her then. The need to save him from himself. She could do it—she *could*!

Everything broke inside her. Slipping her arms around his waist, she laid her cheek on his shirt. His entire body went taut, but he didn't break from her hold, as she feared he would.

"You can't say it, can you?" she whispered unsteadily. "If you could, you would."

His hands wound around her wrists. "Arabella—"

Hot tears spilled unchecked from her cheeks, seeping through the thin cloth of his shirt. "I'm sorry I hurt you, Justin. I'm so sorry."

Justin froze, then twisted around to face her. He peered down into her tortured eyes.

Once she'd started, she couldn't seem to stop. "We've both been such fools! I was wrong to push you away. I should have listened! You said you were different, that you weren't the same man who made that silly wager with Gideon. And I know it now. It's not too late for us, it's not! You won't be rid of me so easily. And I won't leave you again, Justin, no matter what you say. No matter what you do. And I won't let you leave me, either."

"Arabella, do you have any idea what you're saying?"

Arabella sagged against him, weeping openly. "Yes. Yes!"

His arms stole around her trembling form. "Don't cry," he said raggedly. "Sweet Jesus, please don't cry." He smoothed the cloud of her hair. "I love you, sweetheart. I love you."

"And I love you," she cried. "I do!"

He groaned. "You shouldn't—"

"Don't say that! Don't even think it!" Her eyes found his. "You believe you're unworthy of love, but you're not. Oh, don't you see? I love you for what you are, not in spite of what you are. I love you quite madly. And I always will."

He stared at her as if he still couldn't believe it. "Are you quite certain?"

Her eyes darkened. "Yes. Oh, yes." Holding her breath, she laid her fingers against the raspy plane of his cheek.

He didn't retreat, but let her fingers wander where they would—the blade of his nose, the contours of his cheekbones, the sculpted beauty of his lips. Their eyes caught. Trapping her fingers beneath his, he turned his mouth into her palm and kissed it.

Arabella wept once more, but this time she was smiling through her tears. Groaning, he engulfed her in his arms. With lips that were incredibly tender, he kissed away her tears, their hearts streaming together.

Finally he drew back, resting his forehead against hers. "Shall I show you our new home?"

With her slender fingers tucked into his elbow, he showed her through the house. They ended up back in the drawing room. An indulgent smile curling his lips, Justin watched as she peered through the windows, exclaiming delightedly.

"Oh, but I should love to have a little cottage garden there beyond that wonderful little tree. I'd grow primroses and columbine."

A smile grazed his lips. "Actually, that tree was what led me to buy this place. I kept seeing you as a girl—a little monkey clambering through the branches."

Arabella tried to withhold an answering smile of her own and failed. "Well," she murmured, "I daresay this will be the perfect place to raise our family."

"I quite agree." He pulled her into his embrace.

Her fingertips planted lightly on his chest, she looked up at him, suddenly serious. "Justin, do you hear what I'm saying? It's the perfect place to raise a family. *Our* family."

For an instant his brow furrowed. Then his gaze slid down her form. "What," he said blankly, "do you mean that you . . . that we . . ."

"It's too soon to be certain," she said hurriedly, blushing fiercely. "But I'm never, *ever* late," she stressed. "And it's been over a week now." She took a deep breath. "Do you mind the idea of being a father so soon after becoming a husband?"

His reply was not long in coming. "Not at all," he said smoothly. "In fact, if that is not already the case, I believe we should studiously apply ourselves to the possibility."

Her eyes widened, as blue as heaven. Justin laughed and sealed her lips in a binding kiss. "However," he murmured dryly when at last he raised his head, "I do have just one question."

"And what might that be?"

He nodded toward the oak tree in front of the window. "You won't teach our daughter to hang upside down from that tree, will you?"

And he gave her that smile that sent all the ladies to swooning . . . especially her. Arabella laughed and twined her arms around his neck. Oh, how she did love him!

Epilogue

Seven years later

Four-year-old Grayson Sebastian Sterling tugged at his mother's skirts. Arabella smiled down into eyes the color of a warm summer sky. "Yes, sweetings?"

Those eyes gleamed impishly. "Mama," he said with a giggle, "I see Lizzie's drawers." A chubby finger pointed outside.

Arabella turned and looked through the drawing room window.

Upended on the branch nearest the ground, her daughter Lizzie grinned at her mother, then stuck out her tongue at her brother.

Arabella's shriek woke the baby sleeping blissfully against her shoulder. "Justin, she's at it again! Oh, what are we going to do with her? How on earth does she manage to reach that branch?"

Justin glanced up from the newspaper and assessed the situation. "I daresay it has something to do with her pony trotting away minus his rider."

A minute later, she watched Justin stride outside. Lizzie grabbed the branch and wheeled herself upright. She tried to scramble away, but quick as she was, her father was quicker. Strong arms reached up and plucked their firstborn from her precarious perch.

Five minutes later, the three little ones herded into the care of their nurse, Arabella collapsed on the sofa.

"Oh, Lord," Arabella wailed, "I just know she'll do that tomorrow after our guests arrive from London! The Dowager Duchess of Carrington will be horrified! Oh, but that girl's outrageous antics will make my heart fail yet!"

Justin quirked a brow. "Sweetheart," he drawled, "the dowager duchess will not care a whit. Besides, you may as well get used to it—our Lizzie is destined to be the talk of the *ton* just like you."

"You're not helping matters any," Arabella groused. "Nor does it help when Mama and Papa laugh at her frolics. It only spurs her on more."

Justin chuckled and pulled his wife into his arms. His head ducked down and he kissed her, a long, lingering kiss of sweetness that made a tremor of emotion rush through him. Life was good, he decided. No more did he deem himself worthless or undeserving. No more nightmares haunted his dreams. Now his dreams were only of the future, a future he cherished, the way he cherished every moment of life with Arabella. For it was she who had cleansed his soul of guilt, who made each day brighter than the last.

Several hours later, the two of them began the rounds in the nursery, kissing each of their children good night, a ritual repeated each night without fail.

Elise—or Lizzie, as she was fondly called—was still bouncing in her bed when they entered her room. Six years old, she had inherited the same flame-red curls as her mother and grandfather, but her eyes sparkled like twin emeralds; they were the same crystalline green as Justin's.

Gray lay sleeping soundly. Arabella bent and kissed his cheek, while Justin's long fingers tousled silky black hair as dark as his own.

Nestled in her cradle was Tessa, who rather resembled her Aunt Julianna, with fine, dainty features and chestnut hair. Both her parents laughed at the way Tessa sneaked her thumb into her mouth and smacked, wiggling her little bum high in the air before settling over on her side.

Outside in the hall, Arabella slipped her arm through her husband's, resting her head against his shoulder. "We did make the most beautiful children, didn't we?"

"That we did," he agreed.

With their three children snug in their beds, they sought their own. Arabella nestled against his length.

With the tips of his fingers, he traced the outline of her lips. "Why are you smiling?"

"What's wrong with that?"

He raised a brow. "Nothing. Except that you're looking rather secretive."

Arabella walked her fingertips up his naked chest. "Ah, but you know all my secrets, remember?"

"Do I?"

"Yes, well, all but one," she teased.

"And which one is that?"

"Well, I was just thinking," she said blandly, "that we may have to hire another nurse."

"Arabella," he threatened with mock reproof, "do not change the subject."

Her tone was innocence itself. "Oh, but I'm not."

Justin sighed. "I admit, Lizzie is a handful—"

"Not because of Lizzie."

Justin propped himself up on an elbow to stare at her. "Why, then?"

Arabella's smile merely deepened.

His eyes widened. "What," he said faintly, "do you mean to say . . ." He swallowed hard, his eyes meeting hers in amazement. Lean fingers came out to splay possessively on her belly. He shook his head, still a little dazed. "My word—and Tess but four months old. Can you believe it?"

"Well, I did tell you once you would be an excellent father. Which you are," she pointed out. "As well as a perfect husband."

"And?" he prompted, his eyes gleaming wickedly.

"And a most ardent, satisfying lover."

And indeed, he set out to prove it, to her sheer and utter delight.

It was later, just as Arabella hovered on the fringes of sleep, that a sudden shout of laughter erupted.

Arabella raised her head from his chest, peered at him drowsily. "What is it?"

It was his turn to tease her. "I was just thinking."

"Of what?"

"Aunt Grace."

He laughed again, the sound low and rich and husky. Arabella felt her heart turn over.

"What about Aunt Grace?"

"What else? We'll have news for Aunt Grace when she arrives tomorrow, won't we? She'll be ecstatic, you know."

Arabella's laughter joined his. "She will indeed," said Arabella. "Another christening to plan . . ."

If Women Ruled the World . . .

Everyone knows that if women
ruled the world, it would be a better place!
And everyone also knows that in romance,
women do rule . . .
making the hero a better man.

Now read ahead to discover
how the heroines of the
Avon Romance Superleaders—
as created by Jacquie D'Alessandro,
Stephanie Bond, Samantha James, and,
as an added treat, the four stellar authors
of Avon's newest anthology collection—
tenderly, but most definitely, take matters
and men into their own hands . . .

Today's Modern Woman should know that a gentleman hoping to entice her will employ one of two methods: either a straightforward, direct approach, or a more subtle, gentle wooing. Sadly, as with most matters, few gentlemen consider which method the lady might actually prefer—until it's too late.

A Ladies' Guide to the Pursuit of Personal Happiness and Intimate Fulfillment

Tonight he would begin his subtle, gentle wooing.

Andrew Stanton stood in a shadowed corner of Lord Ravensly's elegant drawing room, feeling very much the way he imagined a soldier on the brink of battle might feel—anxious, focused, and very much praying for a hopeful outcome.

His gaze skimmed restlessly over the formally attired guests. Lavishly gowned and bejeweled ladies swirled around the dance floor in the arms of their perfectly turned-out escorts to the lilting strains of the string trio. But none of the waltzing ladies was the one he sought. Where was Lady Catherine?

His efforts to seek out Lady Catherine this evening had already been interrupted three times by people with whom he had no desire to speak. He feared one more such interruption would cause him to grind his teeth down to stubs.

Again he scanned the room, and his jaw tightened. Blast. After being forced to wait for what felt like an eternity finally to court her, why couldn't Lady Catherine—albeit unknowingly—at least soothe his anxiety by showing herself?

He reached up and tugged at his carefully tied cravat. "Damned uncomfortable neckwear," he muttered. Whoever had invented the constraining blight on fashion should be tossed in the Thames.

He drew a deep breath and forced himself to focus on the positive. His frustrating failure to locate Lady Catherine in the crowd *had* afforded him the opportunity to converse with numerous investors who had already committed funds to Andrew and Philip's museum venture. Lords Avenbury and Ferrymouth were eager to know how things were progressing, as were Lords Markingworth, Whitly, and Carweather, all of whom had invested funds. Mrs. Warrenfield appeared anxious to invest a healthy amount, as did Lord Kingsly. Lord Borthrasher, who'd already made a sizable investment, seemed interested in investing more. After speaking with them, Andrew had also made some discreet inquiries regarding the matter he'd recently been commissioned to look into.

But with the business talk now completed, he'd retreated to this quiet corner to gather his thoughts, much as he did before preparing for a pugilistic bout at Gentleman Jackson's Emporium. His gaze continued to pan over the guests, halting abruptly when he caught sight of Lady Catherine, exiting from behind an Oriental silk screen near the French doors.

He stilled at the sight of her bronze gown. Every time he'd seen her during the past year, her widow's weeds had engulfed her like a dark, heavy rain cloud. Now officially out of mourning, she resembled a golden bronze sun setting over the Nile, gilding the landscape with slanting rays of warmth.

She paused to exchange a few words with a gentleman, and Andrew's avid gaze noted the way the vivid material of her gown contrasted with her pale shoulders and complemented her shiny chestnut curls gathered into a Grecian knot. The becoming coiffure left the vulnerable curve of her nape bare . . .

He blew out a long breath and raked his free hand through his hair. How many times had he imagined skimming his fingers, his mouth, over that soft, silky skin? More than he cared to admit. She was all things lovely and good. A perfect lady. Indeed, she was perfect in every way.

He knew damn well he wasn't good enough for her.

Coming October 2004

If Women Ruled the World…

Office relationships would be a whole lot easier

In Stephanie Bond's *Whole Lotta Trouble* three young editors are bound together when the smary creep they all dated is discovered . . . dead. Who could have done it? And, more important, how do they all get out of being the prime suspects?

Felicia Redmon dropped into her desk chair and sorted through her phone messages. Suze Dannon. Phil Dannon. Suze again, then Phil again. She sighed—the Dannons were determined to drive her and each other completely mad. Her bestselling husband-and-wife team had separated under nasty circumstances, but had agreed to finish one last book together. Unfortunately, Felicia soon found herself in the middle of not only their editorial squabbles, but also their personal disagreements. Playing referee was wearing her nerves thin, but sometimes an editor has to go beyond the call of duty to make sure the book gets in on time. Still, she was afraid that if the Dannons didn't soon find a way to put aside their differences, the hostile couple, known for their sensual murder mysteries, were going to wind up killing each other.

There was a message from her doctor's office—an appointment reminder, no doubt—and one from Tallie, who probably wanted to firm plans for getting together at their regular hangout. And Jerry Key had called. Her heart jerked a little, just like every time she heard the bastard's name.

She should have known better than to get involved with a man with whom she would also have to do business, but literary agent Jerry Key had a way of making a woman forget little things . . . like consequences. He was probably calling on behalf of the Dannons, who were his clients. And whatever was wrong would definitely be her fault.

Might as well get it over with, she decided, and dialed Jerry's number—by memory, how pathetic.

"Jerry Key's office, this is Lori."

Felicia cringed at Lori's nasally tone. "Hi, Lori. This is Felicia Redmon at Omega Publishing, returning Jerry's call."

"Hold, please."

Felicia cursed herself for her accelerated pulse. A year was long enough to get over someone, especially someone as smarmy as Jerry had turned out to be.

The phone clicked. "Felicia," he said, his tongue rolling the last two vowels. "How are you?"

She pursed her mouth. "What's up, Jerry?"

"What, you don't have time for small talk anymore?"

Remembering the impending auction of one of his clients' books that she'd be participating in, Felicia bit her tongue. "Sorry, it's been a long day. How've you been?"

"Never better," he said smoothly. "Except when we were together."

She closed her eyes. "Jerry, don't."

"Funny, I believe that's the first time you've ever said 'don't.' "

Her tongue tingled with raw words, but she reminded herself that she was to blame for the predicament she'd gotten herself into. The bottom line was that Jerry Key represented enough big-name authors—some of them tied to Omega Publishers—that she had to play nice, no matter how much it killed her.

"Jerry, I'm late for a meeting, so I really can't chat. What did you need?"

He sighed dramatically. "Sweetheart, we have a problem. The Dannons are upset."

"Both of them?"

"Suze in particular. She said that you're siding with Phil on all the manuscript changes."

"Phil is the plotter, Suze is the writer; it's always been that way. Suze never had a problem with Phil's changes before."

"Suze said he's changing things just for the sake of changing them, to make more work for her."

"Have you spoken with Phil?" Felicia asked.

"Yes, and I believe his exact words were 'You bet your ass I am.' "

She rolled her eyes. "Jerry, the last time I checked, you represented both Suze *and* Phil."

"Yes, but editorial disputes are your responsibility, Felicia, and I rely on you to be fair."

She frowned. "I *am* fair."

"Then you need to be firm. Being assertive isn't your strong suit."

Anger bolted through her. "That's not true." She only had a problem being assertive with Jerry—he had a way of making her feel defensive and defenseless at the same time. "Don't turn this around, Jerry—you know that the Dannons are both hypersensitive right now."

"Which is why, Felicia, it would behoove both of us if the Dannons find a way to patch things up and forget about this divorce nonsense."

"And you're telling me this because?"

"Because I think you should find a way to make this project more enjoyable, to make them realize how good they are together."

She summoned strength. "Jerry, I'm not a marriage counselor."

"But you're a woman."

A small part of her was flattered he remembered, but she managed to inject a bite into her tone. "What does *that* mean?"

"It means that . . . you know, you're all wrapped up in the fantasy of marital bliss. If I tried to talk to the Dannons about staying together, they'd know I was bullshitting them for the sake of money."

"Isn't that what I'd be doing?" she asked.

"No, you actually believe in all that happily-ever-after crap."

Felicia set her jaw—it wasn't enough that the man had broken her heart, but he had to reduce her hopes for the future to the lyrics of a bad love song.

Coming November 2004

If Women Ruled the World . . .

Dating would be a whole lot easier

Even in Regency society, men had a habit of somehow slipping away . . . out of your life. But now, in *The One That Got Away*, four delightful heroines discover that the men of their dreams have never forgotten them. Written by three *New York Times* bestselling authors—Victoria Alexander, Eloisa James and Cathy Maxwell—and one rising superstar, Liz Carlyle, this is an anthology you'll never forget.

Much Ado About Twelfth Night
by Liz Carlyle

In fair weather, the vast estate of Sheriden Park lay but a half day's journey from Hampshire, and this particular day was very fair indeed. Still, the cerulean sky and warm weather did little to calm Sophie's unease. Seated beside Aunt Euphemia, she found her apprehension grew with every passing mile, until their coach was rolling beneath the arched gatehouse and up the rutted carriage drive. And suddenly the stunning sight of Sheriden Park burst into view, snatching Sophie's breath away.

Despite the rumors of ruination, the sprawling brick mansion seemed outwardly unchanged. Row upon row of massive windows glittered in every wing, and already the door was flung wide in greeting. Sophie saw Edward long before they reached the house. He would have been unmistakable, even in a crowded room. But he stood alone on the bottom step like some golden god, his shoulders rigidly back, his eyes hardened against the sun. Sophie's heart leaped into her throat.

A footman hastened forward to put down the steps. "Get out first, Will," instructed Euphemia, prodding at his ankle with her walking stick. "Go 'round and tell Edward's servants to have a care with my hat boxes. I'll not have any broken feathers, do you hear?"

"Yes, ma'am." Will leaped down.

At once, the new marquess took his hand. "Good afternoon, Weyburn," said Edward, using her brother's title. He gave Will a confident handshake, but strangely, his eyes remained on Sophie.

Will turned away to greet Sir Oliver Addison. In the carriage door, Sophie froze. Edward was staring up at her, his gaze dark, and his jaw hard, as if newly chiseled from stone. Well, he did not look quite the same after all, did he? He seemed taller, broader—and anything but glad to see her.

A Fool Again
by Eloisa James

A well-bred lady never ogles a man from behind her black veil, especially during her husband's burial. But Lady Genevieve Mulcaster had acknowledged her failings in ladylike deportment around the time she eloped to Gretna Green with a bridegroom whom she'd met three hours earlier, and so she watched Lucius Felton with rapt attention throughout Reverend Pooley's praise of her deceased husband—a man (said Mr. Pooley) who rose before his servants and even for religious haste went unbuttoned to morning prayer. Felton looked slightly bored. There was something about his heavy-lidded eyes that made Genevieve feel thirsty, and the way he stood, almost insolently elegant in his black coat, made her feel weak in the knees. His shoulders had to be twice as large as her husband's had been.

Recalled to her surroundings by that disloyal thought, Genevieve murmured a fervent, if brief, prayer that heaven would be just as her husband imagined it. Because if Erasmus didn't encounter the rigorous system of prizes and punishments he anticipated, he would likely be discomfited, if not sent to sizzle his toes. Genevieve had long ago realized that Erasmus wouldn't hesitate to rob a bishop if an amenable vicar could be persuaded to bless the undertaking. She threw in an extra prayer for St. Peter, in the event that Erasmus was disappointed.

Then she peeked at Felton again. His hair slid sleekly back from his forehead, giving him an air of sophistication and command that Genevieve had never achieved. How could she, wearing clothes with all the elegance of a dishcloth? The vicar launched into a final prayer for Erasmus's soul. Genevieve stared down at her prayer book. It was hard to believe that she had lost *another* husband. Not that she actually got as far as marrying Tobias Darby. They were only engaged, if one could even call it that, for the six or seven hours they spent on the road to Gretna Green before being overtaken by her enraged father. She never saw Tobias again; within a fortnight she was married to Erasmus Mulcaster. So eloping with Tobias was the first and only reckless action of Genevieve's life. In retrospect, it would be comforting to blame champagne, but the truth was yet more foolish: She'd been smitten by an untamed boy and his beautiful eyes. For that she'd thrown over the precepts of a lifetime and run laughing from her father's house into a carriage headed for Gretna Green.

Memories tumbled through her head: the way Tobias looked at her when they climbed into the carriage, the way she found herself flat on the seat within a few seconds of the coachman geeing up the horses, the way his hands ran up her leg while she faintly—oh so faintly—objected. 'Twas an altogether different proposition when Erasmus stiffly climbed into the marital bed. Poor Erasmus. He didn't marry until sixty-eight, considering women unnecessarily extravagant, and then he couldn't seem to manage the connubial act. Whereas Tobias—she wrenched her mind away. Even *she*, unladylike though she was, couldn't desecrate Erasmus's funeral with that sort of memory.

She opened her eyes to the breathy condolences of Lord Bubble. "I am distressed beyond words, my lady, to witness your grief at Lord Mulcaster's passing," he said, standing far too close to her. Bubble was a jovial, white-haired gentleman who used to gently deplore Erasmus's business dealings, even as he profited wildly from them. Genevieve found him as practiced a hypocrite as her late husband, although slightly more concerned for appearances.

"I trust you will return to Mulcaster House for some refreshments, Lord Bubble?" Since no one from the parish other than Erasmus's two partners, his lawyer, and herself had attended the funeral, they could have a veritable feast of seed cakes.

Bubble nodded, heaving a dolorous sigh. "Few men as praiseworthy as Erasmus have lived in our time. We must condole each other on this lamentable occasion."

A sardonic gleam in Felton's eyes suggested that *he* didn't consider Erasmus's death the stuff of tragedy. But then, Genevieve had studied Felton surreptitiously for the past six months, and he often looked sardonic. At the moment he was also looking faintly amused. Surely he hadn't guessed that she had an affection for him? Genevieve felt herself growing pink. Had she peered at him once too often? *Think like a widow*, she admonished herself, climbing into the crape-hung carriage.

Nightingale
by Cathy Maxwell

A soft rap sounded on the door.

"What is it?" he said, his voice harsh. He wanted to be alone. He *needed* to be alone. Tomorrow, he was going to run Whiting through, and then . . . *what?* The word haunted him.

"There is someone here to see you, sir," the footman's voice said from the other side.

At this hour? "Who the bloody hell is it?" Dane demanded. He went ahead and poured himself another whiskey. To the devil with temperance or being a gentleman. Tonight was for exorcisms, although the whiskey didn't seem to be having any effect. He was feeling everything too sharply. He lifted his glass.

"I'm sorry, Sir Dane, I don't have her name," the footman answered. "She refused to tell me or give me her card but asked to see you on the most urgent of business. I let her in because she is obviously a Lady of Quality."

A Lady of Quality? Out and alone at this hour of the night?

Curious, Dane set down the glass without drinking. “Send her up.”

There was silence at the door as the footman went to do Dane’s bidding. Dane sat quiet. Who would be coming to see him at this hour? It couldn’t be a mistress. He had the last—what was her name? Something French. Always something French . . . although none of them had been French any more than he was. *Danielle.* He had signed Danielle off three months ago and had not had the energy or interest in searching for another.

In fact, for the past year, since he’d returned to London, he had been weighed down by a sense of tedium coupled with a restless irritation over the everyday matters of his life. He’d been going through the motions of living without any clear purpose or desire.

Perhaps he should let Whiting run *him* through?

The idea had appeal. Dane picked up the glass and drained it of the precious amber liquid.

The footman rapped on the door to signal he had returned with this uninvited guest. Dane pushed both the will and his whiskey glass aside before calling out, “Enter.”

The door opened slowly and the footman, dressed in blue and gold livery with a powdered wig on his head, stepped into the room. “Sir Dane, your guest.”

He moved back. There was a moment’s pause, a space of time, three ticks of the clock, and then the woman walked into the room—and Dane stopped breathing.

Before him stood Jemma Carson, the widowed Lady Mosby, looking more beautiful than ever.

The Trouble With Charlotte
by Victoria Alexander

"Bloody hell." Hugh Robb, formerly Captain Robb and now, thanks to his resurrection, Lord Tremont, stared at the figure of his wife in a crumpled heap on the floor. "She dropped like a stone."

"Not unexpected under the circumstances." A man Hugh had scarcely noticed upon entering the room moved toward Char, then hesitated. "We should probably, or rather, one of us should—"

"Probably." Although Char certainly wasn't going anywhere and it might well be best first to know exactly who his competition was. "And you are?"

"Pennington. The Earl of Pennington." The man—Pennington—stared. "You're Captain Robb, aren't you? Charlotte's husband. Charlotte's *dead* husband."

"Indeed, I am the husband." Hugh narrowed his eyes. "And are you her—"

"No!" Pennington paused. "At least not yet."

"Good." Hugh nodded with a surprising amount of relief.

He bent beside his wife and gathered her into his arms, ignoring the flood of emotion that washed through him at the feel of holding her again. The last thing he needed was to have Char's affections engaged right now. Not that it mattered. From the moment he'd decided to return home, he had vowed not to consider anything she might have done while believing him dead to be of any importance whatsoever.

"You might put her down now," Pennington said firmly.

"Of course," Hugh murmured.

He deposited Char carefully on a sofa and knelt beside her. In repose, she was peaceful and serene but she'd always had an air of restlessness about her. It had drawn them together and led them along the edge of scandal. And they had reveled in it. She'd been only eighteen when they'd wed and he a bare two years older. Neither had known anything of life save fun and excitement and high, heady passion.

Had she changed? He was certainly not the same man who had stalked out that very door seven long years ago. He had left a selfish, stupid boy and returned as . . . what? A man at long last willing, even eager, to live up to the responsibilities of his life? Dear God, he prayed he had indeed become man enough to do so. And prayed as well he had not lost his wife in the process.

Her long, lush lashes flickered and her eyes opened, caught sight of him, and widened.

"Char?"

Char's gaze searched his face as if she were trying to determine if he was real or nothing more than a dream. Slowly, she raised her hand to his face and rested it upon his cheek. Her dark eyes met his and he read wonder and awe and . . . fury.

She cracked her hand hard across his face.

The sound reverberated in his head and around the room, and he jerked back on his knees. Even Pennington winced.

"You're alive!" She stared in shock and disbelief and struggled to sit up.

"Indeed I am." Hugh rubbed his cheek gingerly. "You do not appear quite as pleased as I thought you'd be."

"You thought I'd be pleased? Pleased? Hah!" She scrambled off the sofa and moved away from him as if to keep a safe distance between them. "How—"

"It's a very long story." Hugh searched for the right words. "Some of it is confusing and some rather unpleasant and"—he drew a deep breath—"much, if not all of it, is my fault."

"*That* was never in question." She shook her head. "This is impossible. You simply cannot be here looking so . . . *alive!*" Char turned on her heel and paced. "You must be nothing more than a dream—"

"A good dream?" A hopeful note sounded in Hugh's voice.

"Hardly," she muttered. "Marcus, is there a man standing in this very room looking suspiciously like my husband? My *dead* husband?"

Pennington nodded reluctantly. "I'm afraid so, Charlotte."

"I am flesh and blood, Char." Hugh stepped closer. "Touch me."

She stared at him for a moment, then once again smacked her hand across his face.

"Yow!" Hugh clapped his hand to his cheek and glared. "Bloody hell, Char, why did you do that?"

Char stared at her reddened palm. "That hurt."

Hugh rubbed his cheek. "Damned right, it hurt."

"The first time I scarcely felt it," she murmured. Her gaze shifted from her hand to Hugh's face. "You really are alive. Real."

"I daresay there were better ways to prove it," Hugh muttered, then drew a deep breath. "However, you may slap me again if you need additional proof."

"Thank you, but no." She shook her head slowly. "I do appreciate the offer and I should like to reserve the right to smack you again should I need to do so."

Coming December 2004

If Women Ruled the World . . .

There'd be a whole lot less gambling.

And houses would be cleaner too.

In Samantha James's *A Perfect Groom* we discover what happens when a young man believes he can seduce anyone . . . and puts his money where his ego is. But when he's given the challenge of enticing the one known as "The Unattainable" he knows he's in big trouble . . .

A pleasant haze had begun to surround Justin, for he was well into his third glass of port. Nonetheless, his smile was rather tight. "Don't bother baiting me, Gideon," he said amicably.

Gideon gestured toward the group still gathered around the betting book. "Then why aren't you leading the way?"

Justin was abruptly irritated. "She sounds positively ghastly, for one. For another, no doubt she's a paragon of virtue—"

"Ah, without question! Did I not mention she's the daughter of a vicar?"

Justin's mind stirred. A vicar's daughter . . . hair the color of flame. Once again, it put him in mind of . . . but no. He dismissed the notion immediately. That could never be.

"I am many things, but I am not a ravisher of innocent females." He leveled on Gideon his most condescending stare, the one that had set many a man to quailing in his boots.

On Gideon, it had no such effect. Instead he erupted into laughter. "Forgive me, but I know in truth you are a ravisher of *all* things female."

"I detest redheads," Justin pronounced flatly. "And I have a distinct aversion to virgins."

"What, do you mean to say you've never had a virgin?"

"I don't believe I have," Justin countered smoothly. "You know my tastes run to sophisticates—in particular, pale, delicate blondes."

"Do you doubt your abilities? A woman such as The Unattainable shall require a gentle wooing. Just think, a virgin, to make and mold as you please." Gideon gave an exaggerated sigh. "Or perhaps, old man, you are afraid your much-touted charm is waning?"

Justin merely offered a faint smile. They both knew otherwise.

Gideon leaned forward. "I can see you require more persuasion. No doubt to you Bentley's three thousand is a paltry sum. So what say we make this more interesting?"

Justin's eyes narrowed. "What do you have in mind?"

Gideon's gaze never left his. "I propose we double the stakes, a wager between the two of us. A private wager between friends, if you will." He smiled. "I've often wondered . . . what woman can resist the man touted as the handsomest in all England? Does she exist? Six thousand pounds says she does. Six thousand pounds says that woman is The Unattainable."

Justin said nothing. To cold-bloodedly seduce a virgin, to callously make her fall in love with him so that he could . . .

God. That he could even consider it spoke to his character—or lack thereof. Indeed, it only proved what he'd always known . . .

He was beyond redemption.

He was wicked, and despite Sebastian's protestations otherwise, he knew he'd never change.

"Six thousand pounds," Gideon added very deliberately. "And worth every penny, I'll warrant. But there's one condition."

"And what is that?"

"She must be yours within the month."

A smile dallied about Justin's lips. "And what proof shall you require?"

Gideon chucked. "Oh, I daresay I shall know when and if the chit falls for you."

He was drunk, Justin decided hazily, perhaps as drunk as that fool Bentley, or he wouldn't even give the idea a second thought.

But he was a man who could resist neither a dare nor a challenge—and Gideon knew it.

There had been many women in his life, Justin reflected blackly. Having reached the age of nine-and-twenty, thus far no woman had ever captured his interest for more than a matter of weeks. He was like his mother in that regard. In all truth, what was one more?

And if everything that had been said about The Unattainable was true . . . If nothing else, it might prove an amusing dalliance.

He met Gideon's keen stare. "You're aware," he murmured, "that I rarely make a wager unless I stand to win."

"What a boast! And yet I think perhaps it will be *you* paying me. Remember, you've the rest of the horde to fend off." Gideon gestured to Brentwood and McElroy.

Justin pushed back his chair and got to his feet. "Something tells me," he drawled with a lazy smile, "that you know where this beacon of beauty can be found."

Gideon's eyes gleamed. "I believe that would be the Farthingale ball."